THE
DIAMOND
EYE

Kate Quinn is the *New York Times* and *USA Today* bestselling author of historical fiction. A native of southern California, she attended Boston University where she earned a Bachelor's and Master's degree in Classical Voice. She has written four novels in the Empress of Rome Saga, and two books set in the Italian Renaissance, before turning to the 20th century with *The Alice Network, The Huntress, The Rose Code* and *The Diamond Eye*. All have been translated into multiple languages. Kate and her husband now live in San Diego with three rescue dogs.

 /KateQuinnAuthor
@KateQuinnAuthor
@katequinn5975

ALSO BY KATE QUINN

The Alice Network
The Huntress
The Rose Code

THE EMPRESS OF ROME SERIES

Lady of the Eternal City
The Three Fates (novella)
Empress of the Seven Hills
Daughters of Rome
Mistress of Rome

THE BORGIA CHRONICLES

The Lion and the Rose
The Serpent and the Pearl

COLLABORATIVE WORKS

A Day of Fire: A Novel of Pompeii
A Year of Ravens: A Novel of Boudica's Rebellion
A Song of War: A Novel of Troy
Ribbons of Scarlet: A Novel of the French Revolution's Women

THE
DIAMOND
EYE

KATE QUINN

HarperCollins*Publishers*

HarperCollins*Publishers* Ltd
1 London Bridge Street,
London SE1 9GF

www.harpercollins.co.uk

HarperCollins*Publishers*
1st Floor, Watermarque Building, Ringsend Road
Dublin 4, Ireland

First published in the United States by William Morrow,
an imprint of HarperCollins*Publishers* 2022

This edition published by HarperCollins*Publishers* 2022

1

A catalogue record for this book is available from the British Library

ISBN: 978-0-00-852301-5 (HB)
ISBN: 978-0-00-852302-2 (TPB)

Set in Adobe Garamond Pro

Printed and bound in the UK using 100% Renewable Electricity by CPI Group (UK) Ltd

MIX
Paper from
responsible sources
FSC™ C007454

This book is produced from independently certified FSC™ paper
to ensure responsible forest management.

For more information visit: www.harpercollins.co.uk/green

To all the writers who managed to produce a book during the COVID-19 lockdown—to all the creators who managed to make art in the middle of a pandemic. It was really tough, wasn't it?

In the summer of 1942,
as the world was locked in war against Hitler,
a woman crossed the sea from the Soviet Union to the United States.

She was a single mother, a graduate student, a library researcher.
She was a soldier, a war hero,
a sniper with 309 kills to her name.

She was Russia's envoy, America's sweetheart,
and Eleanor Roosevelt's dear friend.

Her story is incredible. Her story is true.
Meet Lady Death.

PROLOGUE

He stood with a pocketful of diamonds and a heart full of death, watching a Russian sniper shake hands with the First Lady of the United States.

"Whoever heard of a girl sniper?" the marksman heard a photographer behind him grumble, craning for a look at the young woman who had just disembarked from the embassy limousine. She'd seemed to flinch at the barrage of camera flashes like muzzle fire, averting her gaze and walking in a phalanx of Soviet minders up the steps of the White House. The photographer snorted, scoffing, "I say she's a fake."

Yet we couldn't resist coming here for a look at her, thought the marksman, idly flipping his falsified press badge. A delegation from the Soviet Union arriving for the international student conference that was Eleanor Roosevelt's latest goodwill project—it wouldn't have merited more than a few lines of newsprint, much less rousted a lot of hungover journalists and photographers out of their beds before dawn and sent them scurrying, pens in hand, to the White House gates, if not for that girl in her crisp olive-green uniform.

"Did they say she had seventy-five kills on the Russian front?" a *Washington Post* journalist wondered, rummaging through his notes.

"I thought it was over a hundred . . ."

"Higher," said the marksman in the Tidewater Virginia drawl he'd grown up with. He'd long since ironed his soft southern vowels out into a flat mid-Atlantic cadence that could belong anywhere and nowhere, but he often let Virginia creep back into his tone, depending on who he was talking to. People trusted a southern accent, and they found themselves trusting the marksman: a loose-jointed man of medium height, medium hair between brown and blond, a bony face, and mud-colored eyes, usually jingling a clutter of uncut diamonds in his trouser pocket. He didn't like banks; anyone who hired him paid in cash, which he then promptly converted to jewels. Lighter than cash, easy to hide—just like bullets. He was thirty-eight years old and had been operating for nineteen years and more than thirty marks. It added up to a lot of diamonds, and a lot of bullets.

"How does a girl like that kill over a hundred Nazis?" a columnist at his side was speculating, still watching the Russian woman on the front steps of the White House, standing to one side in a cluster of dark-suited embassy men as the First Lady welcomed the rest of the Soviet delegation. "Wasn't she a librarian or a schoolteacher or something?"

"Russkies let women in their army, apparently . . ."

Their medical battalions, maybe, the marksman thought. *But even the Reds don't make women into snipers.*

Yet he was here to see for himself, wasn't he? Wanting a look at the woman whose sparse biography he had already committed to memory: Lyudmila Pavlichenko; twenty-six years old; fourth-year history student at the Kiev State University and senior research assistant at the Odessa public library—before the war. After the war, thirteen months of continuous fighting against Hitler's forces on the Russian front.

Nickname: Lady Death.

"Dammit, how many kills *was* it on her tally?" The *Washington Post* journalist was still searching his notes. "Was it more than two hundred?"

Three hundred and nine, the marksman thought, but he didn't believe a word of it. This little junior librarian/schoolteacher was no trained killer. She was a trick pony stuffed with Soviet propaganda, handpicked for the student delegation, and the marksman could see why. A pretty brunette with lively dark eyes and a neat, photogenic face above her bemedaled uniform, nothing like the sort of mannish freak Americans would expect of a Russian female soldier. The Soviets needed American aid; they needed good press coverage on this delegation to American shores, so they'd selected the most winsome candidates they could find. Front and center, this girl sniper who looked so small and appealing beside that tall bony bitch Eleanor Roosevelt.

"Congratulations on your safe arrival in America." The press corps clustered close enough to hear the First Lady's cultured, silver-spoon voice easily as she addressed the Soviet delegation, see the flash of her horsey teeth. "On behalf of my husband the President, welcome to the White House. He looks forward to meeting you all at a later time and invites you to spend your first days in America's capital under our roof. You are some of the first Soviet guests to be hosted in the White House, a historic moment in the friendship between our nations."

She began ushering the Russians inside, and that was that. It wasn't even six-thirty yet, the skies above the capital barely flushed with sunlight as the pack of journalists, photographers, and one lone innocuous assassin began to disperse. "Never thought I'd see the day a Russian sniper got welcomed to the White House," a grizzled columnist grumbled. "FDR will rue the day."

He won't be alive to do it, the marksman thought, eyes still on Mila Pavlichenko's neat dark head as she followed the First Lady toward the doors of the White House. *In nine days—the last day of the international conference—President Roosevelt will be dead.*

"I can see the headlines now," the *Washington Post* reporter muttered, scribbling in his pad. " 'Russian Female Sniper Receives Warm White House Welcome.' "

The marksman smiled, jingling his pocketful of diamonds again. Ten days from now, all the headlines would scream RUSSIAN FEMALE SNIPER MURDERS FDR!

Notes by the First Lady

The President was intending to greet the Soviet delegation with me as they arrived, but he had a fall this morning. I'd just entered with a knock, carrying a packet of memoranda and reports for him to read, and I saw the valet lose his grip as he transferred my husband from his bed. Franklin fell hard on the carpet of his bedroom. Had it happened in public he would have roared with laughter as though it were all a prank, a Charlie Chaplin pratfall, and set about regaining his feet with some hearty, bracing joke. Since he was in the privacy of his bedroom, he allowed his face to twist in agony. I always feel I should look away in such moments—watching the proud facade of President Franklin D. Roosevelt crack with frustration in response to his body's failings feels like a violation.

I reassure Franklin when he is sitting upright again, tell him to take his breakfast at leisure, and offer to greet the Soviet delegation alone. The President already has a packed schedule; I can at least take on this first task. I see the gratitude, even as he makes a joke about his fall. "Better in here than out where all the jackals can see."

"They wouldn't dare cheer," I say lightly.

"But they'd pray I never got up."

Something about his tone bothers me, but he's already reaching for his morning newspapers, girding himself for the day ahead. To the world he appears invincible: a voice full of golden confidence trickling honey-thick from the radio, a profile like a ship's prow cleaving the world, with a jutted cigarette holder rather than a bowsprit. Only a few see the iron will that keeps his facade in place, keeps his body moving ever forward, keeps his enemies at bay.

I hope, moving into the morning light to greet the Soviet delegation—a block of dark-suited inscrutable men, and one unexpected serious-eyed young woman (they say she is a sniper?)—that it will be enough.

FIVE YEARS AGO

November 1937
KIEV, SOVIET UNION
Mila

CHAPTER 1

I was not a soldier yet. We were not at war yet. I could not conceive of taking a life yet. I was just a mother, twenty-one and terrified. When you're a mother, panic can engulf you in the blink of an eyelash. All it takes is that instant when your eye sweeps a room for your child and doesn't find him.

"Now, Mila," my mother began. "Don't be angry—"

"Where's Slavka?" I hadn't even pulled off my patched gloves and snow-dusted coat yet, but my heart was already thudding. There was my son's half-constructed block factory on the floor of the apartment, there was the small worn pile of his books, but no sturdy dark-haired five-year-old.

"His father dropped in. He knew he had missed the appointment—"

"Nice of Alexei to acknowledge that," I gritted. The second appointment I had set up to have our divorce finalized; the second appointment my husband had missed. Each time it had taken me months to scrape up the required fifty-ruble fee; weeks to get an appointment with the backlogged office; then hours waiting in a cold, stuffy corridor craning my eyes for a glimpse of my husband's golden head . . . all to lead to nothing. Anger smoldered in the pit of my stomach. Any Soviet citizen already spent entirely too much time waiting in lines as it was!

My mother wiped her hands on her apron, her big dark eyes pleading. "He was very sorry, *malyshka*. He wanted to take Slavka out for a treat. He's hardly seen the boy these past few years, his own son—"

Whose fault is that? I wanted to retort. I wasn't the one keeping our son out of Alexei's life. My husband was the one who decided only a month or two after giving our son the name of Rostislav Pavlichenko that marriage and fatherhood weren't really to his liking. But my mother's kind, pretty face looked hopeful, and I bit back my hot words.

Mama's voice was soft. "Maybe there's a reason he keeps missing these appointments."

"Yes, there is," I stated. "To make me dance on his string."

"Maybe what he's really hoping for is to reconcile."

"Mama, not again—"

"A *doctor*, Mila. The best surgeon in Ukraine, you said—"

"He is, but—"

"A man on his way up. Rooms of his own rather than a communal apartment, a good salary, a Party member. Not things to throw away." My mother launched into the old argument. She hadn't approved of how Alexei and I had come together; she'd said it happened too fast and he was too old for me and she was right—but she also wanted me safe and warm and fed. "You always said he's no drunk and never once hit you," she went on now. "Maybe he's not the man you dreamed of, but a surgeon's wife won't ever stand in a bread queue, and neither will his children. You don't remember the hungry years, you were just a little thing . . . but there's nothing a woman won't put up with to keep her babies fed."

I looked down at my worn gloves. None of what she said was wrong, I knew that.

I also knew that a part of me was afraid to let my little boy be alone with his father.

"Mama. Where are they?"

THE SHOOTING RANGE wasn't much, just a converted storage space: bars on the windows, a small armory, a line of wooden shields with targets, men on a firing line standing with braced feet and pistols raised or lying on their bellies to fire rifles . . . and in the middle, a tall blond man with a small boy: Alexei Pavlichenko and little Rostislav Alexeivich. My stomach flipped in relief.

"Every man should know how to shoot," I could hear Alexei telling our son as I came closer. He was showing Slavka how to hold a rifle far too large for him, and his voice had that expansive cadence I remembered so well. There was nothing my husband liked better than explaining things to people who knew less than him. "Though inborn abilities are required to be a true expert, of course."

"What kind of abilities, Papa?" Slavka was round-eyed, looking up at this golden stranger he hardly knew. A man who had walked out of his life without a backward glance when he was just six weeks old.

"Patience. A good eye. A steady hand, and a precise feel for the tool in your grip. That's why your papa's such a good shot—he has a surgeon's touch." Alexei flashed a smile downward, and Slavka's eyes got even rounder. "Now you try—"

"Slavka," I called, striding down the firing line, careful to keep behind the shooters. "Give that rifle back. You're too young to be handling weapons that large."

Slavka started guiltily, but Alexei didn't look surprised to see me or my thunderous face. "Hello there," he said easily, brushing a lock of fair hair off his tall forehead. He loomed a head above me: thirty-six, lean and golden, his teeth showing white in his easy smile. "You're looking lovely, *kroshka*."

I didn't bother asking him not to call me that—he already knew it made my hackles rise. For about one week during our marriage I had found it adorable when he called me his *bread crumb*—"Because you're such a little bit of a thing, Mila!"—but it hadn't taken me long to realize a crumb was something that could be flicked away into a dustbin. A piece of trash.

"You shouldn't have taken Slavka out without me," I said instead, as evenly as possible. The pulse of fear was still beating through me, even at the sight of my boy safe and sound. I didn't really think Alexei would try to steal our son away from me, but such things weren't unheard of. At the factory where I'd worked when Slavka was a baby, one of the lathe operators had wept and raged when her former husband swooped their daughter out of school and took her off to Leningrad without any warning. She never got the girl back; her husband had too many Party friends in his pocket. These things *happened.*

"Relax, Mila." Alexei's smile broadened, and that was when the fear in my stomach started curling into anger. He knew I'd been afraid; he knew, and he rather enjoyed it. "Who's going to teach a boy to shoot if his father doesn't do it?"

"I know how to shoot, I can—"

"Anyway, it doesn't matter." Another amused glance. "You're here now. Here to spoil the fun!"

I saw him throw a wink over my head to some friend behind me. *Women!* that wink said. *Always spoiling a man's fun, am I right?* I busied myself pulling off my gloves and disentangling myself from my winter coat, aware I was the only woman standing on the firing line. Females stood at the back, applauding when their brothers or boyfriends or husbands sank a shot. From Lenin on down, Soviet men have always talked a good game about women standing shoulder to shoulder with their men in every field society had to offer, but when it came to children being tended, dishes being scrubbed, or applause being given, I had always observed that it was still female hands doing most of the tending, scrubbing, and clapping. Not that I questioned such a thing overly much: it was simply the way of the world, and always had been.

"Mamochka?" Slavka looked up at me anxiously.

"Give that weapon back, please," I said quietly, brushing a hand over his hair to make it plain I wasn't angry at him. "You're too little for a rifle that size."

"No, he's not," Alexei scoffed, taking the weapon. "Baby him like that and you'll never make a man of him. Watch me load, Slavka . . ."

Alexei's hands moved swiftly, loading the TOZ-8. It was his hands

I'd noticed first, when I saw him at that dance—a surgeon's hands, long-fingered and precise, working with absolute skill and focus. *What, you can't say no when a tall blond man smiles at you?* my mother scolded when she learned I was pregnant—but it wasn't Alexei Pavlichenko's height or his charm or even his hands that had drawn me into his arms. It was his skill, his focus, his drive—so different from the boys my age, all horseplay and careless talk. Alexei hadn't been a boy, he'd been a man over thirty who knew what he wanted—and what he wanted, he trained for; aimed for; *got.* I'd seen that in him that first night, young and laughing as I was in my flimsy violet dress. Barely fifteen years old.

A mother nine months later.

I sent Slavka to hang up my coat at the back of the room, then turned back to Alexei. "You missed the appointment." Fighting to keep my voice even. I was not going to sound shrill; it would just amuse him. "I waited nearly three hours."

He shrugged. "It slipped my mind. I'm a busy man, *kroshka.*"

"You know they require us both to be there in order to finalize the divorce. You don't want to be married to me, Alexei, so why won't you show up?"

"I'll make it up to you," he said, breezy, and one of his friends farther down the line chuckled, seeing my face.

"She doesn't want you to make it up to her!" Laughter rippled behind me, and someone muttering, *I'll let her make it up to me!* Alexei grinned over my head.

"I'll set another appointment to finalize the divorce," I said as coolly as I could manage. "If you can just be there, it will all be over in a matter of minutes." I didn't like the mess I'd made of my own life, a mother at fifteen, estranged within months, and potentially divorced at twenty-one—but better to be divorced than to be stranded in this limbo of the last six years, neither married nor unmarried.

"Ah, don't get all prune-faced, Mila. You know I like to tease."

Alexei gave me a playful dig in the ribs. Only it was a dig that hurt through my wool blouse. "You're looking well, you know. Glowing, almost . . . Maybe there's a reason you want this divorce? A man?"

He was still teasing, still playful, but there was an edge behind the words. He didn't really want me anymore, but he didn't like the idea of anyone else wanting me, either. Much less having me.

"There's no one," I said. Even if there had been someone else, I wouldn't have told him—but there wasn't. Between university classes and studies, Komsomol meetings and caring for Slavka, I was getting by on about five hours of sleep a night. Where was there the *time* for a new man in my life?

Alexei turned the rifle over between his hands, still looking at me. "You're in your third year of studies now?"

"My second." The history department at Kiev University, and my student card had been hard-won after a year of studying at night while working shifts as a turner lathe operator at the arsenal factory. Back then I'd been operating on about four hours of sleep a night, but it was all worth it. All for Slavka, for his future and mine. "Alexei, if I can get another appointment—"

"Alexei!" someone called further down the firing line, looking me over. "This the little wife?"

My husband brought me under his arm with a quick squeeze. "Tell her what a good shot I am, Seryozha. She's not impressed with me anymore. Just like a wife, eh?" Alexei saw the look on my face and leaned down to nuzzle my ear. "Just teasing, *kroshka*, don't bristle."

"Your man's good, watch him with the TOZ-8!"

"Just a simple single-shot rifle," Alexei told me as I wriggled out from under his arm. "We call it the Melkashka."

"I know what it's called." I was no expert, but I'd been to the range before with the factory shooting club; I knew something about fire-arms. "TOZ-8, good 120 through 180 meters—"

"TOZ-8, muzzle velocity 320 meters a second, good from 120 to 180 meters," Alexei said, not listening. "Sliding bolt here—"

"I know. I've handled—"

He raised the rifle, took careful aim, and the crack of the shot sounded. "See? Nearly dead center."

I bit my tongue hard enough to hurt. I wanted to turn my back, gather up my son, and storm out of here, but Slavka was dawdling by the coat hooks listening to two men having some loud political discussion—and I didn't want to depart without some kind of guarantee. A guarantee that the next appointment I set to finalize our divorce, Alexei would *be there*.

"You never used to spend much time at the range. What made you want to get so good at it?" I pushed out a note of grudging admiration for his marksmanship. "You're a surgeon; you know what happens to muscles and organs when they take a bullet. You used to tell me about patching wounds like that."

"Soon there will be war, don't you know that?" Reloading the Melkashka. "When that day comes, they'll need a gun in every hand."

"Not yours." As long as I could remember, my father had been shaking his head and saying, *One day there will be war,* but it hadn't happened yet. "If war comes, *you* won't be a soldier."

My husband frowned. "You think I'm not capable?"

"I mean a surgeon like you is too valuable to waste on the front line," I said quickly, recognizing my mistake. I hadn't lived with Alexei in so long, I'd forgotten how to flatter his pride. "You'll be running a battlefield hospital, not pulling a trigger on command like a blind monkey."

His frown disappeared, and he raised the rifle. "A man sees chances in war, Mila. Chances he doesn't get in ordinary life. I intend to be ready."

He fired off another shot, not quite hitting the bull's-eye. "Good shot, Papa," Slavka said breathlessly, running back up.

Alexei ruffled his hair. Two young girls at the back were watching, winding their curls around their fingers, and maybe my husband saw their admiration, because he squatted down beside his son and said, "Let me show you."

That was the very first thing he'd said to *me*. To little Mila Belova, just past her fifteenth birthday and careening happily through a drafty dance hall, entranced by the music and the laughter and the violet dress swirling about my legs. I was dancing with a girlfriend, both of us eyeing the boys showing off across the room, and then the song changed to something slower, more formal . . . and a toweringly tall man with fair hair pulled me neatly away from my girlfriend and into the curve of his arm, saying, "Let me show you . . ." Later he spread his coat on the grass outside the dance hall for me to sit and told me he meant to be a great man someday. *I'll make the name Pavlichenko resound from Moscow to Vladivostok.* He'd grinned to show he was joking, but I knew he wasn't. Not really.

I can see it now, I'd replied, laughing. *Alexei Pavlichenko, Hero of the Soviet Union!* He burned bright with ambition, so bright he'd dazzled me. Looking at him now in the winter dimness of the shooting range, remembering how he'd taken my hand soon afterward and guided it as he whispered *Let me show you something else* . . . well. I could still admire the fire of ambition in him, much as I disliked him, but I couldn't feel even a flicker of the old bedazzlement.

"No, no," Alexei was telling Slavka, impatience lacing his voice. "Don't let the butt sag, sock it back against the shoulder—"

"He's too little," I said quietly. "He can't reach."

"He's seven years old, he can hold a rifle like a man—"

"He's five."

"Head up, Slavka, don't be a baby. Don't *cringe*!" he snapped.

"Sorry, Papa." My son was struggling to support the heavy birch stock, trying so hard to please this golden father he hardly ever saw. "Like this?"

Alexei laughed. "Look at you, jumpy as a rabbit." He put his finger over Slavka's chubby one on the trigger, pulling. My son flinched at the report, and Alexei laughed again. "You're not scared of a little bang, are you?"

"That's enough." I took the rifle away, pulling Slavka against my side. "Alexei, Slavka and I are going now. And if I set another appointment to finalize the divorce, kindly be there."

I spoke too curtly. I should have been soft, said *Please be there* or *Won't you be there?* The cautious wordsmithing of a woman stepping lightly around a man who has the upper hand, and might use it to lash out—no poet ever agonized over the crafting of a sentence more carefully.

Alexei's eyes took on a hard glitter. "You should be thanking me, *kroshka*. Who else is going to make this puppy of yours into a man?" A glance down at Slavka. "I remember when he was a baby and I'd come back from twelve hours of surgery to find him still awake and crying. *He can't sleep,* you kept whimpering, *he can't sleep.* Not like me, I can sleep anywhere." A glance at me, and Alexei dropped his voice to a murmur, just between us. "What does that tell me, Mila?"

"I can't imagine what you mean." I could feel Slavka trembling as he pressed against my side, uncomprehending but nervous. He wanted his toy train, I could tell—he wanted his grandmother's cramped, cozy apartment, the gleam of the samovar, the spoonful of jam she'd give him off a ladle. I just wanted him out of here, and I began to hand Alexei the Melkashka so I could leave, but his words stopped me.

"This boy doesn't sleep like me, that's all. Doesn't have my hair either, or my eyes . . ." Alexei shrugged, still speaking softly. "A man might wonder things, about a child like that."

"He takes after my father," I said icily.

"He takes after someone." Alexei sank his hands in his pockets, airily unconcerned. "Maybe that's why you want to get rid of me,

Mila. Not a new man in your life; maybe a man you've had in your life since before we met—"

"Go get my coat, *morzhik*," I interrupted sharply, sending Slavka toward the back of the room with a little push.

"—because I look at that boy with my name, and I wonder." Alexei watched our son—*our son*—drag off uncertainly toward the row of pegs again. "I really do wonder."

I still had the Melkashka in my hands, birch stock sticky from Slavka's nervous fingers. I felt my nails digging into the wood and wanted to sink them into Alexei's high-cheekboned face. I wanted to scream that I'd had no one before him and he knew it, because I'd gone straight from the schoolroom to his bed to pushing his baby out of me. But I knew the moment I lashed out at my husband, he'd seize my wrists and squeeze just a little too hard, chuckling, *Women! Always throwing tantrums . . .*

"Your face!" Alexei shook his head, grinning. "*Kroshka*, it was a joke! Don't you know how to laugh?"

"Maybe not," I said, "but I know how to shoot."

I raised the rifle, spun, aligned my aiming eye and front-sight and rear-sight with the farthest wooden target across the range, and squeezed the trigger. My ears rang, and as I lowered the Melkashka I imagined exactly where I'd sunk my shot: the bull's-eye, inside every one of my husband's shots. But—

"Good try," Alexei said, amused. "Maybe next time you'll even hit the target."

A burst of hoots from his watching friends. My cheeks burned. *I know how to shoot,* I wanted to lash out. I'd gone to the range a few times with the factory shooting club, and I'd done just fine. I hadn't dazzled anyone, but I hadn't missed the target either—not once.

But today I'd missed. Because I was flustered, angry. Because I'd been trying to wipe that smile off Alexei's face.

"Look at you, serious little girl with your great big gun." Alexei clipped the Melkashka out of my hand, chucking me under the chin like I was a naughty child, only this clip snapped my head back hard enough to sting. "You want to try again, *kroshka*? Jump for it!" He held it far over my head, smiling, a glint in his eye. "Jump!"

Other men along the firing line began laughing, too. I heard someone call *Jump for it,* coucoushka*! Jump!*

I wouldn't jump for the rifle. I turned to Slavka, coming back to the line with my coat, and began shrugging into it. "I'll let you know when I get another appointment, Alexei."

"Have it your way." Shrugging, he began to load the Melkashka again, flashing a smile at the two girls on the watching line. I saw them smile back. That's the thing with young girls: they're easily impressed. By lean height and golden hair, lofty ambition and devouring dreams. I used to be like that. But now I was twenty-one, an angry mother with the smell of gunsmoke on her hands and cheeks that burned in humiliation, no longer impressed by surface shine on bad men.

SLAVKA'S MITTENED HAND clung tight to mine as we walked through the darkening streets of Kiev. The iron-colored sky overhead sent snow spiraling down to catch in my lashes. "Put your tongue out and catch a snowflake," I told my son, but he was silent. "Hot pelmeni with sour cream when we get home?" I tried next, but he just kept trudging through the muddy snow, shoulders hitching now and then.

"*Morzhik,*" I cajoled softly. It meant *little walrus*—a name I'd given when he was still nursing at my breast. He'd certainly fed like one.

"Papa doesn't like me," Slavka mumbled.

"It isn't you, *morzhik*. Your papa doesn't really like anybody, even me." Feeling my fingers tremble with anger in my patched gloves. "We're not going to see your papa anymore, Slavka. You don't need a papa. You have your babushka, your dedushka." My parents, who hadn't approved of my separation from Alexei, but who had still taken me back in, doted on Slavka with all their hearts, cared for him so I could work a lathe in a factory and study for my exams. "And you have me, Slavka. Your mama, who is always proud of you."

"But who will teach me to shoot? I need a papa to . . ." Slavka floundered. He was only five; he didn't understand those phrases Alexei had flung around today: *be a man, make this puppy into a man, baby him too much.* He just understood that somehow his father had found him wanting.

I looked down at his dark head. "I will teach you."

"But you missed," my son blurted.

I had missed my shot. Because I'd made a mistake, let myself be goaded. But there wouldn't be any more mistakes—I couldn't afford them. I'd already made one colossal error when I fell into the arms of the wrong man, and my entire life had nearly tumbled off its tracks. Now I had a son, and if I made another mistake, his life would come tumbling down with mine. I drew a long breath and let it out. "I won't miss again. Not ever."

"But . . ."

"Rostislav Alexeivich." I addressed him formally, drawing him to a halt by a streetlamp and going to one knee in the snow, holding his small shoulders. My heart thudded again. I'd missed the wooden target at the range, but I couldn't make a mistake here. "From this day, I will be your papa. I'll be your papa and your mama both. And I will teach you everything you need to know to be a fine man someday."

"But you can't."

"Why not?" He looked uncertain, and I pressed. "Do you know what it means to be a fine man, Slavka?"

"No . . ."

"Then how do you know I can't teach you? Women know fine men when we see them." Especially after clashing with men like Alexei. "No one better to teach you to be a good man than a good woman, I promise."

Slavka just looked back in the direction of the gun range, snow veiling those long dark lashes. "You can show me how to shoot?" he whispered.

"Maybe I missed today, but that doesn't matter. Your mama goes to the shooting club sometimes already. Well, with a little more practice I can qualify for the advanced marksmanship course." I hadn't even considered it before—with a full course load at the university already, who would add on a three-times-weekly class in the finer points of ballistics and weaponry? Shooting was just a casual hobby, something I did to prove I was a proper civic-minded joiner in state-approved recreational activities. I'd gone because my friends were going; we'd fire a few rounds after work or after Young Communist League meetings, then we'd go off to a film or more likely I went home to care for Slavka. I'd never taken it very seriously.

That was about to change, I decided. An advanced marksmanship badge—now *that* would wipe the smirk off Alexei's smug face. More important, it would make Slavka believe I was more than just his soft, fond, loving mamochka. Because I had so much more to teach him than shooting, to make a fine man of him. To work hard, to be honest, to treat the women in his life better than his father ever did . . . But that marksmanship badge—yes. That would be a good place to start.

Besides, I recalled that edged, possessive glint in Alexei's eyes as he looked at me. Not wanting me himself, but not really wanting anyone else to have me, either.

Maybe it would be no bad thing if I knew how to defend myself better than I did now. Knew how to defend my son.

"He said I was a *baby*," Slavka burst out. "I'm not a baby!"

My heart squeezed and I hugged him tight. "No, you aren't." *You're not a baby; your father is a bastard. But we don't need him, you and me.* My son had me, and I would give him everything. An apartment of our own someday; a wall of bookshelves; a future. I didn't need my name to resound forever like Alexei dreamed of doing; I didn't need fame or greatness. I just wanted to give my son the life he deserved.

So no more mistakes, that flinty internal voice said. And I promised myself: *Not today. Not tomorrow. Not ever.*

CHAPTER 2

Silence, please." A human saber of a man with a scar on his brow and two St. George Crosses glittering on his chest came striding into the courtyard before the Osoaviakhim marksmanship school, surveying the double line of students arrayed in our new blue tunics. He allowed the stillness to stretch until a few flecks of snow came down from the steely sky, until we were shifting uneasily in our boots, then spoke again in a voice like a rifle shot. "I have heard that you all shoot quite well. But a good marksman is still not a sniper."

For the love of Lenin, I thought, borrowing my father's frequent exhortation whenever my sister and I plagued him. I wasn't here to be a *sniper,* I was here to take the advanced marksmanship course and get my badge. Prove myself worthy of being my son's father as well as his mother. I glanced down at the schedule requirements I'd been handed when I showed up this morning for my first day: twenty hours of political classes, fourteen hours of parade ground drill, two hundred twenty hours of firearms training, sixty hours of tactics . . . it all looked reassuringly academic, which soothed me. I was a history student—I preferred it when action and violence were strictly confined to the pages of a book.

But now the scarred instructor pacing up and down was talking about *snipers.*

"Um—" The girl next to me—there were only three females in this class—raised her hand. "I'm not here to be a sniper. I'm here so I can join higher-level competitions, qualify for USSR Master of Sport."

"In peacetime you will shoot targets in competitions," the instructor said calmly. "But one day there will be war, and you will trade wooden targets for enemy hearts."

Another one like my father, always shaking his head and saying, *When there is war.* Oddly, it relaxed me: I was already very used to men who taught every skill through a lens of how it might be useful in wartime, but the girl who had asked the question looked chastened. She put her hand down, and the instructor continued speaking, eyes raking the double line of students. "A *sniper* is more than a marksman. A sniper is a patient hunter—he takes a single shot, and if he misses, he may pay for it with his life."

That was when I felt myself straightening. Did all these courses and hours of study really boil down to something as simple as *Don't miss?*

Well. That I understood.

"I do not waste instruction on idiots or hooligans," the instructor went on, snow crunching under his boots. "If in one month you have not convinced me that you can acquire the skills and cunning required of a sniper, you will be dismissed from the course."

I stood up even straighter. Because I knew right then and there that if he sent anyone home, it wouldn't be me.

DON'T MISS.

Two years of firearms coursework and drilling squeezed in around my university classes: I'd put in two hours at Kiev University's Basic Archaeology and Ethnography lecture, then struggle into my blue tunic for two hours of Wednesday-night practice assembling and disassembling the Mosin-Nagant army rifle ("Called what, Lyudmila Mikhailovna?" "The Three Line, Comrade Instructor."). I'd go straight from a Komsomol meeting at which we indignantly discussed the German bombing of Guernica in Spain, then put in three hours on the Emelyanov telescope sight ("Break it down for me, Lyudmila Mikhailovna." "It's 274 millimeters with a weight of 598 grams, two regulating drums . . ."). Two years, and all the courses and drilling— the memorization of ballistics tables, the practice hours learning the

Simonov model and the Tokarev model versus the Melkashka and the Three Line—all boiled down to one thing.

Don't miss.

"That construction site," our scarred instructor would say, pointing at a three-story building half raised on Vladimir Street. "What positions could you take to neutralize the site foreman running up and down the plank walkways from floor to floor?" I'd list off every doorway, every line of sight, every window, and then feel tears prick my eyes when he pointed out the window aperture, the stairwell, and the third-floor ledge I'd missed. "Be better," the instructor told me icily. "Come back here in two days and examine how the site has changed: every new wall in place, every window boarded up, every new internal wall that has appeared. Life has a rapid pace, but not through telescopic sights—something is always receding into the background or coming into the foreground, so you must gain the whole picture through the tiniest of details."

I jerked a nod. The instructor had spent twice as long on my mistakes as anyone else's—the other two girls just got a nod!—and I could feel the flush rising out of my dark blue collar. He seemed to sense it, turning his back in scorn. I felt my eyes narrow, and two days later I spent three hours memorizing every single change on that building site, not missing one when I rattled them off in class.

Don't miss. I had those words stamped on my bones, and there were so many chances to miss in this life—to *fail*. As a mother I was forever struggling to hit on the perfect way to raise my son: not too indulgent, not too strict. As a student I was forever struggling to hit the balance that would keep me at the top of my class: flawless note taker, prepared exam taker, dedicated researcher. As a woman of the Soviet Union, I was forever struggling to hit the ideals of my age: productive worker, happy joiner, future Party member. So many gray spaces between those tiny moving targets, so many ways to fail . . . But when I stormed into the firing range after my latest university lecture, asking myself angrily how I could have only managed a Good on a history exam rather than an Excellent, I could put it aside knowing that here, at least, hitting the target was simple—a matter of black and white, not murky gray. You hit the bull's-eye or you missed it.

"A game," the scarred instructor called. He'd begun taking our class into the countryside on Saturdays for lessons on camouflage— how to hide in tangled brambles or stands of trees, or during the wintertime, in drifts of snow. It was winter again now; we'd had a half hour's break for lunch under a cluster of ice-hung birches, stamping our boots, the boys passing flasks of something to warm the belly. Our instructor produced a sack of empty lemonade bottles and was rigging them on their sides in cleft sticks, narrow necks facing toward us as we scrambled upright and got into line with our rifles. "This game's called *bottle base*," he said, rising from his squat and coming to join the line. He set up his own shot methodically, and when he fired, a series of gasps and whistles went up: he had blown out the bottle's base without touching its neck or sides. "Can anyone match that?" he challenged, eyes glinting under the scar.

I could have sworn his eyes stopped on me, deliberate and taunting, but I stood leaning quietly on my rifle and let the younger boys scramble forward. I analyzed their misses: they were shooting too fast, eager to impress.

"You don't want to try, Lyudmila Mikhailovna?" The instructor's voice came at my shoulder, breath puffing white in the frigid air. "Or are you going to hang back posing like a fashion plate?" I had a new winter coat, dark blue with a collar of black fur my mother had painstakingly trimmed from an ancient moth-eaten scarf and restitched to cuddle around my neck like a friendly sable, and the class had been teasing me all morning that I looked too fine and fancy to be toting a weapon.

I ignored the instructor's dig, nodding at the boys as they blasted away. "I'm not joining in because they're showing off. That's not what a rifle is for."

"That could spring from a good instinct," he said. "Showing yourself—that's dangerous for a sniper. You're only invulnerable as long as you're unseen."

"I'm going to be a marksman, not a sniper."

"So you're not hanging back out of good instincts, then. You're not wary of showing off; you're just . . . afraid you'll lose. Afraid to *miss*."

I gave him a level look and went to kneel at the firing line, sinking back on my right heel, socking the rifle into the hollow of my shoulder. Index finger on the trigger, the comb of the butt against my cheek, rifle supported with the strap under my bent elbow as I rested on my left knee and slid my hand closer to the muzzle to steady even further. I stared through the telescopic sight at the bottle in its cleft stick. Even with fourfold magnification, it looked no bigger than the period at the end of a sentence—a full stop in bold type. But I didn't stop. I fired, and in the flash of the shot I remembered the way I'd missed the target when Alexei watched me.

But this time when I lowered the rifle, I saw that the base of the bottle had been blown away in a diamond-sparkle of broken glass scattered across the snow . . . and the neck was intact.

"Well done," my instructor said calmly. "Can you repeat it?"

I felt a grin spreading across my face, barely hearing the applause of my classmates. "Yes."

That was the first day I heard it: the song a rifle could sing in my hands, its stock hard against my shoulder, my finger curled through the trigger. I'd somehow slipped away from my jockeying classmates and their flashy antics and found myself in a place of silence—an island in that raucous atmosphere of fun and games. I blocked everything out, the whole world, all so I could hear the song the Three Line was singing in my hands.

That afternoon I blew the base out of three bottles in a row, setting up every shot with painstaking care, not chipping a single bottle neck. I waited for my instructor to say something—*Scorn that, I dare you*—but he came for me with a fond, surprising hug. "Well done, my long-braided beauty," he said, giving my waist-length plait a tug. "I knew you'd win."

I blinked. "You did?"

"From whom much is given, much is demanded," he quoted. And the day I graduated from his course over a year later, he gave me an autographed copy of his booklet "Instructions for Sharpshooters" inscribed simply: *Don't miss, Lyudmila Pavlichenko.*

"Quite an achievement, *malyshka,*" my father said that evening when I came home and proudly showed my certificate. "My daughter's become a dangerous woman."

"Hardly, Papa." I kissed him on both cheeks: my solid, reliable father in the gabardine service jacket he still preferred to wear even though his military days were long behind him, the Order of the Red Banner worn proud on his breast, hands folded around a steaming cup of tea at the kitchen table. He'd been helping Slavka with his schoolwork, I could tell. My father had helped me with my schoolwork at this table too, as long as I could remember. Even if he didn't get home from work until midnight, he always made time to sit with his children, look over their assignments, and hear their problems—even when we drove him to distraction and he groaned, *For the love of Lenin, you're driving an old man mad!*

Slavka was running his fingers over the round seal crest on my marksmanship certificate. "I can teach you whenever you like," I said, tugging him into my lap and kissing his chocolate-dark hair, the same as mine and Papa's. "Shall we go to the range?"

"Maybe when I'm a Young Pioneer," he said very seriously. "When I get the red kerchief."

"When you're older," I agreed. It didn't distress me that he wasn't eager to learn yet. I had the skills when he was ready; that was what mattered. "Let's see that assignment, *morzhik.* Plant biology, I always liked that at your age. Can you name me all the parts of a leaf?"

I listened to his earnest voice until my slender, beaming mother came home, swooping to exclaim over my certificate. She was proud but a little baffled: "What is such a thing good for, *malyshka*?"

"It taught me not to miss," I said honestly.

"At targets?"

"At anything."

AND THAT IS my secret, if you're curious. You are, aren't you? Everyone is, when they first meet me. Even Eleanor Roosevelt wondered, when we met later on the steps of the White House in August of 1942. I could see it in her eyes: How does a girl like *me*—a mother, a student, an aspiring historian—become a sniper and kill hundreds of men? What's her secret?

Hardly anyone comes right out and asks me. Partly they're afraid I'll be annoyed and add them to my tally—but it's more than that. People love war heroes, but such heroes are supposed to be clean, honorable, white-cloaked. They fight in the open, in the sunlight, face-to-face with their enemies. They deal death from the front. When someone (especially a woman) earns their stars as I have done, people shiver. Anyone who walks in the night, melts into shadows, looks through telescopic sights at an unwary face—at a man who doesn't know I exist, even as I learn that he nicked himself shaving this morning and wears a wedding ring—when I learn all that and then pull a trigger so he is dead before he hears the report . . .

Well. Anyone who can do that over and over again and still manage to sleep at night must surely have a dark side.

You are not wrong to think that.

But you are wrong about *who* has such a dark side, waiting to be tapped. You think that surely someone like me is a freak of nature, gnawing a rifle in her cradle, hunting at five and killing wolves at eight, emerging from the wilds of Siberia (it's always Siberia) fully formed. Americans especially loved to imagine me that way—one of those icy Russian women of dark myth, crawling with bloodied teeth and bloodied hands from some snowbound hellscape: a killer born.

Then you meet me: little Mila Pavlichenko with her wide smile and her bag crammed with books, a student from Kiev only too happy to tell you how she wants to be a historian someday and show you pictures of her adored, chubby-cheeked son—and you are crestfallen. This is Lady Death? This is the girl sniper from the frozen north? How disappointing.

Or . . . and this is your second reaction, the one you won't ever voice . . . how unsettling. Because if a twenty-six-year-old library researcher has such a dark side to her moon, who else does?

I don't know.

I know only that mine awoke when I realized there was no room in my life for mistakes. When I realized I could not miss, not ever. When I heard a rifle sing in my hands as I buried a bullet through the neck of a bottle and sent the base flying into diamond shards . . . and realized who and how I could be.

CHAPTER 3

June 1941
Odessa

Patriotic memoirs have become all the fashion—as the Party would say, they are popular, edifying, and good for public morale (if also somewhat sleep-inducing). But if I were ever to write my memoir. I'd have to modify my story a good deal, or just leave parts out altogether, because there are many, many things about the life of Lyudmila Pavlichenko that would never make it into any memoir. Or at least not the official version.

For example, my account of the day war broke out in the Soviet Union. An official memoir might say, "The day Hitler invaded, I was attending a Komsomol meeting and reflecting on my duties as a future Party member."

The truth? The unofficial version? I was a student in Odessa, and I was at the beach.

"You have *beaches*?" I can just imagine Americans wrinkling their noses. They think Russia is nothing but a vast waste of snow glittering under the white nights—no coasts, no summer days, only ice and wolves. Really, does anyone look at a map? Odessa is farther south than Paris, Munich, or Vienna—and that June day was beautiful, the sky clear and hot, the glittering expanse of the Black Sea stretched flat and shining to the horizon.

I hadn't intended to go swimming, but my friend Sofya rapped my knuckles the day before, both of us enduring the last hour of an endless shift at the front desk of the Odessa public library. "Vika and Grigory are finally back from Moscow, and we're all going to the beach."

"I'm working on my dissertation." I was flipping through my notes at the desk, since we had no patrons to wait on. Not long after getting my advanced marksmanship certificate, I'd passed my fourth-year university exams, all Excellent to Good. I took my results out and looked at them whenever I needed a little internal fortitude. Mila Pavlichenko might have become a mother at fifteen, but her life was firmly back on course, chugging along like a patient little train hitting a predetermined progression of stations. First stop: graduating from Kiev University. Second stop: this assignment to the Odessa public library as a senior research assistant while I sent money home for Slavka every week. Next stop: finishing my dissertation . . .

"The sea, Mila," Sofya cajoled. "It's calling your name, you horrid little bookworm."

"Bogdan Khmelnitsky is calling my name."

"Do not quote your dissertation at me. I do not want to hear one more word about Bogdan Khmelnitsky, the Ukraine's accession to Russia in 1721—"

"—actually 1654."

"—or the activities of the Pereyaslav Council."

"It is *fascinating history*," I said a little huffily. All the library staff were well acquainted with my dissertation topic by now, but somehow no one was excited by it. Sofya regularly threatened to toss my dog-eared pages into the incinerator; I threatened to cram her lipstick up her nose; it was that kind of friendship. "Without the alliance of the Cossack Hetmanate to the centralized Russian state, we would never see a properly unified nation of—"

"Mila, no one cares. Come swimming tomorrow."

So here we were at the beach, striped towels spread out under the sun, a fraying basket full of lemonade bottles parked in the sand. Children careened past shrieking, sand flying up from their feet, but I just flopped back in my navy blue swimsuit that sagged at the thighs. Face turned to the sky, I drowsed to the sounds of the waves, dreaming of the day my dissertation would be done, my degree would be awarded, and I would become a historian in Moscow. I'd have an apartment not far from Gorky Park, where I would take Slavka ice-skating, buy him sugar-dusted ponchiki in a paper cone . . .

"Let's go to the opera tonight," Sofya was saying, flicking sand off her legs. "*La Traviata*—Vika's got extra tickets."

"I've been loaned from *Swan Lake* to fill out the opera dancers for the Act II gypsy dance," Vika said, rolling her eyes. She was a demi-soloist at the Odessa ballet, newly returned from the Bolshoi school in Moscow; she wasn't even twenty, but she had one of those flowery nicknames dancers get—"the Nightingale" or "the Dragonfly," I couldn't remember which. I thought she looked more like a dragonfly, all bug eyes and endless twiggy limbs. "I hate those little ballets in operas," Vika complained. "Substandard choreography—"

"Snob," her brother Grigory teased, flicking sand at her. All of us found Vika a bit of a trial at times, but we adored her twin, who was also a dancer but wasn't so everlastingly *precious* about it. "Let's get dinner after the opera. I'm always so hungry after I get the greasepaint and tights off, I could eat Vika's toe shoes."

"Everything makes you hungry," Sofya scolded, giving me a pang because it was something I was always telling Rostislav. My boy, nine years old now, sturdy and dark and bouncing, forever running up to show me a stone striated with quartz; a whorl in a slab of bark that looked like Comrade Stalin's profile; a baby frog cradled in his gentle hands. I hadn't seen him in months, since leaving Kiev to take up the researcher position at the Odessa library. I didn't have to close my eyes to see him on the train platform with the rest of my family, clinging to my hand. "You could take me with you," he pleaded. "I could help with your work."

"It won't be for long, *morzhik*," I promised, hugging him tight, trying not to cry. I'd never been separated from him for so much as a fortnight, and this would be at least four months. But it would put me on the path toward the future I'd planned so carefully: the apartment in Moscow, the post as a historian; the independence and security. "It's for you," I told my son. "It's all for you—" and heaved my bag of books onto the train before I could break down crying.

And now here I was at the beach on a beautiful day, and it wasn't as beautiful as it could have been because my son was so far away.

Vika was still complaining. "Ballet variations in operas are just a lot of swishing about in red petticoats. A waste of my training—"

"Give it a rest, Vika. You're not being asked to perspire over a lathe in a factory!"

"Ugly sweat work either way!"

"I worked a lathe in a factory," I protested. "It wasn't ugly. Almost beautiful, actually." The days when Slavka had been a baby, barely weaned—as I'd worked the lathe, brushing tungsten dust out of my tight-braided hair and wondering if I'd ever be able to go back to school again, I realized how lovely I found the sight of those blue-violet metal shavings curling out from under the blade.

"Beautiful?" Vika looked scornful.

"No matter how hard the metal, it yields to human strength," I retorted. "Everything does. All you have to do is devise the right weapon."

The dancer snorted, but her twin raised his eyebrows. "Speaking of weapons—"

"I'm not going to shoot a hole in a playing card to win you a bet," I said, heading him off at once. I took regular range practice after earning my advanced certificate, to keep my skills sharp, but I still didn't like showing off. Shooting deserved more respect than that.

"Come on, Mila!" Grigory grinned, dimples showing. He'd been flirting with me all day, and he was certainly good-looking, with those marvelously muscled legs all dancers had . . . but he was still a boy, just eighteen. There was so much difference between eighteen and twenty-four! Becoming a mother so young meant that by the time I'd gone back to school, my fellow students were all five or six years my junior—at times I felt like an old crone in comparison. I went out to plenty of dances and parties now, but none of the men I met there had ever become a long-term prospect. The university boys who invited me to films after Komsomol meetings had nothing more in their minds than fun, whereas I had a child and a future to plan for. As for the older men I sometimes met, they were too trenchantly set in their own futures, and they made it clear they expected me to give up mine if our romance got serious.

Romance later, I told myself whenever the pangs of loneliness stung too sharp. *University degree now.* Once a few more mistake-free stops on my train journey had been safely logged, once the matter of my still-pending divorce had been finalized . . . Alexei hadn't showed up for the third divorce appointment any more than he had for the first two, but when I had a little breathing room after university to finally settle all that, then I could turn an eye to finding a suitable man to share my life and Slavka's. When my feet were on firmer footing there would be time for men, family, more children—all the rest of it.

When you're young and you've known nothing but peace, you assume there will always be time for everything.

"Let's get lunch." Sofya gave me a swack with her towel. "Or I'm going to eat Vika, bony mosquito legs and all. Come on . . ."

That day! A cluster of sandy, laughing young people buttoning summer dresses and old jackets over damp swimsuits, packing up their towels and trailing off to the cheburek café on Pushkin Street. Waiting for a platter of flaky fried meat pastries to arrive, mouths watering; Vika announcing she wasn't going to eat anything because if she gained so much as a gram she'd lose her title role in next year's *Cavalry Maiden*; her brother telling her if she kept complaining about grams and kilos he'd drop her on her head in their next pas de deux; Sofya sipping cold birch juice through a straw; me remembering a footnote I needed to add to my dissertation. All of us surrounded by the noisy, happy clamor of café diners and beach-goers, sticky children and their sunburned mothers. The last day, the last *moment,* before it all went to hell; before the wheel turned and flung all of us into the air, our careful plans shivered into diamond shards and raining down around us. Vika wasn't going to dance the Cavalry Maiden next year; Grigory wasn't going to partner her through any more grand jetés; Sofya would have no sunny afternoons to linger over pale green birch juice, and I wasn't going to defend my dissertation on Bogdan Khmelnitsky, the Ukraine's accession to Russia in 1654, and the activities of the Pereyaslav Council. Within the year, half the people at our table would be dead.

All because of an announcement blaring loud from a speaker on the street just outside, cutting off the café chatter like a knife, informing everyone that at four this morning, Germany had invaded the motherland.

We all froze as if we had been shot. Outside it was the same, all heads turned toward the speaker, listening to Comrade Molotov. *Each of us must demand from himself and from others the discipline, organization, and self-sacrifice worthy of a true Soviet patriot, in order to provide for all the needs of the Red Army, the Navy, and the Air Force, in order to ensure victory over the enemy.* He sounded agitated, but firm. *Victory will be ours!*

He didn't speak long. Just long enough to rearrange the world.

The buzz of conversation started immediately, but the four of us looked at each other around the table, stunned. *Slavka,* I thought. *Slavka* . . . No one moved until our platter of sizzling hot chebureki arrived on the table with a bottle of straw-pale wine, and suddenly we were all talking.

"How far have they advanced?" Sofya sounded sick. "The Hitlerites?"

"I'll enlist," said Grigory.

"You will not," snapped Vika, eyes more buglike than ever with shock. "They won't conscript artists—will they?—so don't go throwing yourself in front of the guns."

"Maybe I can enlist on the medical side," Sofya said, trying to sound brave but only sounding scared. I just stared at my plate. *Slavka* . . . war brought such horrors into the lives of children. Bread lines, bombing raids, queues that stretched for blocks. My parents still spoke of the last war, and the terrible hardships that followed . . .

Vika slammed to her feet, glaring daggers at her brother. "I still have to dance in *La Traviata* tonight, invasion or not. I'll see you all afterward."

"Vika—" Her twin rushed after her, leaving Sofya and me staring at each other.

"We may as well go to the opera tonight," my friend said at last. "Whatever happens, it's not happening yet. Not here."

But over the horizon—yes. Not so far over the horizon, either. I'd learn later that German air raids had pierced as far as Kronstadt near Leningrad; Sevastopol in the Crimea. Outside the café, Pushkin Street was filling up, people gathering under the speaker to argue.

Yet there were still mothers heading toward the beach with excited children, couples ambling hand in hand along Marine Boulevard. It was still a beautiful summer afternoon; no one wanted to skip their plans for the cinema, the theater, the concert hall just because of the outbreak of war. I couldn't decide if it was blind stubbornness or just the Russian way, putting your head down and simply marching ahead, and I still couldn't decide that night when Sofya and I settled in our seats in Box 16 of the dress circle at the Odessa theater, watching over the stage as the hushed opening strains of Verdi's *La Traviata* whispered out over the theater. Such a beautiful theater, all gilded moldings and huge crystal chandeliers—a theater for *us*, ordinary students and citizens, when once people like me would have been left to scrabble at the door while the aristocrats swept inside.

But I couldn't enjoy the opera, the soprano with her white frills and vocal fireworks, the swooning tenor. I stared blindly at the stage, hands flexing in my lap, my thoughts a jumble of random images laced with the ribbon of Comrade Molotov's radio-flattened voice. My son eating hot blini with sour cream and apple jam . . . *German troops have entered our country, without making any demands of the Soviet Union and without a declaration of war* . . . The orderly rows of files I took such pleasure in organizing at the library . . . *They have attacked our borders in many places* . . . The nods from my history professors when I answered a question correctly: "Exactly right, Lyudmila Mikhailovna" . . . *Hostile aerial attacks and artillery barrages have also taken place* . . . Blue-violet shavings of implacably hard metal curling out from under a blade; a shot rocketing from my triggering finger to the center of a target . . .

The curtain descended to a crash of applause. Act I was over, the soprano had renounced love in favor of life (or had she?), and I'd barely heard a note. All I knew was that something was building in my chest, building with implacable steadiness, and suddenly I couldn't breathe, couldn't think, couldn't sit here through Act II and Vika's strutting entrance in her red petticoats. "I need to go," I told Sofya brusquely and rose from my seat, pushing down the great stairs toward the outside until I was taking in great gulps of the warm night air. I stood on the steps of the opera house for a moment, my blue crepe de chine dress stirring about my knees, then began to walk.

I found myself down by the bay, fingers curling and uncurling around the rail overlooking the sea. On the summer stage of Marine Boulevard nearby, a brass band was playing a military march, the notes nightmarishly cheerful. The water glittered, and dimly I could see the outlines of the Black Sea Fleet warships out in the bay. Gunboats, destroyers, an old cruiser that had been re-equipped as a minelayer . . . I wondered if any of them would be here within the week. I wondered if anyone out walking and laughing and clapping along to the band's drumbeats would be here within the week, either, or if it would all be uniforms and grim faces.

This beautiful world. This nighttime wonder that was my city, my country. Slavka's world, the one I wanted to show him, build for him, pour into his hands. Overrun by German thugs with their ranting little toothbrush of a dictator and their smug dreams of world superiority.

"Were you Soviets any better?" a half-drunk American journalist asked me later. "Some nerve you've got, feeling righteous, wanting to make the whole world commie . . ."

There are things my homeland can apologize for. We have a long way to go, and we train ourselves to see not the world around us, but the world as it will become, knowing that world is still a ways away. But whatever our faults, I will never apologize for fighting the war that came to our doorstep in 1941. Germany invaded *us*. Germany wanted *our* oil, *our* cities, *our* flag added to their imperial crown. They wanted to see their damned eagles staked high, from the blue and gold palaces of Leningrad to the icebergs of Lake Baikal, and what we wanted was of no importance, so they invaded. The first shots fired were theirs, the first boots crossing borders were theirs, and if we rolled over and let them do it, my Slavka would be mass-churned into the Hitler Youth and taught to salute a monster.

Is Germany truly so surprised that every mother, every father, every *soul* born in this vast icy land of ours objected to that fate?

Are you?

The anger that had kindled in my stomach upon hearing the announcement of war was burning higher, becoming fury as I thought of swastikas flying over Odessa. The fury clawed and coiled, liquid and molten at the core of me, a tangible white-hot thing being manufactured in the fires of some monstrous factory. Enough rage to churn a sea to boiling fury.

What use is it being angry? whispered the voice of doubt inside me as I stared out at the calm water. *Students like you are no use during a war.* The voice sounded very much like Alexei's. I could imagine him saying *A man sees chances in war, Mila . . . but not little bookworms like you. Go roll bandages.*

And I could—finish my dissertation, dig tank traps, enlist to work at the nearest hospital. Stick to the careful plan, stick to the roles I knew: the library staffer, the researcher, Slavka's mother. These were roles I could fill with never a mistake.

But here, unlike in England and France and America, a woman's fight was not limited to hospitals. And I had more in me than filing and note-taking and far too much seventeenth-century Ukrainian history. *No matter how hard the metal,* I'd told Vika that afternoon, *it yields to human strength. All you have to do is devise the right weapon.*

I *was* a weapon. I'd learned to shoot, after all. And I'd vowed to be Slavka's father as well as his mother.

In times of war, fathers go fight for their children.

So I let out a shaky breath, went home to my student digs for my passport, student card, and marksmanship certificates, and went—still in my crepe de chine dress and high-heeled sandals—to enlist.

CHAPTER 4

My memoir, the official version: *When I arrived at the front on Bessarabian soil, I was impressed by the efficiency and organization of the Red Army officers, and I took on my new duties with stoicism and resolve.*

My memoir, the unofficial version: When I arrived at the front, it was a complete and utter disaster and so was I, because I'd gone to war without saying goodbye to my son.

"NO TIME TO come home?" my mother cried through the telephone line, hearing me say it. "It's not so long a journey—"

"Nearly five hundred kilometers, Mama." I blinked fiercely, keeping the wobble out of my voice. "I leave tomorrow. I didn't know it would be so soon."

"Surely you didn't have to enlist yet." She was weeping, and I heard my father in the background: *Give her peace, our daughter knows her mind.*

The line was silent for a moment, and then I heard his quiet voice. "Did you have trouble enlisting, *malyshka*?"

"A little. The first military registrar I went to wouldn't even look at my certificates." He'd muttered something about women who wanted to be soldiers but had no idea how hard it was and tossed me unceremoniously out of the office.

"They don't know Belov women," my father said, adding somewhat ominously, "Do I need to have a word with someone for you?"

He could, I knew. My father was a good, kind man, devoted to the Party and to his family, but he was also not a man to be crossed, ever.

As the saying goes, he knew people—the kind of people who organized one-way trips into rivers, gulags, or vats of concrete. It was the
reason Alexei had married me when I was fifteen: my father informed
him I was pregnant, then informed him he would do the right thing
by me, and Alexei probably reflected it was better to say yes than to
lose his thumbs. Surgeons need thumbs.

But I didn't want my father pulling strings to get me to the front.
"I found another enlistment officer, Papa." A much more amiable fellow than the first, though I'd still been asked *Does your husband have
any objection to your volunteering for the Red Army*? At least the officer
hadn't made me go get some piece of paper from Alexei. If he had, I
might have wrecked the office.

"Don't pack too much," my father cautioned. "All you need in war
is dry socks, a good pair of boots, and something to read. And be
sure—"

"For the love of Lenin, Papa!" I borrowed his own words to tease
him. "Stop fretting. I have plenty of socks, and I packed my dissertation." Somehow I couldn't bear to leave it behind. Curling my fingers
tight around the handset, I made myself add, "I'm . . . I'm sorry I
didn't come home first to say goodbye, then enlist afterward. I could
have, but—"

"Harder to leave once you've had Slavka's big eyes fixed on you,"
my father said.

I bit my lip savagely. "Yes." How would I ever be able to tear myself away if I had my son clinging to my waist, sobbing and begging
me: *Mamochka, don't go, don't go, please* . . . And what kind of mother
would I be then—a mother who wouldn't fight for her child, for the
world she wanted her child to grow up in?

"I'm proud of you, *malyshka*." My father's rumble brought tears to my
eyes. I cuffed them away. "When you get to the front, just remember—"

"*Belovs don't retreat*," we both chanted, and that gave me enough
strength to bid goodbye to Slavka over the telephone.

What a little life I had in Odessa—packing it away took almost no time at all. Goodbyes to my library colleagues and to my professors; hugs to Sofya. Just a few short days after my enlistment, I found myself crammed into a military train full of jostling new recruits—some in uniform, most still in civilian dress. I searched the car hopefully for another woman and saw none. My heart sank under the lace-edged collar my mother had insisted on stitching to my sturdiest traveling dress to make it pretty. The soldiers around me looked friendly enough, but—

"Here!" A slender hand waved from a bench by a window, and I saw a lanky blonde in a too-big overcoat. "Olena Ivanovna Paliy," she said briskly as I fought my way through. "I'll watch while you sleep if you do the same for me. Personally I'd rather arrive at the front without getting pawed."

I put out my hand. "Lyudmila Mikhailovna Pavlichenko. Mila."

"Lena." She made room for me on the bench by the window, scowling at a big red-haired soldier who tried to squeeze down between us. "Find somewhere else, *blyat*," she said with a casually obscene gesture, and I backed her up with a steely look. We might not know each other yet, but we were two women traveling alone in a compartment full of rowdy young men—such alliances are fast, practical, nearly primal. "Medical battalion for me," Lena Paliy went on. "Last week I was a second-year student in the Odessa medical institute, slicing up shriveled blue corpses on the dissection table. You?"

"Last week, alphabetizing periodicals. Tomorrow"—I thought of my marksmanship badges—"I can be useful wherever they put me, if they just give me a rifle."

"You'd think more women would be here besides us." Lena took a beet out of her pack and began to eat it raw. "Hitlerites pouring over the border like roaches, and we're the only two skirts in this train? Makes you ashamed to be female. If girls want to stay home and cower behind their soup kettles while the men fight, let them move to

England. Prance around Piccadilly with Princess Margaret Rose and put their hair in pin curls."

I grinned, deciding I was going to like Lena Paliy.

The train chugged slowly out of the station, snaking west toward the steppe. The gleaming surface of the Dniester estuary soon shone off to the right, then the string of stations. Shabo, Kolyesnoye, Sarata, Artsyz, Hlavani . . . I choked down a wave of homesickness. *What am I doing so far from everything I love?* But I stamped down on that thought before it could flower into self-pity. *Slavka. This is for him.*

A long night—Lena dozed first as I kept watch; then I put my forehead against the glass and took my turn. An even longer day to follow; more strange depots; more unfamiliar towns. Lena and I traded stories; I admired the scarf her mother had knitted; she admired my picture of Slavka. "Cute," she said, touching his round baby face. "And his father?"

"Not so cute. A real bastard, in fact."

"I sense a story." Lena made a *tell-me* gesture, and I normally wasn't so forthcoming with new people, but I found myself recounting the tale: fifteen-year-old Mila Belova at her first dance, the tall fair-haired man who pulled her away from her girlfriends into a two-step and said, *Shall I show you?*

"That's all it took?" Lena raised her eyebrows. "Must have been some dance."

I grimaced. "Any ordinary night, I'd have danced with him once and gone back to my friends. But right before my eyes, he saved a life."

Alexei and I had circled the dance floor only twice when a stranger by the wall suddenly bent over, red-faced with vodka, eyes wide with panic, choking on something. His friends didn't know it was serious, guffawing even as he slipped to his knees clawing at his throat—but Alexei knew. He melted through the crowd to the man's side and flipped him on his back on the hot dance floor, trying to expel whatever was choking him. By the time I fought my way through the crush, he'd shoved his pristine sleeves up and was yanking a fountain pen and a small knife from his pocket. Seeing me, he tossed the pen into my hands and barked, "Take it apart, give me the barrel!" even as he was seizing a bottle of vodka from the nearest table and using the icy liquor to sterilize the penknife. I went to my knees beside Alexei, heart thudding, and saw he was very calm. He took the disassembled fountain pen, tossing his handkerchief at me. "When I tell you, mop up the blood."

And he cut into the man's throat just under the Adam's apple, down to the windpipe in one firm stroke, and I was mopping blood, terrified but moving under that cool voice, and he was fashioning a breathing tube from the hollow fountain pen, and the man wasn't dying. All because of the steady, long-fingered hands of Alexei Bogdanovich, Dr. Pavlichenko, whose name I didn't even learn until an hour later, when we were sitting under an oak tree in the cool, shadowed garden outside the dance hall, the patient taken away to the hospital.

"You're good in a crisis, little—what's your name? Mila?" Taking my hand in both of his, twining it in those long fingers in a way that rendered me completely breathless.

"I'm not so little," I said, hoping he wouldn't guess my age, feeling relieved when he smiled.

"No, I can see you're not."

("That was a lie," I told Lena. "He made a very accurate guess how old I was, which was too young, which was exactly the age he liked.")

"How did you do that surgery?" I'd pressed. "Save that man?"

"I'm a surgeon. It's what surgeons do." He smiled. "Though I'll be more than a surgeon someday."

"What do you want to be?"

"Great," he said simply. "I'll make the name Pavlichenko resound from Moscow to Vladivostok someday." He grinned, to show he was joking, but I knew he wasn't. Not really. He burned bright with ambition.

"I can see it now," I answered, laughing. "Alexei Pavlichenko, Hero of the Soviet Union . . ."

"Has a nice ring to it." He laughed too, looking at me. "And what do *you* want, Lyudmila?"

Hearing the story, my new friend Lena whistled. "And you swooned into his arms like a plucked lily?"

"More or less." Barely fifteen, poised somewhere between raiding orchards with the local boys and studying for my advanced exams—neither the bookish girl who dreamed of university nor the sunburned mischief-maker who was the best shot in the neighborhood with a slingshot stood a chance against a tall golden Viking who pulled me into his orbit to help him save a life, then asked me *what I wanted*. I did what any girl would have done: leaned in and kissed him before my nerve gave out, and maybe I was caught off guard by how fast everything moved after that, how quickly buttons were slipping free and clothes disappearing, but I was too eager, too dazzled to want to pull away.

"Nine months later," I told Lena now, "there was Slavka."

She whistled again. "And the blond bastard?"

"Moving up in the world. He's the best surgeon in the region, I'll give him that." I'd had to contact him a year or so ago for some piece of paper required for my student enrollment: *Does your husband have any objection to your registration at the University of Kiev?* He'd been amiable enough as he wrote out a brief confirmation that we had not lived together in years. He didn't ask anything about Slavka, just pulled my wrist toward him asking if I'd give him a kiss *for old times' sake*. I'd wanted to say something cutting, but I didn't dare because I needed the paper he'd just written out. So I just smiled tightly, avoiding the kiss, and he grinned and held the paper over my head. *Jump for it,* kroshka! And I actually did jump, because I had to, and he only made me jump three times before he let me have it. The thought of that still made my toes curl in shame.

"Let's not talk about him anymore," I told Lena, swallowing the anger I always felt thinking about Alexei. Rage was no use to a mother, a student, a future historian, and productive member of society, and it certainly wouldn't help me be a calm and effective soldier, either. Alexei was the past, the war was the future, so I nudged Lena with my shoe and said, "Your turn."

"I've got a blond bastard or two in my past . . ." She launched into some colorful story that pushed Alexei out of my mind, hopefully for good.

Nearly forty-eight hours of cold, malodorous discomfort and aching bones before we were decanted from the train: three in the morning, pushing and shoving to line up on a strange railway siding, shivering in the cold damp. Shouted into rough order, we began the long trek down a dirt road. By seven, my feet were blistered inside my canvas lace-ups and I smelled dense pine, tree sap . . . and gunsmoke. The smell of war, or at least my war. My father said his time at the front had smelled of mud and wire, but perhaps every war smells different.

Mine was trees and smoke and blood.

Since that day, I have never gotten it out of my nose.

THERE IS A sameness to how war stories begin, isn't there? The story flows like a film, with suitably themed music. The proud recruit; the family farewells; the donning of the uniform—the music swells, tender and poignant. The taking of the soldier's oath; a dramatic moment— something with patriotic brass is called for. Then the training period as the wide-eyed new recruit learns to handle their weapon—put it to a military march, lots of drums. By then the recruit (and his audience, as he tells this story) is ready for battle.

But I arrived on Bessarabian soil among the rear units of the 25th Chapayev Rifle Division in the middle of utter chaos. There was no time for proper training or measured appreciation of the different moving moments of my initiation; there was barely time to gulp a dish of buckwheat porridge to the sound of far-off machine-gun fire. Mud squelched underfoot, and trees looked down like silent sentinels on the dirty tents, the rattling trucks, the soldiers rushing back and forth like ants. I changed into the uniform that was flung at me, rattled my oath off, and signed my life and body away to the Red Army, absorbing the information that I'd become a soldier of the 54th Stepan Razin Rifle Regiment, 1st Battalion, 2nd Company.

"Goodbye, civilian life," said Lena, cramming her new forage cap over her hair. "Not very many of us, are there? I wonder if that's because it's early days, or because they're sticking the women behind desks or into the hospital battalions?"

I knew there weren't *many* women in the Red Army, but I hadn't expected to be the only one in 2nd Company. I'd always got along well with men; most of my friends growing up were boys, and they accepted me as one of them without question. But it's one thing to run with a pack of boys through a world that was still half women, and another thing to find yourself the lone woman in an entire company of loud, boisterous, overexcited young men, hardly any other females in sight. "Cut my hair," I asked Lena suddenly, pulling my new cap off. "Chop it short at the neck."

"It's nice hair," she objected as I unpinned my thick plait.

"We won't have time here to keep long hair washed and combed." I stamped down the regrets—I was a middling sort of woman, not tall or short, not fat or thin, but the heavy chocolate-brown hair that rippled to my waist was beautiful. *Hair grows back,* I told myself. "Just hack it off, Lena. It's not only the washing—my father said once that the women who get along best in the army are the ones who don't draw attention to being female. Short hair. All business. No flirtation."

"One of the boys." Lena began sawing at my thick plait. "Right. Whack mine off next."

We sheared each other, hurled our severed braids ceremoniously into the nearest campfire, and traded rather grim smiles as they sizzled and stank. "Look after yourself," I told my new friend as she was shunted toward the medical battalion. "Eyes in the back of your head until you make yourself some friends who will watch your back." We didn't have to say why. All women know why.

"You too, Mila." Lena waved over one shoulder as she departed, and with her gone, the officers in my battalion seemed even less certain what to do with the only remaining female in the batch of new recruits. I found myself standing in front of a lieutenant barely old enough to shave, trying to explain that I already knew how to shoot—news he greeted like a mortician confronted by a corpse that had arrived on the slab already embalmed.

"You know how to shoot?" he repeated for the third time. "Well, maybe you think you do. War isn't women's business. I'll petition the battalion commander to transfer you to a medical battalion."

"I would be wasted as a medical orderly, sir." But I was waved off to the command post of the 1st Battalion, where I had the same conversation all over again, and then again when I fetched up—exasperated and stamping in my khaki tunic and new trousers—at the desk of a long-faced, lugubrious-looking captain. "You can shoot?" He looked at my various certificates. "Are you any good?"

"Try me, Comrade Captain," I replied. "A rifle with telescopic sights—"

He pushed his cap back on his thinning hair. "We have no sniper rifles."

"A standard Three Line, then?" Thinking back to the scarred instructor and his lessons handling the Mosin-Nagant rifle.

"We don't have those either, Lyudmila Mikhailovna. Not enough for the new arrivals." I could have been annoyed at the captain's use of my name, but he didn't curl his tongue around it the way I'd already heard some of the officers do. Captain Sergienko was gray, stalky, perhaps thirty years old and looking fifty, and he spoke my name like a man who was two weeks into a war and already felt like he hadn't slept in a year.

"How will I fight then, Comrade Captain?" My helmet clamped awkwardly under one arm, I looked at my artificial leather boots, two sizes too big, and had the distinct thought: *All dressed up, and no way to fight.*

"For you new recruits, the main weapon for now will be the shovel."

A shovel.

Not really a dramatic moment, is it? There isn't a sweeping Pro-kofiev theme for a new recruit heroically digging trenches. But that was my entrance to the 25th Chapayev Rifle Division: a shovel rather than a rifle, and a disorganized scramble into a mass retreat rather than a headlong sprint toward glory.

One of the many ways in which real life is not like a film.

I WOULDN'T SHOOT a single bullet for nearly a month—and most of that month is only fragments in my memory. Clarity came to me with a trigger; before that it was chaos and clods of earth, confusion and clotted blood. Perhaps it's different for the generals, the men commanding large military units who look at nice clean maps and see the bigger picture, the whole machine. For us cogs, only the earth directly under our boots is clear. I'd been flung headfirst into a welter of attacks and counterattacks, surges and retreats—I marched, I obeyed every order shouted at me, I learned to stop flinching at the sound of artillery overhead. What I didn't learn was how to fight, even as battles raged the entire length of our borders. There was no time to catch my breath or even learn the name of the man marching beside me, much less fight.

Fragments.

I remember the regiments traveling in the day and in the night once we began the scrambling retreat across the Black Sea steppes—trucks, horse-drawn carts, on foot. I remember tumbling down to sleep at night fully dressed, too exhausted to watch my back, though it didn't matter because in such chaos the men in my company had no energy to register that Comrade Private Pavlichenko was female, much less do anything about it. I remember the steppe as it looked on the warm summer nights, spread out on both sides of the road like an opened book—and how it looked in the day, booming with cannon volleys, pricked everywhere by fires, the smell of burnt gunpowder lingering bitterly in the nose. I remember civilians retreating with us, whole caravans of factory workers and equipment; farmers prodding herds of livestock from the collective farms; women and children trudging along with laden baskets and knapsacks, shuddering whenever a Focke-Wulf droned overhead.

I remember digging trenches with small sapper spades by the light of the moon, as long-range enemy artillery crackled. I remember realizing I'd been at the front a full month and hadn't yet written my father. *Belovs don't retreat*—yet we were retreating, burying our dead in bomb craters as we went. We were retreating in swaths all along our own diminishing border, falling back before the swastika.

I remember a field of wheat going up in billowing sheets of flame under a flight of German bombers; remember the twisted shells of burnt towns and fire-bombed machinery. The Junkers flying overhead would line up a cratered road crammed with walking families and strafe directly down the center—as my company was ordered off into the trees for cover. One blood-laced twilight, a rawboned woman whose cart had just been bombed to splinters spat at me when I came back to the road with the rest of my company. "To hell with you," she hissed. "Why aren't you fighting these bastards?" I remember lowering my eyes, shouldering my pack, and falling into formation, unable to say a word.

I remember the fear. *Push it away, push it down*, I told myself, but there was no pushing it away, it was everywhere: we lived fear, breathed fear, ate and drank and sweated fear. Every drone of German planes overhead could mean my end, and I had nothing to defend myself with but a *shovel*.

That changed on a July morning along the shattered, cratered hellscape that marked the Novopavlovsk to the Novy Artsyz line. The artillery fire had been sounding in waves; for the moment my regiment was dug in. *Dug in*, a pretty term for *hiding*, sheltering in makeshift trenches and stands of splintered trees, hunkering down on our heels every time another wave of deafening fire rolled through like the footsteps of a giant. The man sheltering next to me in our dugout slit of a trench was little more than a boy, freckled and earnest, fiddling so constantly with his rifle that I wanted to box his ears. Another surge of shellfire crashed; I laced my hands behind my neck and lowered my head, hissing at the boy to keep his head down. "Ride it out," I shouted over the din, nearly choking on my own reflexive terror, "the attacks come in waves, it's like childbirth—" but he just gave me a puzzled look. Of course he did; what a useless analogy to give a man, and I hunted for another one, but suddenly his face was a sheet of blood. He touched his forehead, looking even more puzzled, and I saw the side of his head had been cratered like an egg. He toppled slowly into me; I tried to support him, but he was too heavy, sliding down into the mud.

Leaving his blood-slicked rifle in my shaking hands.

THE SOVIET DELEGATION: DAY 1

August 27, 1942

WASHINGTON, D.C.

CHAPTER 5

f she's ever held a rifle in her life, the marksman thought, watching the supposed girl sniper disappear into the White House after the First Lady, *I'll eat my damn hat.*

The doors closed behind the Soviet delegation, and that was that. "When do we get a crack at the Russkies?" the *Washington Post* journalist wanted to know, riffling his notes. "They're not going to make us wait until the student conference kicks off, are they?"

"There will be a press assembly tonight at the Soviet embassy." The marksman dialed up his Virginia drawl, turning away from the White House in its rosy dawn glow. "Save your questions till then. Unless you scored an invitation to the White House welcome breakfast this morning."

"You got one? Lucky son of a gun . . ."

The marksman smiled. Luck had nothing to do with it; the men who'd hired him for this job moved in high circles, and they'd made sure his name (the name on the immaculately falsified press badge, anyway) was on the list. "Why do you need to see the girl up close?" they'd grumbled. "You need to frame her, not date her."

"I'll need to know how to pull her aside when the time comes," the marksman replied. "If she'll be easy to distract or difficult. If I'll need to bribe someone in her delegation to give me access to her, and if so, who. And I'll only have a week, from the day the Soviet delegation arrives to the last day of the conference, to figure all this out."

"Sounds like a lot of work" the answer had been, and the marksman shrugged. In truth, he'd always rather enjoyed the elbow grease involved in a new job: settling into a well-planned cover identity, backing that identity up with solid research, *living* the job if necessary. He remembered that time in 1932 when he'd worked four solid months in an insurance office to get access to a mark . . . sold a lot of honest insurance, too. Putting those hours in *was* work, no question—meticulous, frequently boring work. But he'd always figured there were two kinds of men in this business: good shooters who thought pulling a trigger was the job and only did enough work to research a skin-deep cover, sweating the whole time . . . and pros to whom the deep cover *was* the job, who put in enough hours and research that they didn't have to sweat by the time it came to pulling a trigger.

He knew which type he was.

"Still a lot of trouble to take for a patsy," his higher-ups' flunky had complained.

Says the man who won't end up in handcuffs if this all goes south, thought the marksman. "Just keep making sure my press-pass name clears all the security and ends up on all the necessary guest lists and travel passes," he'd said, and at least there hadn't been any trouble *there.* He could usually find his own ways to gain whatever access a job needed—after nineteen years, he had a stable of contacts and informants he could pay for just about any information or paperwork—but the men he was working for now could accomplish a great deal more with a little backroom hand-waving.

He had a meeting with his employers in thirty minutes, in fact—or rather, his employers' flunky. It wasn't necessary, but they wanted reassurances, and he had an hour or so to kill before heading back here for the welcome breakfast, where the bucktoothed First Lady would host the Soviets and a handful of press in the small dining room on the first floor of the White House. Idly, the marksman wondered what Mila Pavlichenko was doing now. Was she awed to be standing under that fabled roof or sneering at the capitalist Western decadence of it all? Was she reviewing her cover story about her supposed 309 Nazi kills, or feeling lost, floundering, far from home? He hoped the latter. Lonely women were easy to pick off. He'd targeted quite a few over the years.

He wasn't sure yet whether he'd need to kill her or not. Whatever option proved simplest: all professionals knew that the simpler any plan was, the better. Because as soon as bullets began singing, even the best-laid plans went awry. A certain amount of improvisation was inevitable. Whether he ended up leaving her body as a suicide-note confession on the last day of the conference, or merely fixed a frame around her and let her Soviet-inflated reputation put the noose around her neck, one thing was certain.

When you planned to assassinate a president, you timed it when a Russian sniper was in town to take the fall for you.

The marksman jingled his pocketful of uncut diamonds as he flagged down a passing cab. "The Lincoln Memorial," he told the cabbie, rolling down the window to appreciate the warm morning breeze. The forecast for the week ahead predicted nothing but blue skies, hot days, and perfect late-summer weather. *Miss Pavlichenko, enjoy your first visit to America while it lasts.*

Notes by the First Lady

As I show the Soviet delegation up the White House stairs to their guest rooms, my mind is still lingering over Franklin's words to me this morning after his fall: "They'd pray I never got up." An extra twist on the word they, *beyond his usual amused irony. Bitterness? Worry? I ponder that as I usher Lyudmila Pavlichenko to the rosy chamber that will be hers during her visit.*

My husband has detractors and rivals, of course. Every president is hated. The man who has won an unprecedented third term is hated by more than most. He usually laughs such hatred off . . . but he was not laughing this morning.

Is there a particular cabal of enemies which has him worried?

I blink, startled out of my thoughts as the young Russian woman—who has so far said not a single word—moves across the bedchamber to the window, where the morning light shines through the glass. For an instant I think she is going to exclaim over the view of the gardens flowering below, but instead she yanks the shades down with a snap. "Is something wrong, my dear?" I ask.

She says something in Russian, looking composed enough as she folds her hands at her waist, but I sense discomfiture. "She says she prefers not to have uncovered windows at her back, Mrs. Roosevelt," the interpreter translates helpfully.

Ah. They say she is a sniper—I didn't know what to make of that. In truth, I still don't. But she thanks me for my hospitality through the interpreter and I examine those opaque dark eyes, I wish I could ask her: How do you know when an enemy is lurking? How do you know if it is just nerves or genuine danger?

How do you know if there is a target on your back?

FOURTEEN
MONTHS AGO

June 1941
THE ODESSA FRONT, USSR
Mila

CHAPTER 6

M y memoir, the official version: Every woman remembers her first.

My memoir, the unofficial version: Those words mean very different things for me than most women.

"I SEE YOU'VE managed to get PE sights for that rifle." Lugubrious-looking Captain Sergienko nodded at the weapon now registered in my name. "Have you fired it yet?"

"Yes, Comrade Captain." I kept my eyes forward, wondering why I'd been called to the command post in the long, slanting light just before dark.

He studied me. I shifted in my boots, realizing my lips were dry enough to crack, that my chopped hair was filthy. The Chapayev division had reached the Tiraspol fortified district and dug in. Not a bad place to turn and fight: earthworks, reinforced concrete, and stone firing points; dugouts; deep trenches; machine guns and artillery of our own. The line of Russian defense, strung like a necklace across the throat of Alexandrovka, Buyalyk, Brinovka, Karpova, Belyayevka . . . Had I really been at war less than six weeks? I blinked that thought away.

Sergienko's voice brought me back to myself. "Have you hit anyone you've lined up in those sights?"

"I don't know, Comrade Captain. It hasn't been that kind of shooting." I'd fired like a good soldier—when I was told, blindly, over the lip of trenches and behind trees, as the Chapayev division continued its retreat. You couldn't see what you were firing at in such moments;

you fired because you were being fired on, not because you had anything in your sights. I didn't know if I'd hit anyone; I knew only
that I was less afraid when I had the comforting weight of a rifle
in my hand. Nonsensical, really—having a weapon didn't make me
invulnerable—but I felt less helpless. I couldn't push my fear away,
but I could push it into my weapon.

"Come with me," Sergienko said, and I followed him out of the
command post through the mess of crates and tents, makeshift desks
and earth plowed into bulwarks, some ways distant to a bombed-out
peasant hut where he could point toward the far end of Belyayevka.
Among the distant overgrown trees was a large house with a ridge-
roofed porch, gleaming in the setting sun. "You see?"

I nodded. Two officers in sandy-gray uniforms came out onto the
porch; I could see the gleam of their insignia, their pudding-basin
helmets. Not Hitlerites; Romanians—Germany's ally. So close. I had
not yet seen an enemy so clearly; until now they had all been shadowy
shapes on the other side of trenches, helmeted outlines in the cock-
pits of planes strafing overhead. These two men weren't even half a
kilometer away. Standing there on a porch in the sunshine, *scratching*
themselves, having a laugh. Our invaders.

The fear banked constantly in my stomach began to curl again.
I usually felt the fear cold and blue-violet as a shaving of tungsten
twisting under a lathe, but this time the metal of it was forging from
blue to red. Fear to rage.

"That's likely their staff headquarters," the weary-looking Captain Sergienko was saying. "You showed me your certificates; from
our records you're the only one yet who's come in with an advanced
marksmanship course already under her belt. Now that we've a moment to breathe"—*between retreats*, he didn't say, but he might as well
have—"let me see what you can do."

I was already unslinging my rifle.

Sergienko stood back, watching. I felt the pulse beating under my jaw as I began setting up to shoot at the two men. *Targets,* I told myself, but couldn't ignore the reality that these weren't painted circles on a range or glass bottles in cleft sticks.

They are enemies, the anger inside me said, stoking higher as I moved through my preparations. *Invaders.* I hadn't asked them to come here. I hadn't asked them to ally with Germany, to make grandiose plans for renaming Odessa *Antonescu* once they captured it; to purge any territory they captured of Jews and Gypsies, Ukrainians and Russians, because we were racially undesirable. I hadn't asked for any of this. I wanted to stay home, cuddle my son, finish my damned dissertation. I didn't necessarily want the other side dead; I only wanted them *gone.* But they weren't going, and so help me, I would settle for dead.

I never stopped moving, never hesitated. What hesitation can there truly be, after three weeks of desperate retreat under enemy fire? I just exhaled my rage and let training take over.

A good shooter moves without haste, every movement as deliberate as a clock's hour hand ticking over. *One* . . . Take the first cool, measuring glance through the sights, the moment the soul falls silent and the eye takes control. *Two* . . . Estimate the horizontal sight line; I saw it cover the shoulders of the officer at the top of the porch steps. *Three* . . . Use that benchmark to calculate distance, the equation I'd learned in my shooting course employed in a blink: four hundred meters. *Four* . . . Sliding Ball L light bullets into place. *Five* . . . Finding a firing position in the bombed-out farmhouse where we stood: trying a belly-down angle—not possible; trying a kneeling position behind the half-shattered wall with the stones supporting my rifle's barrel—better. *Six* . . . Settle in: weight resting on the heel of the right boot, left elbow on bent left knee, hold it until you are still, until you are stone, until frost could gather on your lashes. *Seven* . . . Adjust the rifle strap under the elbow, let it carry the weapon's weight. *Eight* . . . Find the target again through the sight, adjust for wind.

Nine . . . Find the trigger, take aim. *Ten* . . . Breathe in. *Eleven* . . . Breathe out.

On *twelve* the clock strikes midnight and the finger squeezes the trigger.

I looked at the invaders through my sights, and on the exhale I fired.

Seven shots later I lowered the rifle, realizing my ears were ringing and my shoulder stung from the recoil. Captain Sergienko lowered his binoculars, looking at me. "You got the rear officer with your third shot, and the front officer with your fourth—even though they were off the porch and scrambling fast by then."

"I saw." My voice seemed to be coming from very far away. I realized my hands were trembling and gripped the rifle's stock harder. When I looked at the captain, his face was still overlaid with the lines of my sights, as though it had burned itself inside my eyes.

The captain looked through his binoculars at the Romanian staff headquarters again. There seemed to be quite a lot of activity swarming that porch now. "Good shooting."

"Not really." My face burned. "It should only have taken me two bullets."

"But you still downed both men." Sergienko looked reflective, retreating from the farmhouse now and beckoning me with him. The Romanians might calculate where my shots had come from and fire back on this position. "I've got feral Siberian boys who can put a bullet through a squirrel's eye at half a kilometer, but when I asked them to show me what they could do, they all froze when it came to firing on a man for the first time. You know the science of it—ballistics, trajectories, all that. More important, you knew how to let the science carry you through when it came to fire on a human target. You might have missed, but you didn't hesitate. That's rare in new recruits."

"It's just training," I said. "I've had some already; the others haven't. That's all."

"Training? Not instinct?"

Sergienko was a smart man, but even he (like many, as I was soon to learn) was inclined to be fanciful about a sniper's *instinct*, about *feeling it in the blood*, about how it was all *in the gut*. Rubbish. I was a good library researcher because I'd learned how to file, catalog, and organize; I was a good shooter because I'd learned range calculation and distance estimation, and knew how far a rotating bullet would drift laterally from muzzle to target. I could do this not because of some inborn instinct, but because I had studied and drilled and practiced until training *became* instinct. I was a good sniper because I was a good student. "Training," I repeated, with a belated salute.

"And you can do it again? I can use long-distance shooters."

"I can do it again." Even after five missed shots, I knew I could. Because I'd trained to be *perfect*, and perfection had become a habit too strong to allow missteps. Life so rarely allowed a woman to be perfect, much less a mother, much less a single mother, much less a single mother in the Soviet Union, which was a beautiful place but not precisely a forgiving one . . . so when I was lashing myself inside for missing an exam question or a chance at a student conference, I could at least go to the range and know that there, I wouldn't miss a thing.

And that compulsion not to miss was so strong, I'd put two live targets down today without hesitation.

I hadn't stopped to examine the enemy faces through my sights, but their features must have made an impression despite me, because I saw them now in my mind's eye with sickening clarity. The first officer had been close-shaven, hawk-nosed; the second had been swarthy with the beginnings of a paunch. Enemies—but perhaps they had also been husbands, fathers. All the quirks and talents, weaknesses and foibles that made up two unique human lives, extinguished in seconds by two bullets.

Suddenly I wanted to put my head between my knees, but I couldn't do that in front of my commanding officer. I swallowed the bile rising in my throat and took a glance over one shoulder toward the building I'd targeted—a building now swarming, so I imagined, with panicked Romanian officers. *Invaders,* I reminded myself again. And despite my moment's queasiness I knew that the next time I fired on my enemies, I wouldn't miss.

"Can you use me, Comrade Captain?" I asked. "As a sniper?"

My scarred instructor had often used that word. This was the first time I spoke it.

"Oh, yes." Sergienko strung his binoculars over his arm, looking suddenly so serious my heart began to thud. "There's just one thing."

"W-what?"

"Seven shots on two Nazis! You need to conserve cartridges, Lyudmila Mikhailovna. Such waste!" His scowl held for a moment, then cracked to a somewhat lugubrious smile. For the first time in weeks, I found myself laughing. A shaky laugh, but still a laugh. Laughter at the front—I hadn't known such a thing could feel so good, be so necessary.

"I'll get it right next time, Comrade Captain." I saluted, smiling but kicking myself, too. Seven shots for two marks—my instructor would have scratched his scar and asked if I wouldn't mind aiming for Moscow next time instead of Paris. "Two lives, two bullets next time."

"Do try. They'll be crawling back soon, and there's no one but us to stamp on them."

"America," I said, because there were rumors: the Americans would join the war, they'd send troops to the east to take pressure off our lines. But Captain Sergienko shook his head.

"The Americans would rather leave us to rot. It's all on us." He nodded dismissal, turning to head toward his command post, but then turned back to me. "You've opened your tally today, sniper. Let the record show that L. M. Pavlichenko's tally now stands at two."

"No," I heard myself say.

My captain raised his eyebrows.

"These two were test shots." They still counted—I'd never forget them—but it hadn't been official, not yet. And I wanted it to be clear that I didn't care about padding a tally at all costs, counting lives like coins. That was another kind of showing off, and I still didn't like it. Maybe this was the moment the midnight side of my moon started to wax from crescent to full, but making some game out of my skills was still distasteful to me. I just wanted to do a job and repel this invasion, not build myself a reputation. "Sniper-Soldier Pavlichenko will open her tally tomorrow."

CHAPTER 7

M y memoir, the official version: Before an attack, you steel your-self with thoughts of the motherland and Comrade Stalin.

My memoir, the unofficial version: Before an attack, you usually feel sick.

THE PRE-BATTLE FIT of gloom—everyone has their own way of combating it. Most of the men in 2nd Company with me relied on a stiff belt of vodka, a bracing exchange of the dirtiest jokes possible, and a rousing chorus or two of "Broad Is My Native Land" or "Over There Across the River." I liked to pull my now-dog-eared dissertation out of my pack and leaf through it. There was something wonderfully soothing about Bogdan Khmelnitsky when I was about to come under shellfire.

A state of siege had been declared in my lovely city of Odessa; it was nearly September, and my sniper's tally was—well, it had been officially opened and I'd been adding to it almost every day, becoming accustomed to that dark and bloody-handed work without too many innate lurches between fear and anger, queasiness and perfectionism. But today I was off with the rest of 2nd Company, not on one of those routine sorties that made up so much of war, but something different.

Smoke drifting over water, screams echoing across the flat plain of the isthmus between the Khajibeisk and Kuyalnik estuaries. The 3rd Battalion was pinned down, hammered by three days of shelling, cut down to no more than four hundred defenders. Romanians spilled over the plain, a sandy-gray mass firing wherever they saw movement, grappling and clawing with anyone they could drag out of the half-destroyed fortifications. Someone was shouting orders; the scream of artillery overhead turned the words to nonsense. I slipped and scrambled into a half-dug trench with a makeshift parapet, set up with my rifle, began taking shots—and almost as soon as I began, the thunder of guns died away.

A silence fell then, drifting across the bloodied ground like the smoke. The Romanians had faded away, fallen back to regroup. Why do these strange pauses fall in the middle of furious fights? Battles seem to be living things, creatures that need to breathe as much as the soldiers who are fighting them. When these silences fall, the impulse is to huddle where you are with your head down, but only novices freeze. The experienced cram a hasty lump of bread down, unfasten trousers for a quick piss, check their ammunition with hands that their friends pretend not to see shaking. I wiped my rifle down and reloaded, flexing my trembling fingers. The man beside me had done the same and then pulled a battered copy of *War and Peace* from his knapsack and calmly propped it against his rifle sights.

"*War and Peace*?" I heard myself asking, bizarrely conversational. "You couldn't bring anything more ironic to war?"

He turned a page. "Wanted to see how the Battle of Austerlitz turned out."

"Napoleon won. Hope that doesn't spoil the book for you." I couldn't remember the reader's name—a blade-thin Siberian, black hair razored brutally close to his skull. "I never finished *War and Peace*. Never got past the New Year's Eve ball."

The Siberian raised his eyebrows. My taste in literature was clearly being judged.

"I prefer history to novels." I shrugged. "Give me a good account of the seventeenth-century Polish-Lithuanian Commonwealth/ Ottoman Empire conflict any day."

The Siberian returned to his book, but I saw the corner of his mouth quirk. "Philistine," he said. I opened my mouth to reply—a vigorous philosophical discussion on the merits of imaginative fiction versus historical documentation seemed like just the way to pass the time in a muddy trench in between artillery attacks—when a strange skein of sound brought my head and the Siberian's whipping round in unison.

The Romanian infantry was advancing again, not spreading out across the steppe, but packing forward in dense columns, feet swinging high to the drums as if they were on parade . . . and they were *singing*. Officers strode between the gaps in the columns, unsheathed sabers on their shoulders; on the left flank I saw a priest in a gold-embroidered gown, three church banners billowing behind. He was shouting, urging the men on under the heartbeat of the drums and the massed roar of the hymn.

Seven hundred meters away.

I marked my field of fire, calculations sliding liquid-quick through my brain: a fence at the edge of a cornfield, six hundred meters; some wolfberry thickets closer, five hundred meters . . . the dull roar of the hymn grew louder, and our mortar battery launched a strike. I saw earth fountain up against the sky among the gray columns, but the living closed ranks and marched over the dead. Bayonets lowered and the blades gleamed like shivers of trapped lightning. I made a quick count—perhaps two thousand bayonets, coming for my stripped-down regiment of four hundred. The priest kept on shrieking, and as my pulse pounded, I wondered what he was saying.

"*Vive l'empereur?*" guessed the dark Siberian at my side, as though reading my mind.

" 'Long live the emperor'? Why—"

He brought up his rifle, and as I did the same, I realized what he meant. Napoleon's troops had roared *Vive l'empereur!* as they marched in massed columns exactly like this, under eagles not so different from Hitler's eagles, closing ranks around the dead and rolling inexorably toward Tolstoy's heroes at Austerlitz . . . and they had marched in the same columns, screamed the same cries against Russians when Napoleon decided to invade the motherland.

Well, we all knew how *that* had turned out.

The rage was stirring in my stomach again, doing its work to drown the fear. Two thousand bayonets were coming right toward me, and my terror died. I waited just until they passed that fence by the cornfield and opened fire.

Click, click, click. Midnight struck on the clock with every second that passed. I was aware of the Siberian beside me firing calm and fast, rifle propped on the thick spine of *War and Peace.* I realized I'd run through all my cartridges; when I called *Out!* he pushed a bag of his own at me, a yellow-tipped Ball D heavy bullet gripped between his teeth, and I reloaded and kept firing. *Got the priest,* I heard someone grunt on my other side.

How long did we lie there firing, our four hundred against their two thousand? Suddenly the sun was setting, lighting the feathered grass of the steppe to flame, and my ears hurt again with the boom of Romanian artillery laying down cover fire. The Romanians were stumbling back over their own wounded, and for the first time in what felt like hours, I lifted my eyes from my sights. I saw those hatched sight lines over my vision again, seemingly burned over anything I saw out of my right eye.

"What—" I began, and that was when a stray mortar shell screamed into the parapet of the trench, not two meters away. My rifle blasted into pieces, ripped straight out of my hands; I heard my own cry of agony that was all for my damaged weapon and not my own flesh. I saw a glimpse of the Siberian leaping toward me as I crumpled into the trench.

A fall of earth slid down over me, and then there was a familiar voice saying, "Wake up, sleepyhead."

I peeled up my gummy eyelids and saw the blunt thin face of Lena Paliy, my friend from the train.

"No, you can't get up," she said, her voice sounding curiously distant—my ears were buzzing as though my head were a beehive. "No, your rifle didn't make it. No, you are not *fine*, it is not *just a sprain*, you have a concussion and damaged eardrums, and your joints and spine got such a rattling, you're going to be stumping around like Baba Yaga for at least a week."

"What can you tell me that starts with *yes*?" I asked peevishly, realizing I was flat on my back in a hospital cot.

"*Yes*, you can go back to your division soon. *Yes*, you are going to do everything Lena Paliy tells you, because she is the best orderly in this medical battalion. *Yes*, you are an idiot for sneaking about under the moon like Lady Midnight." Lena grinned at my frustration, relenting. "You're in the field hospital, Mila. Your regimental mates dug you out and carried you here."

"They shouldn't have, not for a concussion and damaged eardrums," I grumbled. "If I were a man, they'd have told me to shake it off, not rushed me to a stretcher."

"Probably," Lena agreed. "But now that you're here, be sensible and look after your health."

"Fate and fortune grant us health," I quoted my mother. "For everything else, we wait in line."

"Oh, shut up and enjoy the quiet. We're far enough back from the front lines, you'd hardly know there was a war on."

I wondered what had happened to the Tolstoy-reading Siberian, but Lena said no one else had been brought in with me. I wouldn't know till I got back to the front, so I stretched my toes under the clean sheets, wincing as my neck lit up with sparks of pain. Long rows of cots stretched across the floor, and I smelled antiseptic over the coppery tang of old blood. I had the cot on the end, by a window; outside swayed a tangle of tree branches, as if the hospital had been erected near some abandoned orchard. Wind rustled the leaves, and there was a flutter of wings . . . little gray sparrows, black-headed starlings. Out-side the world was tilting toward autumn, and for some reason that made my eyes fill up with tears. The last thing I remembered from the front was the hot spread of the steppe, those massed columns of fanatically singing enemies under the banner of their shrieking priest.

They will never stop, I thought. *Not ever. Not until they're all dead—or so many of them dead that the living can no longer clamber over the corpses.*

"The attack—" I began, but Lena forestalled me.

"Pushed back. That one, at least. They keep coming like roaches, of course."

And my division was still there, fighting without me.

"So," Lena said, seeing how my eyes had filled, "you're starting to rack them up, sniper."

"Who told you that?"

"It's getting around. A woman sniper, that's different. What is it now, twenty on your tally?"

"Twenty-one." I swiped at my eyes. Even that small movement sent a jolt of pain through my spine. "Officially."

"What do you mean, *officially?*" Lena pulled out a pack of Litka cigarettes. "Is it twenty-one or not?"

"It's not like picking apples, and just counting how many are in your basket," I flared. "The only marks added to the official tally are the ones someone else has verified, or the ones that I've verified by bringing back dog tags or papers from—"

She struck a match. "From the bodies?"

"Yes." A part of my new assignment that I loathed, but it had to be done, so I did it. "If there isn't verification, the mark isn't added to my tally. And sometimes I can't tell if I've hit a target or not, so those aren't added, and neither are the ones I hit when I'm fighting along-side my whole company. It's not—clean-cut. It's twenty-one official, and I don't even know how many unofficial." I waited for her to ask if it bothered me. She didn't, just silently offered a cigarette. I shook my head. "I don't smoke."

"I don't, either." She inhaled with a sigh of satisfaction, sitting down on the end of my bed.

I moved my feet for her, feeling another wrench of pain along my back. "Don't you have other patients?"

"I'm on break. And there's a captain on the second floor I'm avoiding until he's done with his rounds. Drooling for a frontline wife, thinks I don't know he has the real thing back in Moscow." She made a certain face. "Officers can be such shits."

I made a noise in agreement, glad not to be talking about tallies and kills anymore. "The rank-and-file boys aren't nearly as bad, are they?" When Lena and I cut our hair on first arriving at the front, we'd both been bracing ourselves for being outnumbered by the men in our companies, but they hadn't turned out to be the problem. You developed your own way of dealing with fellow soldiers: Lena's, I could see, was deft avoidance and blunt profanity; mine was a kind of breezy, no-nonsense toughness I'd perfected as a tomboy running with the local boys. Do it right, and the men in your company came to look at you as a kind of honorary male: cheerful, sexless, useful in a crisis. (The uniform helped, too. Much to the disappointment of the American press I'd meet later, a woman soldier's uniform in the Red Army was not tight, svelte, or alluring. It had all the grace of a potato sack, but itchier.)

No, it was the officers who turned out to be the problem, not the rank-and-file soldiers. Those damned shiny lieutenants and captains who regarded female soldiers as a perk of rank—they'd come prowling whenever they heard a new woman had arrived at the front. There's nothing quite like sitting in a dugout with a needle file, working on the bolt mechanism of your rifle, only to see some amorous bit of brass with three or four bars on his collar come sniffing around with a gleaming smile, a bar of chocolate, and an indecent proposal.

"Have the officers come at you yet?" Lena asked, thoughts clearly mirroring mine. "Or are they just marginally smart enough to steer clear of a woman with more than twenty kills?"

"I've got a good captain. Sergienko shoos the officers off the women in his battalion."

"Some don't like hearing no, regardless what a fellow officer says," Lena warned. "They'll slither at you when his back's turned, so keep your eyes as sharp as your sights."

"Same for you." I struggled to sit up, catching the hiss of pain in my teeth. "Any other news while I've been out?"

"Odessa's changed, from what the locals say. Sandbags in the streets, antiaircraft guns in the squares, windows taped up. No holiday people swanning into the resorts."

I remembered that beautiful day on the beach, the crowded café filled with laughter. "What else?"

Lena hesitated. "Lots of casualties," she said briefly. We traded another set of looks; I took her hand in mine and gave a silent squeeze. Defeatism wasn't allowed; you couldn't go about griping that the motherland was losing to the Hitlerites . . . but Lena had only to count the dead passing through, and I had only to count the waves of artillery fire booming over the steppe. Easily three enemy salvos to every one of ours.

"Looks like I'd better head back to the front and nab a few more," I said, trying to keep my voice even.

"Bag a few for me." She squeezed my hand back, then stubbed out her cigarette in a discarded bottle cap. "I'd better get moving. Hopefully the captain with the wandering eye has gone creeping back to his sewer by now. I'll be back in a few hours—maybe even with mail. Letters find us a lot easier here, closer to the city."

Four letters caught up with me within the week. Darling Mama, scolding me not to drink untreated water on the march, enclosing a precious scribbled scrap from Slavka that began *Dear Mamochka* and brought me to tears . . . Quiet Papa, telling me about his days in the army: *Belovs have always been lucky in battle.* My family was such a long way away from me now, evacuated to Udmurtia—they might as well have been writing from Paris, or the moon.

Another letter from Sofya in Odessa: *Did you hear Vika's twin enlisted in the tank corps? Vika says men who are dancers are usually boneheads, but she never thought her brother was the biggest bonehead of them all. I should dash to the library now; I'm boxing up the more valuable scrolls in case of evacuation. The place is humming!*

For a moment I smelled not antiseptic and blood, but the Odessa library's scent of old leather, parchment, books. My favorite smell in the world. At the front with my rifle, Mila the student seemed very far away, but here I could feel her with me, shuffling note cards and pencils in her bag, organizing her research according to color-coordinated tabs. How had that woman ended up here, with her ears ringing and her spine aching from mortar fire? All that woman wanted was an orderly life with no mistakes in it; to ride the train chugging through her life right to its end because she couldn't afford to miss any more stops.

Well, I'd stepped off that train and found myself on a different set of tracks, with a different set of targets. Only here, the cost if I missed was much higher.

The sterile, stuffy air in the ward suddenly choked me. I reached out an arm and managed to push open the window by the bed, drinking in the breeze. The unpruned branches of the tree outside were nearly knocking on the sill. I broke off a leaf, smoothing along its veins, and picked up my son's letter. He was about to go on his first hike with the Young Pioneers; he was so proud of that new red kerchief that he even wore it to bed, and he was worried he wouldn't fit in with the country lads who knew everything about the woods. *I'm a city boy, Mamochka, I don't know anything about trees and plants . . .*

"What kind of trees are those outside?" I asked the nearest nurse, pointing to the window. She answered, and I wrote Slavka back in a firm hand, stopping now and then to wipe my eyes. *Darling* morzhik, *I will help you learn all about trees and plants. Your mamochka is never too busy for you, even at the front! Enclosed please find a leaf clipping from a pear tree: see the oval leaves, the pattern of the veining? Now you'll know it again when you see it. It belongs to the scientific classification of . . .* I paused, not sure what kind of scientific classification this type of pear tree was, but I was going to find out. I might be hundreds of kilometers away from my son, but I'd make him feel like his mama was still watching.

I sealed the letter and the leaf inside with a kiss, and then wrote another to my family. And this one told them I'd become a sniper-soldier and that I planned to take down a thousand Germans and then return home with pride. Somehow I had to be the woman who wrote both kinds of letters and did not fail at either. The mother and the sniper both, succeeding at both.

"GOOD TO SEE you back with us," Captain Sergienko greeted me when I finally located the command post near a half-destroyed village. Nearly two weeks after I'd been shipped out with the other wounded, I'd cajoled Lena into getting me released and cadged a lift on a truck headed for the Kuyalnik and Bolshoi Ajalyk estuaries. Another half day to find the command post in the mess of dugouts, carts, trucks, and shattered buildings that comprised the front line, but here was my captain with his familiar gray face, looking three-quarters dead as opposed to only halfway there.

I saluted. "Comrade Private L. M. Pavlichenko reporting."

"You are out of uniform, Lyudmila Mikhailovna." I looked down at myself, startled, but he handed me a little gray cardboard box. I opened it and saw two brass triangles. "You're no longer a private, but a corporal. Congratulations."

A thrum went through me, a tangled mix of pleasure—how proud my father would be!—and disquiet. *You are being promoted over corpses.* Quietly I attached the triangles to the raspberry-colored parade tabs on my collar, listening as my captain gave me a list of the dead: the commander of my platoon, thirty other men from my battalion. They couldn't even be replaced with soldier recruits, but with volunteer sailors from Sevastopol, not a lick of infantry experience among them . . . My stomach sank with every new bit of bad news.

"There's a new rifle waiting for you," my captain finished, "given the destruction of your old one. We've received directives for snipers from the high command of the Odessa defense district, and that"— his voice shifted into official cadences—"is to occupy the most advantageous positions for observation and firing, to give the enemy no peace, to deprive him of the opportunity to move freely in the lines closest to the front—and to disrupt and degrade all enemy morale, good order, and discipline among the ranks." Sergienko's face didn't look at all lugubrious now. It looked fierce, and I could feel my still-sore spine stretch hungrily in response. That list of the dead had brought rage curling back through me, where it had slept muted under the pain of the concussion, the weariness, the longing for my son. "We don't have many qualified as snipers," my captain went on, "so look for new recruits who can be trained. For one, you'll need to find yourself a partner." Snipers worked best in pairs, watching each other's backs.

"Yes, Comrade Captain." I saluted, already itching to get my hands on the new rifle. I'd known my last weapon so well she'd felt like an extension of my own flesh; I'd have to get to know this one. I'd modified my old Three Line to suit my exact firing style, removing the wood along the whole length of the handguard groove so it no longer touched the barrel; filing down the tip of the gunstock. Once I did the same for the new rifle and got off some practice rounds, we'd be friends . . .

"Lyudmila Mikhailovna?" Sergienko added as I turned to leave.

"Yes, Comrade Captain?"

He looked me hard in the eyes. "Good hunting."

Two words that helped me put away the mother, the daughter, the student, and let the sniper unfurl her wings.

CHAPTER 8

My memoir, the official version: Rank conveys privileges.
My memoir, the unofficial version: Being known as someone who can put a bullet through a target's eye at five hundred meters also conveys privileges.

"OUT," LENA TOLD the half-naked man in the banya's steam room. "Or face the wrath of the deadliest shot in Odessa."

He rose from the pine bench, towel around his waist, ruffling a hand through sweat-damp blond hair. "Can I at least get dressed?"

"I'm not shooting anyone just so I can get a bath," I protested to Lena, but she was already tossing the tall man his clothes. Civilian clothes, I was glad to see. At least it wasn't an officer or a fellow soldier she was ruthlessly ejecting.

"I usually like to know a woman's name before she sees me with my pants off," he complained good-naturedly as he padded out.

I laughed, and he grinned at me as Lena dragged me into the steam, though not without a cheerful ogle at the fair-haired man's gleaming shoulders.

"I'm having a bite of that when I'm done," she decided, bolting the door from the inside. "Now, strip off and soak in this heat till your hip loosens up."

"No doctor I've ever met said a long steam in the banya did anything for a wrenched hip, Lena Paliy." I eased down my trousers, hissing at the pain in the joint. "You're just using me to get first crack at the bathing facilities."

"Too fucking right, Mila Pavlichenko. You know how long it's been since I've visited a proper banya?" Lena shimmied out of her uniform like a snakeskin, flopping down naked on the long wooden bench. "You're welcome."

The warm baritone of the man we'd ejected came floating through the door. "You ladies just came off the Gildendorf attack?"

"This morning," I called back, stretching out on the bench opposite Lena. The attack had been done by noon, the enemy driven out from Gildendorf and the Ilyichevka state farm, where my company had been happily settling themselves when I came limping in using my rifle as a crutch. Stripped out of my clothes, I could now see the huge black bruise covering my entire flank.

"I can't believe you fell out of a damned tree," Lena scolded, closing her eyes.

"I still pulled off my shot." I parked my Finnish combat knife within arm's reach—not that I believed I'd need it, but only an idiot would strip naked in a camp full of men and not have a weapon at hand. Sweat was already running freely down my face in the dark, enclosed space.

The baritone voice through the door again: "Are you the woman sniper who took out the entire machine-gun nest?"

"Four shots." Quite a bit of preparation had gone into those four shots: a day to reconnoiter the site, then a morning wedging into a maple tree with a clear line of fire over the Gildendorf cemetery to the road—but the result was one dead adjutant, two dead machine gunners, and one final armor-piercing bullet through the breech of the MG 34 to render it useless before my regiment advanced down the road. "They were using telescopic sights—the entire day before, our boys couldn't so much as wiggle a finger without seeing it shot off." I'd seen three men from my company go down, boys I'd traded jokes and smiles with over evening mess tins.

"How many is it now on your tally?" Lena asked after a half hour's silence, rolling her neck.

I massaged my shooting hand, reflexively checking that the post-shooting tremors had worked themselves out. September was more than half over; fighting was continuous and my nights had been busy. "Officially, forty-six." I still disliked that question. I didn't want to count the dead; I didn't do this for bragging rights. It was simply a job I had to do. And I was doing it. Suddenly the heat felt stifling, and I sat up. "Let's sluice off."

In the village where I was born, my family always went to the banya together: my parents and sister and me all sitting in the steam, then everyone racing out to plunge whooping into the icy stream—or if the stream was frozen, the nearest snowbank. No snow here yet, and I wasn't plunging into any stream naked with an entire regiment around, so Lena and I rinsed off in the bolted changing room with pails of icy water. The man outside called through the door again, just as Lena upended a bucket over my head.

"Not to lurk around your bath, ladies, but one of the corporals just came by and left a rather nice pile of gifts for L. M. Pavlichenko."

"Gifts?" I sluiced icy water off my steaming skin, shivering. The good kind of shivering, the banya's magic where hot met cold and sweat met ice, and your flesh remembered it was violently, beautifully alive. Buried in the dust and blood of the front, making do with tepid washes out of a basin, I hadn't realized how much I'd needed this. I gave my head a shake, feeling the dust and dried blood stream out to puddle at my feet.

"Don't think that's getting you in here, lover boy," Lena shouted through the door, turning around so I could upend a pail over her in turn. "This door's staying shut till we're dressed—"

"I guess you don't want this nice cake of bath soap, then. I can certainly—"

"Give me that!" Lena wrenched the door open, just far enough for a big brown hand to pass the soap through.

"Quite a motley assortment here," he continued as the door closed again. "Another bar of soap, a little flask of scent, a pear from the farm's orchard . . . the note says: *From the men of 2nd Company.*"

Not courting gifts, simply the kind of small luxuries given in wartime as a thank-you. My eyes pricked as I lathered up the cake of soap. My job now was to take lives—I sometimes forgot that I was also saving them. My company had been able to march up that road today without being mowed down by machine-gun fire, because of four shots fired by my hand. I'd forgotten that for a moment, but the men hadn't. Their rough, simple thank-you felt better than the suds lathering my skin.

"You must be one of the civilian guides," I called through the door to the man outside, soaping my hair. "Do you know what's happening in the rest of the eastern sector?"

He gave me the results of the attack as I finished washing my hair. "My company is south a ways from Gildendorf," he finished. "What's a name like Gildendorf doing so near Odessa, anyway?"

I smiled, rinsing off. "That's very interesting, actually—"

"You'll be sorry you asked," Lena groaned, stealing my soap.

"I found out the town was settled eighty years or so ago by German settlers—hence the Teutonic influence. You can see it in the local nomenclature on their gravestones," I added, brightening at the bit of historical trivia I'd managed to glean.

"Gravestones?" The baritone voice now sounded bemused. "When were you sightseeing cemeteries in between taking out machine-gun nests?"

"When I was reconnoitering the best position to fire. I've been reading *Combat in Finland*; you know in the Karelian forests, the Finnish snipers did target shooting from trees? Very interesting. It's why they got the nickname *cuckoos*—"

"You're the one who's cuckoo." Lena pitched my shirt at me, and I pulled it over my scrubbed, glowing skin.

"—so I found a graveyard," I went on over her, still talking through the door. It had been so long since Mila the student had had a chance to emerge from her cave, instead of Mila the sniper (when I was fighting) or Mila the mother (when I was writing letters home). "Germans, I tell you, those settlers couldn't even dig graves without putting them all in fanatically straight lines like rulers. I staked out with my rifle in the tree, right over the tombstone of Bürgermeister Wilhelm Schmidt, who died in 1899—"

"Would that explain this fetching outfit piled at the door?" Definitely laughter in the baritone voice now. "I've seen camouflage before, but this stuff . . ."

"I worked all night on that!" Bits of netting and brown sackcloth and old green uniform material, cut painstakingly into ribbons and sewn down all over my jacket—I'd remembered my lessons from the scarred instructor, who used to disappear into a meadow in a pair of unspeakable yellow-green hooded overalls sewn with leaves, and challenge the class to spot him. We'd give up after an hour, eyes aching, and he'd invariably pop up from a bush three feet away, smirking. I hadn't had a chance to use my camouflage skills on the steppe, since there was hardly anything to camouflage in*to*, but the wooded areas around Gildendorf had given me trees and foliage to hide among. "And you shouldn't laugh at it, because I got the machine-gun nest."

"Then she fell out of the tree," Lena called through the door.

"Nine meters." I buttoned up my shirt, yanked my trousers and belt into place. "Right on the tombstone of Bürgermeister Wilhelm Schmidt, died 1899."

"Next time you read a book that tells you to climb trees dressed like a Finnish cuckoo," Lena said, "don't assume you can *fly* like one."

I made a face and swung out of the bathhouse, carrying my boots. Leaning up against the banya wall was my pack with my hat, the little packet of wolfberry leaves I hadn't been too busy to pick for Slavka, and my rifle, twined in maple leaves and vines to disguise her sharp clean lines. I slung her over my shoulder, then looked up at the man I'd been chatting with through a door. He'd shrugged into dilapidated boots, old trousers, and an even older shirt missing a button at the throat, and he looked about thirty-five in contrast to all the uniformed boys of nineteen and twenty. Definitely one of the local civilians drafted as army scouts.

"A nine-meter fall?" He looked me over, searching for damage, and I found myself looking him over, too. Tall, broad-shouldered, laugh lines around the eyes . . . "You're lucky that hip's not broken."

I shrugged. "Injuries happen." It's only new recruits who look at the wounded and think, *That can't happen to me.* A soldier who's been under fire thinks, *That could happen to me, so I need to be more careful.* And a soldier who has seen comrades die regardless of how careful they were thinks, *This will someday happen to me—but not today, if only I can get out of here.*

Lena came out of the banya still toweling her hair, and she gave the fair-haired man a loud smack of a kiss. "That's for cutting your bath short, *zaichik.*"

He looked at me with a raised eyebrow. "Well worth it if I get one from the lady sniper, too."

I laughed, stood on tiptoe, and slung an arm around his neck. "Why not?" I didn't ever respond to the flirtations of fellow soldiers, but civilians were something different. It had been a long time since I felt admired, felt complimented, felt *female,* so I planted a kiss on his cheek. He turned his head, diving after my lips unashamedly, and I pulled back with a grin before his mouth could land on mine. He smelled like pine.

Lena wolf-whistled, scooping up the little pile of gifts by the door. "Come on now, or we'll miss the chow line!" I let her drag me off and winced again as the pain in my hip flared.

"Lover boy wasn't wrong when he said you could have broken that. You need a partner, Mila. Someone to cover your back, lend a helping hand when you have to dive out of sniper nests."

"I haven't found one yet." I'd gone looking in my battalion, following Sergienko's orders to find recruits who could be trained as snipers, but I hadn't found anyone I wanted at my back longer than one night's sortie. A boy from Kiev shot well but moved like an ox; a lanky Leningrader had the keenest eyes I'd ever come across, but couldn't stop flinching when he pulled the trigger.

"Forty-six kills . . ." Lena pulled the golden pear from my pile of presents and inhaled its fragrance. "You're living on borrowed time. Get a partner, or next time you fall on a gravestone, it might end up being your own. So, can I eat this pear?"

FOURTEEN MEN, ALL sizes, all ages: my new recruits stood in a rough cluster, laughing, looking about for their officer. I let them wait, resting my still-sore hip against a crate of shells, flipping through the signed instruction booklet from my old instructor. The word was we'd be transferring soon, retreating through Odessa, but not yet—and I'd received another set of orders about training up new marksmen, this time handed down from General Petrov himself. He wanted more snipers, and he wanted them soon. *You can't train a sniper in just three or four days,* I'd protested, only to hear from a sour-faced major standing behind Sergienko: *You have a week.*

I eyed the men before me over the top of my manual, dubiously. A few were riflemen orphaned from slaughtered platoons and folded into new companies, but two-thirds were volunteer sailors from Sevastopol. I had my doubts that any man in wide-legged pants who was more used to a pitching deck than the smooth, brutal heft of a Mosin-Nagant was going to have a marksman's eye.

The biggest of the sailors finally called to me. "You're serving here too, *kukulka*?"

"Yes," I said, still perusing the manual.

"Smashing medic they've given us, eh, boys?" I couldn't see him winking at his friends, but I could just about feel it. "Let's get acquainted, beauty—I'm Fyodor Sedykh, and your name is?"

I made a mark with my pencil. "Lyudmila Mikhailovna."

"Well, Lyuda, don't frown. Be nice! It won't do you any harm."

I had a sudden flash of Alexei saying *Give me a smile!* I shoved the memory out of my head, but my voice came out with an icier edge as I said, "I'll *be nice* when you all stand at attention and announce your presence to the commander as you are supposed to do in accordance with the military code."

He blinked. "Where's the commander?"

"I'm the commander."

"Quit having us on, Lyuda, that's no way to—"

I unfolded fully, lowering the manual so they could see my corporal's tabs and raising my voice to my father's bellow. *"At. Attention."*

A dark-haired man stepped from the back and came to, smartly. A long silence fell; I tried not to hold my breath. Then the sailor named Fyodor Sedykh stepped into line beside the first man, still looking puzzled, and one by one the rest fell in.

"You're here because snipers will be needed in the push to come," I continued, walking the line, meeting each pair of eyes one by one. Some blue and some brown, some insolent and some curious. "Let's see if you have what it takes. Cartridges over there, take five each." I came to the last recruit, the one who had come to attention first. "Let's start with you." He was older than the others, nearer thirty-five than twenty-five, a compact razor of a man pared down to sinew, bone, and whiplike tendon. His cap sat on black hair razed down to stubble like a winter wheat field, and when he met my gaze, I knew him.

"Did you get past Austerlitz in *War and Peace*?" I asked the Siberian I'd last seen in the trenches before I was first wounded.

He gave a single nod, not smiling, but there was a smile folded into the corners of his eyes.

I nearly smiled back. "Name, Private?"

"K. A. Shevelyov." His voice was quiet, steady, educated.

"Let's see what you can do." I stood back as he began loading in swift movements. I already knew from our first meeting in the trenches that he could shoot, but I wanted the others to see him following my orders. "Then the rest of you, starting with Fyodor over there with the smart mouth." A smile, to let him know I was willing to joke as long as he fell in line. "If any of you are any good, I'll take you with me on a sortie and see how you do in the field."

"If you're Pavlichenko," Fyodor challenged, "are you the one with a tally of forty-six?"

"Fifty-one. Load your rifles."

They began to load, some looking impressed, some looking resentful. Either way, I knew they were mine.

PARAPHRASING TOLSTOY SHOULDN'T be allowed, but I can't help it: unsuccessful hunts are all alike; every successful hunt is successful in its own way. (I didn't finish *Anna Karenina* any more than I finished *War and Peace*, but even I knew the first line.) A successful day for a sniper might involve ten kills or a tense standoff with no kill at all. An unsuccessful day for a sniper is the day you miss and end up dead. So the eternal question—*What is it like, to be a sniper?*—has no answer. Every day was different. If it was a day I lived, it was a good day.

But what is it like? I could hear my trainee snipers asking, silently. I saw that question in Eleanor's eyes a year later—even the First Lady of the United States wasn't immune to morbid curiosity. *What is it like, Lyudmila?*

You are asking too, aren't you?

All right. Come with me.

Watch now, as I take you on a sortie. Not a particularly important sortie—I didn't bag an adjutant that night or a Gestapo colonel carrying secret plans from Hitler. I'll take you along on the night where I found my partner, the other half of my dark moon—for a sniper, a discovery far more important than the night you meet your true love. Husbands, as I have had cause to know, cannot always be trusted. A sniper puts her life in the hands of her partner, night after night after night. He had better be someone she trusts more than a husband.

I'd sited the hideout earlier during the day, everything reconnoitered down to the last blade of grass. A thicket of shrubs—one hundred and fifty meters long, twelve to fifteen wide—in the broad no-man's-land stretching beyond our front line, the narrow end piercing the Romanian defensive line like a spear, ending in a shallow gully near the enemy's second echelon.

"Machine gunners?" The recruit I'd decided to take along tonight kept his voice quiet as we set out from the dugout in the hour after midnight.

"Raise your spade, and our gunners will lay down fire for us to retreat." That was all we said, ghosting along in the warm night from the dugout to the thicketed hideout. Slithering like shadows under the cloudless sky, hauling our rifles and our bags of cartridges. An hour to cover six hundred meters.

Watch now, as my recruit and I do our homework. The dull, painstaking part no one imagines when they think of this dark work done under a dark sky. This isn't like the demonstration Captain Sergienko asked me to give in the bombed-out farmhouse; and it isn't like my stakeout in the maple tree, either, where I'd camouflaged myself to blend into the leaves. This is ground that has to be prepared, and that means hours in the pitch-black digging trenches and small parapets, reinforcing them with stones and turf—because snipers are more likely to fire from hidden ground positions than lofty rooftops or trees, contrary to popular belief. Then the hours of lying down in our nests, placing rifle barrels to find optimal stability, testing the direction of the wind, calculating the distances. And then the wait, two of us folded into the torn earth as the stars wheel and the enemy sleeps. The waiting is where green snipers show their inexperience; they fidget and rattle their cartridges, break down enough to reach for their cigarettes. The dark Siberian lies quiet an arm's length away, calm-blooded, his eyes just a gleam in the starlight.

Watch now as dawn comes. As movement stirs the enemy like heat roiling the surface of a soup kettle, soldiers walking about, calling to each other, thinking themselves safe. The field kitchen sets up, officers give loud orders, a medical station swarms with the gleaming white smocks of medics. One gesture to my new recruit—I'd target the left flank, he'd take the right. A returning nod.

Watch now as the day warms. Fingers flex, loosening, becoming pliant. The heart stirs. The sun climbs. The rifle sings softly to me, and artillery fire rumbles overhead. I begin the countdown to twelve, to my midnight.

Watch.

The first kill is mine. A Romanian officer in a cloth kepi topples over; the Siberian snaps off his first shot before my first target has even finished falling, and I see a second officer stagger. Our shots are masked in the rumble of artillery; for a moment no one can see who or what is dropping their officers, and we pick off two more before they all begin to panic. I fire and fire and fire, the Siberian racking shot after shot at my side, and it isn't until machine-gun rounds begin to thrash the thickets around us that we pull up and slide back into the brush, raising our spades for covering fire.

Back behind our own lines, gasping from the final sprint, I look at my companion. "Seventeen shots, sixteen kills. You?"

"Seventeen shots, twelve kills." The first words he'd spoken in the last twelve hours, and he sounds angry at himself for those five shots that missed.

"I took seven bullets to drop my first two. It happens." We settled in the dugout in the steel-gray morning light, stripping and cleaning our rifles. "Congratulations—your tally is opened."

A nod, and he went back to oiling the barrel. His hands were trembling just slightly; he was trying to hide that from me.

"Hold your hand out," I said.

He hesitated.

I held up my own so he could see it was shaking. "Nervous tension," I said. "It comes on after the sortie is done, but it goes away." I'd learned that by now, but he hadn't yet. "You weren't shaking when there was shooting to be done, were you?" I asked gently.

"No. But I still missed five shots." He didn't scowl, but his face darkened. "I've hunted since I was a child. I haven't missed like that since I was eight years old."

"Firing at a human being for the first time—it's not the same as firing at a deer. There's no pretending it is."

"I've fired at men, too. Hundreds of times with my battalion, aimed at hundreds of enemies."

"This is different. The way *we* kill, you see their faces. If they've washed that morning, if they're meticulous with their uniform or sloppy; if they've had a haircut recently." I was the one to hesitate now. "It's—intimate. You feel that afterward."

"Not during?"

"Not for me. When waiting in a hideout . . ." I hesitated again. "I don't feel any emotions then. I fold into place, and I wait there. Telling my rifle to be sure and steady."

"You talk to it?"

"Oh, yes. I know her better than I know myself. She's a little more ornery than my last rifle, a little fractious." I kissed the barrel's cool black metal. "But she's reliable."

He looked at me. He smelled of gunsmoke, and so did I. "Do you see their faces afterward?"

"Not anymore." Not often, anyway.

"But you still—" Nodding at the tremor in my hand.

"I know enough now to know it goes away in a little while. Same as the eye fatigue." I rummaged for my cigarette case. "This helps. I didn't used to smoke, but my friend Lena said it would only be a matter of time, and she was right." I lit up, drawing the calming smoke into my lungs.

"This helps, too." He pulled a flask from inside his breast pocket, offering it to me.

"Get yourself a cloth-covered flask." I swigged. The rough vodka tasted like pine sap. "You don't want the metal glinting, giving away your position."

"Rifle, flask, knife, two ammunition pouches—" He ticked his way through a list of a sniper's gear. "No helmet?" Glancing at my bare head.

"Not for me. Shell damage during that Romanian attack with the priest—my ears aren't quite what they were." Almost, but not quite, and *almost* was a drop-off as deadly as a Caucasus ravine for someone like me who dealt in fractions. When you lived by *Don't miss*, there was no room for *almost*. "A sniper has to become all ears, and a helmet makes it harder for me to detect faint sounds." I laid my rifle aside. "Hand?"

He held it up, fingers stone-still. His eyes smiled.

"Good." We sat, passing his flask back and forth, looking over the busy encampment. The battalion would be pulling up stakes and retreating through Odessa very soon now. Word was we'd be merging with two other battalions from the 54th. There'd be a big push then.

"Will you be my partner?" I asked simply.

He answered just as simply. "Yes, Pavlichenko."

"If you've got my back out there, you can call me Mila." I offered him a cigarette. "What's your name, K. A. Shevelyov?"

"Konstantin Andreyvich." He lit up, drawing down a curl of smoke. "Kostia."

Watch, now. That's a day in the life of a sniper. One hunt. Twenty-eight kills. And I'd found my my partner, my shadow, my other half.

CHAPTER 9

My memoir, the official version: On the morning of the second day of October, our mighty military machine moved crisply into action at Tatarka, organized and efficient.

My memoir, the unofficial version: It was about as organized and efficient as a monkey shit-fight in a zoo.

THE MORTAR BATTALIONS and rocket installations struck the invaders first—a roar as deafening as a dragon's, and the huge yellow blazes of flame enveloping the enemy positions to the west and southwest of Tatarka might have come from a dragon, too. I went in with the rest of my battalion a few hours later, across black earth baked into a hellish dreamscape. Dugouts, communication passages, firing points, all surrounded by tall grass and hazel bushes and wild apple trees—everything scorched into ash. My squad of newly trained marksmen followed me in silence. They'd boasted before the battle of how many enemies they'd take down, but now in the face of victory they were white-faced. There is nothing pleasant in such a horrifying triumph of death over life, even the death of a hated enemy. Half my men vomited when they first smelled the strange sweetish aroma of the dead.

"Look at it all," I told them quietly, stepping over the smoldering fragments of a gun placement. "But then forget it. Because we will have to do it all again." All this fire and blood had bought us only a kilometer and a half of ground, and the Romanians still had eighteen divisions to our four.

That was the battle, and I fought in it, and when I read accounts of it, I could remember the broader strokes. But Tatarka would forever be bound up for me not in a battle, but in a girl named Maria.

"The Kabachenko homestead." Captain Sergienko's thumb marked it out on the map. "Overlooking the road from Ovidiopolye to Odessa, not far from the railway tracks, used as a command post by the enemy machine-gun battalion. They've abandoned it for now. You and your squad"—nodding at me—"take two hundred cartridges each, hold it as long as you can." He went on to divvy up the other advance posts, and I went to prepare my informally grouped squad. I was a sergeant now, and of the fourteen men I'd been given to train, I'd cut four. Of the ten left, I had eight decent shooters, and two who might make real snipers.

They were singing as they swung along behind me toward the Kabachenko homestead—"Merry Wind," from the Vaynshtok film *The Children of Captain Grant*. "Never saw that one," I remarked to Kostia, who was padding along in his usual place at my elbow, and he gave me his silent smile. He was my partner now, and he was rarely more than an arm's length away from me, but I still knew nothing about him except that he'd come from Irkutsk and now had a tally of thirty-six. He didn't boast of his numbers or his kills any more than I did—that, even more than his sharp eyes and wolf-prowl tread, was what told me I'd chosen my partner well. War highlights the true essence of every person, and as little as I knew about Kostia, I knew his essence was bedrock.

The homestead was single-storied with a red-tiled roof, an orchard spreading beyond up a gentle slope. Secure that slope and we could keep a watch on the road, fire on any who advanced . . . My squad split around the burnt-out wreck of an enemy truck and overturned motorbike, an armored transport with a torn track. The woman who answered my knock at the door looked fifty, erect and bitter-eyed in a gray headscarf. "I don't often see soldiers in the command of a woman," she answered my greeting stiffly. "Serafima Nikanorovna. Come in." She must have known we'd have to come in and avail ourselves of her stores regardless of whether she invited us or not, but she made a rigid little gesture of welcome anyway. "Of course you may share what we have."

What they'd had, before the fascists came, was one of those beautiful little farms you see all over the countryside: a cozy farmhouse with a husband and wife, sons and daughter, all tending the vegetable garden, the chicken coop, and the pigpen. Then the enemy had come, and they'd rifled the vegetables, rounded up the chickens, and slaughtered the pigs. As for the family, the two sons had been beaten black and blue, the father had an arm in a clumsy sling, and the daughter was sitting wrapped in shawls beside the window, staring vacantly at the field behind the homestead. One of my men approached her with a friendly bow—the young ox named Fyodor Sedykh who had first challenged me, and the next best shot I had after Kostia—but she shrank away with a wordless cry. Fyodor, a nice boy and not too bright, withdrew with a puzzled look as the girl's mother gave him a sharp glance.

"Our military units all withdrew from this area in September." Serafima's voice was hard as she slapped down a plate of sauerkraut and salted pickles. "They left us to the mercy of the fascists. I made my Maria hide behind the pigpen, but the invaders found her anyway. My Maria, who used to dream of going to Odessa and becoming an actress in films. They—" The girl's mother broke off abruptly, looking at me with furious eyes. "Four of them. Four. Where were you then, Comrade Sergeant?"

I wanted to tell her the war wasn't lost; that it was just beginning. I wanted to tell her we had been holding the line at Odessa for over two months; that thousands of invaders had died trying to take the Black Sea steppes. But the words crumbled to dust on my tongue. I stood and let her harangue me as long as she wanted, and when she was done, I crossed to the window where seventeen-year-old Maria sat with her eyes like fields of ash. She'd shrunk from Fyodor, but she let me kneel beside her.

"Maybe you can help me with something, Maria," I said quietly, unfolding a handkerchief from my pocket. It held a handful of different leaves, which I now laid across her lap. "I'm collecting samples from the trees here to send to my son. He's learning all about plants in the Young Pioneers, but I'm no country girl and I don't know what kind of trees these came from. This one here—is that birch?"

Her voice was a bare whisper. "Black alder."

"And this one?"

"Chalk pine."

"And that?"

"Sessile oak." She named the rest for me, one by one, as her mother watched, and my men.

"Thank you, Maria." I tucked the leaves away for later, for when I could put aside the sniper and write to Slavka. "May I show you something?"

She nodded like an old, old woman. The pang that went through me was so far beyond pain, so far beyond grief, it left me breathless. Gently I took her hand where it lay in her lap.

"See the black streaks there on the slope?" I pointed to the field beyond the window. "That's from the rocket shells of our Katyushas. They can burn fascist soldiers down to black cinders. We don't bury them, Maria. We let their dust vanish into the earth, so no one will remember their faces and names. That's the way invaders ought to die."

Her eyes pierced me. May I never see such a look in the eyes of my own child. No mother should see such a thing. "Are you a good shot, Sergeant?" the girl asked.

"Yes. I've got a rifle with special gun sights."

A breath everyone in the squad seemed to hold together, and then:

"Kill them," said Maria. "However many you see, kill them all."

• • •

MURDERESS. SLAYER OF innocents. Cold-blooded killer. Later some
of the American journalists called me that. To them, a woman who
had overcome her natural feminine sympathies to become a sniper
must be nothing but an icy front-line murderer, hunting poor defenseless German soldiers who were after all only following orders of
their own. I wanted to tell those self-righteous typewriter warriors the
truth: *You* didn't look into the eyes of Maria Kabachenko after she
had been pinned down by four men who invaded her country, then
her home, and then her flesh. *You* didn't see the desperate, grieving
fury in her gaze. *You* didn't hold her clutching hands in yours as she
begged you, *Kill them all.*

If you had, you would have done what I did. Squeezed her hands
back, with all the gentleness in your soul, and then with every drop of
rage you could summon, say: *I promise I will.*

I shot five when my squad ambushed three motorcycles with sidecars. I dropped eight more when we stopped two enemy trucks rum-
bling past; Kostia took out the wheels and I picked off the invaders
as they spilled from the cabs. My men dug a trench at the foot of the
slope behind the homestead, past a hillock overgrown with wild roses,
and I lay there between Kostia and Fyodor when we watched Romanian tanks roll past; heard the dragon roar of our artillery opening
fire on them, and then picked off the survivors retreating back across
the slope. Every day I brought a handful of leaves and flowers for
Maria to identify, and as she told me the names, I told her how many
I'd downed that day. For her, I would care about my tally. Because
every day, I saw her smile.

"I'll pray for you," she whispered when she heard we'd be returning
to our battalion tomorrow. "Our Lord Jesus Christ will protect you."

I don't believe in God, I nearly said. Like most city families, mine
had always put its faith in the state and the motherland rather than in
empty religious trappings. Even if I had been devout, as remote rural
families like this still often were, this war and its horrors would have

killed my faith stone dead. But I squeezed Maria's hand and thanked her for her prayers.

"Do you believe, Kostia?" I asked my partner that night. Everyone had gone to bed except those on watch—and us. I'd wandered out to sit in the long grass before the darkened house, savoring the crisp autumn air, and Kostia followed with a jug of the cloudy home brew Maria's mother had uncorked for everyone this evening. Leaning back on our elbows in the grass, rifles lying alongside us like pet dogs, stars wheeling diamond-silent overhead . . . it was the kind of night to talk about God, about souls, about the great mysteries.

A long silence as my partner rolled a stem of grass between his fingers. "I believe in books," he said finally.

"Just books?"

"Books—and friends."

"But you're a loner like me." Fyodor and the others were always wrestling and joking in a pack like friendly dogs, but Kostia could usually be found by himself, reading or tending his rifle in his own patch of silence. I was the same way. I liked company, I liked to laugh, but after a point I needed solitude.

"We're loners," Kostia said. "But we have friends who would die for us. And we'd die for them."

I wondered what merry Sofya was doing right now back in Odessa, or prickly Vika. "I don't think my friends from before the war would know me anymore." Mila the library researcher was a long way from Mila the soldier.

"You'd start talking about Bogdan Khmelnitsky." A smile gleamed briefly in Kostia's shadowed face. "Then they'd know you."

I laughed, picking up the jug of home brew. At supper that night, we'd drunk it out of cut-glass goblets Serafima had proudly taken out from a chest that had somehow escaped the German raid. Now I swigged directly from the jug and coughed. "I swear this is tank fuel."

"Give it over." Kostia took a long swallow, looking back up at the slow dance of stars. "What do you believe in, Mila?"

I thought about that, feeling the burn of rough liquor in my throat. "Knowledge, to light the path for humankind," I said at last. "And this"—patting my rifle—"to protect humankind when we lose that path."

"You lead us down the path," Kostia said, "I'll have your back."

THE 1ST BATTALION had driven the enemy out of Tatarka, but my squad and I found ourselves in the thick of the fighting when we rejoined the ranks, flung headlong against three enemy battalions by the railway line. Bombs were falling like summer rain all around our trench; half-deafened and half-blinded, I was struggling with my rifle's dust-fouled bolt when something sang very close to my ear, a silver chime of warning. And suddenly I couldn't see; blood was ribboning down my face, sewing my left eye closed, sliding over my lips. I tasted copper and salt.

Just need one eye to shoot, I thought sluggishly, still tugging at my fouled bolt. The blood kept coming, and I wasn't hearing anything at all out of my left ear. Dimly, I watched my hands drop the rifle and fumble for the first-aid kit at my belt; I managed to clap a wad of bandaging to my face but winding it round my head seemed impossible. If this din would let up, this dust—I couldn't *see*—

"Mila." Kostia's voice, very calm. "Look at me." My partner pressed what was apparently a cut in my hair above the forehead; pain went through me in a bolt. He wound the bandage around my head, and I wanted to joke: *You've had my back—now you have my head!* But everything around me was sinking into fog. And for the second time, I woke up in a hospital cot.

"Want a souvenir, sleepyhead?" Lena dropped a blackened piece of jagged-edged metal into my hand. "That's what sliced your scalp open."

I looked down at the mortar splinter, hardly bigger than a matchstick. A little lower and it would have gone through my eye socket—I'd be one of the hundred and fifty of my regiment who would never leave Tatarka.

"Who's gone?" I asked Lena, folding my fingers around the splinter. "Who died this time, while I was unconscious?"

She lit a cigarette, gaunt and gray-faced after what I could only imagine were frantic, endless hours tending the nonstop flood of wounded. "Private Bazarbayev took a bullet to the heart."

One of my sniper trainees. He hadn't been very good, but he'd tried—how hard he'd tried. I felt the metal splinter's sharp edges dig into my palm as my fingers tightened. "Who else?"

"Your company commander—what was his name?"

"Voronin." A good man, one of the few officers I liked. I remembered a trench-side discussion once about favorite museum collections; the young officer had waxed eloquent about the Scythian-gold collection at the Hermitage, and I'd told him about the archaeological excavation I'd been lucky enough to attend after my first year at university. Just one brief hour in which I'd talked tenth-century grave barrows and the Kostromskaya stag, feeling like a student rather than a soldier. And now he was gone, and I'd be carrying my rifle to yet another hasty funeral between sorties, marked by a few mumbled words and a red plywood star.

"Kostia?" I asked, dreading the answer. "Is he—"

"Promoted to corporal. He's been underfoot looking in on you, whenever he's not leading sorties."

"He should have stitched me up on the front line rather than rushing me here," I grumbled. But at least my makeshift squad was in good hands while I was gone. "When can I go back?" I tried to rise from my cot, but a wave of dizziness nearly flattened me. Lena reached out with one finger and pushed me down onto my pillow.

"When I need two hands to shove you back down and not my pinkie, you can go back. At least a week."

"A *week*—"

"Are you that eager to add to your tally? I hear you're over a hundred now."

I was. Well over a hundred. But the last thing I wanted to do was discuss my tally. "Lena, speak to the doctors. They can sign off on—"

She drew a long hard pull on her cigarette, reached into her pocket for a battered compact, and held the mirror up to my face. I hadn't looked at myself in so long, and I recoiled at the sight. My cheeks were gaunt, my eyes shadowed in their sockets; a patch of hair had been shaved away to treat the splinter wound, which marched parallel to my hairline in a centipede of black thread. The area had been daubed with brilliant green antiseptic. I looked like . . .

"Death," supplied Lena. "You're not going anywhere, Mila, because you look like death."

I pushed the mirror away. "I am death." To over one hundred invaders, anyway. *Not enough,* the thought whispered.

Too many, whispered an answering thought.

Lena pocketed the compact, rising. "You can still be killed, Lady Death," she threw over one shoulder as she resumed her rounds.

"Lady Death?" I said to Kostia when he visited the following day. I'd braced myself for a lot of "thank goodness you're not dead" heartiness, but my partner just pulled up a stool without a word, leaning his rifle against my bed. "Why did Lena call me that?"

"They're all calling you that." He looked at the dried flowers I'd scattered across half the sheet: the latest batch of samples for Slavka. "Iris, chamomile, rhododendron," he said, naming them.

I began folding each one into its own piece of paper, marking the name in large clumsy letters. My hands weren't quite steady yet, so maybe Lena was right that I needed more time. Before anyone else I'd have been embarrassed of those shaking hands, but not my partner. "Lady Death—like Lady Midnight, Baba Yaga's servant?" Polunochnitsa, servant of the fabled witch in the old lore before the revolution swept away superstitious myths.

"Was she your favorite from the old stories?"

"I preferred Lady Midday. But really they're the same thing. I wrote a paper once on how such pre-revolutionary folkloric figures represented the opposing faces of pre-Soviet womanhood." Tucking another dried flower into its envelope. "It got a grade of Excellent."

"Of course it did." My partner's trigger-calloused fingers sorted through some dried daisies. "When I was growing up, I thought my father was old man Morozko."

"You thought your father was Father Frost?"

"He was a Baikal fur trapper . . . He came to Irkutsk only once a year with the first snows, and he sprouted knives from everywhere like icicles. He always left in a huge violent gust like an avalanche."

"He sounds noisy. Winter is quiet." It was the first time Kostia had ever said anything about his family. "You're Morozko, not him."

Kostia smiled under his eyelids. He picked up my hand where it lay among the scatter of flowers, unfolding my fingers and then folding them back inside his own, and he pulled it against his chest. He didn't say anything—he just held my hand against his tunic, where I could hear the steady beat of his heart.

Gently I disengaged my fingers and sat back. I didn't say anything, either, just looked at him with steady regret. This wasn't like flirting with that fair-haired scout for a lark—I was Kostia's sergeant, and maybe a difference in rank didn't stop most officers from fraternizing with their inferiors, but it didn't sit right with me. Even more important, he was my *partner,* the one I relied on above all others during the deadly dance in no-man's-land every night. I didn't dare introduce any chaotic rush of new passions into that delicate, critical balance, or we both might end up dead. So I just let the silence fall and gave a small shake of my head.

"Let's get you up and walking," Kostia said as if nothing had happened, and helped me off the cot so I could totter around the room. By the next day I was standing alone, peaked cap crammed over my battered, bandaged head, limping determinedly outside. The medical battalion had been stationed at what had once been a rural schoolhouse; skirting the cots and the rushing doctors, the stretchers with burned men and unconscious men and moaning men clutching stumps of arms and legs, I managed to find my way to the garden surrounding the schoolhouse.

Just days ago the autumn sun had been shining bright from a blue sky, warming the whole vast surface of the steppe. Now winter was coming in a bluster of lead-colored clouds and cold northern gusts, old man Morozko stealing closer on snow-scented feet. Even here, as far back from the front lines as we were, I could hear the rumble of guns.

I turned away from the sound, inhaling the smell of fresh-turned earth and wild roses. Juniper grew here straight as a green wall; tulips and roses bloomed in the borders—despite all the bombing and shelling, someone was looking after this garden. I gave silent thanks to whatever soul cared enough to nurture this humble patch of flowers in such a living hell. I picked up a fallen red-gold leaf for Slavka, nearly falling in my dizziness, and tried to uncurl it in my hand. It broke, dry and dead. I dropped it, feeling another wave of weakness, wondering why I was fighting so to stay upright. Why not just fall, lie down, close my eyes? I was *tired*. When I got back to the fight, I'd have to rekindle the rage and carry on, but for now it was ash in my stomach, dead and cold after three and a half months of sorties and battles. I sat on a garden bench and pulled out my dissertation, hoping dear old Bogdan Khmelnitsky would cheer me up, but I couldn't make my eyes focus on the words. The letters crawled off the page like ants, and the heading that little library researcher Mila Pavlichenko had typed with such pride earlier this year was now half-obscured by a bloodstain.

For the life of me, I couldn't tell you whose blood it was.

A purring sound slid into my one good ear, and I looked up to see a khaki-colored staff car ooze through the open gates toward the school. A flurry of uniforms; by the time they came marching toward the front doors, I had stuffed my dissertation pages back into my pack, limped up the drive, and drawn myself up at attention. It wasn't the first time I'd clapped eyes on Major General Ivan Yefimovich Petrov, commander of the coastal army, but this was the first time I'd seen him so close. Perhaps forty-five, red tinges in his hair, bags under his eyes . . .

I expected him to sweep past, but one of his officers caught sight of me, whispering something, and the general halted. "Pavlichenko, yes? I've heard your name—the woman sniper."

I saluted. "Yes, Comrade Major General."

He surveyed me. "A head wound, I see."

"On October 13, with the 1st Battalion at Tatarka."

"Are you being treated well?" He nodded at my assent. "Well, get ready to move, Lyudmila Mikhailovna. We're off to Sevastopol, orders of the supreme command."

Shock rocked me to the soles of my feet. I'd known the retreat from Odessa was coming, but hearing the order become official was a different thing entirely. "We're not going to surrender Odessa to the enemy? They'll raze it to the ground." My beautiful Odessa of the sparkling sea and blue skies, the striped umbrellas and outdoor cafés. The city I'd helped defend, holding my firing lines, taking my shots. I stared at the commander of the coastal army in stark horror, and I saw a flicker of sympathy in his gaze. It hurt his soul too—he just hid it better.

"It's the duty of a soldier to carry out orders to the letter." He gave me a clap on the shoulder, surprisingly gentle. "My orders to you now? Don't mope, have faith in victory, fight bravely. How many in that tally of yours?"

"One hundred and eighty-seven," I said dully. The enemy attacked in such dense ranks, I could nearly get two with one bullet. Who knew what my real tally was when the battles and the skirmishes and the unconfirmed shots were added to my official sorties, but officially I was at 187.

Low whistles from the staff behind General Petrov, and his grip on my shoulder tightened approvingly. "That's champion," he said. "Sevastopol needs that rifle. We'll cross the sea and defend the Crimea." I could see him visibly searching for something stirring to say, something to put fire in the blood, but the general looked as exhausted as I felt. "Everything will be fine," he said at last. "You'll see."

Off he swept with his entourage, going to survey the wounded, evaluate morale—and probably, oversee this evacuation of his military units to Sevastopol—leaving me standing frozen before the useless fragrant borders of flowers.

WE WOULD LEAVE by sea, and that meant retreating through Odessa itself to the port.

I begged to be released so I could travel with my squad, but was refused. Kostia and my men left in advance of me; I departed with the medical battalion, which had been loaded onto road transport, skulking in the falling dark under the camouflage fire of the rearguard battalions, which would remain in their trenches until the last. "Retreating," I spat to Lena. "We're fucking cowards." I'd never used such a word in my life, but I felt as though I were choking on a throatful of thorns.

"Not so loud," Lena hissed. "Do you want to be shot for defeatism? They've executed more important people for less." She was called off to rebandage an amputee on a truck, and I knew she'd be too busy with the wounded to listen to me brood. I had nothing to occupy me but putting one foot in front of another as I took what was perhaps my last look at the city I loved.

How changed it was since the day I'd taken a train out of here to the front. The autumn twilight covered the parks and boulevards like a shroud, but the shroud couldn't hide how many buildings gaped roofless, how many black holes instead of windows looked down like mournful eyes on the retreating defenders. Our column halted at an intersection blocked by artillery wagons, and with a start I saw the two-storied enlistment office where I'd gone to join the Red Army. Only the building wasn't there anymore, just collapsed beams and soot-blackened walls, the twisted bones of the iron staircase I'd tripped up in my crepe de chine dress, bent on seizing fate by the throat.

"Mila?"

A voice called me from the silently watching onlookers. Turning, I saw a woman hugging herself against the cold night, wrapped in a too-short coat. For a moment I didn't recognize her, but then I registered the protuberant eyes and endless dancer's legs. "Vika?" I blinked, and with a word to my lieutenant, stepped out of the column to join her. I hadn't seen her since the day war broke out, the day she'd pirouetted in red petticoats with the opera ballet.

"You're retreating?" she said, sounding stunned.

"Withdrawing to a place of better strength," I said, repeating the official line, hating it.

"Retreating." Her voice flattened out. "Abandoning Odessa."

"At least I'm fighting," I flared. "Didn't you dancers get evacuated to safety? Must be nice to be a Bolshoi-trained demi-soloist." I knew I was being unfair, but her contempt stung me.

"I've quit the ballet. My brother, I—" Vika drew an unsteady breath. "Grigory's dead. He didn't even make it two months in the tank corps."

Her twin, her dance partner, her other half. "I'm sorry," I said, regretting my sharpness.

"Sofya's dead too. A stray bomb."

"Sofya?" I whispered, feeling my stomach wrench.

"She wanted to be a teacher," Vika said tonelessly. "She had all these didactic little studies on group play that were going to encourage cooperation in the four-to-seven age group. Who kills someone like that, Mila? A *teacher*? Or a boy like my brother, who could dance the Bluebird variation like an angel?"

"Fascists," I said. Fascists had now killed half the little quartet who'd been sitting at the Pushkin Street café that afternoon war broke out. I'd thought the rage banked in my stomach had subsided to ash, but it turned over in a flicker of renewed heat as I saw Vika's bleak eyes.

My column was starting to move; the blockage with the artillery carts had been cleared. "Take care," I told her awkwardly. "Can't let the invaders stop the Dragonfly from dancing. Or was it the Nightingale? The Star?"

"Does it matter? No one needs dragonflies and stars now. What we need is killers." She gave a bleak smile. "At least we have you."

The dancer turned and walked up the shattered street, head erect, toes turned out, and I continued my retreat toward the sea.

The port looked like Babylon before the fall: army trucks swarming everywhere, tractor units pulling howitzers and tanks, thousands upon thousands of soldiers. The water was choked with ships from the steamer service and the Black Sea Fleet; in the pitch-dark I shuffled up the gangplank of the *Zhan Zhores,* which loomed before me like a long black wall rising sheer above the quay. The heaving mass of wounded funneled below, down to the crew mess room. I sat clutching my pack and fighting waves of dizziness as the tugs began leading the vessel away from the wharf, the ship shuddering like a whale lumbering toward the open sea. Through the porthole I saw leaping flickers of red and gold—Odessa's huge portside warehouses were aflame. Deliberate, to leave nothing to the fascists, or an accident with the gas cans? Either way, no one was rushing to put the fires out. There was no one left; everyone who could leave Odessa was abandoning her. My last sight of the city where I'd enlisted as a soldier was to watch it going up in flames as I slunk away over the Black Sea.

My rage rose, and rose, and rose.

"Comrade," the third mate scolded, seeing me take out my cigarettes in shaking hands. "No smoking down here."

"Then tell me where," I snarled. The mess room already smelled of sweat and nervousness, the air loud with shouts and the shuffle of boots. My skin crawled, crying out for solitude.

"Quarterdeck, at the stern."

"Quarterdeck? What's that? How do you have a quarter of a deck?" He began some deeply technical answer; I exhaled the last of my patience. "Tell me. Where. I can *smoke*."

He saw the look on my face. "The back of the ship, at the top."

I fought my way through the crowd out of the mess room, continuing above deck to the smoking area. Sailors and medical orderlies stood in clusters, smoke curling upward. We weren't just leaving Odessa, I thought—we were leaving Gildendorf, the Kabachenko homestead, Tatarka; the battlefields that had turned me into what I was now. Whatever that was. Sergeant Pavlichenko, as I heard every day? The woman sniper, as General Petrov had called me? Lady Death, as Lena called me? I shook the names away on the wind, squinting over the dark ocean toward where Odessa was vanishing like a mirage.

"May I borrow your binoculars?" I asked the nearest man, and then dismay froze me to the deck as he turned.

"Little Mila," said Alexei Pavlichenko, looking down at me with that amused flick of his mouth. "Look at you."

THE SOVIET DELEGATION: DAY 1

August 27, 1942
WASHINGTON, D.C.

CHAPTER 10

The marksman sat on a grassy verge overlooking the Lincoln Memorial, fanning himself with his hat. His employer was late, but Washington types liked to play such games, to remind you how important they were. The marksman tipped his face to the sun, covertly observing the trickle of visitors trailing in and out of the huge marble edifice. It was early, but a handful of tourists were already coming out to beat the summer heat: a family clutching brochures, some vacationing parents dragging sullen teenagers, a couple wandering hand in hand to look up at the giant contemplative marble figure inside.

A shadow fell across the marksman's hands. "Did we have to meet here of all places?" a peevish voice demanded.

The marksman replaced his hat, smiling. "What, overlooking a monument to another president who was assassinated?"

"Keep your voice down." The new arrival was middle-aged, balding, packed into an expensive suit with a faint pinstripe and a blue pocket square.

"No one's listening." It was why the marksman preferred to do this sort of thing outside. In the middle of a broad expanse of grass, not a soul in earshot, surrounded as they were by the bustle of a busy city, no one would pay attention to the idle chatter of two men lounging on a warm morning. "Sit down."

Pocket Square spread out a handkerchief to protect his suit from the grass, sitting with bad grace. The marksman didn't know his name, or the name of the men behind him who'd selected him as the go-between. The marksman didn't care, either. It wasn't his business who his customers were or what drove them to pay for death. As long as they paid promptly and kept their mouths shut, none of the rest mattered. "Well?" Pocket Square demanded.

"I'll know more after the White House breakfast in an hour, but the girl and the rest of the delegation are already scheduled for a press conference this evening," said the marksman. "My name is on the list of attending press?"

"Yes, but my employers don't see any reason for you to attend."

"I need to establish myself on the fringes of this delegation as a security-vetted and innocuous part of the scenery, so I can cozy up with someone who can get me access to the girl when the time comes." It wasn't the usual way he worked—normally the marksman put more distance between himself and his targets, worked through layers of anonymous informants—but with a presidential target in his sights, he wanted as few people and complications built into the plan as possible. Perhaps superstitiously, he wanted his own eyes on everything. "I'll need a list of the attending delegation members—not her fellow students, they'll be in the spotlight, but the little people."

"You'll get it." Pocket Square mopped his face. The day was already heating up, but even if it had been cold, the marksman suspected he'd be sweating. Some people just didn't have the nerves for assassination. "When are you going to—do it?"

"September fifth. The last day of the conference."

"But you can guarantee success?" Pocket Square pressed.

"No." Death was never guaranteed. "Failing the desired outcome, I can guarantee embarrassment, public outrage against the President and his Soviet guests. I was given to understand this would be an acceptable secondary outcome."

"For some of my bosses," Pocket Square muttered.

"The America Firsters will be pleased enough, and so will the anti-Soviets." The marksman smiled at the other man's startled expression. It wasn't hard to figure out who, in this carnivorous capital city, would want Franklin Delano Roosevelt dead. Even popular presidents had enemies, and FDR was no exception: American fascists who loathed *President Jewsevelt*; bitter political rivals in Congress; isolationist tycoons who opposed war with Germany; Communist-hating millionaires so rabidly anti-Marxist that even beating Hitler wasn't worth allying with Stalin—not to mention righteous idealists who saw any third-term president as a tyrant in the making. Who knew what occasion or event had brought enough seething men together, what match had lit the wick as they aired their grievances, what events had stoked the flames until someone was brave enough to whisper the word *assassination . . .* but it had happened, and the marksman's telephone had duly rung with an offer.

Pocket Square now looked positively ashen. "You can't possibly know who they are. The greatest care was—"

"They're suits," the marksman said calmly. "Men in expensive suits who want the world to run in their favor. That's always who hires me—some shadowy compact of powerful discontented suits. And they know I can get the job done."

He rose, giving a mental tip of his hat to the distant marble figure of President Lincoln inside the monument. A theater performance spattered with presidential blood and brains; now that had been an assassination with style. "If you'll excuse me," the marksman told his employer's flunky, "I have a breakfast to attend."

Notes by the First Lady

I have very little time before the welcome breakfast for our Soviet guests, but I look through an invitation to address the U.S. Committee for the Care of European Children, examine the minutes of a meeting of the advisory committee of the American Federation of Negro College Students, review the schedule for the commissioning of a new battleship in the Brooklyn Navy Yard, read over a report from the Civil Aeronautics Administration concerning the use of women in their CAA pilot training, and check on Franklin. He's sitting up in bed where he always takes his breakfast, old blue cape thrown over his pajamas, breakfast tray set to one side with its scatter of toast crumbs and coffee dregs. Newspapers litter the bed—he always takes the Baltimore Sun, *the* Washington Post, *the* Washington Times-Herald, *the* New York Herald Tribune, *and the* New York Times *with his breakfast—and on the floor by his bedside table is the Eleanor basket, where I leave reports and communications earmarked for his attention. He groans sometimes—"More homework, Eleanor?"—but he knows he cannot see everything and counts on me to fill the gaps. He's already gone through the notes I left earlier, and he must be about to get dressed, because I hear the valet rustling in the wardrobe. Franklin is sitting with his eyes closed, face set in exhausted, determined lines.*

I know what he's doing. He's imagining himself as a boy back on the family estate in Hyde Park, standing with his sled at the top of a snowy hill overlooking the Hudson far below. In his mind he tips over the brow of the hill and careens down, wind rushing past his face, steering every curve in a shower of diamond-bright snow crystals. At the bottom he brakes to a halt, throws the rope of his sled over one arm, and strides back up on strong young legs. He relives that hill, that exhilaration, that climb, until it is real and the vigor of it flows through him.

Normally he saves this memory for restless nights, using it to calm his mind and bring sleep. This morning he has taken it out to banish weakness before he faces the day ahead. This morning he has need of it. His lean strong hands brace his weight on the bed—it is like he is braced for a bullet.

What is it you fear? *I want to ask.* What—or who? *But the gong sounds below, and I tiptoe away to welcome our Soviet guests.*

ELEVEN MONTHS AGO

September 1941
THE SEVASTOPOL FRONT, USSR
Mila

CHAPTER 11

My memoir, the official version: I hadn't seen Alexei Pavlichenko for at least three years before enlisting in the Red Army. I'd write it that way not because I wanted to lie, but because then I could dispense with him in one line, and not waste the page space that real life had allotted him.

Because in my memoir, the unofficial version? That rot-gut, oily-tongued bastard turned up in the middle of the war like what the Americans would call a bad penny. The most unwelcome penny in the world.

I STOOD GAZING at him, large as life and three times as unpleasant on the deck of the ship bound for Sevastopol, my stomach suddenly roiling. "Look at you," he said, and noted the rank on my collar. "Sergeant? I hope you didn't steal your boyfriend's tunic just to keep warm, *kroshka*. There are penalties for impersonating rank!"

I'd forgot how tall he was. Most of the soldiers on the *Zhan Zhores* looked disheveled and weary from the retreat, but Alexei's uniform was crisp, his cap perched on his fair hair at a rakish angle. "This is my uniform," I said as coolly as I could manage. "I am a sergeant."

"Not bad, I suppose, for such a little girl." He didn't ask about Slavka. I didn't want him to ask—I didn't want him anywhere near our son—but it still made my blood boil that he had not even a stray thought for the beautiful boy he'd fathered. That Slavka meant so little in his eyes. He wore a lieutenant's triangles on his collar—of course he was an officer; of course he outranked me.

"Medical battalion?" I made myself ask. He must have enlisted in

Odessa around the same time I did. Surgeons of his skill were worth their weight in silver at the front.

"That's right. I told you once, didn't I? A man sees chances in war—this is mine." He nodded out to the black expanse of sea ahead of us. "I have a good feeling about Sevastopol. Great things lie in wait, you'll see."

So confident, not a doubt in the world. He must have seen hellish things if he'd had months in the hospitals of Odessa, operating on battle wounds from dawn to dusk, but clearly it had made very little impression. He hadn't gone to war to heal his wounded countrymen or preserve this land for his son to grow up in—he'd gone to war for a chance to rise. He clearly still had his dreams of greatness. "Alexei Pavlichenko, Hero of the Soviet Union?"

My voice came out hard and mocking. He frowned. He was used to seeing me deferential, pleading, frustrated—the wife who hated to ask him for things and kept having to ask him for things anyway. The little woman who jumped when he told her to. He was used to having the upper hand over me . . . but not anymore. I'd seen too much blood and terror in the last few months to be impressed by a man with a mean streak. He could still make me seethe, but he couldn't make me tiptoe, and he could no longer make me jump. Alexei leaned on his elbow against the ship's rail, and he looked like he was seeing me now. "Chapayev division?" he guessed. "We'll be seeing more of each other in Sevastopol."

"I doubt it." I couldn't resist a jab. "Unlike doctors, I don't operate safe behind the lines."

Another frown. "But you're in the medical battalion, yes?"

"No." I smiled at him. "I'm a sniper."

He laughed. "Nice to see you've finally developed a sense of humor, *kroshka*."

I shrugged. If he was stupid enough to miss the rifle slung over my shoulder, that was not my problem.

"No joking, now." Alexei's smile disappeared. "You're not a rifleman."

"Why not?"

"That's no position for women, even in war. No matter what the state says."

"Tell that to all the enemy dead I put in the ground while defending Odessa."

I threw it at him, wanting to see the surprise in his face. Instead he just chuckled. "Aren't you all grown up. Still want to borrow my binoculars, for one last look at Odessa?" He held them high up in the air, over my head. "Jump, little Mila!"

I didn't stop to think. I slung the rifle off my shoulder, nipped the barrel through the loop of his binoculars, and with a wrench and a twist flipped them out of his hands over the ship's rail. "Jump for them yourself," I said, hearing them splash far below, and turned to go.

Not so fast I didn't see the flash of anger go through his eyes, didn't hear his final words behind me. "Still can't take a joke, can you?" His voice laughed, but there was real anger underneath. "Still pretending *you* aren't a joke."

"One hundred and eighty-seven dead enemies know I'm no joke," I shot back, and stalked off across the quarterdeck.

Alexei Pavlichenko here. My heart pounded. My husband, back in my life after years of barely thinking of him at all. On the same ship, headed to Sevastopol.

It doesn't matter, I told myself, going below. I wasn't afraid of him, not anymore. And in the chaos of the front it would be easy to avoid each other. I could stay out of his way and he—if he was smart— would stay out of mine.

Surely.

SEVASTOPOL. I CAME to the white city with my red hands and my battered heart, and I stood in wonder. It wasn't even a quarter of the size of bustling, cosmopolitan Odessa, but its public gardens and lanes of red-gold trees were still untouched by war. The stone walls of the ancient twin forts guarding the entrance to the main bay hadn't yet been pocked by German mortars; the blue dome of St. Vladimir's Cathedral gleamed whole and pristine. People strolled the streets after work, went to public baths, bought tickets to see *Tractor Drivers* or *Minin and Pozharsky* at the local cinemas. A beautiful city—and one I quickly tired of, because I couldn't get *out* of it.

First I was ordered to recuperate with the medical battalion until my scalp wound healed. Then to my exasperation, I couldn't find a single officer who could tell me where my regiment had *gone*. "You can't just lose an entire regiment," I protested to a harried-looking staff officer. "Did you lose the whole coastal army as well?"

"That is defeatist talk," he said stiffly. "Don't you have friends in high places, Pavlichenko? Go talk to *them*." But October was over by the time Major General Petrov arrived in Sevastopol along with his staff at the coastal defense command post, and more days yet before I could obtain even a three-minute meeting.

"Greetings, Lyudmila Mikhailovna." He was doing about eight things at once, white dust of the Crimean roads still frosting his general's stars, but he smiled through the pince-nez perched on his nose. "How are you feeling?"

I was yearning for Kostia and my squad like a missing limb, but that wasn't what he was asking. "Fully recovered, Comrade Major General." My stitches were out, and my hair was already growing back over the shaved area around the scar. If I placed my cap carefully, you'd never know it was there.

"So, are we going to beat the Nazis in Sevastopol?"

"Absolutely, Comrade Major General."

"I'm making you a senior sergeant, and I want you commanding a sniper platoon when you rejoin your regiment. Which is"—followed by some murmuring from an aide—"somewhere on the road between Yalta and Gurzuf. See the staff headquarters for your documents, and the quartermaster for winter gear." He hesitated. "Make sure you get a pistol."

"I have my rifle, Comrade Major General—"

"Get a Tula-Tokarev for close quarters. Eight shots. Seven for the enemy, if they come on you by surprise. The last one . . ." His face was suddenly stony. "It's the Hitlerites we're fighting now, not the Romanians. Germans don't take snipers prisoner; they shoot them on sight. And for the women . . ."

Better not to be taken alive. The unspoken words hung in the air like drops of ice. Was that what awaited me in Sevastopol—death at my own hand, to avoid gang rape and execution? Even with my tally of one hundred and eighty-seven dead enemies behind me, a thread of fear wormed through my stomach. I'd done all my shooting in flat steppes where visibility was excellent, and my targets had been thickly bunched, easily flustered Romanian soldiers. This was the Crimea, a dense wooded country full of secrets, and my targets were Hitlerites. Highly trained Germans captained by fanatical officers drilled into hatred of anyone who didn't belong to their master race. Who shot or starved captured Russian soldiers in their prisoner-of-war camps rather than treat them like the British or French soldiers. Who would rape a woman to death if they caught her alive, just for the sin of stepping outside *Kinder, Kirche, Küche* to kill an enemy who had invaded her country.

I swallowed, saluting. "I'll make sure I'm never without a pistol from now on, Comrade Major General."

Nearly another week before I could rejoin my regiment in the Mekenzi Hills—the third defense sector, lying between the Belbek and Chornaya Rivers, more than twenty kilometers outside Sevastopol. I made my way first by truck in a group of new arrivals, then on foot as they dropped me at a nest of dugouts and thickly forested paths, asking directions from the rushing soldiers around me. I was longing to see Sergienko's familiar lugubrious face and tease him about how if he got any grayer he'd look embalmed, but I got a shock at the command post.

"Captain Sergienko has been gravely wounded and dispatched home. Comrade Lieutenant Grigory Fyodorovich Dromin commands the battalion now." Before I could manage more than an inhalation of shock and grief for my captain, I was meeting his successor. Dromin was new, slim, immaculate, and thirty-five; not one hair on his smooth head did anything but shriek *fresh meat*.

He flicked through my documents as I saluted. "You wish to become a platoon commander, Comrade Senior Sergeant? Are you really up to it?"

"That's not for me to decide, Comrade Lieutenant," I said evenly, "but senior command."

"Which senior command do you mean? I am your senior commander, and I am opposed to women occupying field positions in the army."

At least he *said* it. Plenty of officers thought the same thing but refused to admit it. They just smiled when they saw women arrive in their commands, then refused to make use of them.

"You're a sniper, apparently." Dromin tossed my documents back. "Fire away at the Nazis by all means. But commands will be issued by those who are supposed to issue them."

"Who would that be, Comrade Lieutenant?" I couldn't resist replying.

"Men, of course. Proper officers."

He would have dismissed me from his presence right then and there, but a laughing voice came from the rear of the command post where a cluster of officers was working. "Give her a platoon, Dromin. Or do you want to argue with General Petrov?" A man unfolded from a too-small stool, and for a moment I thought it was Alexei and nearly recoiled. A junior lieutenant, tall and fair-haired—but he wasn't my husband, though he did look familiar. "She already had an unofficial squad," the lieutenant continued, leaning against my new battalion commander's table. "Give her more men and call it a proper platoon."

"Do we really believe this nonsense about one hundred and eighty-seven kills?" Dromin spoke as though I wasn't there. "If she had even a quarter that many, she'd have an Order of the Red Banner by now."

"Petrov still gave her a platoon." Cheerfully. "Fork it over or go argue with him."

The lieutenant smiled at me, and I realized who he was: the fair-haired man at the banya outside Gildendorf, the one I'd kissed on the cheek. He'd been in civilian clothes, so I'd assumed he was a scout or a guide . . . that was the only reason I'd let myself flirt with him. Now here he was in the damned *command post.* I felt myself flush, not even bothering to hope that he didn't remember. His eyes were sparkling. He remembered, all right.

I was only too happy to obey Dromin's curt dismissal, marching out with eyes fixed on the middle distance. The bickering continued behind me, and I distinctly heard: ". . . Petrov's little pet, she's probably warming his bedroll—" My face flamed as I stamped through the unfamiliar mess of trenches, communication passages, machine-gun emplacements. New front line to defend, new enemies to understand, new terrain to learn, and now a new commanding officer who thought I was a front-line whore. An impression for which I had only myself to blame. Well, if lieutenants wouldn't traipse around dressed like civilians . . .

The army sappers had constructed good, deep dugouts in the thickly forested hills. Making my way down the winding trail leading me to the lines of 2nd Company, still swallowing my embarrassment down like hot coals, I heard a whoop and found myself suddenly seized in bearlike arms. "Mila! Mila, there you are—!" I saw the broad beaming face of that young ox Fyodor Sedykh as he set me back on my feet. "We thought maybe the Romanians got you after all. I told Kostia—"

I turned from Fyodor and registered my partner's still, carved face. "Kostia," I said, and his arms came round me like a band of iron. I hugged him back hard, only pulling back to look him over. He was thinner than when I'd seen him last, and his trigger hand was bandaged. "You're wounded?" He shrugged, and then Fyodor was drawing us both down by the nearest stove.

"It's a tangle out here," he said frankly, heating some water in a mess tin for tea. I sat on an upturned crate, my shoulder hard against Kostia's as he rewound the bandage on his hand. "Second Company's down by half. We came up against the Hitlerites at the end of October near Ishun—beat them back, but their mortars and Messers ground us down, and we were being deployed almost on the open steppe. Too exposed; that was where Sergienko got it. Direct hit on the battalion command post; completely shattered his leg."

"Will he make it?" Throat tightening for the man who'd elevated me to sniper; kept his amorous fellow officers from pestering me; given me my first promotion.

"He'll make it, but he won't walk again. It's a desk for Sergienko now."

At least he'd survive this war. I already missed my calm, competent captain—badly—but at least he was *alive.* "And the regiment?"

Fyodor passed out the tea along with some precious hoarded sugar and plain biscuits. "Down to six, seven hundred."

Six or seven hundred, from the three thousand it would have been in peacetime. "And my squad?" I asked, taking Kostia's injured hand and tying off the wrapping, since he was having trouble doing it one-handed. In my pack I'd brought gifts for each and every one of the men I'd trained, bought while waiting in Sevastopol—mostly flasks of brandy or bars of chocolate, though for Fyodor I had a tin of his favorite sardines in oil, and for Kostia a secondhand copy of Tolstoy's *Sevastopol Sketches* bought in a bookshop, remembering his much-battered *War and Peace* . . . but now my heart clutched, realizing I hadn't seen any of the other men I'd trained. The Kiev boy with the acne-scarred face, the lanky sailor from Minsk . . . "How many are left?"

Kostia spoke for the first time. "Us."

I'd commanded ten, I thought sickly. Now I had two. These Germans were a different kettle of fight. "When can we get more men?" I said more to myself than the others. "More men, more rifles . . ."

"I'll see what I can get for you," a cheerful voice said behind me, and when I looked over my shoulder, I was surprised to see the big blond lieutenant. Any last lingering hope that he didn't remember me shriveled as he said, "You look different with dry hair, Pavlichenko."

"So do you," I said stiffly. "Comrade Lieutenant."

"I was on leave when we last met, hence the civilian clothes. I didn't transfer to 2nd Company until I arrived in Sevastopol—Comrade Lieutenant Kitsenko, at least in the command post." He offered a hand. "Off-duty, Alexei."

The name made me blink. It wasn't his fault he was a tall, blond, blue-eyed lieutenant like my husband, but did he have to be named Alexei, too? Then I blinked again, as Kostia jumped up with a broad grin and embraced the new arrival as though they were brothers.

"You'll get your platoon," Kitsenko told me, thumping Kostia's back with a friendly fist and coming to sit on an old oil drum. "Dromin's just kicking and squealing. He knows he can't argue with Petrov."

"Thank you, Comrade Lieutenant." He was being friendly, but I couldn't help wondering if his had been the voice speculating that I was General Petrov's bed warmer. All because of one careless kiss . . .

"My friends call me Lyonya," Kitsenko said with a grin, feinting at Kostia, who slipped the mock punch and threw one back. "And you're Lyudmila Pavlichenko. When I met up with Kostia here, I asked him about this brunette vision I'd seen come out of a bathhouse like Venus from a clamshell, and Kostia told me all about you."

The breezy flattery caught me off guard, but not as much as this unexpected camaraderie. "How do you two know each other?"

"Met years ago in Donetsk, in technical school," Kitsenko said, reaching for a biscuit. "I see this skinny kid from Irkutsk come prowling into the classroom like a nervous wolf—"

"Everyone in the class poking fun at my accent," Kostia said. "Except him—"

"Oh, I made fun of your accent, too. Siberian vowels that could cut ice. But I thought, *That's a feral little bastard that will be useful in a hockey scrum; let's be friends.*"

"And then an ox from Leningrad said my mother was a whore, and Lyonya broke his nose." Kostia shook his head, still grinning, and I stared. I hadn't heard my silent partner volunteer so many words in—well, ever. "So I invite this big-city boy here to Irkutsk to visit, that fall—"

"—and his father took us on a hunt, and I saw *that* was the real wolf," Kitsenko finished, shuddering. "Something out of Baba Yaga's nightmares."

I wondered how one man could be a lieutenant and the other a corporal considering they must have joined around the same time, but Kostia said, "Lyonya took the accelerated course for middle-rank officer corps under the coastal army general staff."

"And now I get to give him orders," Kitsenko said with another feinted punch. "Now let's hear about you, Lyudmila Mikhailovna. If you've got a hundred and eighty-seven scalps, why haven't you earned an Order of Glory or two?"

"I don't do it for glory," I said, not quite able to keep the edge out of my voice.

"She does it for the liquor." Fyodor laughed, passing a cup of the rot-gut army vodka. "Not to mention the luxury accommodations around here."

Kitsenko smiled but persisted. "Really—why not a single decoration on that tunic?"

I shrugged, but Fyodor answered for me. "Sergienko passed her name up for commendations, but they must have died on someone's desk. Someone over his head, who didn't like our Mila here—"

"Someone who didn't feel like pinning stars on a woman's tunic," Kostia observed.

"They'll get used to the idea," said Kitsenko. "You know Comrade Stalin's ordered three all-female combat regiments formed in the Red Air Force, under Marina Raskova? They'll be pinning red stars and gold stars on hundreds of ladies by the new year." He smiled at me, frank and admiring. "You'll get your share, Mila."

I paused, looking at him over my mug of tea. "Sir," I said at last, wondering how not to give offense, but wanting this line drawn here and now before his flirtatious first impression of me turned into an assumption that I was *available*. "Kostia and Fyodor call me *Mila*. They've guarded my back, and I've guarded theirs. We've killed together, fought together, bled together. I don't give my nickname unless it's to a brother in arms."

"Then until we bleed together," Kitsenko said without rancor, and raised his mug of tea in salute. "I imagine Sevastopol will give us the opportunity."

He was certainly correct about *that*.

CHAPTER 12

My memoir, the official version: I was given the responsibility of recruiting and training a proper platoon of snipers—the first woman of the Red Army so honored.

My memoir, the unofficial version: I have no idea if I was the first Red Army woman to lead a platoon, but someone in the propaganda office decided it sounded better that way, so there I was with my ragtag little band of fumble-fingered amateurs that was absolutely nothing like a proper platoon.

A REAL RIFLE platoon would be fifty-one troops commanded by a lieutenant and a deputy senior sergeant, the men beneath them divided into four sections each with their own sergeant. There would be a mortar section, a dispatch rider, clear lines of organization. Mine was a handful of raw recruits grudgingly pointed in my direction by Lieutenant Dromin, who culled them from the marine infantry battalions when reinforcements arrived in November. The scene played itself out exactly as it had when I was given my first batch of trainees: the men argued with me about whether or not I was their commander; they argued about whether I had or had not killed one hundred and eighty-seven enemies; they argued about whether or not women belonged on the front line. But frankly you have heard enough of that sort of thing by now, and so had I, so let us move on to the point when they were listening, more or less, and I had a platoon, more or less.

Although I nearly didn't have any corporals to help me lead it, because Fyodor and Kostia were both no help at all with the new recruits that first day. In fact they considered it hugely amusing to sit back and watch me get my temper up stamping all over the new men, and I threatened to send the pair of them up to Dromin for laughing at their commander. "I wasn't laughing," said Kostia, statue-faced, his eyes dancing, and as for Fyodor, he could barely be peeled guffawing out of the mud. I made them dig latrines for three hours.

So I had riflemen under my command again, but there weren't many proper sorties to get them seasoned. The first half of November was a series of furious skirmishes trying to push back against the Hitlerites, who had fortified Mekenzia in hopes of using it as a base to push toward the rear of the city's defenders. They were now driving like an arrow for Sevastopol, which meant not sniper work but blind firing, counterattacking under heavy mortar fire . . . weeks of German attacks and our own counterattacks, not only when we were at Mekenzia but all up and down the defensive lines of Sevastopol.

"Twenty-five days," Kostia said, and I heard the speculation in his voice. Twenty-five furious days the Fritzes had attacked Sevastopol, never wavering, never faltering until they'd pushed us back a few precious kilometers. The attackers around Odessa would never have had such steely will, not under the rain of death we were pouring down.

"They'll have to regroup now," I said, scanning no-man's-land through my binoculars: a neutral strip laced on either side with trenches, communication passages, machine-gun nests, minefields, antitank ditches. "Things will be quiet for a bit. So you know what that means."

Kostia pointed out the spot I'd already marked, along the high ridge of the Kamyshly gully. It wouldn't be a crossing point ordinary troops could make without withering fire pouring down, but snipers at night? I nodded. "There."

"They'll be sending theirs through, too," Kostia noted. "Scouts, reconnaissance teams." But the first man my platoon and I barreled into on evening patrol was one of our own, not a Hitlerite.

The forest here was like a maze once we were past the excavated stretches of trenches and barbed wire. It sprang to life in a living tangle of juniper, hornbeam, garland thorn, wild rose—plants I could identify by sight now, after gathering so many leaves and flowers for Slavka. I'd been leading my platoon along the ridge, where we'd just flushed a dozen German submachine gunners armed with Schmeissers. Though out of our range, they hastily retreated, and we had no orders to follow minor patrols. For the sake of training, I had the men target-shoot at the distant gray dots of German uniforms until they vanished into the trees. Gunsmoke was still wreathing the hills, the last shots resounding around the gullies, when a white-haired man melted out from a thicket.

Fyodor snapped his rifle up, but I shoved the barrel down. The old man's hands were raised, showing what looked like a Soviet passport; he was shouting, "Friend! Friend!"

"If you're a friend," I called without moving a step, "what are you doing on the military lines of the 54th Regiment, and how did you get past the enemy lookouts?"

"It's not difficult." He spat into the leaves at his feet. "The Germans are afraid to venture too far into the woods, and I know the hidden tracks. I've been a ranger here for thirty years."

"A ranger?" I echoed, dubious. In his gray civilian jacket and knapsack, his white beard growing dense and scraggly nearly up to his eyes, that thin stooped figure looked more like an elderly wood sprite than a woodsman.

"I was." The old man met my eyes, and his whole face screwed up in a paroxysm of grief. He swiped at his eyes before the tears could fall, saying gruffly, "I'm known as Vartanov here. And if you listen to me, I can give you the German staff headquarters at Mekenzia."

THERE'S A HOUSE. Caterpillar armored transports with aerials beside it, machine guns on the roofs of the cabs, tractor-borne cannons, motorbikes with sidecars. That's the one."

"Troops?" I asked.

"The usual gray-green uniforms." The ranger hunkered on his heels in one of our watch trenches, shoveling down a dish of hot barley porridge. "Others in short black jackets, berets."

"Tank crew." I made a note. "Who's giving the orders overall?"

"Big officer, about forty, pale eyes. Parade tunic, braided silver epaulets, black-and-white cross under the collar. Every morning he comes out to wash at the pump and go through his calisthenics. They have everything at their pleasure, those Krauts." Vartanov's face rippled, hatred passing deep under the surface. "But they're afraid of Russians."

"Why?"

Vartanov's eyes went to my weapon, never more than an arm's length away. "I'm told there are rifles with special sights."

"That's true," I said, neutral.

"Then use them." He scraped up the dregs of the porridge from his mess tin. "It's not far from here—through the forest, about five kilometers using a shortcut. I'll show you."

I exchanged glances with Kostia. He drew me aside with a flick of his eyes.

"Trap?" He put the question bluntly, and it was a distinct possibility. Not all the local populace here was loyal to the motherland; even with news spreading of how Germans treated our civilians and captured soldiers, some rural idiots saw the Hitlerites as liberators who might save them from Comrade Stalin's food shortages. I had no desire to get walked into an ambush and shot.

"We'll take this to the head of reconnaissance," I decided. "We get firm confirmation of this man's allegiance and identity, I'll risk taking him out to reconnoiter."

Kostia's face tightened. "Not alone."

"We need a guide," I said. "The front lines are stabilizing; the Krauts likely won't mount another major assault for weeks. It's time to send the platoon out hunting." And there was no way to start them off if I didn't know the ground, didn't know how to navigate this dense forest that stood like a green wall and rustled in the unruly wind from the sea.

So, two days later, approval secured and Vartanov's identity and loyalties satisfactorily vouched for, the old ranger and I moved into the Mekenzi Hills at first light.

He passed through the trees like a ghost, following a nearly invisible hunter's track. I wound along behind him through the bent sycamores, wondering how I was going to shoot in these trees. Good for hiding—better than the brutally wide-open steppe—but not for sharpshooting. What were my bullets supposed to do, zigzag between tree trunks?

"Pavlichenko," Vartanov grunted, sounding out my name. "You're Ukrainian?"

"I'm Russian," I answered levelly. These questions of nationality always irked me. We were all Soviets, weren't we?

Another grunt. I doubted Vartanov agreed, but at least he didn't argue. "From the bent sycamore to the well is eighty-five meters," he said, forking right, and as I followed, a garland thorn snagged my jacket. Yanking loose, I froze to hear a flock of tomtits take off noisily from the nearest tree. "Careful," the ranger hissed, and moved off through the growth again like an eel. By the time the sun rose we'd reached Mekenzia, and I climbed into the nearest tree with my binoculars.

German trucks and mouse-colored uniforms moved ant-like along the road stretching between Mekenzia and the village of Zalinkoi. Among all the Teutonic gray I saw the Crimean Tartars with the white armbands of the Politsei, the pro-Hitler collaborationist force, guarding the barrier at the cordon. At noon a field kitchen appeared, and my mouth watered at the smell of potato stew and ersatz coffee.

"There," Vartanov murmured from the ground below, and I saw the officer. I knew enemy decorations better than the old ranger—through my binoculars I saw the tabs of an artillery major and a recipient of the Knight's Cross. I watched him light a cigar and set off by car toward Cherkez-Kermen. *Main staff headquarters probably up there,* I thought. Colonel General Erich von Manstein himself might be residing there, not that I'd get a shot at *him*. But this smug major with his morning calisthenics and his silver epaulets—yes. *You are mine,* I told him as his car jounced away over the road.

I sketched the homestead on a rough firing map, jotted the distances, began calculating the wind. *Speed medium, four to six kilometers per hour.* "What's all this?" Vartanov said, looking at my figures when we were retreating safely back toward no-man's-land. "This is about wind?"

"The rifle fires the bullet, but the wind carries it." I quoted the old proverb. "We choose that position, we have a breeze from the side blowing at a ninety-degree angle. At 100 meters from the target, the horizontal lateral correction for a sniper is several milliradians. Now, in locations high above sea level"—I brightened, unable to resist the technical tangent—"the atmospheric pressure changes and the distance of the bullet's trajectory and flight increases. But in hills under 500 meters in height, and here we're at 310, one *can* ignore a longitudinal wind as long as one takes the lateral into consideration, since it can cause significant—"

Vartanov had that wary, hunted look the Odessa librarians used to get when I started talking about Bogdan Khmelnitsky.

I sighed. "You calculate the wind so you can make allowances in your aim and not see your shot blow off target."

"Why didn't you say so?" He sounded offended. "I can take down a buck at two hundred meters; I know how to compensate for wind!"

"I'm sure you can, but there's still value in understanding the science behind it."

He waved that off. "This time of year, expect strong blows from the north and northeast. You'll attack tomorrow?"

No sense waiting, I thought. We could bag the entire nest here with a little luck and some cool heads . . . not a job for my whole platoon, though. Some of them had barely mastered their ballistics tables, much less cross-wind calculations, and this would be tense, precise work.

"Take the dark one," Vartanov said, reading my mind. "Your partner. He's the only one among you who moves quietly."

"Him, and Fyodor Sedykh, and Burov." The best of my sailor recruits. "I'll borrow a couple of hand-to-hand types from my reconnaissance officer as well, in case we get rushed."

"And me," said Vartanov.

I stopped beside a tangle of garland thorn. "You aren't a soldier of the Red Army, dedushka," I said gently. "I can't take civilians hunting."

"That homestead the Germans turned into their headquarters was mine." The ranger's eyes over the thicket of beard were like knives glinting from underbrush. "I lived there with my son and his wife, my own wife and my younger children. We had a banya, a barn, greenhouses, we all worked dawn to dusk; I couldn't tell you where the war even was, or what it was about. I was off to the municipal authority offices ten days ago, to register some supplementary expenses—and that was the day a party of Hitlerite scouts came along, lined my family up alongside my house, and shot them all." There were tears in his eyes, but he wouldn't let them fall. "I will be there to watch those beasts die, with your permission or without."

Slowly I reached for the rifle slung across his bent shoulder. He let it fall into my hands. An old Berdan II, almost an antique. I looked the ranger in the eye. "You can borrow a Mosin-Nagant from one of my platoon. I can spare you twenty rounds to get comfortable with her before tomorrow."

He bared his teeth. "I'll only need ten."

WATCH NOW, AS a party of seven shooters approaches the village at first light the following morning.

Kostia isn't at my side for once, and he's not happy about it. He doesn't argue with my orders to stay with the less-experienced platoon members, but there's a line sharp as a whip cut between his dark brows. "I'm staying with the old man," I say, nodding at Vartanov. "If after all this he ends up playing us false, I'll put him down. If he's everything he says he is, he's still the newest to a firefight and I want to be there to steady him. You steady the others. Shoot true—" and Kostia nods, slipping away through the shadows. It's strange having him leave my side. He's become like another limb since we found each other after Odessa; I'd be less uneasy if I settled in for duty without my shadow than without Kostia. He and the rest of the platoon take position fifteen paces to my left; I take my place in the middle with Vartanov, and the two extra soldiers I borrowed from the reconnaissance officer plant themselves fifteen paces to my right: a triangle of fire we'll pour down on the Nazis. Wind at right angles to my position; I correct the dial of the lateral on the tube of my telescopic sight and quietly pass instructions down the line. Vartanov follows my every movement, eyes glittering.

Watch now. The Germans gather at the same time, the same place, the same numbers. For the love of Lenin, their iron adherence to schedules and rules may have conquered empires but it makes them prey to a lynx pack like us. The sun climbs, the mobile kitchen comes out at 11:37 on the dot, the men cluster . . . at least sixty officers and specialists.

A sniper platoon's commander always fires first, signaling the rest. My rifle sings, sending her first hot gift through the eye of an officer berating a private in a loud voice, and he's barely begun to crumple before shots begin to thunder to my right and left.

Watch now as the Nazis fall like scythed rye. They're pinned under three points of fire: my side-line shooters all work from the outside in; I target anyone coming out of the middle, and Vartanov aims for anyone crossing left or right toward my zone. They came to the mess line without their weapons, too tightly packed to run, and I feel not a drop of pity. It was this crew that murdered Vartanov's family, and if my tiny band of seven lets up for even a moment, we'll be charged, overrun, and outnumbered eight or nine to one. If that happens, my men will all be executed. As for me, I'll be gang-raped and then executed, if I don't manage to shoot myself first . . . but that's not our fate today, because we're winning this, numbers be damned.

The artillery major charges out of the house, still in his singlet from his daily calisthenics, and a bullet drops him between the eyes. I think it's Vartanov's. The old ranger is firing slow but steady beside me, teeth bared in his harsh old face. Kostia across the way is snapping shots with cool precision like the block of ice he is. My platoon trainees and the borrowed reconnaissance soldiers are aiming and reloading without hesitation, and I am so proud of them all. Not one of them hesitates. They're my men, my pack of deadly, silent, softprowling lynxes.

Watch now, and don't blink—it's all over in moments. Close to fifty dead on the ground, another dozen fled into the nearest truck and careening away. We do a fast raid of the headquarters, stripping whatever we can find in the way of staff papers for our officers to analyze, supplies to supplement our meager rations, an MP 40 submachine gun we can turn back on its makers. Then we're fleeing into the trees. Fyodor lumbers along with soft whoops as though he has

just won a football game, the great ox, and Kostia glides like a shadow
at my elbow again, and Vartanov is weeping as he runs, but he never
stops smiling.

And neither do I.

WE WOULDN'T BE able to cross no-man's-land and return to our
barracks until nightfall, so we made camp at a place Vartanov had
marked for me on our reconnaissance run: a plank shack half dug
into the earth, protected by a stand of conifers and prickly juniper.
We were nearly there, blowing from a kilometer and a half's worth of
sprinting, when a buck crashed through the underbrush ahead. "No
time to go after it," I said as it disappeared, before any of the men
could start dreaming of fresh game.

"Never mind venison, I'd take it just to put on the wall." Fyodor
watched the crown of antlers disappear into the trees, wistful.

"A sniper doesn't have to kill everything in sight," I retorted as we
moved back into a jog.

"Hunt to fill your soup kettle and put a pelt on your bed, not just
to put a trophy on your wall," Vartanov grunted unexpectedly. "The
forest is like a temple: observe the old customs, be respectful, don't
kill for amusement, and the woods will reward you for it."

"I don't believe in forest spirits, but I don't enjoy hunting animals.
They're defenseless against these." I patted my rifle as I ducked under
a low-hanging sycamore branch. "It's not like the days when the bo-
yars went out with spears. At least with that kind of duel, the animal
had a fighting chance."

"We just slaughtered fifty men from the cover of shadows." Kostia
spoke for the first time all morning. "We certainly didn't give them a
fighting chance."

"But we're at war, and wars are mankind against mankind. Not
innocent beasts."

Vartanov bared his teeth again. "Those men we killed today were beasts."

To my surprise, someone had already lit a campfire outside the plank shack when we reached it. "I was off duty, so I offered to meet your sniper party," Lieutenant Kitsenko called, brushing pine needles from his breeches as he rose. "See if you recovered any critical intelligence."

"You're avoiding the command post," Kostia guessed, thumping his friend on the arm as we pressed inside.

"All right, I'm trying to get away from Dromin before I jam the officious little sprat headfirst into a tank turret." Kitsenko looked to me. "Good hunting today?"

"Not bad." I grinned, and he grinned back. I could hear Lena's appreciative whistle in my head: *That's a smile!* "You can stand watch, Comrade Lieutenant," I suggested as my men began making themselves comfortable all around the shack. "We can't cross back until nightfall, and my platoon needs sleep."

Kitsenko watched as we all flung ourselves down on the pine needles and stretched out. Fyodor was already yawning hugely and I felt an answering yawn climb up my own throat, the fast-running blood of the long night and tense morning giving way to that sudden familiar exhaustion that fell on my platoon after action like a curtain. "All the waiting and watching you do, staking out a shot." Kitsenko looked thoughtful. "I hadn't realized that could be so tiring."

"The most exhausting thing in the world is being on high alert for hours." I thumped my pack down, leaning against it for a pillow. "A sniper's eyes get tired from focusing so much."

"One eye, or both?"

I laughed. "Good snipers don't close one eye—you just focus on the dominant one; it fights eye fatigue. But fatigue happens anyway after awhile, and the eye starts slipping in and out of focus." Like mine were doing now. I yawned. "If you don't mind, Comrade Lieutenant, I'm going to pass out for a bit." And I did, until late afternoon when I peeled my gummy lids open and saw that a thick autumn mist like milk had rolled through the trees.

Kitsenko was digging a firepit under Vartanov's instruction, my other men were rising and yawning, and I couldn't remember the last time I felt so pleased. My platoon was coming together: we'd had a successful night; no one had died or even been injured. Days like today were days to treasure. I looked over at Kostia, still sleeping an arm's length away with his head on *War and Peace*—he took it everywhere, even on hunts—and gave him a poke. "Come on, you. Let's see what goodies we got off the Germans—unless your officer friend already had a rummage?"

"You think I'd risk annoying a woman who can drill an eye socket at 300 meters?" Kitsenko asked. "I leave the honors to you, Comrade Senior Sergeant."

All the men gathered round as I opened up the artillery major's pack, and moans of ecstasy rose. Biscuits, bars of chocolate, tins of sardines, a log of salami the size of my forearm, a liter-and-a-half flask of brandy . . . I looked up to see my platoon gazing at me soulfully like starving puppies and raised my eyebrows at Kitsenko.

He scratched his jaw. "You take that back to the command tent, and it'll be confiscated. So we clearly have no choice but to—"

"Eat every bite?" I tossed a tin of sardines at Fyodor. "You heard the lieutenant, boys. Eat up."

Nothing makes a party sing like the knowledge that death awaits you tomorrow, but you've dodged it today. In no time Vartanov was boiling water over the fire in a mysteriously procured pot, tossing in pea puree cubes to make soup; hunks of ration bread were being toasted on sticks. Kostia set up a proper table on a big flat rock and sliced the salami. I took charge of the brandy, dividing it into standard-issue tin mugs as we all gathered around the rock and the men looked at me in the dancing firelight. "Well done, lads," I toasted them, sitting between Kostia and Vartanov. "May we always have such luck."

"To Lady Death and her pack of devils," Kitsenko answered, raising his own mug. "I've never seen anything in my life as terrifying as you lot melting out of the trees this morning with your rifles. Well, except the time I walked into the latrine and saw Dromin's bare ass shining like a searchlight; *that'll* drive a man screaming into the night."

A laugh went around the rock, and we bolted the brandy as one. It fired its way down to my stomach, and I closed my eyes in dreamy peace as the first spoonful of soup slipped down my throat, and the jokes and laughter began to fly. *I could die here,* I found myself thinking. *I could die here and at least I would be happy.* And I opened my eyes, drinking the rest of my soup and wondering when it was that I'd started to think of death as something not just possible, but inevitable.

The men were ahead of me, done with their soup and now sucking down the sardines, chins slick with oil. The brandy had clearly gone to Vartanov's head; he was proclaiming, "'S easy to find your way among trees, even you townies . . . trees are like *people*, each has its own soul . . ." When the last scrap had been eaten, Fyodor stripped to his undershirt and rose to challenge one of the reconnaissance soldiers to a wrestling match as catcalls rose. I smiled and rummaged further into the German major's pack, gnawing on a bar of chocolate as I turned over the packet of papers.

"What did you find?" Kitsenko leaned to look over my shoulder.

The spiky German script was hard to read, but I could make out the man's name. "Klement Karl Ludwig von Steingel." His decorations spoke of a career that had led through Czechoslovakia, France, Poland.

"That's a lot of war under one man's belt," Kitsenko said. "All that, and then he came here."

"Here he came, and here he stays," Kostia said from my other side.

"Kostia!" someone called from the campfire. "Come give Fyodor a run, you mangy wolf—"

"Who are you calling mangy?" Kitsenko challenged even as my partner rose and began stripping off his jacket. "Tear his arms off, Kostia! Just you wait," the lieutenant added low-voiced to me. "Everyone will bet on that ox Fyodor because he's twice as big."

The two stepped in to circle each other, my partner smiling faintly. "I'll wager a chocolate bar the young ox takes it!" Vartanov called across the fire.

"I'll take that bet," Kitsenko called back, adding for my ears, "Now watch our wolf eat him alive."

"You've played this game before," I said as Kostia began to circle round Fyodor, hands poised, eyes alert. Fyodor was the size of a boulder, but he was fleshy and rash; my sparely built partner wasn't much taller than me, but he was made out of tungsten and patience.

"You know how many classmates we rooked out of their pocket money with this game when we were students? Every Moscow golden boy with a Party bigwig for a daddy thought he could wipe the floor with the skinny kid from Siberia." Kitsenko rested his elbows on his drawn-up knees. "By the time they spat out a tooth or two and learned how wrong they were, we'd have raked in bets at five-to-one."

I watched Kostia side-slip a rush from Fyodor and come back in an armlock that doubled his opponent's wrist up behind his back. "So you were the bookie and he took the punches?"

"Oh, we both took the punches. Moscow golden boys with Party bigwig daddies don't like losing, so usually Kostia and I would end up in another fight when the official one was over. But we'd still come out of it with more rubles than bruises."

I smiled. "That's friendship."

"The best."

His glance held mine just a touch too long. *Don't flirt with officers,* I reminded myself, and was glad when Kitsenko jumped up to shout encouragement to my partner: "Go for his knees, Kostia!" Kostia threw a bow back, and I smiled. I couldn't help but like Kitsenko for bringing such an unexpected light side out of my taciturn other half.

Biting off another square of chocolate, I went back to the German officer's pack again and found something more disquieting: a photograph. A pretty, fair-haired woman with her arms around two gawky boys, all beaming at the camera. On the back was a woman's writing: *Mein Herz! Mit Liebe, Anna.* There was a packet of letters in the same feminine script, and another in a man's writing—the major had written his wife back, but not had time to post the letter. Even Nazi devils had families who loved them. I wondered how Anna would feel, if she'd known about Vartanov's murdered family and whatever other crimes her husband had committed here.

A roar went up around the fire. I looked up in time to see Kostia flip Fyodor neatly on his face, pinning that huge arm behind him. Fyodor tapped out, and Kostia handed him up with a grin. Swiping his jacket from the ground, he waved off calls for a rematch and shadow-boxed briefly with Kitsenko, who was then hauled off to an arm-wrestling match with old Vartanov. My partner flopped beside me again, growing still as he saw the photograph in my hand.

"I wonder when she'll get news of her husband's death." I tilted the picture. "Or how he died."

Kostia slung his jacket over shoulders that had already begun prickling with gooseflesh in the chilly mist. "Handsome family."

"It's not their fault their father came here and walked into my sights." I grimaced, looking at the major's young sons: perhaps fourteen and sixteen years old, standing proud in Hitler Youth uniforms. "Will we end up fighting them, if this war goes on long enough?"

"If it comes to that." Kostia did up the last of his buttons "I didn't ask them to come here and fight me. Any more than I asked their father."

The wrestling and catcalling died down around the fire now, as twilight fell. Once it was full dark we'd have to douse the firepit and be on the move, but a soft lull descended as purple dusk hovered. "Who's got a song?" Kitsenko asked from the other side of the fire, and Vartanov began to sing in a cracked but still strong bass—a minor-key ballad in a Russo-Armenian dialect I could barely understand. One of my sailor recruits responded with a melancholy sea chantey; then unexpectedly Kostia's low baritone rose. *"The pale moon was rising above the green mountain . . ."* Startled, I realized he was singing in English. I spoke some English—my mother had taught languages at the local grammar school—but not enough to understand all the verses. Something about *Amid war's dreadful thunder, her voice was a solace and comfort to me . . .*

"What was that?" I asked my partner when he finished, and Kitsenko began singing "The Women of Warsaw" in a resonant tenor. " 'The Rose of Tralee.' " Kostia poked at the fire with a stick. "My grandmother used to sing it."

"She spoke English?"

He hesitated, then lowered his voice even further. "She was American."

"What?"

Kostia said something long and fluent in English, smiling at my surprise. "An Irish girl from New York who came over with a missionary group in czarist days. She'd read too much Tolstoy, had romantic ideas about Russian snows and white nights . . . Of course she fell in love with the first Siberian revolutionary she came across, and married him." He leaned back on one elbow. "She lived a long time, past the revolution. I learned English from her."

"Is that her copy of *War and Peace* you lug around everywhere?" I guessed.

Kostia looked at me, face abruptly serious. "Mila, I don't tell people about this. Even my grandmother kept it hidden. She and my mother made sure all our documentation was lost when the family moved to Irkutsk, so it's not on record anywhere."

I could understand why. Contact with foreigners who had counter-revolutionary purposes—it was something the authorities took seriously. Just receiving an innocuous letter from the decadent West could be enough to land you in an interrogation room, much less having blood ties to a capitalist nation. America wasn't exactly a friend to the motherland, especially now when they were dragging their heels on offering even a lick of support against the Hitlerites. "Does anyone else know?"

My partner nodded across the fire at Kitsenko, still singing as the men beat time. "Only Lyonya."

That surprised me. "He's that trusted a friend?"

"The best," Kostia said, echoing what Kitsenko had said to me earlier.

"Well, I won't tell, either." I bumped Kostia's shoulder with my own, not knowing how to answer such a tremendous gesture of faith except to make light of it all.

"Just don't go singing 'The Rose of Tralee' where any of the other officers can hear, eh?"

He smiled.

"So where exactly is New York?" I asked, mentally searching a map of the American east coast. "North of Washington, but where?"

"I'm not too sure. I'd like to see someday. Where do you want to go, after the war?"

There is no after *for me,* I thought. *I won't be going anywhere but a grave.*

It was the first time I let myself admit what I'd come to believe: that I was never going to make it home. That this war, at least for me, was the end of the road.

CHAPTER 13

My memoir, the official version: *Snipers must be calm in order to succeed.*

My memoir, the unofficial version: Snipers must make themselves calm in order to succeed, and that is why women are good at sharpshooting. Because there is not a woman alive who has not learned how to eat rage in order to appear calm.

"NO," LIEUTENANT DROMIN snapped at me. "You cannot have that relic Vartanov in your platoon. The motherland is not so desperate we will stuff decrepit old grandfathers into uniform and send them tottering out toward the enemy on canes."

I took another long, calm swallow of fury, keeping my voice reasonable. "He has requested permission to join, and his knowledge of the local terrain makes him invaluable." My written petition to accept the old ranger into my platoon had been denied, and I was at the command post to plead his case. "It was with his scouting assistance that my men wiped out twelve Hitlerites in no-man's-land over the last two days."

"I heard the resulting mortar attack from the other side," Lieutenant Kitsenko said from where he was leaning against Dromin's desk. "Quite a concert they put on. Bit heavy on the brass; blame Wagner for that—"

"Who?" Dromin said irritably. "Never mind," he added as Kitsenko opened his mouth.

Kitsenko just laughed, arms folded across his chest, cap pushed at a cheerful angle over a rumple of fair hair. I remembered Lena saying *I'm having a bite of that!* when she eyed his shoulders outside the banya, and I was trying not to notice the shoulders now. If you get distracted by a man's shoulders, it's better if he's not the new commander of your company in the middle of a war zone, and it's even better if you're wearing a nice dress so you can be admired back. I was just back from a morning's hunt and was wearing my camouflage jacket, which had been draped and stitched all over with tendrils of garland thorn, so I looked like an ambulatory bush.

"I say let Vartanov in if he's keen to serve," Kitsenko was saying. "Maybe he last saw service under Catherine the Great, but who cares? If there's still sap in the tree, it may as well wear a uniform."

"Your company, your decision," Dromin said with an air of washing his hands of the matter. "On your head be it when he dodders off a cliff. As for you, Comrade Sergeant Pavlichenko . . ." I could see his eyes wandering with distaste over my camouflage and my rifle, which had been bundled and thorn-twined until it looked like a load of kindling. Clearly he did not find my horticultural couture appealing, and clearly he thought I should care about this. "You will represent 2nd Company tomorrow afternoon at the command post of the 54th Regiment in the Kamyshly gully, when Major General Kolomiets will be presenting government awards."

Dromin had a spiteful gleam in his eye, and I bit back a curse. An afternoon ceremony meant I'd get no sleep after a night spent scouting, digging, and camouflaging a nest in no-man's-land, and a morning spent tensely waiting for a shot. Instead of toppling into my bedroll I'd have to get sleeked up in my parade uniform and make the trek across the gully all so I could stand and yawn through hours' worth of speeches . . .

But I'd have Vartanov in my platoon, and he was worth losing a few hours of sleep. "Thank you, Comrade Lieutenant," I said, saluting smartly, and rustled out in my leafy splendor.

Kitsenko came out behind me and sauntered along at my side. "I'll give you a ride in the staff car tomorrow," he said. "I've been sent along to the ceremony as well. Giving you a lift will make up for all the droning."

"Why do you want to give me a lift?" I swatted a tendril of garland thorn out of my eye.

"So I can steal a kiss," he said. "Last time you kissed me. I feel I should return the favor."

"I knew that kiss was going to come back and haunt me," I retorted.

"Hopefully your daydreams, not your nightmares. Would you shoot me if I laid a smack on you, Comrade Senior Sergeant Pavlichenko?" Kitsenko went on, grinning.

"I might." I paused to yank some of the vines off my shoulders, making my tone polite but unyielding. Flirtation is all very well in a more civilized place—intermission at the opera, say, while wearing yellow satin instead of a shrub. For a moment I wished that was exactly where I was. But we weren't at the opera, and I didn't have the excuse now of not knowing he was my superior officer. "Thank you, Comrade Lieutenant, but I can make my own way to the ceremony tomorrow."

"Are you sure? I've always wanted to attend an awards ceremony with a hedge on my arm. We'll be a very dashing couple; I sprig up nicely as a spruce."

My lips twitched despite myself, so I busied myself pulling more bits of camouflage off. "Thank you for speaking up for Vartanov back there. He'll be delighted to learn he can officially join as a soldier of the Red Army." Actually, Vartanov had no love for the Red Army, the motherland, or anything else he considered an oppressor of the Ukrainian people, but he hated Hitlerites more than he hated Comrade Stalin. "He's longing to kill fascists," I added with complete honesty.

"I like the old bastard," Kitsenko said cheerfully, hands in the pockets of his overcoat. "He could sneak up behind Father Frost and cut his throat, you can tell. Glad he's on our side. What's that?" he continued as I disentangled a flask and a rubber tube from my ammunition pouch. "An enema bag?"

"Another tool from the sniper's bag of tricks. Vartanov showed me a trail down to a very small section of no-man's-land—it overlooks a dirt road running within half a kilometer of the German front line. When I fill this with water"—I held up the flask—"and then bury it in the earth around my nest and run a tube through the mouth of the flask up to my ear, I can hear the rumble in the ground that means motorcycles or staff cars are approaching up the road." I'd lain all night and half the morning next to Kostia in a shallow trench, covered by a scrim of wild rose vines and hornbeam bushes, passing the tube back and forth until we heard the vibrations of a good-sized convoy. "Kostia and I shot the wheels out on the staff car and downed three officers and a gunner."

"You really are terrifying. Are you sure I can't kiss you?"

I was tempted to let him, remembering that he'd smelled like pine, and it annoyed me that I remembered that so clearly. "Quite sure." I resumed walking, trailing vines.

"Why not?" He kept pace easily at my side. "Do you not like junior lieutenants?"

"I shoot junior lieutenants. I shot one this morning. Iron Cross, acne."

"Is it junior lieutenants named Alexei, then?"

"The man I married at fifteen is a junior lieutenant named Alexei, Comrade Lieutenant, and I'm not very fond of him." I hadn't seen hide nor hair of Alexei Pavlichenko since arriving in Sevastopol—no surprise given that he'd be up to his elbows in blood and disinfectant in the hospital battalion. As long as I didn't get wounded, surely I wouldn't *have* to see him again. Now there was an incentive to dodge German bullets.

"My nickname is Lyonya," Kitsenko pointed out. "Because my mother wanted to name me Leonid and not Alexei, and *Lyonya* was how she got around my father. If you'd use that, there shouldn't be any negative associations with my name."

"Nicknames are for—"

"Comrades in arms, yes. Do I need to rustle up a battle for us to march into by tomorrow noon?" My company commander squinted at the sky as if checking the hour. "The timing's tight, but—"

"Comrade Lieutenant, I prefer not to fraternize with officers," I said firmly. "I mistook you for a civilian when we first met, but that doesn't change the fact that regulations—"

"I prefer not to fraternize with sergeants. Just exceedingly lovely hedges. I dated a hawthorn for a while; oooh, she was prickly. I had better luck with a viburnum, but her affection withered. A garland thorn, now—"

"Good afternoon, Comrade Lieutenant . . ." and I marched into the latrine where he couldn't follow, before he could see that despite myself, I was smiling.

"DEATH BY DRONING." It doesn't matter whether you're attending a Komsomol discussion of "The Communist Youth of Tomorrow" or an Order of the Red Banner presented in honor of the gallant defense of Odessa: any meeting of officials held anywhere in the motherland always includes speeches. I used to think that no one could beat Soviet men for endless speeches, but when I came to America, I realized men of *all* nationalities like the sound of their own voices, especially the kind of man who spends long hours behind a podium. Whether in a Washington park or a Sevastopol battle zone, it's all the same: after the first speech you're afraid the boredom will kill you; after the fifth speech, you're praying it will.

To keep awake at the awards ceremony the following day, I mentally thumbed through the pages of my dissertation and wondered if there was any way, here on the front line, to get it retyped. Too many trenches and sniper nests had left the pages soft and creased, and my section introducing the Pereyaslav Council had been splattered with blood when Kostia took a splinter wound across the back of his neck. He hadn't been badly hurt—he stripped off his jacket and offered up his neck so I could stitch the cut myself, disinfecting the needle with vodka so he wouldn't have to register at the medical battalion—but my poor dissertation, like Bogdan Khmelnitsky, had been through the wars . . . I snapped out of my musing when it came time to deliver my own (short!) speech of congratulations on behalf of 2nd Company.

Lieutenant Kitsenko delivered a longer speech, just the right combination of official language and wry wit, which brought grins to faces. He was good at that, as I'd had a chance to observe by now. It was a rare officer who could be friendly without losing his authority, and I was willing to concede Kitsenko had the gift. I'd seen him break up a brawl between a cluster of soldiers with fast efficiency, and rather than put them all on punishment duty, he delivered a combination lecture of scolding and joking that had them half laughing, half cringing, and vowing like naughty children that no, Comrade Lieutenant, they'd never do it again, Comrade Lieutenant.

The speeches were over at last, and then it was just watching ribbons and stars being pinned to tunics. One of the decorated soldiers was a woman, a pretty machine gunner who had helped five hundred fascists into their graves. *Good for you,* I thought approvingly, watching her beam as the Order of the Red Banner was fixed to her breast. Then the line shifted, and I saw Alexei Pavlichenko in line to be honored. I wasn't sure what ribbon or star they were pinning to his tunic, but there was something about *exceptional efficiency in the restoration of the wounded to the front lines* and I saw the pleased curve of his lips. Of course he'd been decorated. Men like Alexei always got the right kind of awards. He'd climbed fast at his hospital as a civilian; he'd climb fast in the hospital battalion as a lieutenant.

I made a quick escape when the assembly was dismissed. Somehow I knew Alexei would be looking for me—he'd have lined me up like a trick shot the moment he saw me step forward to make my speech— and I made a bolt into some tangled brush at the side of the makeshift parade ground. "Mila?" His voice floated over the air, the voice that still had the power to make my teeth grit, and I sank down noiselessly against a toppled tree. I'd outwait him, sit here until he got tired of the game and went back to his battalion. After so many stakeouts I could outwait Father Time, much less an irksome husband.

I didn't dare smoke until I saw Alexei's fair head move away. Lighting up and inhaling gratefully, I remembered what a prig I'd been when I came to the front, turning my nose up with a sniffy *I don't smoke.* I looked back on that woman—the library researcher, the graduate student, the aspiring historian—and barely knew her. I'd been nearly six months now in the school of war.

"This is the first time I've ever seen a woman smoke a pipe," Kitsenko said behind me. I could have told him I preferred to be alone, but if I was sitting with my company commander, my husband couldn't hunker down if he found me, so I didn't object when Kostia's friend leaned against the tree at my side. It had nothing, absolutely nothing, to do with his shoulders.

"Where'd you get that?" he asked, nodding at the pipe in my hand as he took out a pack of cigarettes.

"Vartanov. He gave it to me after our first sortie." It was an old Turkish pipe carved of pear root, with an amber mouthpiece—a beautiful thing, clearly the last object of value he possessed. I preferred cigarettes, but he'd offered it with such fierce, tremulous pride, I knew better than to give it back. It was a decoration earned and won; I'd take it over Machine Gunner Onilova's Order of the Red

Banner any day. "I'm trying to learn how to pack it, so I can at least use it where he can see."

"Isn't that shag tobacco a bit strong?" Kitsenko lit up a Kazbek cigarette.

"I've got used to it."

"It's funny," Kitsenko said, exhaling smoke into the frosty sky. "Good-looking women usually don't smoke pipes."

"In other words, I must be ugly and unusual." I said it with a grin, because I was feeling anything but ugly right now. In fact I was feeling delightfully feminine for the first time in months. Maybe since we'd first laid eyes on each other, flirting at the banya's door.

"The fact that you're *unusual* is well known to the entire 54th by now." Kitsenko blew a smoke ring. "The question of looks, well, that's complex. Ideals are dictated by time, fashion, custom. For me"—he looked at me very seriously—"I've never met a prettier hedge."

I couldn't help it; I burst out laughing. He punched the air as though he'd won a victory lap.

"Why are you trying so hard with me?" I asked, still laughing, giving up on the pipe. "There may not be many women in the regiment, but there are enough. And they're all softer targets than me."

"Less interesting targets."

"Why?" I took the cigarette he offered. "Do you have some romantic idea about snipers? Felling the woman who's felled more than two hundred men?" I was starting to encounter this notion among some of the more idiotic young officers. Some vaguely articulated notion that a woman who had killed so many in cold blood had to be, I don't know, hot under her knapsack?

"That's the thing." Kitsenko surveyed me, thoughtful. "A woman sniper with two hundred marks in her tally—it conjures up a very specific image. And you . . ."

"I match your imaginings?"

"Not in the slightest. I pictured someone a bit like Kostia's half sister. I met her last year when I visited him in Irkutsk; no idea how I survived the experience. You'll have to get Kostia to tell you about his complicated family history, but his father didn't exactly marry his mother. The old man lives out on Lake Baikal with a pack of Kostia's half brothers and sisters, one of whom came to Irkutsk for flight school—"

"Is this going somewhere, Comrade Lieutenant?" I asked, out to sea.

"Bear with me. So Kostia and I bumped into this half sister Nina in Irkutsk; he barely knew her himself, but he introduced me. That girl just about gave me nightmares. Little feral thing with eyes like razors, practically picking her teeth with a human bone, absolutely capable of tearing your throat out with her bare hands. That," Kitsenko concluded, "is the kind of woman you imagine when you hear the words *woman sniper with two hundred kills*. Some wild thing from the Siberian wastes with icy eyes and no more conscience than a wolf."

"What leads you to conclude that?" I tilted my head. "Why imagine *that's* what a woman sniper would be—cold, unemotional, savage? You don't know me or any other woman sniper, so what makes you think we have to be a certain way? Look a certain way?"

"It's just surprising to meet a woman with two hundred lives to her name and find a history student with the world's most boring dissertation in her pack and the softest brown eyes ever to paint crosshairs on a man's heart."

I didn't know what to say to that, except that my own heart was thumping in a way it usually didn't bother to do unless I was just back from a hunt. "How do you know anything about my dissertation?" I finally managed to say. "For your information, it is not at all boring."

"Your dissertation is famous throughout the entire *company*, Sergeant. Brave men leap into live fire zones when they see you haul it out. Soldiers with the Order of Lenin falter and grow pale—"

"Insulting my dissertation, now that's a sure way into a woman's bedroll!"

His smile quirked. "Did you miss the bit about your eyes?"

"Even if you have very pretty compliments about my eyes, I'm not interested in being anyone's front-line fling. For all I know, you've got a wife at home, or a fiancée, or a whole string of would-be-either."

"I'm not seeing any other hedges at the moment, on my honor. I'm a very monogamous sort of shrub."

"They all say that."

"I suppose they do," he admitted.

"Then sometimes if you say no, they threaten to demote you."

"I won't do that, Lyudmila. If you say no from now until the war's end, I won't do that." He cocked his head. "You've really been threatened with *demotion* if you didn't—"

"Of course I have." Twice, in fact. I'd been less concerned with being demoted and more concerned about being raped by my own officers if I continued to say no. Such things happened. Lena patched those women up afterward in the hospital battalion, but of course no report was ever made.

"With your record, you should have been standing up with that little machine gunner getting an Order of the Red Banner of your own, not fending off demotion from your own officers." For the first time since I'd met him, this lighthearted lieutenant looked angry. It took the form of a cloud with him, as though rain gusts had rolled behind those blue eyes and broad high cheekbones and crystallized into a storm front. "I'll put your name up. With a tally like yours—"

I shrugged, drawing deep on the cigarette. "I'll take any decoration I've earned, but that's not why I do it."

"Why do you do it, then?"

"Really, now. Would you ask any of the men that?"

"I would, and I do," he said, surprising me. "I ask all new men why they volunteered, if they did. I want to know who the patriots are, who are the fanatics are, who the desperate are . . ."

"But they'll all say the same thing. *I do it for Comrade Stalin and the motherland.*"

"Yes, but it's how they say it—that still tells me something." He nudged me. "So why did you enlist?"

"For Comrade Stalin and the motherland," I intoned.

He gave me a serious look, waiting. I hesitated.

"For my son." That I admitted it surprised me. Hardly anyone outside my platoon knew I had a son. I didn't talk about Slavka; *couldn't* talk about him. It felt like I was soiling him, bringing his name into this reeking world of death and mud and gunsmoke. "If I don't fight, he won't have a world to grow up in."

Kitsenko tapped ash off his cigarette. "Do you have a picture?"

I pulled it out, surprising myself again. "My Slavka." A formal photo taken when he was seven, sitting upright with his favorite wooden boat clutched in his hands, dark hair brushed sleek. "He looks nothing like that now," I said softly. "So much taller, getting gawky . . . at least he was when I last saw him. Who knows how much he's changed by now?" If I was killed here—and more often these days, I thought *when* I was killed here—I'd never learn the answer to that question.

If Lieutenant Kitsenko had attempted to put his arm around me then, I would have bristled and snarled like a badger. He just gazed at the photograph, pretending not to notice me fighting for self-control. "A beautiful boy," he said, handing the photograph back when I had my face straightened out. "He looks like you."

"I . . ." Another fight to push the tears back as I tucked my son's picture back into my breast pocket. "I promised him I'd think about him every day. But days go by when I don't think of him at all. Does that make me a bad mother? Even—" I had to stop, breathing unsteadily. "Even when I'm collecting leaves and flowers to send him in my letters, I don't think about him. I *can't* think about him, not here. He doesn't *belong* here. So I put him away in a locked room in my mind, and I seal it off."

"You do what you have to. We all do." Kitsenko cocked his head down at me. "How old is he?"

"Nine." I could see Kitsenko doing the math. "I was very young when he was born, yes." Hearing my voice grow brittle as I dashed at my eyes. "Too young."

"I couldn't help notice a Lieutenant Pavlichenko in the receiving line for a decoration." My company commander exhaled smoke. "Your former husband?"

I didn't answer, not wanting to get into the complicated history of the divorce that never quite happened. I just took a long, savage draw of smoke down into my lungs. We leaned against the tree side by side until the last of the voices faded in the distance, the last of the cars drove away, and then Kitsenko tossed his cigarette butt down and ground it out. "I'll give you a lift back."

"I'll make my own way." If Kostia rode back with his company commander, everyone would know they were friends when rank wasn't in the way. If I rode back with my company commander, everyone would assume he was sleeping with me.

"I'll drop you off two hundred meters from camp so you can walk in alone," he said, reading my mind perfectly.

I hesitated. "Thank you."

His cheeks creased. "About that kiss—"

"You're not getting a kiss!"

"Is that a wager? Remember, I used to be a bookie."

"You'll have to catch me off guard, and I'm never off guard."

"I'm patient. You can't always have that rubber tube in your ear."

"Sneaking up on a trained sniper to steal *anything* she doesn't want to give you seems quite a stupid idea to me." I saluted. "Good luck with that, Comrade Lieutenant."

"Ah, but you're smiling . . ."

CHAPTER 14

M y memoir, the official version: *At ten past six in the morning of December 17, 1941, ten days after the Americans entered the war, the Hitlerites unleashed a fury of artillery and shellfire on Sevastopol's defense positions. The intent was to split our defensive front and come out at Sevastopol in four days exactly—on December 21, the sixth-month anniversary of war between Germany and the Soviet Union.*

My memoir, the unofficial version: *My luck ran out.*

FLICKERS, LIGHT AND dark. Pain, dark red and midnight black. Confusion, a muffling blanket.

I couldn't move.

—*armored transport approaching, followed by two battalions of riflemen and submachine gunners*—The crackle of the report comes in from the military outposts. The men of my company flow into position. Orders—from Dromin? From Kitsenko? *Soldiers in the sniper platoon to stand with the machine gunners. Pavlichenko*—that's Kitsenko speaking, his hand on my shoulder, eyes blue sparks in a gunsmoke-grimed face—*you take the concealed trench covering the flank, aim for machine-gun nests and mortar crews . . .*

I blinked blood out of my lashes. I still couldn't see, couldn't move. I lay on my stomach, pinned flat.

—*The machine-gun nest, take it out*—The order, screaming out in a voice that cracks hysterically over the din. More screams as the armored transport vehicle slinks into the clearing on its caterpillar tracks, the machine gun chittering like some malevolent insect behind the armored shield on the cab roof, crawling toward the broken trunk of a young elm and raking 1st Battalion's trenches with bullets. I hear a roar of crashing timber from a trench giving way, a man shrieking in pain . . .

I blinked blood again. Something trickled across my side, something weighted me down across the back. Kostia. Where was Kostia? My platoon? *Kostia.*

—let me come with you, Kostia shouting directly into my ear to be heard over the din, catching my arm as I head for the concealed trench, but I point him back toward the platoon. *You have the platoon, take them—*Vartanov open-mouthed, trying not to tremble in the din and smoke of his first pitched battle; some of the others looking on the verge of bolting unless they have a steadying hand. *Kostia, TAKE THEM—*and I dive into the shallow trench half covered by the fallen leaves of an acacia tree. The armored transport droning forward, spitting death; I rack a round into place and line up my shot, and I have less than sixty seconds . . .

Blink, blink. I lay pinned in the dark like a butterfly to a board, tasting blood and iron on my lips, but my mind helpfully produced the calculations I'd run in a matter of frenzied seconds just a few minutes—hours? days?—before. *Heads of the machine gunners over two meters above ground level; rifle propped on a twenty-centimeter parapet; between aiming line and weapon horizon, a 35-degree angle . . . distance of two hundred meters to moving target; bullet traveling two hundred meters in .25 seconds; in that time target would have traveled four meters . . . adjust windage drum on sights . . .* Calculations had coiled and crossed as my internal clock wound the shot-count down to midnight.

—Fire. My bullets spanging through the eye slots of the armored shield; one body falling—two. A German lieutenant actually climbing out of the cab to see what has hit his gunners. What does he have to fear, after all, when he is covered by the shield and all the Soviet fire

is coming from the trenches in front? My bullet comes from the side, takes him in the temple . . .

Blink. I still couldn't see, but I tried to get my hands under me, push myself up. A wave of pain roared up my spine, flattening me into the earth. Dirt, was I still on the ground, in my trench, or—?

—*Scharfschütze, Scharfschütze*—is that the German word for sniper; is that the cry going up from the command post of the German reconnaissance battalion? Gunfire suddenly thrashing the trees over my head, German bullets plucking the ground, trying to find my hiding place. I grab my rifle and roll up out of my trench to the left, once, twice—there's another, deeper sniper's nest dug just a few paces over; one more roll and I'll drop into it—

But the world drops on me first, a shell that rips the air and swats me sideways like a swipe from some massive clawed beast. I have time, feeling myself flung up among the clods of earth and shards of trees branches to think *No, no, not wounded* again—

But I am. Which I realize when the veiling cold brings me back to full consciousness, when I blink the blood from my eyes, and finally come back to my torn body in the falling grip of night.

THE FIRST THING that really came into focus was my rifle. My Mosin-Nagant with her shining lines looped in camouflaging layers of garland thorn . . . the wooden stock was cracked in half, the barrel bent, the telescopic sight shivered into splinters of metal and glass. She'd never fire another a shot, my lovely rifle who had sung to me so sweetly, and I pulled her shattered body against me and began to weep numbly. I could move my arms but nothing else—the crown of an acacia tree overhead had been torn loose by shellfire and plunged down to pin me against the ground. The pain stabbed between my spine and my right shoulder blade; I couldn't tell if it came from impaling branches or mortar wounds, but I couldn't rise or wriggle or reach around to stanch my own bleeding. I could only lie in the mud clutching my broken rifle, icy twilight falling softly around me like a pitiless mist, and feel blood pooling under me as the daylight faded. My undershirt and tunic were drenched.

So quiet. The trees rustled almost noiselessly; the tide of battle had clearly swept on toward the next sector—I could hear shellfire echoing from somewhere distant. *My platoon*, I thought, my regimental mates—how many were dead this time? How far had the Fritzes managed to push? If the Germans found me here, I'd never be able to put a bullet through my brain before they took me—I couldn't reach down past my own shoulder; the TT pistol at my belt might as well have been in Moscow.

This is where I die, I thought, still clutching my useless rifle. Trees tossing overhead against the winter sky, stripped black and leafless from mortar fire, casting strange shadows on the ground in front of my blurring eyes . . . I saw my mother leaning toward me to smooth the hair off my face; then the twist of shadow turned into my father, saying sternly, *Belovs don't retreat!* I wanted to tell him I'd tried, that I was still a Belov even if I had to drag Alexei's *Pavlichenko* behind me like a poisoned anchor—but my father was gone before I could tell him, and it was Slavka who now stood before me. My little walrus in his red Young Pioneers kerchief, turning toward me with his hands full of all the dried leaves and flowers I'd sent him. *Mama?* No more plump walrus cheeks; the bones of his face were coming through to show the adolescent he'd soon become, but I'd never see it. I'd never see *him*, not in this life. I was bleeding out.

"Slavka—" I managed to get through my blood-gritted teeth, but when I blinked he was gone. He was gone, and I saw a man's dark shadow, the sun's last shiver of daylight touching a gleam off his helmet. Lieutenant Kitsenko, an overcoat over his uniform and a submachine gun slung over one shoulder.

"Mila," he was saying. "*Mila*, tell me where it hurts—"

Everywhere. Soldiers behind him, but they were just shadows helping shift the splintered acacia. *Don't bother*, I wanted to tell them, *I'm done.* Maybe I'd finally get a medal, something posthumous my son could remember me by.

"Don't talk horseshit, you're not allowed to die yet." Kitsenko again, turning me over and sliding his arms under my knees and shoulders. "You haven't submitted the necessary paperwork to your company commander, and that's me, so dying's going to have to wait. Hold steady—" and he was lifting me up, carrying me back toward the trenches.

"*Fuck*." Lena Paliy's tired exhortation came at me the same instant I felt shears slitting seams down my back, my coat and undershirt peeling away like a bloody carapace. "It's dug clear down her back—"

"I can have her at the medical battalion in twenty minutes. Fighting in my sector's lulled." Kitsenko again. "I have Dromin's car."

"That prick lent you his car?"

"Let me put it this way: if you bandage her fast and I drive faster, I can have it back before he realizes it was ever gone."

Jouncing over shell-pocked roads, my strapped torso a blaze of agony. Kitsenko's hand on my lolling head when he could spare it from the wheel. "Come on, Mila, you're not letting a few splinters take you down . . . talk to me, tell me about Bogdan Khmelnitsky. If you die, who's going to drone at me about the Pereyaslav Council?"

A brief side-slip into unconsciousness, and then the shadowed hell of Medical Battalion 47, a complex maze of bandaging rooms, isolation wards, and sickrooms dug into underground tunnels like a kingdom of moles. "She needs blood—" a doctor's voice, weary. "Fuck, how many more coming in? The blood reserves are—"

I don't need blood, I tried to say, *I'm dying.*

Kitsenko was rolling up his sleeve. "I saw her tags; we're the same blood type. Tap a vein."

"She'd be better off getting stabilized and dispatched to unoccupied territory. The next transport ship—"

"My company loses Lyudmila Pavlichenko, they'll riot. Get her an operating table, then a bed here."

"But—"

"You need blood? Her whole battalion will be in here rolling up their sleeves, just *keep her here*." An operating theater: blinding lights overhead, four surgeons slaving over four separate tables. The last thing I saw as I was wheeled in, before I tumbled down a tunnel of darkness, was a man shrieking as a burly aide held him down and an artery gouted; an exhaustion-slumped surgeon turning with blood down the front of his smock. Even with my hearing receding into the black after my eyesight, I recognized the voice: "*Kroshka*, what are you doing here?"

Oh, for the love of—

And I was gone.

THE FIRST FACE I saw when I woke up was Alexei Pavlichenko's, and I recoiled so hard he nearly had to peel me off the ceiling.

"Not very flattering, *kroshka*." He put a hand to the base of my throat and pushed me back flat on the hospital cot, sitting closer beside me than I would have liked. Of course, if he'd been sitting on a bed in Vladivostok he would have been closer than I liked. "Considering I saved your life three nights ago."

I started to say that it was Kitsenko and Lena who had saved my life—he by carrying me out of the front lines, she by strapping me up so I didn't bleed out on the way here—but I went into a fit of coughing instead, every cough a stab of agony. Alexei took my pulse as I coughed, counting beats, watching me hack with a detached expression.

"How bad is it?" I managed to gasp out at last. "My wound?" I had about as much strength as a kitten; my elbows were pocked with needle marks from blood transfusions; and my back and shoulder felt like they'd been dipped in acid, but if it was three days later, I didn't seem to be dying very fast. I yanked up my blankets, realizing that I was freezing cold.

"A splinter the length of your foot plowed from your right scapula to your spine," Alexei said matter-of-factly. "A few centimeters deeper, you'd be dead or paralyzed. I dug it out, stitched you up, pumped blood into you."

"Thank you," I said, in part because he paused pointedly, in part because he'd without doubt done a fine job. Alexei Pavlichenko might be a bastard, but he was also a superb surgeon.

"It was the blood loss that nearly did you in," he continued, noting my various vital signs. "That lieutenant who brought you in, he dropped about a liter straight into your veins . . . who is he?"

I ignored that, trying to sit up. "The German attack, is it—"

"Ongoing, but we're holding them off. Von Manstein won't be toasting the new year in Sevastopol as he planned."

"When can I get back to my company?"

Alexei pushed me back down. "It'll be two weeks before your stitches are even out."

"Ten days," I rasped. "On the eleventh I start ripping them out with the nearest broken bottle."

"You would, wouldn't you?" My husband regarded me, thoughtful. "On the boat I thought you were having me on, all that guff about one hundred and eighty-seven kills. I've heard things since then . . . You weren't joking after all, were you?"

I pressed my lips together, looking up at the ceiling.

"What is it now, *kroshka*? Over two hundred? Considering the little breadcrumb I once married, I can hardly—"

"You will please address me by my rank, Comrade Lieutenant Pavlichenko."

"Just teasing, you never could take a joke—"

"Is our problem patient making a nuisance of herself?" Lena, to my intense relief, breezed up with a basin of water. "I'll check her stitches, Comrade Lieutenant, they need you back in the operating theater."

Another long thoughtful look, and Alexei strode off in a parade-ground swing. His absence seemed to widen and lighten the whole room; suddenly I was aware of the other cots in my row, the patients stone-still or thrashing under their blankets, the smell of antiseptic and copper. Suddenly I could draw a deep breath, even if it made my stitches feel as though they'd been doused in fuel and set alight.

"All the surgeons in the battalion, why is he the one who ends up working on me?" I demanded, coughing again.

"Because he asked to be alerted if you were brought in. All the doctors do that for the soldiers they know. Same with the orderlies— why do you think it's always me checking your stitches? Speaking of which, turn over." Lena helped me onto my side, pretending she didn't notice the hiss of pain I couldn't suppress. "So that's the husband, eh? He's a looker. Half the women in the medical battalion are trying to get in his pants."

"They can have him." I braced, feeling the cold air on my naked back, the bandages unwinding. "Does he ever give you any trouble?"

"I have a feeling I'm too old for him," Lena said, very dry. "He's always chasing the young, dewy, wide-eyed ones. He did pretty work on these stitches, though, I'll say that. The other surgeons, if they're young they're inexperienced, and if they're old they're drunks. Your Alexei did twenty-hour shifts this past week and never fumbled a single incision."

Cold conceited bastards make good surgeons, I thought. "The attack—do you know anything about 2nd Company? My platoon?"

"Your partner came by to give blood, stalking around like a wolf until they said you weren't going to bleed out on him. He left to take command of the platoon, but he gave me this for the moment you woke up." Lena passed me a folded square of paper. "The casualties."

Bless you, Kostia. I scanned the names in his handwriting, which was small and square. I'd never seen it before—strange how you could fight beside someone for months, know every intimate detail about them from how they yawned to how they exhaled to how they tapped their fingers against a thigh to expel fear, yet not know what their handwriting was like . . . I breathed shaky relief. Only one death, my youngest recruit, and the rest unscathed except for minor wounds. Old Vartanov had made it, and thickheaded Fyodor, and Kostia . . . and me.

I still didn't entirely believe I'd made it. I'd been so sure my time was up.

"You'll heal faster than you have any right to," Lena was saying cheerfully, bandaging me back up. "You lead a charmed life, you lucky bitch."

"Charmed." I eased back into my hard pillow, closing my eyes. I loved Lena, but right now I didn't want to talk to anyone, even her. *Lucky.*

It was something people kept saying, over the next week. Vartanov said it, tugging his gray beard: *The feet of a lynx and the luck of the devil!* Fyodor said it, wringing my hands between his huge paws. The rest of my platoon said it when they managed to trek in on their off-hours, giving news from the front. "Don't you say it," I warned Kostia when he appeared. "Don't you tell me how *lucky* I am."

The corner of his mouth tilted, and he unslung a gleaming Mosin-Nagant from his shoulder. "Your new rifle. I insisted on a Three Line. They tried to stick you with a Sveta."

"Who on earth thinks a rifle with a muzzle flash like a searchlight is a good weapon for a sniper?"

"That's what I said." He sat at the foot of my bed without another word, taking out his Finnish combat knife and needle file. I could see he'd already put considerable time into making it battle-ready. He'd watched me strip and oil my old rifle hundreds of times; he knew I'd removed the wood along the length of the handguard groove so that it no longer touched the barrel; he knew I preferred to insert padding between the receiver and the magazine; he knew I kept the tip of the gunstock filed down. I nearly wept, watching his hands work, and felt the words hovering at the tip of my tongue: *When I get out of this bed and take that rifle up, I'm going to die.*

But I couldn't say it to Kostia; he was my partner, my shadow, the one who was supposed to keep me from dying. When my fate came for me, he was going to blame himself—so I let the words wither, letting myself sink instead into Kostia's snow-soft silence whenever he visited my hospital cot, sliding in and out of a doze, feeling the comforting weight of the new Three Line's barrel against my leg as he worked on it through each of his visits, patiently making it mine. When a leader has doubts about herself in wartime, even if she's just a sergeant, she can't reveal them to her men. I'd learned that, leading my platoon.

I shouldn't reveal such doubts to my officers, either, but Kitsenko had a way of surprising things out of me.

"You're not dying," he said from the doorway on my sixth day in hospital, startling me as I frowned at a bowl of broth. "Have some chocolate," he added, taking out a paper-wrapped bar as he came to sit on a too-low stool by my cot. "Proper Belgian stuff. One of my sergeants plucked it from the pack of a dead German lieutenant yesterday afternoon. I pulled rank unashamedly and stole it for you."

I blinked, surprised to see him here. "The German attack, aren't you—"

"The attack on the 54th eased yesterday. I'm free and easy until they come pulsing back at us like the maggots they are." His face was grained and his uniform rumpled and splattered as though he'd come right from the front lines, but his smile was still cheerful as he looked down at me. "You're not dying," he repeated, unwrapping the chocolate for me.

"Why do you keep saying that?"

"Because when I was hauling you off the front lines, you wouldn't believe me. Kept muttering, *I'm dead, I'm dying*. I thought I'd try to pound the truth into you now that you're a bit more conscious. You're not dying," he finished, and broke a square off the bar.

I slipped it into my mouth. Belgian chocolate, the real stuff, not the chalky blocks of army chocolate I was used to. The sweetness in my mouth brought tears to my eyes. "Maybe this time didn't kill me," I found myself saying, almost inaudibly. "The next one will."

I expected him to say something hearty: *You'll bag many more for the motherland, don't you worry!* Or perhaps I'd get a stern reprimand about defeatism. Instead he broke off another piece of chocolate and pushed it at me, asking, "How do you figure that?"

I chewed, swallowed. Tucked my ragged hair behind my ear. "They say the third wound kills you."

"Who's *they*, and who says *they* know everything?"

"You know what I mean."

"Well, your count's off. This is already your fourth time injured."

"The first two don't count." An impatient shake of my head. "A concussion, then a strained hip . . . those were little nothing wounds. The last one was the first, really. Now this. The next one—"

"But last week you were convinced you'd be dead on this one," Kitsenko pointed out. "So it sounds to me like you're changing your story. Are you so determined to be a martyr that you've forgotten how to count?"

I tried giving him a sour look, but it was hard with a mouth full of chocolate.

"You're not dying," he said. "What can I say to make you believe that?"

"I can't—shake it." My voice came out thready, uneven. "Maybe it's not the number of wounds. Third, fourth . . . at some point, I'm done. My luck's almost out."

"I don't think that's how luck works, Pavlichenko." He pushed his cap back on his rumpled fair hair. "You're not issued a certain amount, like bread in the chow line."

"Run the numbers," I said brutally. "I can calculate wind shifts by the milliradian; you think I can't run the odds on whether I'll ever see my son again?"

"I think you have a good many more dead Nazis to go before that has any chance of happening." Kitsenko pushed another square of chocolate into my hand. "Here. My mother always said when a woman is upset, give her chocolate and tell her she's beautiful. In your case, I think I can amend that to give you chocolate and tell you you're dangerous. You are beautiful," he added, "but something tells me you'll be more comforted by the thought that you're still danger-ous. And that the Hitlerites know it."

Maybe the compliment shouldn't have mattered at a moment like this, but it did. I hiccupped a laugh.

"We all have that feeling from time to time," he added. "The feel-ing that we're doomed. It comes and goes, like fever. I had it when I first came to the front—I thought the first battle would kill me, and I'm still here. Kostia had a bad patch in Odessa at the end, he told me, convinced he'd be cut down before the evacuation."

"He didn't tell me that."

"He needs to be invincible for you, just as you are for him. And now you're having a bad case of the forebodings, and that's perfectly natural. You've dealt so much death, you feel it breathing at your shoulder."

"You're going to tell me it's *not* breathing at my shoulder?"

"It's breathing at all our shoulders. We could all die tomorrow. So eat your chocolate, Pavlichenko." He gave me the last square. I rolled it around my mouth, savoring the last drop of sweetness, not sure what to feel. Except . . . lighter, a very little. For everyone else—my family, in my letters; my men, in my platoon; even Kostia, in our partnership—I had to be invincible. But before Kitsenko, I could be afraid. Be tired. Be *human*.

The relief of that stabbed so sweetly.

"Mila," I said at last.

"What?" He linked his hands between his knees.

"We've fought together now." I lay back in my hard cot. "Call me Mila."

He smiled. "If you call me Lyonya."

THE SOVIET DELEGATION: DAY 1

August 27, 1942
WASHINGTON, D.C.

CHAPTER 15

S ay, Mrs. Pavlichenko, can we call you Lyudmila? *Pavlichenko,* that's a mouthful!"

The marksman watched the hungry ripple of curiosity that rose up as the girl sniper entered the first-floor White House dining room. Another barrage of camera flashes—he hid his face behind his own borrowed camera—and through the lens he saw her flinch. Lyudmila Pavlichenko was not a tall woman, and she looked smaller now that she'd changed out of her olive-drab uniform into a blue-sprigged day dress that probably passed for stylish in Moscow. The marksman watched her eyes drift over the smart frocks of the sleek Washington women in the room, their pearl necklaces, their carefully set waves and curls; for an instant the Russian girl's hand stole up to her bluntly chopped hair.

Timid, the marksman filed away, still fiddling behind the camera to hide his face. *They'll eat her alive.*

"I hope you have all rested." The First Lady stepped forward with a gesture of welcome for the whole Soviet delegation as the dark-suited men filed in behind their girl sniper, trying not to gawk at their surroundings. The room was big despite its being called the *small* dining room, with a glittering chandelier, gracious molded ceilings, and tall windows draped in elegantly tied-back curtains. Interpreters on both sides murmured introductions, and the marksman paid close attention to the murmurs of Russian. He didn't speak the language well, but he could understand it. Useful for when he had to sit through American Communist Party meetings, waiting for a chance to pick off the latest Red agitator who had sufficiently alarmed someone in Washington or New York. Arranging fatal accidents for American

Marxists had paid the bills nicely in its day—not so much now that the Soviets were allies . . .

Although the people he worked for weren't at all convinced they should *remain* allies, a prospect which the marksman thought might mean a great deal of future employment.

The First Lady continued, gesturing everyone toward the long table with its forest of china, crystal, and silver. "I thought you might begin your acquaintance with the American way of life by trying a traditional American breakfast."

"Is there always this much food at an American breakfast?" the marksman heard the head of the Soviet delegation mutter in Russian as everyone took their places. The dishes had already been laid out: fried eggs, grilled bacon and sausage, marinated mushrooms, jugs of cold orange juice, and carafes of hot coffee. "What are those, oladi?"

"Pancakes," Mila Pavlichenko murmured back, also in Russian. The marksman had angled himself into a seat two down from her, where he could hear her clearly but she'd have no view of *his* face at all. "Americans call oladi *pancakes*. Don't stare, or they'll think we're yokels."

"The one they're staring at is you. Maybe they think you're the yokel." The head of the Soviet delegation sounded peevish, and the marksman hid a smile as chatter erupted across the table. The Soviets had sent two other Russian students turned soldiers to attend the international conference, both of whom sat at this table, along with a phalanx of minders and embassy staff—but they were all blocky charmless men in dark suits, and no one was interested in them. All the eyes were on the girl sniper, who had started to empty the marmalade pot into her cup of tea, then stopped with a deprecating little shrug as she realized her neighbors were staring.

"I wish they'd stop calling me the *girl sniper*," the marksman heard her mutter in Russian as she took a slug of tea laced with marmalade. "Only in America can you be a soldier and twenty-six, and still be a *girl*."

Thin-skinned, the marksman noted, crunching bacon, increasingly glad that he was here to make his own evaluation of Lyudmila Pavlichenko. Normally he'd have obtained any information he needed about her from some well-bribed third party; kept a careful layer of distance between himself and a patsy being set up for a fall. But with a top-shelf cover identity in place thanks to powerful backers, not to mention a throng of avid newsmen and glittering Washington functionaries to keep the girl from focusing on one more innocuous face at a table of loud strangers . . . well, he'd thought it merited the slight risk. He could already feel his internal sketch forming of this pretty Soviet propaganda pony: who she was, what made her tick, how to pull her strings. He didn't think it would be much of a challenge.

"A woman at the front lines, serving as a soldier!" A slim blonde leaned across the table toward the Russian side, eyes avid. "You can't imagine how strange that is to American women. I suppose the measure was only passed to defeat Hitler, desperate measures for desperate times and all that?"

"On the contrary," the girl sniper replied in Russian once the question was translated. "Our women were on a basis of equality long before Hitler rose. Our full rights were granted from the first day of the revolution—that is what makes us as independent as our men, not the war."

Practiced, thought the marksman, as her words were translated into English. Naturally she would be. Soviet envoys were always stuffed with canned answers and memorized slogans.

"Do you miss borscht, Lyudmila?" one of the First Lady's aides asked, leaning across the orange juice and bacon.

"Nobody in their right mind misses beets," Lyudmila Pavlichenko said through the interpreter, and got a laugh.

Funny, thought the marksman, in some surprise. He hadn't anticipated a sense of humor.

More questions began to fly. "I understand you rode in on the

Miami-Washington train this morning, Lyudmila—first time on an express? Were you shocked how fast it was?"

"The only thing I was shocked by was the sign on the carriage saying FOR WHITES ONLY." The girl sniper forked a mushroom off her plate. "It's a strange thing to see in a country that started with 'All men are created equal.' "

Prickly, thought the marksman. He was fairly certain the head of the delegation gave her a kick under the table, but she just chewed her mushroom, looking bland. The interpreter looked relieved when the blonde leaned forward with another question.

"Tell me, are unmarried women allowed in the Red Army? I noticed you were *Mrs.* Pavlichenko."

Married, the marksman noted. He wondered where the husband was.

"I can't imagine Soviet husbands being any more keen than American ones about the idea of their wives heading off to war." The blonde chuckled. "Men! My husband fusses so much when I'm off to chair a committee meeting, you'd think I *was* abandoning him for the Russian front!"

"Some husbands don't like much of anything a wife does," said the girl sniper. More chuckles around the table.

"I don't know about that." The First Lady spoke up unexpectedly. "If I decided to head for the Russian front, I imagine my husband would simply say, 'Don't get yourself killed, Eleanor, and bring back some Nazi scalps for the office.' "

The girl sniper laughed—before the interpreter murmured a translation. *Understands English,* the marksman thought with yet another flicker of surprise. And clever enough not to advertise the fact.

"I say, Mrs. Pavlichenko, you're doing well for your first trip to the USA," a hearty-looking man across the breakfast table boomed. "Look at you, managing that silverware like a pro!"

Lyudmila Pavlichenko's voice grew edged. "Thank you," she said brightly. "We just received silverware in the Soviet Union last week. Up until now it's all been stabbing our food with sticks!"

Angry, the marksman thought, fairly certain she'd got another kick under the table. He watched her apply herself to her plate again, spearing her sausage with more force than necessary. *Behave yourself and smile,* the delegation head muttered in Russian, and she just gave back a narrow-eyed stare. *Very angry, in fact,* the marksman amended. Not so smooth and controlled as he'd assumed a propaganda poster girl would be. Lyudmila Pavlichenko didn't want to be here, didn't like smiling on command, and hated idiotic questions.

The marksman smiled, making a note of that. *Be angry, little girl,* he thought, sipping his coffee. *Lose your temper, lose your poise, lose your script. The angrier you look over the week to come, the more these people here will be willing to believe you pulled the trigger on their president.*

Notes by the First Lady

Franklin will be interested to learn that our Soviet guests speak more English than they let on—or at least the young woman does. "Those rascals," he'll say, chuckling around his cigarette holder. I'll enjoy painting the scene for him later—not for nothing do they call me the President's eyes and ears. He'll pretend his fall this morning did not happen, he'll wave away any suggestion of mine that the ill will of his enemies might be worrying him, and he'll ask me to talk. "Describe it, Eleanor!"

How often has he said that, drumming his lean fingers on the arm of his chair, eyes bright and ravenous to understand, to absorb, to learn? Often I tell him entirely more than he wants to hear, and he becomes annoyed about my persistence in the matter of my pet causes, but that has never stopped him from asking for my descriptions or me from giving them.

So I watch the Soviets over the breakfast table, compiling impressions for my husband even as I think of a thousand other things that will demand my attention the moment I am released from this room (the column I need to finish, the letter to Hick, the planned banquet for the National League of Women Voters, following up with the fund for Polish relief . . .). Our Russian friends are dignified, grave, conscious of making a good impression—yet under the dignity I sense fragility. The Soviets did not only send students for my international conference, and they did not send granite-hard Soviet supermen, either. They sent war-weary veterans who have suffered. Look at us, *they are saying with every move and every gesture.* We eat bacon and pancakes with the same delight you do; we laugh at the same jokes you do; we plan and hope and dream just like you do . . . and we're being bled dry by Hitler's tanks and bombs and planes. See us as the allies you call us. Help us.

That is the real purpose of their visit, of course. To make us understand how much they need aid, how much they need a second front . . .

And there are those here in Washington who will do anything— anything at all—to stop Franklin from giving it to them.

NINE MONTHS AGO

December 1941
THE SEVASTOPOL FRONT, USSR
Mila

CHAPTER 16

My memoir, the official version: *Being a woman in the army has its difficulties. In male company one must be strict: no flirting, no teasing, no games, not ever.*
My memoir, the unofficial version: *Well. About that . . .*

"STOP," I WHEEZED, wiping at my eyes. "My stitches are killing me."

Kostia and Lyonya paid absolutely no attention. They were fighting a mock duel up and down the ward, brandishing rolls of bandaging for sabers and bedpans for shields. "Yield, you cur!" Lyonya shouted with some Errol Flynn sweeps of the bandage roll—something told me he'd managed to sneak a look at a forbidden Western film reel or two. The entire ward was cheering: patients calling encouragement from their cots, Lena and the other orderlies staggering with mirth in the doorway. I tried to catch my breath and went off in another fit of laughter. I couldn't remember when I'd laughed so much.

Kostia and Lyonya couldn't visit me more than every few days, but when they did, elaborate high jinks always seemed to ensue. Last time Kostia taught us some labyrinthine dice game with a set of caribou-bone dice carved from a buck he'd shot when he was nine, and Lyonya fleeced us both out of every ruble we had before we figured out he was cheating. The time before that I was in need of a blood transfusion, and Lena ran a line directly from Kostia's elbow into mine while Lyonya told ghoulish stories about night-walking *upyr* who sucked blood to survive: "Mila, keep an eye out if you start growing fangs. Of course Kostia won't be able to tell, not with those wolf incisors . . ."

And today—

"Disarmed, you villain!" One of Lyonya's wild parries sent Kostia's bedpan buckler flying, and my partner gave a ghastly scream as the bandage-roll sword plunged dramatically toward his gut. He folded up around it, collapsed across the foot of my cot, and writhed there for a while in some obliging death throes as Lyonya took a bow and the ward cheered. A month ago I'd have sworn my taciturn partner had no gift for horseplay; now I applauded his dramatic demise as loudly as anyone else.

"You'd better not be too dead," I told him. "I still need a partner when I get out of here."

"And I need to make sure you have a platoon to come back to." Kostia looked at his watch, rolled upright, and retrieved his cap. "I should get back. Your rifle's almost battlefield ready," he added.

"Can't wait to get back to it." I lay drumming my heels under the sheets, thinking of my men heading out to hunt without me to look after them. "Tell the boys to look sharp." I watched wistfully as Kostia thumped Lyonya's shoulder and padded noiselessly out. "Aren't you going, too?" I asked Lyonya as he flopped into the chair by my cot.

"I'm not on this nocturnal schedule you *upyrs* are, thank goodness. How does anyone accomplish anything at three in the morning besides brooding over old mistakes?"

I began rotating my arm and shoulder to get some of the motion back, something Lena had encouraged even if it did make my stitches pull painfully. "What mistakes do you have to brood over?"

"I was married once," he said unexpectedly. "Divorced within a year. Do you think less of me?"

"That depends on why you divorced."

"Oh, I was young and stupid." He shook his head, rueful. "Eighteen years old, letting my mother push me into marrying the girl next door. I knew nothing about women, not even to tell Olga she was beautiful and hand her chocolate when she was crying, and after a few months it seemed like all she did was cry. We both realized it was a mistake, so we parted ways before there were any children to get hurt. Olga's an engineer now, with another husband and two babies. We're friendly enough when we meet."

"How civilized," I said, thinking of Alexei's mocking *Jump for it!* My stitches pulled again, and I flinched.

"I know you married young, too." Lyonya leaned back in his too-small chair, elbow hooked around the back. "What went wrong?"

"He decided being a husband and father wasn't for him." I hesitated. "If he hadn't . . . well, I'd have left him anyway, eventually. He was bad for my son, and he made me feel small."

"You are small. A pocket-sized sniper." Seeing me strain for a harder stretch through my shoulder, Lyonya caught my wrist—his fingers overlapped my narrower bones easily—and gave a slow, firm tug. "But I've seen you when your Lieutenant Pavlichenko comes by on rounds. You shrink around him; I don't like to see it. Here, tell me when it hurts . . ."

I gasped, feeling the torn muscles stretch. "I don't like to feel it, believe me."

Lyonya released my wrist when I nodded, and I eased back into my pillow, not wanting to talk more about Alexei. Lyonya steered the conversation into happier waters for another half hour or so, then glanced at the time. "I should go. Allegedly I'm a lieutenant with serious responsibilities; I need to go shirk them for a while so Dromin will have an excuse to glare at me."

I laughed. Lyonya leaned close to speak into my ear.

"Your former husband is hovering at the door. Shall I steal that kiss now, to make him jealous?"

I choked back another laugh, tempted. "No."

"Worth a try." Lyonya sauntered off whistling, fair hair gleaming under the harsh hospital lights, and I turned hastily on one side and pretended to go to sleep before Alexei could come over and begin making conversation. I heard him standing over my cot for a long moment, though. Just breathing.

What do you want? I thought, listening as he finally strolled away.

Lena, coming to sit by my cot on her break, was blunt. "He wants to know if you're tossing the bedroll with Lyonya or Kostia or both. He's grilled all the nurses and orderlies about you three."

"It's none of his business," I protested. "And why does no one believe I might just be doing my *job,* not hopping in and out of bedrolls?"

"Because men are worse gossips than old women, that's why. The rumor is you're screwing both of them." Lena gave me a shrewd look. "So, which one's the lucky fellow?"

"Neither, and you know it. For the love of Lenin, I just had a foot-sized splinter excised from my back."

"You could have either one of them, and *you* know it. Amazing they haven't started punching each other."

"They wouldn't. They're friends." Lyonya was the only one I knew who could crack Kostia's silence, bring out his elusive, tilted grin. "And they're *my* friends. Nothing more."

"Kitsenko's got plenty to do in the command tent without hustling up here every other day, with gifts." Lena nodded at the little vial of scent my company commander had brought on his last visit, wrapped in a lace-edged handkerchief. "Red Moscow, not cheap. First a liter of his own blood, then perfume . . . He'd be bringing you diamonds if he had 'em. He's courting, Lady Midnight."

"You're an advocate for front-line romance now?" I leaned forward so she could check my stitches. "After all our talks about fending off officers?"

"Fending off the asses and the brutes, yes." Her fingers were icy; it was the eve of the new year, and the weather had turned biting. The only comfort in this bitter chill was that the Germans with their soft Bavarian childhoods would be feeling it far worse than we were. "The officers who think they're entitled to have us flop on our backs if they so much as crook a finger, those are the ones to run from. But if a nice, decent fellow comes asking, I don't always run." She waggled her eyebrows. "Or at least I run slow enough so they can catch up."

"I hope you're careful."

"I tell them straightaway they can glove it up or they can put it back." She tugged my smock over my stitches. "It's nice having a warm body to curl up with now the nights are cold, Mila. Give it a try. Either your lieutenant or your Siberian would be thrilled down to their socks if you climbed under their blankets."

"Kostia doesn't—"

"Don't even *pretend* to be one of those stupid women who doesn't notice when a man's head over heels!"

"But he's my partner," I said softly. Hard to explain the bond between sniper partners to someone who wasn't one. When we fell in at each other's side at the dark hunting hour after midnight, we didn't just move in unison: we breathed in unison, thought in unison, felt our blood beat in unison like a pair of soft-padding lynxes sliding through snow. We lived by the heartbeat whisper of *Don't miss*. Introduce anything to disrupt that perfect working partnership, and one or both of us might make some infinitesimal, lethal error—might end up tossed in a hastily dug grave with our names misspelled on a red plywood star. *No.*

"Your lieutenant, then. He's a dish, and no mistake." Lena spritzed herself with Red Moscow. "Now, you'll be out of here in two days. Promise me you'll try to go at least a week without getting blown up again?"

"I don't walk in front of mortar splinters just to keep you in suturing practice, Lena Paliy." I didn't tell Lena my superstition that the next wound would kill me. She'd just smack me with a bedpan.

That didn't mean I wasn't still feeling it, though: the hovering dread, the gray certainty that my luck had run out. *Don't be a coward,*

I lashed myself fiercely, but I didn't think it *was* cowardice, precisely. Put a Hitlerite in my sights, I knew I wouldn't freeze pulling the trigger. No, this was just a matter-of-fact voice in the back of my head, saying, *Get as many as you can now; do as much as you can now—because your sand has almost run through the hourglass.*

Well. Would that be so terrible, if Mila Pavlichenko did not survive this new year of 1942, did not live to see the age of twenty-six? I'd have done my part for my homeland, fought as long and as hard as I knew how. My son could be proud of me, and he would grow up with my mother and father, cherished with all the love I wouldn't be there to give him.

And if Germans overran the motherland and subjected everyone I loved to live under a swastika, I'd never see it.

I was discharged in a steel-gray twilight a few days into the new year. Buttoning up my uniform, I saw how it hung loose on me, and in the sliver of mirror I could see how grained and ashy my skin had grown. "You look pretty," Alexei said from just behind me. "Do you have much of a scar?"

"You're losing your touch, Alexei." I arranged my cap over my hair, feeling the puckered ridge on my scalp from my last trip to the hospital battalion. "Telling a woman she looks pretty while bringing up her scars."

"At least this one doesn't show, under that uniform." He came a step closer. "You could show me, you know. Later, maybe. After dinner."

"The scars under my uniform are none of your business. You are never, ever, going to see them." I made a point of not stepping away from him. Alexei had done that so often when we were married; moved just a hair too close so I felt the urge to back up. I was done backing up. "If you'll excuse me, Comrade Lieutenant." Turning away from the mirror.

"I'm trying to compliment you, *kroshka*." His hand dropped to my arm; he sounded irked. When Alexei Pavlichenko exerted himself for a woman, he expected his efforts to be greeted with smiles. "Can't you appreciate that?"

"And I have invaders to target." Yanking away. "Can't you appreciate that?"

He laughed, the indulgent sound raking my ears. "Mila, really. You should—"

"Be going? Yes." I straightened my collar, lifting my chin. "I don't want your compliments. I don't want your dinner invitations. I don't want anything from you at all."

"You want that blond lieutenant instead?" Alexei asked, conversational. "Maybe I should give him a few tips. How to handle the girl sniper . . . it's been a while, but I still remember what makes you writhe and moan."

Rage made me light-headed as I strode off down the corridor with its harsh-flickering lights. Around the corner I had to stop and steady myself against the wall, shoulder throbbing. Beating the rage into submission didn't help; the wound kept beating in a pulse of pain I felt right down to my feet. It really wasn't done healing. If this had been peacetime, I'd have been given another week in bed, but if it had been peacetime, I wouldn't need it. The second German assault had been pushed back, at the cost of 23,000 dead, wounded, or missing . . . but there would be another soon enough. I stood there mentally framing my husband's smirking face with imaginary telescopic sights as he chuckled and said, *Just teasing, Mila!*—now that would be a shot I wouldn't miss. I mentally pulled that trigger until the dizziness of rage passed. Then I made my way aboveground from the dugout medical center.

As I shaded my eyes in the fading winter light, I saw a mud-splattered official car pulled up by the entrance. Lyonya leaned against it, reading a battered Gorky novel. "I thought I'd drive you back to 1st Battalion's lines," he said when he saw me. "Have dinner with me when we get there?"

And I shoved Alexei's jeering voice out of my head and said simply, "I'd like that."

EVEN A COMPANY commander doesn't get much in the way of living quarters on the front line. Lyonya had a private dugout like a tiny cellar, earth walls and packed dirt floor and three layers of logs overhead for a ceiling he had to stoop under . . . and when I saw how he'd made it ready, all that came out of me was a quiet "Oh."

"It's not much," he said anxiously, hovering at the entrance. He'd knocked a table together out of rough planks and covered it with a canvas drape for a tablecloth; the battery-powered lamp showed dinner laid out on tin plates—the kind of front-line feast that meant a week's worth of bartering and trading of favors had taken place. Black bread and hard salami, a can of meat stew, soft-cooked potatoes in a mess tin, vodka . . . In the middle was a 45mm shell case he'd turned into a vase, crammed with green fronds of juniper and sprays of maple twigs glowing with red-gold leaves. "I thought you could send them to your son later—I know you collect leaves and flowers for him."

I lowered my face toward the sprigs, inhaling winter, feeling suddenly short of breath again. *He's courting,* Lena had said.

Yes, it appeared he was.

"What would you have done if I hadn't agreed to dinner?" I asked, raising my face.

"Invited Kostia," said Lyonya. "I've heard he's a *great* lay."

Laughter spluttered out of me, breaking the tension, and I let him pull out a stool for me at the makeshift table. "I'm starving."

"Good, because you're officially off duty tonight."

"But—" I hadn't seen my company yet, or my platoon, or been back to my usual dugout.

"You can wait till tomorrow night to go stalking back into no-man's-land, Comrade Senior Sergeant." Lyonya forestalled my objections, spooning meat stew onto my plate. "Tonight you'll eat well and get a good night's sleep, orders from your company commander. And that's the last thing I'm saying as your company commander tonight."

"Why is that?" I dug into the feast.

"When I propose marriage after dinner," Lyonya explained, "I'd prefer the offer not be overlaid with any sense of obligation, coming from a lieutenant to a sergeant. Vodka, my one and only?" he offered as I choked on a mouthful of stew.

"You can't be serious." I managed to swallow the chunk in my mouth, which was more gristle than stew meat. A dinner invitation and flowers were one thing; I knew he was hoping to romance me into his bedroll, but— "You're proposing *marriage*?"

"No," he said, pouring vodka for us both. "I'll do that later, on a full stomach."

"You're teasing," I decided.

He looked across the table through the lamplight. "You dazzle me," he said.

My hand stole up to my chopped, stick-dry hair. "You've known me six weeks."

"You dazzled me within six seconds, Mila."

I knocked back my vodka, chasing it with a bite of black bread and salami. "It's too soon. I've only known you—"

"Then say no. I'm still going to ask. Later," he added, swallowing his own portion of stew down. "Right now I'm nervous. Most fellows feel nervous at this point, but I feel fairly certain I'm the only fellow in history proposing marriage to a woman who has personally dispatched over two hundred men."

I laughed again, despite myself. "How do you always do that?"

"Propose marriage to homicidally gifted women?"

"Make me laugh."

"I display a distressing tendency to levity and bourgeois sentimentalism, or so my Komsomol leader told me, growing up. I will never rise high in the Party unless I strive for objectivity in my personal relations, rather than mirth."

"Clearly a hopeless case."

"At thirty-six? Utterly."

I smiled, relaxing despite myself, vodka unfurling in my stomach. I couldn't remember the last time dinner had been taken for pleasure, with conversation and leisure in mind, rather than a simple refueling exercise between bouts of dealing death. "Tell me something, Lyonya." Deciding on a change of subject, something a little less weighty than marriage proposals and kill counts. "As an officer, would you have any idea where I could get access to a typewriter here at the front?"

"A typewriter?" He addressed the winter bouquet on the table. "Give a woman a romantic dinner; she wants a typewriter . . ."

"I want to retype my dissertation. It has blood all over it—"

The crash overhead nearly deafened me. The shriek of mortars—normally I was impervious to the sound of German artillery, but two weeks in hospital away from the clangor of the front line had softened my ears. Maybe softened my spine too, because at the scream of shellfire overhead, I erupted out of my chair as if I had been electrified, grabbing desperately for my rifle, which wasn't there.

"Mila—"

The table rocked as I dived under it, clamping my arms to my ears, heart hammering through my chest.

"Mila—"

I couldn't tell if there were more mortars coming; my damaged ears were ringing and roaring. I shuddered, my eyes screwed shut. Were the German bastards starting again so soon? Did nothing *stop them*?

"*Mila.*" Warmth around me, a voice vibrating low and soft beside my ear. He sounded calm, but his muscles were tense. "It's not an attack, just the Hitlerites giving us a little night music. Trying to keep us scared."

I'm not scared, I tried to say, but the words jammed in my throat. What an idiotic thing to say, anyway—I was clearly afraid; I was under a table with my arms around my ears. My company commander had had to *crawl under the table after me.* I felt his arms tight around my shoulders, gripping me against his chest. I'd felt such relief in hospital when I'd realized I didn't have to hide my fears from him . . . but I was out now, I was supposed to be recovered, not still cowering and petrified. Such a wave of shame swept through me that I nearly sank through the floor like a *domovoi,* one of those old hearth spirits people made offerings to in the days before the revolution, before education and rationality conquered fear and superstition. Except of course, such things are never conquered, no matter what the Party says.

"I'm sorry," I muttered, trying to pull away, trying to shrivel into my collar, but Lyonya just tucked me more firmly into his shoulder.

"Believe me, I'm the frightened one here. I was right behind you getting under the table."

We were both huddled against the floor now, the canvas drape of the makeshift tablecloth curtaining off the rest of the world. My heart was still racing in misplaced alarm; I peeled my hands off my ears and watched my fingers sink into the front of Lyonya's jacket instead. "They're—they're not attacking."

"Doesn't sound like it."

I listened hard. Boots walking past outside, the occasional low laugh, the clink of tin cups. A company going about its evening routine, no screams or shouts or chatters of machine-gun fire. "Don't tell them," I whispered into his jacket. "The company, the men and the officers, don't—"

"Don't tell them what?"

"I—this." Lyudmila Pavlichenko curled in a shaking ball. The girl sniper, sniveling under a table.

"You've killed more than two hundred men while looking them square in the face as you pulled the trigger." Lyonya's hand moved over my hair. "No one thinks you're a coward."

I do. "Do I still dazzle you?" I managed to say harshly.

I could feel him smile against my temple, pressing his lips over my ear. "Utterly."

We disentangled, climbing out from under the plank table. The tin plates were safe, but the shell-case vase had been knocked over, the winter bouquet scattered on the dirt floor. "It's all right," Lyonya said, but I scrambled to retrieve the juniper fronds, the maple twigs. Those bright leaves like fire cupped in my still-shaking hands, jammed into a 45mm shell case—if that wasn't wartime life in a nutshell, I didn't know what was. A stray frond of beauty here and there, jammed into something mass-produced and violent, usually toppled and trampled underfoot before too long. Dead and withered tomorrow, but still glowing with life today.

Like us.

I was still trembling when I reached up and pulled Lyonya's face down to mine. "Do you have something?" I asked, and kissed him. He tasted of vodka and pine.

"Something?" He was already kissing me back, hands in my hair, both of us lurching against the dugout wall.

"You know." I pried at his collar; he pried at mine as his mouth traveled down my jawline. A button spanged off the table. "Do you have—"

"I don't have a ring," he confessed. "It was hard enough getting a loaf of decent bread and a damned can of stew."

"For the love of—" I pushed him into the chair, climbed into his lap, put my forehead against his so we were eye to eye, dark eyes drowning in blue, and locked my other hand around his belt buckle.

"I will not get *pregnant* on the front line, Lyonya. Do you *have something?*"

"Oh," he said. "Yes," he added, producing a small packet from somewhere.

"Good," I said, and our mouths nailed back together as my jacket and then his hit the floor. Maybe this wasn't a good idea, not with my company commander, not after knowing him less than two months, but I had no idea if we'd be alive next week or not. *This,* I thought, kicking off my boots, *give me this while I'm still alive to enjoy it.*

"I've never had to disarm a woman before bed," Lyonya murmured into my collarbone, tossing aside my combat knife, my pistol, my belt with its ammunition pouches, pulling me back into his lap in the chair as trousers were shoved away. It was too cold to be naked like this, we were both shivering despite the little dugout stove, breath pluming in the air between us and melting again in every kiss. He was broad-shouldered, long-flanked, his hair soft under my hand, his wide hands steadying my hips as I tore the little packet open.

"It's been a while," I murmured as we fitted ourselves together, thinking despite myself of the boy last year with whom I'd enjoyed a laughing romp on a visit to the Lenin All-Union Academy of Agricultural Sciences. That had been good fast fun, a little perfunctory, nothing serious on either side. There was nothing fast or perfunctory here. Lyonya smiled into my eyes the entire time, palms sliding the length of my spine, my throat, the back of my neck, our bodies rocking breast to breast in silence, the prosaic muddy world of the regiment moving by outside in its nailed boots.

I love you, his lips murmured soundlessly into mine, and his hand against my throat must have felt the stutter-stop of my pulse in response to those simple, terrifying words, because he smiled and said it out loud so I couldn't mistake him: "I love you," simple and stark as he moved in me, as my eyes brimmed. The terrifying lock of our eyes didn't break until the end, when he saw me biting my lips fiercely as the tide built in us both. He put his broad hand to my mouth and let me cry out into it, stifling his own shout in my shoulder.

We clung silently after, still coiled together in the chair. "Marry me," he whispered against my throat. "Marry me, Mila."

"I can't," I muttered, still trembling in his arms.

He pushed my hair back. "Do you trust me?"

"Yes, but—" There was a conversation we'd need to have, but did it have to be now? "Do we have to talk about the future, Lyonya? Can't we just—"

Can we have this? Just this, for now? Because I felt more alive than I'd felt in months.

"We'll work on the marriage part." He kissed my temple as we began to disentangle. "I'll ask you again tomorrow. In the meantime, do you want to sleep over?"

"Sleep *over*, like we're on holiday? We're in a dugout. Shells may cave the roof in at any moment."

"Well, you can't say it doesn't add excitement . . ."

CHAPTER 17

My memoir, the official version: Lieutenant Kitsenko sent in an application to our superiors to formalize our new relations in the official way. It would need to be stamped and signed by Lieutenant Dromin and the regimental commander, then given the regimental seal of approval and filed for implementation at the staff headquarters of the 25th Chapayev Division.

My memoir, the unofficial version: "Lyonya, we should talk . . ."

"YOU'RE STILL MARRIED?" my new lover repeated for the third time.

"Only technically." I took a deep breath, trying to calm the flutter in my stomach—we were sitting at the rickety little table in his dugout, two days after our first night together, and the topic I'd been dreading was spilling out all over the table like a messy, invisible oil slick. "The divorce was never finalized."

Lyonya scratched his jaw. "But divorces are so easy to get."

"My father made things complicated." I sighed. "He can be old-fashioned . . . He didn't entirely approve of my leaving Alexei. Papa let me move home but asked me to wait and think about the divorce, make sure it was the right choice. I let it go because I thought Alexei would divorce *me*, one of those no-fuss postcard legal splits—what I should have realized was that having an absentee wife he didn't have to support suited him just fine." All the freedom in the world to mess about with young girls and then say mournfully, *I can't marry you, kroshka, I've already got a marital noose around my neck.* "Then before I knew it, Slavka was four and the new laws came through." The laws requiring payment of a fifty-ruble fine, and the presence of both parties before officials to dissolve the marriage. I explained how Alexei had missed every appointment I set.

"So you put it off till later?" Lyonya guessed. "When things weren't so busy?"

"But when you're juggling a child and factory work and night school, and then university classes, and then a researcher job, well, things are *always* busy." There had never been a day I thought, *Now is just the right time to pay money I can't spare to wrangle my husband whom I can't stand into an office he'll pretend he can't find, to sign papers he has no intention of signing.* And it hadn't made any difference to my daily life or Slavka's, whether Alexei was divorced from me or merely separated.

Only now I was sitting opposite a man who wanted to marry me . . . and I felt myself wanting to say yes. I scanned Lyonya's face, looking for signs of anger, but he leaned across the table and kissed me, smiling. "This does put a wrinkle in my wedding plans, I admit."

"You're not upset?"

"Upset? I'm relieved. I thought maybe you didn't *want* to marry me. If it's just a matter of a still-living husband, well, I can work with that."

I raised an eyebrow. "What, do you mean to kill him?"

"I'm not ruling it out," Lyonya said cheerfully, going to the stove to heat up some tea. "It would cost the Red Army a good surgeon but save on the paperwork. And if he's such a schoolgirl-chasing swine, we'd be doing the world a favor."

"It's not funny," I protested, but found myself laughing anyway. It was Lyonya's gift, I'd already come to realize—he could bring laughter like a stray thread of sunshine to brighten even the most shadowed room. He grinned over his shoulder, and I grinned back, propping my chin in my hand. "What really isn't funny is that you started all that front-line marriage paperwork for nothing," I said, enjoying the sight of his broad back under his uniform tunic. "What's that, sixteen pages in triplicate?"

"I'm sure there's another sixteen pages I can fill out in triplicate, which formalize a nonlegal front-line union so you can billet here with me. I'll find out."

I wrinkled my nose. "Surely there isn't paperwork to document who's living as your dugout girlfriend?"

"*Milaya,* this is the Soviet Union." Lyonya pushed a tin mug into my hand—tea, hot and sugared just the way I liked it. "There's paperwork for everything."

"For the love of—"

"Don't worry, we'll handle Alexei one way or another—later. For the moment, I'm due back at the command post." Lyonya bent down and kissed the corner of my mouth. "See you in the morning. Kill lots of Nazis. Don't die."

He kissed me again, so hard the tea nearly went flying, and then he swung out whistling. "Sixteen pages in triplicate," I muttered, but I couldn't stop smiling. In the face of Lyonya's jokes, Alexei and our strung-out legal status didn't seem like such a mountain. And even if it took another few months to wrangle the divorce, I had Lyonya here and now. It had been only a few days, but I'd already grown addicted to sleeping beside the solid warmth of his body, the arms that wrapped me up when I blew in cold and snowy from a night huddled in a sniper's trench, the pot of water he always had ready on the potbelly stove for me to wash my chilled face and aching hands.

"Can I kill these wretches, Comrade Senior Sergeant?" old Vartanov grumbled as I came to join my platoon. He waved at the handful of new recruits he was teaching to fieldstrip their SVT-40 rifles. "Worthless, every one of them. Younger than new butter."

I surveyed the new men, looking for the resentful gleam in the eye that meant trouble, but they all seemed either cowed or awed at the sight of me. "You used to be younger than new butter, remember."

"When I was that young and dim, Russia still had a czar."

"Well, things have improved since then."

"Have they?" Vartanov wondered.

"Of course they have!"

He tugged at his ragged beard. "I don't know, Comrade Senior Sergeant. The little men are still out here taking the bullets while the big men sit safe and dry. That doesn't change no matter who's in charge."

"Shut *up*, Vartanov." I headed him off before he could slide into one of his patriotic Ukrainian moods and start making not-too-veiled anti-Soviet jabs. "Again," I called to the new recruits, and had the old ranger strip the Sveta as I called out the stages. "Detach the ten-cartridge box . . . Remove the breech cover . . . See how he releases the catch and puts his weapon down with sights upward? Then push the cover forward—left hand, there . . ." Patiently I walked them through it. "Again, on your own. You'll be able to do this in the dark soon enough."

"Not *very* soon," Vartanov muttered as they fumbled back into motion. "You tell that commander of yours to get us some better recruits."

I waited to see if the mention of Lyonya would come with a leer or a wink, but it didn't. I'd been bracing for mockery or obscene jokes, dreading the moment I'd hear jeers from my platoon—I'd guarded my reputation for so long, been so careful not to cross that line—but so far, my men seemed to be taking it in stride.

As if reading my mind, Vartanov said, "The boys feel like they can rest easy now you've got an officer in your bedroll, Lyudmila Mikhailovna."

"It's not their business, Comrade Corporal," I said coolly. But I couldn't deny I was relieved. Maybe this could all be managed without fuss, after all. If anything, I seemed to be getting *fewer* impudent looks or flirtatious remarks than I was used to.

"Having a young woman walk around a war zone without knowing who she belongs to, that unsettles the lads." Vartanov was surely the only man in my platoon who'd dare be so blunt with me, but age had its privileges, even on the front lines. "You settled it, now they can settle down."

For the love of Lenin, I thought. *Men.* "Again," I called to the new boys with their Svetas. Away they went, fumble, fumble, fumble.

"Kostia's back, by the way," Vartanov added, wincing as he saw a breech cover drop off a Sveta into the grass.

"Kostia?" I hadn't seen my partner since his last visit to the hospital—the morning after coming back from Lyonya's quarters for the first time, smiling and floating and undeniably kiss-flushed, I'd found my new rifle propped up in the dugout where I usually slept, polished to a diamond gleam, with a note in Kostia's small square writing. *Yours,* it said simply. And then Fyodor told me my partner had put in for a little of his long-overdue leave now that the German assault had finally tailed off, and had headed into Sevastopol as though an entire Panzer division was on his tail.

"He's back," Vartanov repeated, scratching his rough white beard. "Wouldn't say he's in the best mood. I've never seen a boy that hungover, and I've seen a few in my day."

"Tell him to come find me when you see him." I knew why my partner had taken off, but there wasn't anything to say about it, so I just called out to the new recruits: "Again—" and began thinking about a foray into no-man's-land tonight, maybe taking Vartanov for a lookout, when an orderly appeared with a message: I was to report to the regimental command post at once.

I half expected to see Lyonya there, but it was Major Matusyevich and a sturdy red-faced colonel introduced as the commander of the 79th Naval Rifle Brigade. They took my salute, the colonel eyeing me curiously. "They say you're the best shooter in the division, Comrade Senior Sergeant Pavlichenko. Your picture's on the divisional board of honor."

That was news to me. He went on.

"A first-rate German rifleman has appeared in our defense sector.

Over the past two days, five of our men have been killed—three soldiers and two officers, one the commander of our 2nd Battalion. All single shots to the head."

I could feel every nerve in my body prick. "His nest?"

A shrug. "Our best guess, he's tucked himself somewhere in the wreckage of the bridge over the Kamyshly gully."

I felt myself smile, the kind of smile Lyonya had never seen. The kind of smile no one saw, except maybe Kostia, because it was the smile I wore only when the count went down to midnight and it was time to fire. "I know that bridge."

I knew it because I'd marked it as a sniper's paradise. The gully in the middle of no-man's-land was covered in reeds and overgrown, splintered apple orchards, two slopes rising up from the stream meandering down the center. The steep, pine-furred southern slope was held by our division; the gentler northern slope was held by units of the Germans' 50th Brandenburg Infantry Division . . . and the two high sides of the gully were spanned by a bombed-out railway bridge. A span or two survived on either side, giving way to nothing but soaring air in the central section, concrete pilings topped by a spider's web of tangled, twisted metal overlooking the ravine.

"He'll have found a place on one of the surviving spans and hidden among the metal wreckage." There was a map on the table; I tapped the place. "Six hundred, eight hundred meters . . . perfectly possible for a good shot. He's been able to fire at leisure if he's up there."

"Can you put an end to it?"

I looked up, still smiling. "Yes."

"GERMAN SHARPSHOOTERS." LYONYA sounded matter-of-fact. "I'm not surprised they're starting to turn up."

"Why?" My fight was such a narrowly focused thing, I saw little more than what was in my sights—or at most what was directly embroiling my company, my regiment, my division. Lyonya's war, seen from the company command post, had a wider angle.

"The first assault on Sevastopol, the Hitlerites expected to bull straight through our defenses." Lyonya pushed aside the remnants of our supper, which the orderly had fetched from the mess kitchens, and unrolled a map. "Their second assault, they realized how we've dug in—they've had to reexamine their situation. We're a first-rate fortress here, so they'll be bringing in specialists to nibble at morale. In the command post we're hearing talk of German snipers being sent in from Poland, even France."

"Who do you think he is?" Kostia's voice sounded behind me. I turned and saw my partner leaning against the doorjamb like a dark shadow. His black eyes were a little sunken but steady. "This German sniper."

"I don't care who he is." I shrugged. Some icy-eyed Alsatian who grew up hunting boar on his family estate; some fanatical flaxen-haired Reich soldier who had burned through a special training course so he could take his place on that shattered bridge and pick us off—what did it matter? "He's mine."

"You're not going alone," Lyonya protested.

"No." I looked at my partner. "Kostia, would you rather I asked Fyodor or Vartanov?"

It was a careful question, and I needed a blunt answer. If he felt awkward with me now, if he couldn't be my other half as soon as we went hunting, it would be no good out there. If that was the case, I needed to hear a no, and I needed to hear it now before it got either of us killed.

Kostia took the third place at the table with Lyonya and me, looking at the map. "We stake it out tomorrow. Get him the old Russian way—"

"Cunning, persistence, patience," I finished with my partner in unison. I couldn't stop the smile that broke over my face. Lyonya pushed a glass of vodka across the table with a tilted grin. Kostia drank it in a neat swallow and bent back over the map, drawing my attention to a spot on the bridge's northern end. The two of us put our elbows on the table and our heads together and made our plan, while Lyonya sat back and watched us work, contributing the occasional observation. And when the hour before dawn arrived and the car rolled around that would carry Kostia and me to the command post of the 79th Naval Rifle Brigade, Lyonya loaded it with our kit bags and rifles, buttoned my overcoat for me, scolded Kostia for not taking down his earflaps until Kostia swatted at him and the two men started shadowboxing in the dugout. "Quit it," I scolded, swatting them both, and Lyonya stopped, merriment fading as he caught Kostia's shoulder.

"Watch her out there," my lover said. "Watch her for me."

"Always," my partner said, and there was a moment of silence I interrupted with a cough.

"No long goodbyes," I said briskly, "it makes the heart sad in wartime!" and we piled out outside. But when the car bore us away, I had the strangest sensation in my life—the sensation, new to me, of leaving someone behind to worry through the night. Heading off to fight as a man who loved me stood with his hands balled in his pockets and fear for my life flickering in his eyes as he watched me go.

And then I forgot all about Lyonya, because that was what I had to do.

KOSTIA AND I stared at the bridge for three straight hours before either of us said a word. "Tricky," he said at last.

"Just when I got used to shooting among trees," I answered, thinking of the Crimean forest tracks Vartanov had taught me to walk like a shadow, but this was something new: crumbling arches of bridge topped by charred timbers, splintered sleepers, twisted railroad tracks rising to spear the whitened sky. My partner and I lay our stomachs on the snowy earth on the other side of the ravine, camouflage smocks pulled over our heads, eyes hawk-slitted through our binoculars.

"He's there," Kostia said.

"Not now."

"No, he's got his shot and he's gone till nightfall. But he's been firing from a nest up there."

"Lazy." I let my binoculars trace a tangle of corkscrewed metal beams. "He's fired from that position two days running. I'd have found a new nest by day two." A good sniper didn't form habits. Habits got you dead.

"Germans like patterns." Kostia's binoculars traced the bridge. "It's worked for him twice. He'll think he can get one more."

"I'm thinking his nest is there—" I pointed.

"—or there." Kostia pointed to another spot.

"Agreed. One of those."

We wriggled back on our elbows, carefully, till we were back behind our own lines. I sat up, rolled my neck, arched my back to stretch out the aches of a long stakeout. Kostia pulled out our night rations: a heel of rye bread each, with two strips of rosy fatback sprinkled with salt and ground black pepper. We chewed, both still looking in the direction of the bridge.

"Trench?" he said at last, swallowing the last of his bread.

"Trench," I agreed. "And you know who else we need."

Kostia looked at me and grinned, his teeth a sudden gleam of white under the quarter moon. "Ivan?"

"Ivan."

The colonel of the 79th was dubious, but he agreed to lend us a team of sappers. Hidden in the frosty thickets of juniper and hazelnut bushes, the men dug out a trench after nightfall, in the early hours of darkness when the day's shellfire had lapsed but before the German sniper would return to his nest after midnight. "It's deep enough," one complained, chafing the blisters on his hand from spading the frozen earth.

"Eighty centimeters deep, ten meters long." I waved my papers. "I've done the calculations."

"I'll show you what you can do with your calculations," the man mumbled.

"I've reached 226 right now in my sniper's tally," I remarked. "Keep talking if you want to be 227."

Trench dug, Kostia and I unfolded a metal frame and canvas drape over it and spent a full eight hours camouflaging it with twigs, brush, and armfuls of snow. And we worked on another little sniper's trick we'd long ago nicknamed Ivan. "He doesn't have much in the way of personality," I said, standing back and surveying our work.

"Don't criticize Ivan," Kostia said. "He's my brother in arms."

"Speaking of which . . ." I held up my rifle, the one my partner had customized for my hands, my eyes, my habits while I was laid up. "I didn't have a chance yet to thank you for this. It's perfect, Kostia."

"Let's get 227 with it," he said, the smile back in the corners of his eyes, and we crawled into our nest.

The best time for a sniper begins an hour and a half after midnight. That's when a shooter usually moves into position, and my partner and I were fully concealed in our trench and lying in wait for the German sniper to move onto the bridge and make for his nest. But the night passed and dawn broke through our binoculars, and finally we looked at each other. "Go back?" Kostia asked, because the German wouldn't move on his nest now, in the light of day. I envisioned Lyonya's dugout, the potbellied stove, the mess tin of hot potatoes and stew he'd put down for me while I peeled out of my uniform. The compress he'd prepare for the still-healing scar on my back.

I shook my head, looking across the ravine at the bridge. "I'm staying until we bag him."

"I'll keep watch till midmorning. You sleep."

I hesitated to curl against Kostia the way I usually did, but my winter uniform—thick underwear, tunic, padded vest and trousers, overcoat, white camouflage smock—didn't do much for warmth beyond keeping you from freezing to death. I curled into Kostia's back and slept till he woke me and took my place, alternating through the day until the sun fell again, the shrinking moon rose, and we were both back at our binoculars. *Come on, you Kraut bastard.*

Another long, empty night. Another morning alternating sleep and watch, relieving ourselves in an empty can as the other politely turned away. Lyonya would be ripping the floor of his dugout to bits pacing, I thought, but I couldn't abandon the stakeout—not yet. "What if he's dead?" I asked as another midnight rolled over the ravine. "What if our side finished the sniper off in the forest somewhere after he retreated from his last sortie here?"

Kostia passed me a pinch of dry tea and a lump of sugar wrapped in foil. Chew the sugar and the tea together, it helped keep you awake on a long stakeout, and without pouring tea into your belly that you'd have to pee out into a can. "You want him badly," my partner observed. "More than the usual target."

"Yes." I thought about why for a half hour or so. Kostia and I could have four-sentence conversations that stretched over hours; there was no need to hurry in a sniper's nest. "I don't have any ridiculous notion that what snipers do is unfair," I said finally. "The Hitlerites invaded and then started exterminating us—we're stopping them however we can. They already have the upper hand in so many ways. So I don't have time for anyone who says firing on them from the shadows might not be fair."

"No one says that," Kostia observed, and he was right. A few weeks in the chaos and cruelty of the front lines was enough to turn even the most ardent lover of fair play into a soldier who would do *anything* to beat back the swastika. The whole notion of what constituted a fair fight wasn't a question to be entertained during a brutal invasion; it was an academic argument for peacetime. But I was an academic at heart, and in long empty nights like this, theoretical questions still sometimes floated through my mind.

"A sniper against a sniper . . ." I paused, thinking for another silent half hour. Kostia waited, chewing tea. "This is about as close to a truly fair fight—whatever that's worth—as we're going to see in this ugly war," I finished at last.

"It's two against one," Kostia pointed out.

"Fine, spoil my theory. It's not much of one anyway." And I was all right with that. I just yearned, looking at the bridge where I hoped to trap my enemy, to win this duel.

The moon climbed. The tea ran out; the bread ran out. Hunger raked at my stomach with steel claws, but I dozed despite myself, chin drooping as I squatted with my shoulder hard against the trench wall—and that was when Kostia touched my shoulder. I came awake with a snap as he pointed at the bridge.

Watch now. The duel begins.

The first frozen light of an approaching January dawn is just creeping over the bridge, barely enough to see the shadowed figure of a man picking his way through the iron tangle of beams. He's late, rushing but still keeping low—he vanishes almost as fast as he appeared in the first place, too fast for me to fire.

Kostia and I trade looks. He gestures with one thumb; I nod. My partner begins slithering on his stomach back along the trench toward the front line as I watch the bridge through my sights. Across the gully, the German sniper will be settling into his nest out of sight, setting up his own rifle, finding familiar markers to gauge today's kill shots. Only there won't be any. Mine should take him from below.

Half an hour ticks past as day brightens in utter silence. No chatter of mortar fire this morning as the guns on either side clear their throats; no fighters or bombers rising into the sky. The war has withdrawn from view, like a swan folding her wings. There is only a gully, and a sniper on either side of it. I put two fingers to my lips and let out a low, crooning birdcall Vartanov taught me. A moment later I hear Kostia answer with a whistle of his own.

I never take my eyes off the bridge, but my mind sees every move my partner makes, clear as day. He's pushing Ivan into position: a mannequin we fashioned with a stuffed torso on a stick, dressed in winter overcoat and a captain's helmet. From across the bridge, it should look like a Soviet officer has abandoned his post for a moment and gone to the edge of the ravine for a morning stretch.

Old trick, Kostia had said as we wrestled Ivan into a spare uniform.

Good trick, I'd responded.

The shot from the far side of the bridge sounds muted, a gong from a cracked bell. I see a brief glitter of light in the tangle of shattered iron beams, and my sights hone in. *There you are*, I think even as Kostia lets Ivan's stuffed body fall. *There you are, you Nazi bastard.* The German sniper sitting on the heel of his right leg, rifle propped in the crook of a bent branch, almost completely hidden by a metal beam. Through my sights I see him pull the bolt of his rifle, pocket the spent cartridge . . . and raise his head to look out of his nest.

Midnight, I think.

And fire.

"SO WAS HE a big name?"

"Very. Helmut Bommel, Iron Cross, 121st Infantry Regiment, 50th Brandenburg Infantry Division, Oberfeldwebel—" I let out a groan as Lyonya's hands worked at my aching feet. The minute he'd put me down after pulling me out of the staff car and hugging the breath out of me, he bore me off to his dugout, peeled me down to my undershirt, wrapped me in a blanket, and parked me beside the glowing stove, hunkering down on a stool to pull my feet into his lap.

"Stop squirming, *milaya,* your feet are like blocks of ice. How were you able to find out his name and rank?" Massaging my tingling toes.

"His soldier's book." The sniper's body had plummeted from the bridge to the ravine below like a falling star; Kostia had covered me with his own rifle as I slipped and slithered down the brush-choked gully to search the corpse for usable intelligence. "It said he'd fought in Poland, Belgium, and France, and that he served as a sniper instructor in Berlin. He had 215 kills," I said, thinking of that cold-stippled, rosy-cheeked face on the dead man lying among the frost-white reeds.

"What's that grimace for?" Lyonya's hands worked up to my calves, knotted and aching.

"I don't like looking at their faces afterward," I admitted.

"Lady Death is human after all." Lyonya smiled. "Don't worry, I won't tell the brass."

I snorted. "The colonel of the 79th? He assumed Kostia made the shot. Looked right past me and asked how he'd done it."

"Turn around, let me at those shoulders . . ."

I turned, groaning again as Lyonya's strong thumbs began digging circles beside my neck, carefully avoiding my still-healing shrapnel wound. "You never saw a man look more embarrassed than that colonel when Kostia jerked a thumb at me. Fell over himself asking, *How is it this Hitlerite has two decorations and you have none, Comrade Senior Sergeant Pavlichenko?* Then it was Dromin's turn to look embarrassed. Ouch!"

"Two days in a sniper's nest chewing dry tea at negative thirty degrees Celsius, and you grouse at a shoulder rub?" Lyonya pressed a kiss between my shoulder blades, letting his mouth stay there a long moment. "I was terrified for you, *milaya,*" he said quietly. "I'd rather fight a hundred Hitlerites with bayonets than pace the dugout wondering if some blasted sniper instructor with a copy of *Mein Kampf* over his heart is going to make you his two hundred and sixteenth."

I felt my shoulders tense. "Lyonya . . . I won't give it up if that's what—"

"No. I'm not asking that." He turned me so we sat face-to-face. I already knew his face so well: the broad, high cheekbones; the clear blue eyes; the mouth that quirked on one side. No quirk now. "Just— be cautious."

"I can't be cautious," I said honestly. "Caution makes you miss. You can be cautious or you can be good, and I'm very good."

"You are good, you little killer." He pulled me into his chest, rubbing my arms, which were still prickled with the bone-deep cold of two days in that trench. "The world is about to know it."

"What do you mean?"

"I think Dromin's days of sitting on your achievements are done. You"—Lyonya kissed the tip of my nose—"are about to become famous."

CHAPTER 18

My memoir, the official version: I was congratulated by General Petrov in the matter of the sniper duel, and he told me he hoped I would not rest on my victories but would continue to crush the foes of our socialist homeland. He also informed me that an account of the sniper duel would be broadcast throughout the Sevastopol defense district, and I would have my picture taken for some combat leaflets. I was pleased to comply, in the name of inspiring our brave soldiers of the Soviet Union.

My memoir, the unofficial version: Combat leaflets? For the love of Lenin.

I DON'T KNOW why anyone wants to become famous. It's utterly maddening. First the visit from the senior political officer, and then hordes of press, each visit more annoying than the last.

From the chirpy photographer of the coastal army newspaper *For the Motherland:* "You're very photogenic, Comrade Senior Sergeant. Try a smile—"

From the correspondent of *Beacon of the Commune:* "Details of the duel will be most helpful . . . Are you sure that's how it happened? Wasn't it a little more dramatic? Try to look more friendly for the camera—"

From the writer sent by *Red Crimea:* "How about a smile for your partner? I'm sure he helped you make that fateful shot!"

From the war cine-cameraman Comrade Vladislav Mikosha: "I'm looking for the right *angle* for this footage; I'm just not *seeing it.* Look,

climb up that apple tree there and strike a pose with your gun. Big
smile—"

"No," I snapped, finally cracking. "I'm not climbing up an *apple
tree*, and it is a *rifle*, not a gun."

My lover and my partner were no help. Lyonya was laughing so
hard he could barely stand; Kostia had to hold him up, eyes dancing.
I shot them both a filthy look as the cameraman fiddled with his
camera.

"Look," I said, trying to lay it out for a civilian, "I don't shoot from
trees in Sevastopol, so any picture of me like that is misleading. And I
can't answer questions about marksmanship, camouflage techniques,
or my methods for hunting—anything printed in a newspaper will
end up in enemy hands."

He gave a blithe wave. "We don't need technical details, Comrade
Senior Sergeant, we need excitement! Tell us about the cold gray eye
of the fascist oppressor as you locked gazes through your sights—"

"We didn't lock gazes through our sights. That isn't how this
works."

"—tell me how you trembled with hatred for the invader Helmut
Bommel before overcoming your rage to pull the trigger—"

"I don't feel rage when I pull the trigger. That would be distract-
ing. You come to firing position with a heart at rest and the knowledge that you are in the right, and I guarantee that Helmut Bommel
felt the exact same way." I gave Lyonya a *Help me* glance, but he just
stood there, broad shoulders shaking with laughter.

"Look, Lyudmila Mikhailovna," the cameraman finally said,
sounding amused, "I don't care what you felt when you pulled the
trigger. People need heroes right now, and you've been picked for the
role, so say a few nice things about how inspired you are by the bravery of your comrades in arms and the leadership of the Party and
climb up in that damned apple tree with your rifle. And *smile*."

I bit my tongue. The whole circus was absurd, but he wasn't wrong about the need for heroes. I didn't think I was one, but maybe Slavka would read the accounts and be proud of his mother—who he hadn't seen now in more than a year. So I climbed the damned tree, posed with my rifle, and bared my teeth in what you might, in a charitable mood, call a smile.

At least after this it will all be done, I thought, ignoring the muffled chortles from Kostia and Lyonya as I tried to figure out what exactly "Put a heroic gleam in your eye!" meant. *They'll all go away and leave me alone.*

"Wrong, *milaya*," Lyonya said when the stories came in. "I'm afraid this is only the beginning."

"They got it all wrong," I nearly wailed, pacing up and down the dugout as I read one of the newspaper clippings. "Listen to this: *In the pale light of dawn, Lyudmila saw her enemy behind a tree root . . .* They reset everything in the forest; apparently the bridge wasn't dramatic enough? . . . *Suddenly she caught in the lines of her sight the Hitlerite sniper's deadened eyes, flaxen hair, slab-like jaw . . .* That's not what he looked like, and I never tried to describe him anyway! *Life was decided in an instant—by a mere second, she beat him to the shot. Taking the Nazi sniper's notebooks, she read that more than 400 Frenchmen and Englishmen had perished at his fascist hands.* It was 215, not—"

"*Beacon of the Commune* put his tally at 600 Soviet lives alone," Lyonya said, reading away.

"Who is going to believe that?" I stuffed the clipping into the stove. "No German sniper has had a chance of racking up that many Red Army kills by this point in the war. Entrenched fighting and long sieges, that's where sharpshooting come into play. The Hitlerites have been here only half a year, and they've been pushing forward with tanks and aircraft, not digging in with telescopic sights. Positional fighting—"

"I love it when you start footnoting yourself about positional fighting." Lyonya tossed the clippings aside and tugged me into his lap. "You can take the sniper out of the student, but you cannot take the student out of the sniper."

"It's all absolute rubbish," I grumbled, thumping my head on his shoulder.

"They're propagandists, *milaya*. They deal in rubbish. They're determined to make you a heroine—"

I made retching noises.

"—and personally, I quite like the thought of marrying a heroine. You earn the glory, I bask. I've already been asked what it's like to live with the girl sniper herself—"

I groaned but could feel a smile starting to creep over my face. "What did you say?"

"I was very complimentary. I told them you were lethal on the battlefield yet an utter disaster in the kitchen, and what man could possibly want more in a wife?"

"You don't even know if I can cook or not—"

"I'm sure you have a box of recipes somewhere, and they're all beautifully footnoted. With blood splatter," Lyonya added, and as I exploded into laughter, he picked me up and slung me over one shoulder. "When can we get married?" he asked, tossing me down on his army cot.

"Later." I pulled him down on top of me, taking his face between my hands for a long kiss. "Come here . . ."

"Why later?" he asked afterward when both of us were still breathing hard, damp with sweat, our limbs interlocked. "Why not get things finalized with Alexei and marry me, Mila?"

My hand was still tangled in his hair, brushing slowly up and down from the soft strands at the crown to the short velvety buzz down his neck. "I love you, Lyonya—but are you sure I'm what you want? It's so soon . . ."

"It's been a month since you started here with me. A month in front-line time? That's a year in peacetime." He gave me a shrewd look. "I think you're just dragging your feet at the idea of facing Alexei about the divorce."

I was dragging my feet, and I hated that. I knew, I just *knew*, that Alexei would make trouble when I told him I wanted a divorce so I could marry someone else, and it felt unlucky to invite even a drop more trouble into life when Lyonya and I were already living in a war zone. "What's the rush?" I asked, ducking the subject. "What do we get by marrying that we don't have now?" I indicated the little world of the dugout: the stove that warmed our evenings; the table where we ate supper; this cot where we burrowed against the cold.

"If we were married, you'd get my pension if I die," Lyonya pointed out. "Come on, Lady Death—marry me for the money."

"Maybe you're trying to marry me for mine," I teased. "My ever-so-luxurious senior sergeant pension if I cap it here on the front line."

"I would like to know you're taken care of, after all this." That quirk of Lyonya's mouth. "Things get lean and hungry after wars. I'm eleven years older than you; I probably remember the hungry times after the last war a bit more clearly."

"Don't worry on that score." I traced the outer edge of his eyebrow. "I won't ever starve. My father knows people. The kind of people who never die of hunger, but make sure their enemies do."

"Then marry me so your father won't accuse me of despoiling his daughter and decide to take steps." Lyonya rolled onto his back, grinning, arm still around my waist. "Make an honest man of me before I'm found floating in a river."

"If a man ever ends up floating in a river on my behalf, *I'll* be the one who put him there, not my father!" I burrowed into Lyonya's shoulder. "Though Papa would probably like it if you ask for his approval."

"I'll make you a trade. I'll write to your father if you tackle Alexei."

I took a long breath. Yes, I could do that. I'd faced down far worse in this war than Alexei, so this heel-dragging was inexcusable. "I'd like a chance to write to Slavka first, get him accustomed to the idea. You haven't even met him, and he's part of any decision I make."

"I may not know him yet, but he's yours, so I'll love him, too." Lyonya quirked an eyebrow. "You don't think I'd refuse to raise a boy I hadn't fathered?"

I'd run across men before who felt that way. And Alexei hadn't even wanted to raise the boy he *had* fathered. But no, I didn't think Lyonya was like that. "Alexei left us," I said slowly, "and it hurt Slavka to grow up knowing his father didn't want him. If I bring someone else into Slavka's life and it goes wrong, he'll be hurt all over again. So you need to be sure, Lyonya. Are you?"

He plaited his fingers slowly with mine, one finger at a time. "I've been sure since the moment I met you, Mila. Why?"

"Because it's wartime. This isn't normal, this life we're leading." The only time we saw each other was a few hours in the evening: Lyonya was long asleep at midnight when I was tugging on my boots to head out into no-man's-land; by the time I returned with my rifle by noon or so and tumbled yawning into bed, he would be long gone on his lieutenant's duties. The only time we really saw each other was after twilight, when he came in from the command post and woke me up with "Dinner's here, *milaya*." We might have a few hours in bed after eating, but when he dropped off to sleep tonight I'd be climbing into my uniform and heading off to hunt with Kostia. "This isn't real life—yet we're talking about making a real life to-gether." I made myself say it, the thing I feared. "What if we find out we don't suit each other in ordinary times? What do ordinary times even look like?"

"Well, I'll tell you." Still plaiting my fingers with his own. "I'd find work in Moscow—I have my electrical certification, technicians like me can always work. You'd finish your dissertation, get your degree, become a historian or a librarian. We would live on the same clock, go off to work at the same time every day. I'd put jam in your tea for you every morning while you packed us lunches, and if we worked close enough together, we'd meet on our lunch hour. And when Slavka comes home from school, he and I will bash hockey sticks around in Gorky Park." Lyonya smiled. "The only real difference in our lives, Lyudmila Mikhailovna, is that instead of asking 'How many Nazis did you kill today?' I'd be asking 'How many footnotes did you annotate today?' "

I sat up, pulling the blanket round my shoulders to hide my shiver. Not a shiver of cold—a shiver of *yearning*. I could see it, feel it, almost touch it: that shared apartment, the tea with jam, the lunches and games in the park. A golden, glorious *then* on the other side of our bleak, bloodstained *now*.

If there is a then, my thoughts whispered. Because it wasn't gone, that fear that still sometimes clutched my throat. The certainty that the next bullet would kill me . . . that all Lyonya's talk of the future was pointless, because the only future for me was a coffin.

"By the way—" Lyonya kissed the side of my neck. "I've rung the sergeant major to find you a parade uniform in the regimental stores."

"I spend most of my days dressed as a bush," I said. "What do I need a new parade uniform for?"

"FIRST TIME?" COMRADE Senior Sergeant Onilova condescended to ask. "I suppose I was nervous the first time I made a public speech. I've done so many now, I can't remember." She straightened her Order of the Red Banner; I wanted to say I'd seen them pin it on her for her machine-gun heroics, but I was too nervous. Nervous or not, my orders were clear: *On February 2, 1942, platoon commander Senior Sergeant Pavlichenko, L.M., is to leave the front line and join a conference of female activists in the defense of Sevastopol, where she is to give an address of up to fifteen minutes on the operations and activities of snipers.*

"A formal public address?" I'd said, highly dubious. "I shoot people from long distances away, doing my best never to be seen, and they want me to stand in front of a packed audience hall under glaring lights and give a speech? I mean, I'll try, but—"

"Shut up, Mila, you'll be brilliant," said Lyonya.

"The brass haven't thought this through at all. What if I fall on my face? What's *that* going to do for morale among female activists in the defense of Sevastopol?"

"The brass never think *anything* through, and you're not going to fall on your face. You shoot Iron Cross sharpshooters through the eye socket for a living; don't tell me you're afraid of a little public speaking."

"Not a bit," I lied. And here I was in the regimental commander's car, wearing a uniform skirt and stockings for the first time in eight months, nervously flicking through my talking points, which were looking stupider by the minute.

"You're the girl sniper, aren't you?" Onilova continued, looking mildly interested. "Don't tell me you have *notes*? Goodness, I haven't needed notes in ages. Don't read off your page, that's fatal. And don't hunch at the rostrum—"

She went on rat-a-tat-tatting like her machine gun, all the way from the front lines into Sevastopol, as I chewed my lip and picked at my stockings, which both sagged and itched. I should have been drinking in the sights of the city as the car rolled through its heart—it had been so long since I'd seen houses, spires, anything that wasn't olive-drab and made of metal and canvas—but I was too nervous. A whirl through the Teachers' House, where the conference was being held, and then suddenly I was in a hall full of women. Machine Gunner Onilova was carried off at once by a crowd of eager fans, but I stood staring. I hadn't seen so many women in one place in months: blue dresses and rosy blouses, long braids swaying against bony hips . . . and like drab spots among the finery, the severe uniform tunics of the servicewomen like me. Narrow-eyed lynxes in a crowd of gentle house cats.

Or maybe not *so gentle,* I thought, seeing the fierceness on the civilian women's faces as they gathered to sit. They were carrying on life in the middle of a siege, after all—they knew what the cost would be if the city fell. After some official droning from the brass, it was women getting up to speak, one after the other, and suddenly I was riveted. Some had notes like me; others extemporized as they told their stories. A yellow-kerchiefed woman taught a classroom full of children in a bomb shelter every day; a stout apple-cheeked matriarch put in twelve-hour shifts stamping out hand grenades. A woman who had lost her left arm in a bombing raid had still stayed in the city to work—she met her quota every day, she said fiercely, because it was her part to play in fighting the enemy. Her empty left sleeve was pinned to her dress like a decoration, worn as proudly as Onilova's Order of the Red Banner. I was supposed to follow her with a dry account of Nazis wiped out in Crimean forests?

When it came time to get up and address them, I had tears in my eyes. I crumpled my talking points in my hand and heard myself saying, "The thing you have to know in your bones is that you can never miss. Not ever, not in war, not in civilian life, or that mistake will be your downfall."

And I spoke from the heart.

"How did that go?" Lyonya asked when I returned.

"Dreadfully," I admitted. "I fumbled. I backtracked. I hemmed and hawed a great deal. But they gave me a round of applause anyway, and told me to kill a Hitlerite apiece in their name, and I promised I would. So I must have done something right." I began peeling gratefully out of the parade uniform, looking forward to my padded trousers and camouflage smock.

"You have the best legs on the front line," Lyonya admired, watching me carefully roll down my stockings.

"That is an unbacked supposition. How can you possibly know I have the best legs at the front without extensive gathering of further data?"

"I have no intention of gathering further data. No interest at all in seeing Kostia or old Vartanov in a skirt. Are you really going to kill one more apiece for all those women?"

"They'll hunt me down if I fail." I pulled up my trousers, buckling the belt around my hips. "They nearly asked me to bring them ears as proof."

"Women are bloodthirsty creatures. The English and Americans are utter fools if they think females are too delicate to send to the front." Lyonya handed me my boots. "So, your first public speaking engagement—that's a milestone."

"First?" I snorted, pulling out my heavy socks. "After my performance today, no one's ever going to put me in front of a crowd again."

Fate must really have had itself a laugh, there.

CHAPTER 19

My memoir, the official version: March 4, 1942. The day that . . .

My memoir, the unofficial version: . . .

SPRING! I DON'T remember ever greeting a season's shift with more joy. A week ago had brought us storms of low clouds, flurrying snow, frost crunching underfoot. Today the snow had melted, the sun shone down, the temperature bloomed well north of zero. In the Crimean heights you could glimpse yellowed grass, new shoots of juniper, cypresses and cedars putting out bright green growth—I'd be able to start taking leaf and flower samples for Slavka again. I scanned the valley through my binoculars, nearly beaming.

"Spring means another assault soon," Vartanov growled at my elbow. "They've been quiet too long."

"Then let's shake them up." I had seven of my platoon with me today, because an entire group of Nazi snipers had nested themselves on a hilltop our maps had simply labeled No-Name Height. They'd targeted traffic on the dirt road passing below; half the personnel of a 45mm antitank gun had been downed yesterday, and answering with artillery fire just made the German sharpshooters change position and resume picking us off. "Take your boys, Lyudmila Mikhailovna," I was ordered—so here we were with almost the whole platoon.

"Eyes on our bushes," I ordered. Last night in Lyonya's dugout, Vartanov and Kostia and I had crammed in to make six decoy bushes, wiring long juniper branches together in bunches. *We look like brides making garlands,* Lyonya remarked, pitching in to help, *but with more khaki.* Kostia fired back with *You're the ugliest bride I ever saw, Kitsenko,* and I'd plunked myself down between them before they could start trying to arm-wrestle among the bushes, scolding *You two!* as Lyonya kissed my neck and Kostia lobbed a juniper frond at me. Lyonya had hugged me goodbye on the dugout steps at three in the morning when I set out, then more formally returned my salute when we stepped into the open. It was always like that: the minute we put a toe over the dugout threshold we were no longer lovers. We were regimental comrades who gave each other a formal farewell and a call of "Good hunting."

And now the long night of setting the trap was done, and I watched through my binoculars for the German snipers to take the bait: our decoy bushes, which would stick out like obvious decoys to the enemy who knew every centimeter of this hill by now, and who could be counted on to notice when six new bushes appeared on the slope overnight. And I couldn't stop myself from beaming when daylight broke, as the Hitlerites saw the conspicuous new brush we'd placed in the dead of night and began to thunder fire down on our wired juniper branches, which they assumed we'd brought to hide behind.

"There—" Kostia pointed out one of the hidden German sniper nests, tracking it from the downward angle of fire. "And there—and there—" And when the German fire ceased and the Nazi snipers put their heads up to survey the damage, a hail of Russian bullets greeted them.

"*Up!*" I shouted when everything went still. "*Forward!*" and we flowed up the last hundred meters of No-Name Height, over the top and down into the enemy trenches at the crown. Not just a complex of sniper parapets up here, but an entrenched net of communication passages and machine-gun nests, three MG 34 machine guns with loaded ammunition belts trained on the road below . . . Vartanov fired off a red flare, which meant *We've captured it*; a green flare bloomed in response on the Soviet side of no-man's-land, meaning *Well done!* The road below would soon be swarming with our troops, but my platoon looked at me, poised and hungry.

"Wait here," Kostia asked, "or clear it out?" There were undoubtedly more Hitlerites in there, who'd ambush us given half a chance.

I grinned at my partner. "Clear it out."

We tore through like methodical wolves, one dugout after another. Pitching hand grenades through doorways, shielding ourselves from the blast, then fanning through with snapped shots and wary eyes on each other's backs. A corporal with a Walther charged me with a shrill cry; I snapped my pistol up, but Kostia dropped the man with a thrust of his Finnish combat knife. A German captain went down after clipping Fyodor's earlobe with a wild shot. When we finally cleared out the underground staff quarters, we whooped with triumph to see a portable radio set with transceiver and batteries, rod aerial spearing through the dugout roof. "The reconnaissance officer will dance a jig," Vartanov chortled, disconnecting the radio for transport—a working enemy radio was such a prize, and here we had earphones, codebooks, and record books. I began dividing them for my men to carry, the blood beating in me: *Keep going, keep going.*

"Mila!" Kostia's shout came from the eastern side of the dugout, and rushing to his side, I saw the team of German submachine gunners, at least twenty, struggling up a narrow track through hazel bushes. My platoon closed around me, eight rifle butts hitting shoulders, eight barrels smacking parapets. I called out the calculations that had spliced through my head in a half second, finishing with *Adjust for downward aim, boys, don't miss*—and snapped the first shot off, bringing the storm of bullets down.

"How many did you get?" the young captain who relieved us from our position said a few hours later.

"Thirty-five," I said, and my platoon clustered around me with fierce cheers. I kissed every one of my men on both cheeks like a brother, too choked to speak. Lumbering Fyodor and my silent Kostia, who were both junior sergeants now, old Vartanov and the other men whom I'd nurtured from fumbling green recruits to cool, capable shooters . . . there wasn't a one who couldn't move like a shadow through brush or woods now; not a one who couldn't hold himself motionless in the dark and the cold for six hours straight if that was what the shot required. "Let the Germans bring that third assault," I yelled over the din as my shouting men carried me on their shoulders back toward our division. "Give my platoon the high ground and enough ammunition, and we'll stop the whole eastern advance in its tracks!"

"You'll be decorated for this one," Lyonya told me that night. "You and Kostia. Dromin is yowling like a kitten in a rain barrel, but he can't stop the awards coming down from Petrov. You'll soon have enough tin on your tunic to make a dinner service, *milaya*. How many does that make on your tally now?"

"Two forty-two." I went on tiptoe in my combat boots to kiss him. "Being in love is good for my shooting. I swear, every bullet zings along the right trajectory when I know I'm coming home to you . . ."

"For the love of Lenin, woman, did you just say you loved me as you *tallied your dead*? Classic Mila Pavlichenko." He kissed me back, and I nearly puddled down into my boots. "You've been awarded a leave pass for Sevastopol. I can take leave, too—what do you say to an afternoon in town?"

"A day off? Together?" I'd spent my last half day off trying to find Alexei at the hospital battalion, finally leaving a note for him that I wanted to discuss the finalization of our divorce as soon as possible. I still hadn't had any response, and I knew I'd have to go track him down, but I wasn't going to waste a leave pass on Alexei when I could spend it in Sevastopol with Lyonya.

It felt like the strangest thing in the world to walk with him along the winding waterfront path that weekend, an old floral skirt rippling around my knees instead of my greatcoat, Lyonya in an unraveling knitted jumper rather than his epaulets. Arm in arm like any

ordinary couple enjoying a Sunday afternoon, looking at the sweep-
ing expanse of the sea, stopping periodically to kiss the salt from each
other's lips. He bought me a posy of early-blooming hyacinths, then
rescued it when I started gesturing a little too vigorously at the Monument to the Sunken Ships: "Erected to honor the scuttling of the
Black Sea Fleet during the Crimean War! I wrote a paper about that
once. One of the few monuments from czarist days to eschew ostenta-
tion for simplicity—just that single granite column on a spire of rock,
and the lapping waves all around. You know it was designed by—"

"I do not know who it was designed by, and I have a feeling there's
nothing in the world that will stop you from telling me," Lyonya said,
wrapping his arms around me from behind and resting his chin on
top of my head as I chattered, waving at the monument.

"History lives all around," I concluded happily after Mila the student came out of hibernation with a really-quite-curtailed lecture on
the works of Amandus Adamson and his influence on the Russian Art
Nouveau style. "You can breathe it in on every street corner. Can we
go to the museum on Frunze Street? One of the women at the conference told me there's a special historical exhibit. The first siege of 1854
through the revolution—"

"Life with you is going to mean trudging through a great many
museums, isn't it?" Lyonya complained.

"—the factory exhibits! Did you know the lathe operators association has a special—"

"Yes, yes, I will take you to the damned museum . . ."

I WAS STILL thinking about the museum the next morning, after we'd
returned to the front line. That evening I'd get back to my usual nocturnal habits, but for today I could wake up with the sun and wander
outside in the spring sunshine to enjoy my breakfast like any ordinary soldier. Yawning, pondering the exhibit on Sevastopol's role in

the revolution and wondering if there were parallels I could draw to my dissertation topic, I took my cup of lukewarm coffee and joined Lyonya, who was already sitting on a fallen log with his mess tin, teasing Kostia.

"My father does not transform into a wolf by the light of the moon," Kostia was saying as he sewed down a loop of shaggy netting on his camouflage smock. "You met him once, and you're convinced he's a *bodark*?"

"I swear he had incisors that lengthened whenever he smiled, and so did that sister of yours."

"*Half* sister—"

"The wolf half. Your family is all feral, you Siberian miscreant—"

They kept ribbing each other as I sat down on the log. Lyonya draped an absent-minded arm around my shoulders—*You soft southern boys wouldn't last a day on the Siberian taiga, Lyonya—I should order you to take your boots off, Kostia, I'll bet we'll find wolf claws instead of toes*—and I stole a wedge of black bread off Lyonya's mess tin, scattering crumbs for the Sevastopol sparrows. They hopped around my boots, twittering and pecking, utterly unafraid. How could such tiny, fragile things have no fear at all?

"Ah, the morning chamber music," Lyonya remarked as the usual scattering of long-range German artillery fire began. "Will it be Brahms or Wagner today?" We listened to the first shells explode, far in the rear. "Wagner," Lyonya decided as the second salvo appeared to fall short. "I'm definitely hearing the timpani come in."

I was laughing, Kostia was laughing, Lyonya was laughing as he gave my shoulders a squeeze and said, "How'd you sleep, *milaya*? You're not tired, are you?" and then a shell from the third German salvo exploded directly at our backs.

The three of us hit the ground, arms around heads. Lyonya's arm dragged me down beneath him as splinters and shrapnel tore the air. My ears rang, and I coughed as I was crushed between the hard earth and Lyonya's heavy chest. I unlaced my fingers from around my head and looked up when the din cleared.

"Mila?" Kostia was doing the same, looking around. He had a shrapnel cut on his forehead streaming blood, but he was already rising. Lyonya uncurled from around me with a groan, pulling to a sitting position against the log, and I crawled clear with my ears still buzzing.

"You half crushed me," I started to say, smiling, and then I saw the pallor on Lyonya's broad, handsome face. Saw the red wetness soaking his right shoulder, saw that something was wrong—terribly, horrendously wrong—with his right arm hanging limp inside its sleeve. Then my entire rib cage felt like it was collapsing on itself as I rose and caught sight of the red ruin of my lover's back.

Splinter wounds, driving deep through tunic and undershirt to the flesh below as he wrapped his body around me, to protect me.

"Listen to that brass section," he said, trying to smile, and then he toppled slowly sideways into the earth.

THE MEDICAL BATTALION again. I knew it so well now, it was like home. Only this time I wasn't the one being wheeled into the operating theater on a stretcher. "Lyonya, breathe, just breathe. You're in good hands now." My hand hadn't left his pale, sweating forehead on the entire jolting, rattling ride to this underground hell of disinfectant and glaring lights; now he was wheeled away from me and I felt his soft hair glide out from under my fingertips like a phantom.

Stupidly I started to follow and Kostia pulled me back. "Let the surgeon work." He'd helped me carry Lyonya to the first-aid station on a blanket, and now he was pulling me away.

"Blood," I babbled, remembering when it had been me who was wounded. "They'll need blood for him, we're the same type—" I tore my sleeve open, giving the nurse my arm for the needle. I'd have opened my veins with my teeth and funneled my blood right into Lyonya's body if they'd let me. He wasn't supposed to be injured, not a lieutenant who spent his days at the command post, and this wasn't even a proper assault—it was the morning *chamber music.* Why then was he *injured*?

"Mila." Kostia took me by the shoulders, his face blurring in and out, streaked with dried blood down one side like a harlequin mask. He had one sleeve pushed up too; the nurse was taking a pint of my blood and pint of my partner's into the operating theater. "We wait now."

And we waited. I paced the underground corridor; Kostia sat against a wall with his elbows on his drawn-up knees, frozen still as though he were on stakeout. Maybe there were others waiting with us; I don't know. I just paced, counting the minutes as they ticked past like beads of frozen amber.

And then two surgeons came out, gloved in blood up to their elbows.

"Bear up, Lyudmila Mikhailovna." The older man gave my hands a squeeze, face drawn. "His right arm had to be amputated. It was hanging by a single tendon."

My breath went in and out, but I couldn't breathe. Dimly I heard Kostia saying, "He can live without an arm."

The other surgeon spoke up then, and with dull shock, I saw it was Alexei. "What's much worse are the seven splinters in his back. I've taken three out, but the rest—"

I don't remember what happened then. I don't remember. I don't remember. I came back to myself in a room somewhere, sitting on a narrow cot. My hand fell to my holster automatically, and found it empty. "Where is my pistol?" I asked the nurse.

"Your weapon will be returned later when you aren't so—"

"No." With a wrench I managed to stand. "Give it back. Give it back right now."

"Mila, stop." Kostia's voice, Kostia's arms keeping me from lunging at the nurse.

"You think I'm going to shoot myself?" I screamed. "No. No, that won't happen." I stopped fighting, seizing my partner by the collar and yanking him toward me until our noses nearly collided. "Give me. My *pistol*."

Kostia got it for me. I could see the terrible doubt in his eyes, the tension that coiled through him—but I only buttoned it back into its holster with numb fingers. I didn't know how to be calm without a weapon at hand. I looked back up with swimming eyes. "Now take me to him."

My love lay white-bandaged and still in a curtained-off cot. So still. I went to my knees at his side, reaching out to touch his one remaining hand. "Lyonya." I tried to say it, clear and calm, but no sound came out, only my lips moving silently. His entire torso wrapped in bandages, his right arm ending in a gauze-capped stump just under the shoulder. His face was drained, empty, no sign of the laugh lines that crinkled his eyes or the humorous vitality that quirked his smile.

I unholstered my pistol, feeling Kostia tense again, but I only folded Lyonya's limp hand over it and then enclosed both between my own. It wasn't my Three Line, but it still knew the same song. "You're going to make it," I whispered, my eyes blurring. "And then I'll down another hundred Nazis just for the one who fired that mortar at you."

I squeezed his hand, but there was no answering squeeze. No flicker in the vacant face. Throat choked, I put my pistol on the nightstand and crawled onto the cot beside him, my head on his shoulder. I'd lain like that so many nights . . . no. Not so many. It had been only three months since we came together. Not enough time. Surely we were going to have more time. He would make it.

"He might wake," the nurse said, sounding flat. "You could try reading to him, speaking to him."

I tried. I tried so hard, but the only sound I could squeeze out was a strangled sob. I just lay shaking against Lyonya's shoulder. Kostia sat down on the other side of the cot, his eyes like black holes burned in snow, and I saw the same helplessness in his carved face. We were snipers; the world of silence and darkness was where we lived. This terrible place of bright lights and loud voices had us both flailing.

Seeing I still couldn't speak, Kostia reached into his pack and took out his battered, bloodstained *War and Peace*. His voice was hoarse as he began to read, translating the English edition to Russian. " *'Vera,' she said to her oldest daughter, who was clearly not a favorite, 'how can you have so little tact? Don't you see you aren't wanted here?'* "

Kostia kept reading as the nurse faded away and my tears began to slide. *You aren't wanted here,* I told death, breathing faint and inexorable over my shoulder. *You were supposed to take me. Not him.*

Death didn't care. He stood at my shoulder, implacable, immovable, as the hours of day slipped into night, as Kostia read and read and read, as Lyonya sometimes stirred in delirium and opened blind, blank eyes, and sometimes lay still as a headstone. Once he turned his head in my direction—I thought perhaps he smiled at me. Kostia stopped then, so hoarse his voice was almost gone.

I took Lyonya's hand between my own, kissed his papery cheek. "We're getting married," I whispered. "Remember?" He didn't move, didn't smile, didn't speak. Death kept on breathing at my shoulder. "I got the divorce. I can marry you now." Anything I could say to keep him here, keep him with me. "We can marry now. I'll marry you tomorrow."

I kept saying it long after he was gone.

THE SOVIET DELEGATION: DAY 1

August 27, 1942
WASHINGTON, D.C.

CHAPTER 20

The White House welcome breakfast was almost over. Teacups were being drained, smears of maple syrup were being mopped up, the buzz of chatter through the small dining room was dying away. The marksman was swirling the dregs of his coffee and laying silent plans when someone finally got up the courage to ask the girl sniper what everyone had been thinking since the moment she arrived.

"Mrs. Pavlichenko, I'm simply ravenous with curiosity . . . Is it true you are a . . . a *sharpshooter*? That you've, um, well"—no one wanted to say the word *killed*—"*dispatched* 309 enemies?"

The whole table fell silent then, and every American eye went to Lyudmila Pavlichenko. Some were disapproving, some disbelieving, all were curious. The marksman sat back in his chair, every bit as curious to see how she would reply.

The Russian girl's neat, pretty face showed no sign of annoyance. She turned a polite smile across the table and said through the interpreter, "Yes, it's quite true."

Bullshit, thought the marksman. He knew women who could shoot: backwoods wives who filled their family soup pots with whatever they could bag; society belles who enjoyed a little gossipy target practice before a three-martini lunch; sporty girls who lined their rooms with competition ribbons for marksmanship. But he did not believe a woman could shoot 309 men—and if she did, she'd be in handcuffs or a straitjacket. No woman could shoot 309 men and be capable of sipping tea with the First Lady, cool as a cucumber.

The buzz that swept the table sounded skeptical; evidently the marksman wasn't the only one with doubts. Eleanor Roosevelt, however, looked thoughtful, sitting with her chin resting in her hand. "Can you see their faces?" she asked.

Her interpreter, a young officer in lieutenant's epaulets, murmured a translation as the girl sniper answered. "Their faces, Mrs. Roosevelt?"

"Of the men you shot. If you had a good view of the faces of your enemies through your sights, but still fired to kill . . . well, it will be hard for American women to understand you, Lyudmila dear."

For a long moment, the girl sniper stared at the First Lady. Long enough for people to begin shifting in their seats, long enough to make the marksman's blood prickle in his veins. He had the urge to reach into his jacket for a weapon, but of course he hadn't brought so much as a pocket knife to the White House. Yet suddenly, here and now, he wished he had a gun.

"Mrs. Roosevelt," Mila Pavlichenko began, and with a jolt the marksman realized she was speaking in English. Her accent was marked, and she was clearly struggling to express herself correctly, but every word came slow, clear—and furious. "We are glad to visit your beautiful country. It is prosperous—you all live far from the struggle. Nobody destroys *your* towns, cities, fields. Nobody kills *your* citizens, your sisters and mothers, your fathers and brothers. I come from a place where bombs pound villages into ash, where Russian blood oils the treads of German tanks, where innocent civilians die every day."

She caught herself up, exhaled slowly as she marshaled her next words. No one moved, least of all the marksman.

"An accurate bullet fired by a sniper like me, Mrs. Roosevelt, is no more than a response to an enemy. My husband lost his life at Sevastopol before my eyes. He died in my arms. As far as I am concerned, any Hitlerite I see through my telescopic sights is the one who killed him."

A frozen silence fell over the room. Only the marksman's eyes moved as he looked around the table, cataloging responses. The Soviet delegation leader sat clutching his butter knife, looking like he wanted to saw off her head and bowl it through the window into the White House gardens. The smart Washington women in their frills and pearls looked appalled. The First Lady looked . . .

Embarrassed? the marksman wondered. Did that horsey presidential bitch look *embarrassed*?

"I'm sorry, Lyudmila dear," she said quietly, laying down her napkin. "I had no wish to offend you. This conversation is important, and we will continue it in a more suitable setting. But now, unfortunately, it is time to disperse. My duties are calling, and I understand you have a photographer waiting at the embassy."

She rose from the breakfast table, made some farewells, and was gone before the girl sniper could essay a response. "What did you say?" hissed the delegation leader. "We have orders not to offend them!"

"They offend *me*," Lyudmila Pavlichenko whispered back in furious nearly inaudible Russian. The marksman, looking after the First Lady's departure as though oblivious, strained to make out every word from two seats down. "I came here to help solicit aid for my comrades in arms, my friends at the front, men and women dying every day in their dugouts, and the President's wife sits there worrying that her husband's constituents won't find me *likable*?"

"Lyudmila Mikhailovna, you will obey directives—"

The back-and-forth hiss of Russian got too rapid for the marksman to follow, and the Soviet delegation was rising to leave anyway. Chairs were pushed back, pleasantries were exchanged in both languages, an aide hovered: "Mrs. Roosevelt has instructed me to give you a brief tour of the White House before you depart for the embassy . . ." The marksman faded into the departing throng of guests, turning to give one last thoughtful glance over his shoulder at the girl sniper. Color burned high and angry in her cheeks as she turned to follow the aide, and her eyes were molten.

For just one instant, the marksman wondered: *What if she actually is everything they say she is?*

Notes by the First Lady

"She put me in my place," I tell Franklin later ruefully. "No other word for it."

"I'd like to see the Russki who could do that." He grins.

"I wasn't intending to belittle her . . . if anything, it was American women I was thinking of less favorably. I want the Soviet delegation's time here to be a success, but the average Virginia housewife or Washington hostess will not make that easy for a woman like Mrs. Pavlichenko." I frown at myself as I pass my husband a new pen. It's not like me to stumble so with a guest, but my nagging worry about Franklin has me distracted this morning.

"Never mind American housewives. She'll have her hands full with the American press." He uncaps the pen, looking full of vim and vigor, which relieves me. "We'll see if she puts the journalists in their place at the press conference tonight."

He taps the pen against his leg brace, looking thoughtful even as we make notes for his upcoming tour of the western defense plants. He's wondering if the girl sniper can be useful in his crusade to swing public opinion in the matter of aid to the Soviet Union. He hopes she will be, not only because he wants his second front in Europe—and has been facing opposition to it given our setbacks in the Pacific—but because he has a most unusual liking for useful women. He collects us, and what a varied constellation of females we are. The shy, awkward wife he turned so efficiently into his eyes and ears . . . his impervious secretary Missy LeHand, who could organize that second front as efficiently as she organizes everything else in the White House . . . his labor secretary, Frances Perkins, the iron hand behind his New Deal, who dispatches strong men reeling from cabinet meetings . . .

Franklin's women. He collects us, admires us, hones us, and then he does not hesitate to use us up, burning through us body and soul until we flame out. If some part of us rises up in silent protest at such treatment—as it does sometimes in me, for things between us are not always easy—then it dies unspoken when we see that he burns himself up no less ruthlessly. We would all die for him, because he is killing himself for all of us.

Do they realize that, the men who are his enemies, who call him class traitor and communist lover and tyrant? The men he worries about now, whether he will admit it or not? Do they realize this man in leg braces is the bulwark against the fall of the West?

Or do they wish to topple him anyway, just so they can see the crash?

FIVE MONTHS AGO

March 1942
THE SEVASTOPOL FRONT, USSR
Mila

CHAPTER 21

My memoir, the official version: The funeral of my husband Lieutenant A. A. Kitsenko was attended by my entire platoon and all the officers of the 54th Regiment who were not on duty; the speeches were powerful and the salute heartfelt.

My memoir, the unofficial version: He was not my husband in law—I missed my chance for that, missed, and the mockery of the loss cored me. But Lyonya was my husband in every way but law, and I knew I'd call him that until the day I died.

"POST-TRAUMATIC NEUROSIS." ALEXEI Pavlichenko said it without bothering to examine me. "I'm giving you two weeks in hospital."

"This is absurd." I tried to push up from the chair.

He pushed me back down. "You nearly throttled the political instructor at Kitsenko's funeral."

I stared stonily, not speaking. The instructor had pressed into my face after the salute was fired over Lyonya's coffin, demanding to know why I hadn't fired my pistol with the rest. I'd seized him by the collar and grated, *My salute will be directed at the Nazis*. It was the only thing I remembered from the entire occasion.

"It took half your platoon to get you off him," Alexei continued. "He wants an apology. Your partner persuaded him you were suffering from shock."

"So why is a surgeon examining me, not a neuropathologist?"

"It doesn't take a specialist to identify post-traumatic neurosis. Besides, I told the man I was your husband, and so he should leave you to me." Alexei smiled easily, looking as golden and healthy as a sun.

"I know you wanted to finalize that divorce of ours, but we didn't quite get around to it, did we? And maybe that's not so bad. I'm in a position to help you here. I can make that political officer forget about the apology. If you ask nicely."

"I will walk to Vladivostok barefoot before I ask you for a thing." I wanted to leap up and sink my hands into his throat, but they were trembling too badly. I kept them clenched in my lap so he wouldn't ask to see them and I wouldn't have to admit they hadn't stopped shaking in three days.

"Two weeks' rest," Alexei went on, ignoring my venom. "Valerian root infusion and a bromide solution to calm your nerves—"

"Did you kill him?" I asked.

For the first time since I'd known him, Alexei looked truly startled. "What?"

"Did. You. Kill. Lyonya." The words jerked out in near gulps. "You had him on your operating table. You knew we wanted to marry. He comes in with seven splinters, and you can only get three of them out—" I stopped, rage boiling in my throat. The suspicion had haunted me since I saw Alexei coming blood-gloved out of the operating theater. "You son of a bitch, did you kill him?"

Alexei's face shuttered. I saw anger there, but a vast, exhausted sadness as well. "You think I'd do that? Murder a man on my operating table?"

I refused to look away. "Did you?"

"Look, maybe you think I was a shit husband, and maybe you think I'm a shit father—"

"You are a shit father," I hissed.

"—but you can *never* say I am a shit surgeon. I put in fifteen hours in that operating theater every day; you think I notice names and faces anymore? I didn't realize it was your golden-boy lieutenant until it was done. I broke the news to you myself as a *courtesy*—"

"You are never getting thanks from me. Not for doing your sworn duty by a wounded man. *If* you did—"

"I couldn't have saved him if he'd been hit by those splinters right on the operating table in front of me. Saint Nicholas the Wonder-worker couldn't have magicked them out of his lungs." Alexei pushed back from my chair. "Believe me or not, Mila."

He walked away, looking like the weariest man in the world. I simply sat there. My head ached dully. I didn't know whether to believe him or not. I barely knew what I was saying or seeing or thinking; I hadn't slept in three days and nights. When I tried, I just lay aching and exhausted on the cot in Lyonya's dugout, which I'd probably have to vacate soon for the new company commander.

"We have a bed for you, Comrade Senior Sergeant." An orderly helped me up when it was clear I wouldn't rise on my own. "Two weeks' hospital rest, starting now."

No, I thought. *I want to be out hunting. Killing the men who killed Lyonya.* But I wasn't up to it, and that was the terrible truth. The day of the funeral I came back to the dugout, ripping off my parade uniform for my camouflage smock, picking up my Three Line . . . and I realized my hands were trembling too badly to push a single bullet into the chamber. They kept spilling from my fingers as I tried. The rifle might as well have been a club, not my deadly midnight partner with her inaudible song. If I tried to take her out, I'd miss every shot I tried. I'd get myself or my platoon killed.

Get over it, Pavlichenko, I tried to tell my shaking hands as the orderly showed me to my cot—but all I could think was that if I hadn't dragged my damned heels on my divorce for so long, I'd be calling myself *Kitsenko* instead. "I should have married you," I whispered, sinking into the cot.

Too late now. Too late to marry him, too late to avenge him.

Too late for everything.

• • •

AT SOME POINT in the next two weeks, I realized the hand holding out my daily dose of valerian didn't belong to Lena or one of the nurses. It was a man's hand instead, tough and olive-skinned, with a sniper's calluses. "Hello, Kostia," I rasped, the scratch of my unused voice surprising me. He looked thinner, sunken-eyed, terrible. I looked down into my cup. "I wish it were vodka."

"I have vodka," he said, indicating his pack.

I nodded slowly. "Can . . . can we get drunk?"

He looked around. "Not here."

It was midafternoon, the orderlies and nurses mostly assisting the surgeons, the wounded lying quiet. "How long have I been here?"

"Nine days."

"The platoon?"

"They need you back."

I held up my hand. Still shaking. Every day I worked, I tried, and it wouldn't go away. "I want to be out there," I whispered. "But I can't. Not like this. I'll get you killed."

Kostia rose. "Let's get out of here. I borrowed a car."

"I can't drive." Alexei could, and he was very proud of that. But I'd never had cause to learn.

"I'll drive."

Kostia drove us fast and loose, rattling out toward the fourth defense sector. I knew where we were going before we were halfway there, and I bit the inside of my cheek savagely when the wall of Crimean limestone with its imposing iron gates loomed before us: the Fraternal Cemetery.

We entered through the southern side, parked, and began to climb on foot toward the ancient, bombed-out church at the crown of the hill. The church had been consecrated in czarist days to Saint Nicholas the Wonderworker, which made me think of Alexei's angry words. Now it wasn't a church, it was a ruin. I could have used the blackened, crumbled dome for a sniper's nest.

At the funeral over a week ago I'd had no eyes for the old graves with their white-and-black-marble stones, much less the new graves marked by nothing more than wooden stars. I took a long, steadying breath as I saw Lyonya's. It had been painted more carefully than the others, and the inscription was longer, his birth and death and full name inscribed in neat, square letters I recognized. "You did this?" I asked Kostia around the lump in my throat. He nodded, and I traced the lettering with a fingertip. "I wish it could say something about how he could make anyone laugh. Even me."

"He was my best friend in the world," Kostia said.

"Tell me." There was a tree stump beside the grave, wide enough for two. I sat down, pulling Kostia to sit beside me. "I—I want to hear more about him."

For a long time I didn't think Kostia would speak. "Boys can be cruel," he began finally. "*Konstantin Andreyvich Shevelyov*—everyone knew my father wasn't Andrei Shevelyov. My mother married him because my father was a hunter out on Lake Baikal, and by the time I was coming, she'd found out he had a wife and family back there, not that he'd ever told her when he came to Irkutsk to sell furs. But the boys all knew my father was mad old Markov out on the lake, and even when I went far away to school in Donetsk, someone found out and they all called my mother a whore and me a bastard." A breath. "Except Lyonya . . ."

My partner and I sat arm against arm on the stump, and in Kostia's spare, honed words I saw Lyonya as my partner had first seen him: a broad-shouldered, loose-limbed, golden young athlete, all hockey sticks and poorly graded tests, with a streak of kindness most golden young athletes utterly lacked.

"He was good at making friends," Kostia concluded quietly. "I never was. But that didn't matter, because I had him."

We'd been passing Kostia's flask of vodka back and forth as he talked. I took another swallow, gazing at the row of graves. Lyonya's was still heaped up, the earth black and tumbled, but it would soon be just another mound of drying earth topped by a forlorn fading star. I didn't have any flowers, so I took a heel of bread from my canvas gas-mask bag and crumbled it over the earth so the Sevastopol sparrows would circle and sing here. For my golden front-line husband.

Kostia poured a stream of vodka over the grave. "Rest in peace, brother."

I tried to reply, but my throat closed on the words. We fell into silence then, sitting in the cooling afternoon for more than an hour, passing the vodka again. The sparrows swooped down, fluttered, swooped away. Such a beautiful day.

"I heard you're a senior sergeant now," I said at last. Kostia nodded. "The platoon's yours."

He shook his head. "We need you, Mila."

I held up my hand. Still trembling. He put the flask into it and I drank, feeling the scorch down my throat and into my stomach. "You don't need me. You need someone who can shoot."

"We need *you*. Mila—"

"Stop." I gave him a sudden furious shove; he went off the stump but came to his feet at once, standing with his hands open and his eyes black and steady.

"You're the best." His voice was implacable as granite. "The Hitler-ites fear you. The platoon believes in you. We need you back."

"I can't *shoot*," I shouted, erupting to my feet and shoving him again. He braced, taking it. I hit him this time, a closed fist to his sternum, and he took that, too. "All I want is to kill them, and I can't *shoot*—"

"You have to," he said. "We need you."

I drained another long swallow from the flask and hurled it at his feet. "It's not that I'm afraid." My tongue fumbled the words, and I realized how hard the vodka had hit my empty, burning stomach.

"I didn't say you were." Kostia took a step closer. I slammed my fists into his chest again; he was my height; I didn't have to reach up. "Mila—"

My eyes were swimming. I staggered when I raised my hands again, looking down at the grave. "I was the one with the dangerous job. It was supposed to be *me*."

"It wasn't," my partner said simply.

"I'm going to get you all killed," I whispered.

"Then we die like Lyonya." I saw the tears in Kostia's black eyes then. "We die like soldiers."

"In agony, with iron splinters in our lungs?" My voice slurred. I was so drunk. Why didn't the vodka ease the pain?

"We die brave. Like him." Kostia reached out and took my shoulders, as much to steady himself as me. He could put it away like a Siberian, but he was drunk, too. "And you and me, Mila? We die shooting."

He pulled me into his chest as the sobs exploded out of us both. He wept into my neck and I wept into his, the two of us grappled together swaying over Lyonya's grave. I don't know how long it took that explosion of grief to tear itself free, only that we ended up back on the tree stump, leaning against each other, faces salt-streaked and chests still heaving, gulping the last of the vodka and watching twilight fall. In the darkness we kept on sitting in a sniper's silence, motionless as death. Which still hovered at my shoulder, breathing black and silent.

Kostia looked at me. "Comrade Senior Sergeant?" he asked formally.

I took a long breath and held up my hand. I hadn't slept in a week; my eyes were swollen to slits; I had a belly full of vodka, a heart full of hatred, and a soul full of grief—but my hand was steady as a rock.

"Tomorrow night," I told my partner. And I was back.

CHAPTER 22

My memoir, the official version: *Thanks to the valiant spirit of the Red Army and the leadership of our brave officers, none of us believed Sevastopol would fall.*

My memoir, the unofficial version: *I remember the exact moment I knew Sevastopol was doomed.*

A QUIET MARCH, April, May, when I hunted every night in no-man's-land and slept like the dead through the day . . . and then the sudden savage Nazi attack that claimed the Kerch Peninsula in mid-May; the massive air strikes afterward on the main naval base of the Black Sea Fleet, turning the city into a sea of fire and smoke—and then the main assault itself, long-awaited, long-dreaded, in the first week of June.

"Psychological attack," Kostia said as we watched the massive wave of German infantry advancing on the front line of our defenders. He was thinking, I knew, of the Romanians advancing in a Napoleonic column under their shrieking priest, looking to overwhelm us with fear as much as numbers.

I stared through my binoculars over the lip of the sniper trench where the two of us lay on our bellies, taking in the tanks sliding forward like centipedes, German riflemen with Mausers, submachine gunners with MP 40s, all half hidden by coils of black smoke from the dawn artillery bombardment. "New arrivals," I said, noting well-fed bodies in those Nazi uniforms, not yet whittled down by Russian cold and Russian resistance. "Imperial Germans. Probably transferred from Donetsk, the 17th Army." I tossed the binoculars, set my rifle into my shoulder, and saw an officer marching at the side of his troops, striding right into my sights. I fired, the rifle kicked, and down he went. "This batch won't be any luckier than the first two assaults last year."

I believed that. I was still in the grip of the agonized fury that had taken me in its jaws after Lyonya; I'd spent three months killing Hitlerites six nights a week and spending the seventh trying to write letters to Slavka, folding dried flowers into torn end pages of my dissertation. The third assault began, and I joined the firing with my platoon, and it didn't occur to me that we would lose.

But every day the hammer fell: five-hour mortar attacks, tanks and infantry columns pushing along the road that led toward the Mekenzi Hills railway station. Every day the Nazis nibbled at our defenses like the rats they were, pushing centimeter by centimeter toward the northern side of the main bay. Ten days, maybe eleven of continuous fighting, and I was staggering along a path in the Martynov gully, wondering where I could get a cold meal and an hour's sleep, when I nearly collided with a line of boys struggling along under the exhortations of the regimental Young Communist League organizer. "Comrade Senior Sergeant Pavlichenko," he hailed me. "Look lively, boys! Our very own girl sniper, a true hero of the motherland. How many is it now, Lyudmila Mikhailovna?"

"I don't know," I said wearily. Three hundred? Who cared?

"The Hitlerites fear the shadow of her rifle," the organizer told his boys, who just stared at me in exhaustion, white-eyed and blank-faced. They looked so young—surely some weren't any more than fourteen. I snapped off a salute, tried to smile, and the organizer's cheer suddenly broke. He put a hand to his mouth to hide its tremble, and I drew him aside.

"How bad in your sector?" I asked, low-voiced.

"The Fritzes have the entire Kamyshly gully," he muttered. "The railway station, Verkhny Chorgun, Nizhny Chorgun, Kamary . . . battles are raging around the Fraternal Cemetery."

My gut twisted. Lyonya's grave—it might be vandalized by Germans now, his red star splintered.

The Young Communist League organizer went on in a monotone. "This is all that's left of my lads—" waving a hand at the swaying, gray-faced line of boys. "I lost two-thirds of my entire league in nine days. We've no more ammunition coming in. Foodstuffs and water, well . . ."

We will lose, I realized then, gazing at those doomed boys in their deathly exhaustion, swaying under the scorching hot sun. They looked barely older than my Slavka, who in his last letter had told me he got an *Excellent* for Russian dictation and a *Good* for mental arithmetic; that he missed me and that he was making a book of all my plant samples—he was the best in his Young Pioneers troop at biology, Mamochka . . .

If my Slavka had been here in Sebastopol, he might have been carrying a rifle, because the city was going to fall.

"Do you have a word of encouragement for my boys?" the organizer begged. "Just a word?"

I had no encouragement, no hope at all. But I looked at those boys, making myself remember their faces, and I said, "I swear I will fight for you all till the last drop of blood."

"We swear—we so swear—we also swear." The oaths rippled from them like a wave of hot, dying wind through grain. We saluted each other and passed by, on our way to defend our city as it entered its death throes. When I returned to my platoon, and we faced the next wave of Nazi soldiers advancing in their smug, well-fed ranks, the wave of hatred that came over me nearly turned me blind.

"Don't aim for the first rank," I ordered my men. "Aim for the second, aim for the gut—and don't miss." Rifles began to spit bullets, and Hitlerites in the second ranks began to scream, doubling over; the third rank tripped on them, and the first rank turned as they heard the shrieks; the column lost its unity. "Keep it up," I shouted, sinking steel into one soft German belly after another—me, the woman who prided herself on clean, quick, merciful kills, shooting now to maim. "Break their focus. Make them hurt. Slow them *down*."

They were going to take Sevastopol, but Mila Pavlichenko was going to make them pay for it.

It took nearly a month for the city to fall, and it took 300,000 German soldiers, over four hundred tanks, and more than nine hundred aircraft. But I wasn't there to see it.

On what turned out to be my last day of battle on the Black Sea front, I trekked wearily down from the heights of a shattered church I'd been using to pick off German spotters. They were like crows, nesting in trees, on hilltops, in upper floors of buildings—I should have had Kostia at my back, but we were spread too thin now to double up, and I saw him come down from the building across the street, face streaked in grime. "Got nine," he said.

"Got twelve." Not that it did any good. Shoot twelve spotters and twelve more took their place, calling strikes down on the city in walls of fire—Luftwaffe planes were now strafing individual cars and pedestrians on Sevastopol's ruined streets. The city where I'd walked arm in arm with Lyonya, admiring the Monument to the Sunken Ships and planning our future, had become a slaughterhouse. "Fyodor?"

"One block over, on the bakery roof."

We fell into step, rifles in the crook of our arms. Neither of us flinched at the crackle and boom of artillery thundering overhead, at the shrieks of the dying and the roar of collapsing masonry following it. This wasn't just the morning chamber music anymore; it was a symphony of death. A symphony that never ended.

We clambered up to the bakery roof where Fyodor Sedykh had wedged himself behind a chimney to pick off more spotters, Kostia pulling me up through the hole in the bombed-out roof as I called out, "Fyodor?" But my huge lumbering ox of a junior sergeant was beyond answering; an air strike had hit the roof, toppled the chimney, and pinned him in a welter of shattered beams and broken bricks. The whole lower half of his face was gone, but his eyes begged. Kostia and I went to him, either side of that big, hopelessly broken body, and Kostia took Fyodor's hands and murmured the question we all knew to ask, if a day like this ever came. Fyodor nodded, writhing, eyes not leaving mine, and I nodded back. "Hero of the Soviet Union Fyodor Sedykh," I rasped, "the honor has been mine—"

And I fired a single, merciful shot.

Kostia and I were too ravaged to weep as we climbed down from the shattered rooftop. We just clung to each other for a few numb seconds, then disentangled and made our way toward the regimental staff headquarters. There were only four left in my platoon besides us. "Check on Vartanov and the others," I told Kostia as we waited for new orders from the reconnaissance officer, and that was when a shell hit the dugout.

No time to shout a warning to my partner.

No time to shelter myself.

No time.

SWEAT. OIL. STUFFY air and unwashed bodies all around me. Even with my eyes still glued shut, I knew I was crammed into some claustrophobically small space, a space that buzzed my bones with the throbbing hum of churning diesel engines. I was panicking before I was even fully conscious.

"I thought you were dead," a voice said dully somewhere beside me.

I peeled my eyelids open. A low ceiling not far above me; a floor spread with cork mattresses and metal partitions, soldiers jammed everywhere they could sit, lie, or curl into fetal positions. Most were bandaged, all seemed to be staring with blank eyes at some unknown distance. Only there was no distance; this room was as windowless and cramped as the inside of a rifle's barrel. "Where are we?" I rasped, looking around to see a skinny corporal from 54th Regiment whom I'd chatted with in the mess line from time to time. "You're Misha— Comrade Corporal Sternov, right? Third company? Where—"

"Cruising underwater toward Tsemes Bay in Novorossiysk," he answered. "L-4—she used to be a minelayer, now she's a transport submarine. Captain Polyakov took her down at dawn—you've been out cold since they loaded you in here on a stretcher."

I couldn't make sense of what he was saying. Submarine? Dimly, I remembered hearing a rumor that a handful of submarines were coming into Sevastopol's bay with ammunition, fuel, and provisions, but no one knew anything more. If they'd arrived and unloaded, of course they would depart with as many wounded as they could carry . . .

Kostia. Vartanov. My platoon. I tried to sit up, and a wave of splitting agony cratered my head. I knew what it was: concussion, eardrum damage, shell shock. I heard a whimper that seemed to be coming from me, and reaching up, I found a row of neat stitches along my earlobe.

"Looks like a blast knocked you out and a splinter nearly took your ear off." Corporal Sternov looked at me a little spitefully. "I'd like to know who you've got in your pocket back in the medical battalion, getting on the evacuation list for a splinter wound."

Lena—was she here? "Do you know Lena Paliy? The best medical orderly in—"

"Dead, so I heard. Mortar fire on a first-aid station."

No, not Lena, *not Lena*. "My platoon." I moistened my cracked lips, trying to sit up despite my throbbing skull. "Sergeant Shevelyov, Corporal Vartanov—"

A shrug.

"Second Company?" Names of friends and comrades in arms fluttered through me like trapped bats.

"Probably all dead." With shocking suddenness, Sternov's face screwed up in a sob. "My company was overrun, too. I don't know if I'm the only one who . . ."

I reached out and took his hand, hardly aware of what I was doing. "I can't be here," I whispered. What was I doing here when my partner was back there, my men were back there, Lyonya's grave was back there? How could I have been magicked onto a stretcher and into a submarine, fleeing my doomed city like an underwater rat? If I'd been conscious when the evacuation order came through, I'd have fought with every bone in my body. I'd have pried myself off the stretcher and crawled back into Sevastopol on my bloodstained hands and knees. "I have to get back."

"You think they'll turn the submarine around just for you?" Sternov snarled tearfully. "Even Lady Death doesn't get that privilege."

"Don't call me that!"

He pulled away sullenly, tears still leaking. I turned over, facing the humming metal wall, and felt a sharp corner poke me. I'd been lying on my pack; probably the only reason it hadn't been stolen. My rifle was gone—that would have been tossed to someone still able to defend Sevastopol. The beautiful Mosin-Nagant Three Line Kostia had turned from a standard-issue rifle to a sniper's weapon just for my hands . . . but my shaking fingers found the rest of my things. The packet of letters from my family; Slavka's picture; my battered dissertation; the pear-wood pipe Vartanov had given me. And something else.

It slid out of the pack into my hands: a bloodstained, oil-smeared English copy of *War and Peace*. Kostia's. I'd seen him prop his rifle on it if there wasn't time to construct a parapet; he pulled it out to read on long stakeouts; he carefully tore a strip from its blank end pages to light our cigarettes when we were out of matches. We'd teased him that he loved it more than his babushka. "It was my babushka's," he retorted.

I didn't know if he'd left it with me as a farewell when I was carried off the battlefield for the last time, or if he'd died back there and some well-meaning orderly tucked it among my things as a memento. I didn't know, and maybe I never would know. *My partner.*

I doubled over weeping, clutching the book, as the submarine slid through the alien waters toward a safety I didn't want, away from a death I would have welcomed, abandoning everyone I loved.

"LYUDMILA MIKHAILOVNA, IS that you?"

I turned as I approached the Novorossiysk commandant's office. At first I didn't recognize the grim-faced, weary-looking man in his fine greatcoat and cluster of aides. Then I saw his rank and hastily saluted. "Comrade Major General Petrov, sir."

Twelve days since the submarine slid into Novorossiysk and off-loaded its wounded to the hospital wards, me among them. Just one day since I had been released from my cot there, told to come to the commandant's office and testify to my recovery—at least, testify that I had recovered enough to hold a rifle again. And here was Petrov himself, turning away from his idling staff car and coming toward me with a smile. I remembered meeting the man before evacuating Odessa, and I knew he'd been the one to put my name up for my first combat medal after the duel on the bridge, but we hadn't traded any further words. If he'd recognized my gaunt, unsmiling face with its centipede of stitches still marching up my neck and ear, he had a good memory.

He spoke baldly, no niceties. "You've heard?"

"Yes, Comrade Major General." The *Pravda* had printed the news yesterday: *By order of the Red Army Supreme command dated 3 July, Soviet forces have abandoned the city . . .* I'd been knocking on every door I could find for the last twenty hours, begging for information on Sevastopol's survivors. There had to be survivors. The rest of my platoon . . .

"Who else from Chapayev division made it out with you, Lyud-mila Mikhailovna?" General Petrov had been there until the end, so I'd been told—evacuated with the rest of the top brass right before the city fell. I gave him all the names I could, the soldiers I'd been evacuated with on the submarine, the ones I'd seen in the hospital wards afterward. I saw him filing each one away. "I have one name for you, Comrade Senior Sergeant. Your doctor husband, Alexei Pavlichenko, was on the last transport out. Headed for Krasnodar, I think." A smile. "He's being decorated for his service to the wounded. A valiant servant of the Red Army."

"Valiant," I echoed. Kostia's quiet stoicism, Vartanov's bitter en-durance, Lena's humor under fire—*they* were the valiant ones. But I couldn't deny Alexei's surgeon hands had probably saved hundreds if not thousands of lives, and the general clearly thought he had given me good news. So I nodded my thanks and asked the question I'd dreaded to ask. "The rest of my division, the ones in Sevastopol when I was evacuated at the end of June?"

"There is no more Chapayev division," Petrov said gently. "They fought to the end—burned their staff papers, buried their seals, threw their standards into the sea. The Hitlerites won't be parading your division's colors through Berlin as trophies."

My eyes filled with tears again; I managed to keep them from brimming over as I gave a stiff nod. The general managed a smile, more like a death's-head rictus. I remembered hearing a rumor that he'd tried to shoot himself rather than flee Sevastopol, and someone from his military council had prevented him. Just one of those wild army rumors that fly everywhere like chaff, but suddenly I believed this one. General Petrov looked haunted, a dead man walking. "Tell me, Comrade Senior Sergeant, have you received new orders?"

"Not yet." I had to swipe at my eyes, to my shame. "I hope to be posted back to the front as an officer."

Petrov's aide glanced meaningfully at the waiting car, but the general turned back to me. "An officer?"

"Yes. I think I've earned it by now." I shouldn't have been so blunt, but I was too drained to be anything but honest. "I've learned over this last year how to command troops, Comrade Major General. To think about them in combat, to be responsible for them. And I still haven't got even with the Nazis for the deaths of my friends." Lena, Fyodor, Lyonya. Oh, Lyonya. If I were an officer at my next posting, responsible for giving more of the orders, perhaps I could save more of my men next time. "The Hitlerites are still advancing. The things I saw done to civilians at Odessa and Sevastopol . . . The earth should burn under their feet."

The general surveyed me for a moment. "In three days, I'm leaving Novorossiysk for Moscow. You will accompany me—to receive your new posting."

CHAPTER 23

My memoir, the official version: Moscow was the perfect incarnation of the Soviet imagination encapsulated in stone and steel.

My memoir, the unofficial version: Moscow was huge, austere, and hellish. But my mother's eyes were the size of saucers when she laid eyes on it—and me.

"LOOK AT YOU: a war heroine, a lieutenant, *and* a Moscow girl!" Mama was skinnier than ever on wartime rations, but her long plait and bright eyes were the same as I led her into my quarters at the Stromyn Street hostel. I'd been living here since arriving in Moscow—more than a month now. "You should have seen your father when he heard about your Order of Lenin. He strutted to work like a rooster."

My eyes pricked. I wished my father could have come to Moscow too, but there was a pass only for one—and he couldn't have taken so much time from work, to travel more than a thousand kilometers simply for a visit. Nor could a child take that journey, and I took a deep stabbing breath before asking, "What did Slavka say?"

"Proud as punch." Mama stowed her wicker traveling case under the table. "And before you ask, he thinks I'm off visiting a cousin."

"Good," I jerked. If he knew I was back from the front, he'd plead to visit me, and I couldn't inflict that on him. I'd heard from other soldiers that it was devastating trying to visit your children if you could stay only a short while—they went completely to pieces when it was time to leave again.

"Oh, *malyshka*, don't cry. It's the right thing to do." Mama gave me the hug I was craving, folding me into her arms like a child. I leaned into that hug, and I felt the moment she gave a quick inhale, catching the scent of vodka I hadn't quite been able to scrub away from last night.

That was the other reason I'd asked her to leave Slavka home: I didn't want him to see that his laughing mamochka, the woman who checked his schoolwork and told him stories of Lady Midnight running errands for Baba Yaga, had become a woman of hard shining boots and pitiless brass stars, a woman without smiles. A woman who managed to sleep the night through only because of vodka.

But my mother didn't mention the vodka. "Such luxury," she said instead, admiring my room. "Sixteen square meters all to yourself! How long will you be here?"

"I don't know. They're giving me a sniper platoon in the 32nd Guards Parachute Division, but I don't have orders to the front yet." I'd had to bottle my frustration since coming to Moscow; now it spilled over as I began pulling out sliced black bread and pickles. "Mama, I'm stuck doing instruction duty at the local training center. When I'm not at a chalkboard, the secretariat of the All-USSR Young Communist League's central committee wants me doing *speeches.*"

"And why shouldn't they?" Mama smiled. "You're a heroine, aren't you?"

"I'm not a speaker." That was what I told the secretariat, but he just waved my objections aside. *People need to be told about this war. Just do it with an optimistic note!*

Optimistic. As if there was an *optimistic* way to tell the story of losing my entire platoon . . . none of whom I'd heard any news of, no matter how often I beat on doors looking for information: *Konstantin Shevelyov speaks very good English, perhaps he came out of Sevastopol and was put to work as an interpreter at one of the embassies? Anastas Vartanov, is there any news of an old ranger from the Crimea?*

Nothing.

"I think you've been doing more than just making speeches and teaching ballistics!" My mother beamed, and for a horrible moment I thought she was going to ask if I had a man in my life. *No,* I nearly shouted, *I don't have a man. I go to sleep every night aching for Lyonya, and I think I always will.* But I caught my angry words before they could spill out. My mother didn't know about Lyonya; he'd been killed before I wrote to my family about him—I'd wanted to wait until the divorce from Alexei was final before telling my parents about a new son-in-law, and after he died, I couldn't bear to put his name to paper. Mama didn't know I was grieving, and she didn't seem, in any case, to be asking about romance, because she prompted, "The Lavrenyov pamphlet?"

"Oh," I said. "That."

That damned pamphlet, commissioned by the Red Army central board of political propaganda, part of the much-read Frontline Library series: the wartime heroics of sniper Lyudmila Pavlichenko, to be written by none other than famous novelist Boris Lavrenyov.

"What was he like?" Mama wanted to know. I'd been trying to lay out snacks for her, but she pushed me into a chair and insisted on slicing the salami herself. "I've always loved *The Forty-First*—so romantic! Did he interview you himself?"

Ha. The great man had looked me up and down through his iron-framed spectacles, cut me off in my first sentence, and explained to me his *Vision* for how to present my life to the masses. (He had a *Vision.* I sensed the capital letter.) "You're just like my Maryutka," he said kindly. "My heroine in *The Forty-First*, of course you know of her. Just a few details about you, and I'll finish the pamphlet in a week."

I admit I didn't react well. I was hungover, I was tired, and the self-satisfied flashing of the man's spectacles was making my temples throb. "I'm nothing like your dumb fictional factory girl," I'd told him flatly. "Your novel's entire premise is contrived, and if you think I want a hack like you writing about me—"

Things went downhill from there, if not quite downhill enough to cancel the pamphlet. It would release at year's end and I'd already had an advance look. *The girl sniper and I went down the boulevard on Commune Square one fine morning, the wind ruffling her cropped silky hair over her maiden's brow as we sat on a bench. Her delicate, high-strung face pulsed with a deep passion of character. Her eyes seemed sad, but sparked under my skillful questioning with a childlike eagerness.*

I wondered if that part was supposed to happen before or after I told him he was a prosy hack and he told me I was a rabid Ukrainian bitch.

"Before I forget, Lyuda—a letter came last week for you." Mama fished in her drawstring bag. "I'd have forwarded it on, but when I knew I'd see you so soon . . ."

I slit the envelope, unfolding the square of smudged paper as my heart began to thud. I'd traded family addresses with all my platoon; we swore to write to one another's families if one of us fell or was sep-arated from the company. I'd dispatched letters to the families of all my men. Who was now writing to me?

Small square writing, familiar as my own pulse.

Mila,
I'm alive. Last evacuation out of Sevastopol, shattered knee. Re-cuperated in hospital ward in Krasnodar; about to be shipped to Moscow military district for reassignment. Where are you?
*   —Kostia*

"Are you all right?" My mother's hand flew to my forehead. "You look so strange—"

"I'm all right, Mama." I looked up from my partner's letter with a smile that felt like it stretched all the way down to my toes. "You just brought me the first good news I've had in months."

Kostia alive. My partner, my shadow, my other half. Some dark bottomless ache in me eased, as though one of my legs had gone to sleep and now blood was flowing back through it, prickling me with the painful yet welcome sensation that it was still there and whole.

Kostia, alive.

I hugged my mother so hard her toes left the ground. "Put on the finest dress you've got in that bag, Mamochka. You're going to see everything in Moscow this week, starting with the ballet."

"Ballet!" Mama chuckled. "Remember your ballerina friend Vika? I heard she walked out of a starring role in Odessa to drive a T-34 in the tank corps! A ballerina becoming a tank driver, the things this war does to us. Thank goodness you're home from the front . . ."

I didn't tell her that all I wanted was to go back there. Collect my partner, get him assigned to my new platoon, and then go back to war. Because the job wasn't done yet, and right now I wasn't good for anything else.

"GOOD NEWS, LYUDMILA Mikhailovna! You're headed back to war."

I blinked exhaustion-gritty eyes, surprised. I had served a twenty-four-hour shift on instruction duty at the training center, done my rounds of the various personnel offices inquiring if Kostia had reached the Moscow military district yet, then helped organize four trucks of newly arrived weaponry. And now here I was summoned to the first secretary's office, looking at an entire cluster of men, some in uniform and some in suits. "My orders are in? Orders to the front?"

"Not that war." The secretariat laughed. "The most important war of all—the war of propaganda."

I stared at him in utter confusion.

"You're going too fast," a familiar voice said behind me, and I turned to see Alexei's smiling face. I hadn't seen him since Sevastopol or thought of him since Petrov told me he'd been evacuated. I'd assumed he was off polishing his shiny new decoration and angling for a better post. Now he was *here*?

"Hello, *kroshka*." He kissed both my cheeks in breezy greeting. "We're going to America."

THE SOVIET DELEGATION: DAY 1

August 27, 1942

WASHINGTON, D.C.

CHAPTER 24

I f there was anything the marksman disliked, it was having to reassure nervous clients. *You want to be soothed, go see a headshrinker.* He didn't let his impatience show, strolling down a hot Washington sidewalk with Pocket Square, but he was annoyed. He'd already given the man an update this morning before the White House breakfast; a second meeting was excessive. He preferred to keep contact with his employers minimal, for God's sake—the fewer points of connection, the safer they'd all be. Yet here he was, being required to soothe and reassure.

"We need to *know*." Pocket Square glanced behind him, perspiring more than ever. He was already in agony because the marksman had refused to meet in some dark whiskey-scented bar to discuss all this, but bars had eavesdroppers, which was why the marksman kept his business discussions outside. "You said you'd know more after the welcome breakfast. Well?"

"Things are in hand." The marksman picked up the pace as they turned the final corner toward the Soviet embassy. In one hour, the Soviet delegation would address the nation on live radio.

"But we want *details*," Pocket Square hissed.

"You're paying me for results, not details." The marksman had already fleshed out his plan for September 5, the last day of the conference. That horsey bitch of a First Lady was intending to invite all the international students to a farewell reception on the White House lawn. The President would be in attendance, as would a full cadre of press . . . including the marksman, thanks to the strings Pocket Square's employers had already pulled behind the scenes. "Everything's in place on my end." Almost, anyway.

"What have you learned about the Red girl?" Pocket Square kept glancing around him, drawing glances from a pair of middle-aged women hurrying past with their shopping. "You can guarantee she'll take the fall?"

"No guarantees in this business." The marksman fed a little more Virginia drawl into his voice, soothing. "But your people were right to have me look into her. We couldn't ask for a better patsy."

Pocket Square peered up at the stony bulk of the embassy, now looming overhead. Journalists and photographers were already hurrying inside, showing their press badges to embassy security. "Is she really a sniper?"

"No." The marksman had had a moment's doubt at the end of breakfast, looking at Lyudmila Pavlichenko's furious face as she said *An accurate bullet fired by a sniper like me, Mrs. Roosevelt, is no more than a response to an enemy* . . . but on reflection he'd dismissed it. An angry woman didn't make a sniper. "She's a propaganda poster girl who gets flustered easily and loses her temper at idiotic questions, and God knows the press can be counted on to ask plenty of those. The Russkies made a mistake, cooking up the sniper cover story. They think it will make her admired, a war hero." In the Soviet Union maybe, but not in America, where pretty brunettes were supposed to bake cookies, not kill fascists. "Mrs. Pavlichenko won't be the sensation here that they're hoping for. Everywhere she goes, she'll be viewed as a freak and a monster."

In fact, he was counting on it.

"MRS. PAVLICHENKO—"

"Mrs. Pavlichenko—"

"Mrs. Pavlichenko—"

I tried not to flinch. Flashbulbs were going off in my face like grenades—had none of these journalists ever questioned soldiers before? Setting anything to explode with a flash of light in a battle veteran's face was just *asking* to get stabbed.

"Smile," the delegation head murmured. Three of us had been chosen for this delegation, all of us students, all of us soldiers, but he was in charge: Nikolai Krasavchenko, twenty-six and square and earnest. He'd fought well at Smolensk, but that wasn't why he'd been chosen to lead the delegation. He'd been chosen because he was a pompous young bore who could be counted on not to have a single original thought on this entire trip. *No surprises here,* I imagined them saying as they stamped approval on his folder. *Backbone of the Party!*

Maybe Krasavchenko was delighted to have been chosen, but not me. I'd stood (dumbfounded, incredulous, increasingly angry) through a great deal of droning about Eleanor Roosevelt's international student conference, that first night I heard about it in Moscow. How it provided Comrade Stalin with an opportunity to send students as the most progressive element of the population to speak out against fascism to the Americans . . . How we had been chosen among hundreds of candidates in the Moscow military district, not only as former students and current soldiers but as Young Communist League personnel . . . How we would advocate for our country, our party, and for the dire need of American aid . . .

"Smile," Krasavchenko repeated now, glaring at me. He wasn't happy about my angry outburst at the White House breakfast this morning, and his were the orders I was supposed to follow, so I faced the cameras and obediently pulled back my lips. The conference wouldn't begin for a few days; tonight's address to the American press would broadcast live over radio, from the embassy to the whole of America. I swallowed my nerves, looking out over a sea of cameras and chatter. This whole scene seemed as foreign to me as the moon. All I'd wanted was to find Kostia and go back to the fight, and instead I'd been packed off to a continent full of oblivious capitalists on a *propaganda mission*? Americans didn't like Russians. They called themselves our allies, but so far they were leaving us to die in the hundreds of thousands. How was anything I said at this press conference supposed to change that?

"A glass of water, *kroshka*?" Alexei murmured, hovering.

"I can get my own water. I don't require the delegation doctor to get it for me."

That was the post he'd landed: official physician for the Soviet delegation to Washington. "How did you manage to worm your way onto this mission?" I'd sputtered back in Moscow, still reeling from the surprise of seeing him again. "What does a student delegation need with a combat surgeon?"

"They want a Soviet doctor to attend to any of the delegation's health needs, another soldier with a sterling record, and I've done my share of general doctoring." Alexei had looked golden and confident in his immaculate uniform, not a smudge of Sevastopol's horrors on him. "As for how I got this assignment . . . well, naturally I kept my ear to the ground for any news of my wife." Straightening the Order of Lenin at my breast, fingers lingering on the proud red ribbon. "And naturally, a husband would wish to accompany his wife overseas if she were sent on such a long journey—"

"You are *trading on my name* to get out of frontline service and into a cushy post," I'd hissed, but there was no undoing it. Even halfway around the world, I wasn't going to be able to escape my husband.

And he'd been solicitous ever since: first in Moscow, those few frantic days we were all being briefed and prepared for the journey; then on the long flight from Moscow to Tehran and then to Cairo, cadging the seat beside me as I clutched the armrest during takeoff, offering to hold my hand if I felt afraid.

"What do you want?" I'd asked bluntly.

He just smiled. "Can't I tell my wife how brave she is? Your first flight; you're doing so well, *kroshka*."

"Oh, and you've flown on airplanes *so* many times, yourself," I scoffed. But his smile didn't waver, and after we flew from Cairo to Miami he knocked on my hotel room door and asked if I wanted to walk on the *beach*—"Let's get some sun on that pretty face." All this niceness was making me twitchier than a two-day stakeout.

I swatted him away now, looking back to the bank of microphones and cameras as we were herded into position. "If you three will take your seats, Mrs. Pavlichenko in the center . . ." I did as I was told, banishing my husband from my thoughts if not my presence. Krasavchenko was shuffling the pages of his statement on my right, at my left lounged Lieutenant Pchelintsev, our third student delegate, looking haughty. "You have coffee on your tunic," I said, and he nearly overturned his cup in his haste to brush himself off. I couldn't really dislike Pchelintsev—in some ways he wasn't so different from me, just an earnest university student before the war turned him down a different road and made him a sniper. But it was hard not to regard him a little cynically all the same, because he was three years younger than I and his official tally was half mine, but he was a senior lieutenant to my junior and he'd been made Hero of the Soviet Union and not just Chevalier of the Order of Lenin. I wasn't eaten up with jealousy for his gold star, but it was hard not to look at the burnished young Lieutenant Pchelintsev and wonder if I'd be where he was if I'd simply been born a man.

Hit four hundred on your tally, little boy, I thought the first time I met Pchelintsev's superior gaze in Moscow. *Then you can look down your nose at me.*

But it wasn't my impressive tally that had won my place here with Pchelintsev and Krasavchenko, and I knew it. I'd heard two of the Moscow suits arguing over my appointment while I was getting fitted for the uniform skirt I was now wearing: "Should have chosen that tank driver from the Leningrad literary program, Vassily Something. Who wants a woman on a delegation? Too emotional, too difficult to control."

"But this one's pretty, and she'll present the USSR in a more favorable light . . ."

"We're beginning." Krasavchenko's whisper across the table snapped me back to the present. "Remember, listen to our interpreter, not theirs."

And a lump rose in my throat as I saw Kostia take his place quietly before the table.

If Alexei could pull strings to get a position on the delegation, so could I—and I'd maneuvered to get my partner back at my side, the moment I'd heard Krasavchenko drone about bringing our own interpreters. I hadn't formulated any kind of plan, just blurted, "I can recommend an excellent interpreter, newly transferred to the Moscow military district. Decorated soldier and fluent speaker of English and Russian." Because if I was going halfway around the world with the possibility of new enemies in front of me and the certainty of at least one old enemy behind me, I wanted my partner at my back.

And here he was, my partner, almost unrecognizable in a pressed uniform and a clean shave, standing beside the delegation table, leaning on the cane he still needed after a splinter had nearly blown his knee apart in Sevastopol's fall. I willed him to look over and smile, but he was shuffling papers, adjusting his microphone. *After the press conference,* I thought. *We can finally talk*—but flashes were going off again all over the room as the broadcast began.

I shifted in my seat as the introductions rolled, trying to get rid of that feeling of being exposed, unarmed, locked in unfriendly gunsights. Krasavchenko seemed polished and at ease in this kind of setting; I'd rather be dressed as a bush with my Three Line in hand. But my way back to the front led through this tour. *The Americans need to be shown the truth of our struggle against Nazism,* we had been lectured in Moscow as we prepared for the trip. *Our need for reinforcements— that is the real purpose of your delegation, not merely sitting in sessions with international students. This directive comes all the way from Com-rade Stalin.* A stern look all around. *We cannot miss this chance.*

My spine had straightened at that. Maybe I wouldn't have a rifle in hand, but apparently this mission still boiled down to the same directive: *Don't you dare miss.*

"Propaganda ponies," I heard an American journalist snicker in the front row as the broadcast rolled on, not bothering to whisper, since he assumed none of us could understand. "Let's see 'em go through their paces."

I put up my chin. *Yes, let's.*

At first it wasn't so bad. Krasavchenko read a statement: the dire plight of our country, the unity of our civilians. Pchelintsev read a statement: the readiness of the Red Army to strike back against the Germans. I read a statement—first some Party-approved fluff about greetings from Soviet womanhood, and then I was glad to get to the meat of it. "The Soviet people send thanks for your aid, but the strug-gle which our nation is leading demands more and more from us. We await active assistance and the opening of a second front." I heard Kostia's voice translating in a quiet murmur; saw pencils scratching as the journalists took notes. I straightened in my chair. "As a Russian soldier, I extend my hand to you. Together we must defeat the Nazi monsters." That was the end of my printed statement, but I added in English, with a smile, "Forward to victory!" A nice little slogan that could wrap up just about any speech. People need a signal that you're finished, and that they can clap now.

The ambassador opened the floor for questions, and I began mar-shaling facts and figures, though most questions would probably go to Krasavchenko.

But the questions were almost all for me, and they weren't about the war.

"Is it true your nickname is Lady Death?"

I began to say that another interpretation could be Lady Midnight, but I was already sensing that no one here wanted complicated answers; they wanted simple comments that fit easily into newspaper captions. "Yes," I said, through Kostia. I'd been instructed to use the interpreter for all questions, even if my English was up to it. (Because who knew what a volatile female might say, without a man to sift her words if she gets out of hand? I'd rolled my eyes at that, but on the whole I preferred to be underestimated by the press, so all to the better if they thought I spoke little English.) "I am sometimes called Lady Death. Also the lynx, for the way I move through trees."

"Lyudmila, can you take hot baths at the front?"

I blinked, surprised partly by the question and partly by the fact that he didn't bother using my rank. "What?"

"Baths," the man repeated, a lanky fellow from the *Washington Post*. "Hot." He mimed sweating.

I stared at him. "Yes, I get a hot bath two or three times a day, whenever I'm sitting in a trench and there's an artillery attack. That's a real bath for you, only it's a dust bath."

A ripple of surprised laughter answered my response. Then a man in a checked tie rose. "Are you women soldiers able to wear lipstick?"

I glanced at Krasavchenko. He made a little urging motion. "With bullets coming at you, you're more likely to reach for a rifle than a lipstick." Kostia translated me with an impassive face, but I could hear his buried amusement.

A woman journalist came next, pursing her lips at me. "Is that your parade uniform or your everyday uniform?"

"We have no time for parades at the—"

"The cut is very unflattering. That skirt length makes you look fat! Don't you mind?"

I let my breath out slowly as anger licked through me and leached the color out of the room. My briefing in Moscow had warned me:

Some Americans will be convinced a woman cannot do what you have done, Lyudmila Mikhailovna—that you're an actress prepped by propagandists. Disabuse them, but gently.

I'd already decided this morning at the White House breakfast that if the questions were insulting enough, I wasn't going to bother with *gentle*.

"I am proud to wear the uniform of my army," I answered the woman journalist. "It has been soaked by the blood of my comrades who have fallen in combat." A sudden, horrendous flash of Lyonya's blood drenching my tunic as splinters drove like spikes of ice into his lungs; of being spattered with the gray slurry of Fyodor Sedykh's brains when I put him out of his agony on a Sevastopol rooftop. *Breathe. Breathe.* "I wish you could experience a bombing raid, ma'am. Trust me, you would forget about the cut of your outfit."

I couldn't even see the next journalist through the blur of fury fogging my eyes, only hear the faint leer in his voice. "Lyudmila, what color of underwear do you prefer?"

Kostia didn't translate that. The embassy interpreter did, as my partner sat radiating cold rage and so Krasavchenko and Pchelintsev on either side of me. Oddly, that checked the furious beat of my pulse. Perhaps I had a platoon around me after all.

I looked at the journalist, and I smiled. It was the smile that made new recruits back up a few steps, if they had even a thimble of sense. "In Russia," I began, nodding at Kostia to translate, "you'd get a slap in the face for asking any such question. That's an inquiry for your wife or your mistress. I'm neither to you, newsman, so if you'd like to come closer, I'd be happy to give you a slap."

To my surprise, the room burst into outright guffaws. Even the man who'd asked the question shook his head ruefully, as if he knew he'd earned my sharpness. I didn't trust myself to say anything more, so I rose before the applause could cease. "We're done here."

I braced myself for a reprimand from the Soviet ambassador

as we retreated into the corridor, but he only gave me a look of grim amusement. "Well said, Lyudmila Mikhailovna. Washington cockroaches . . ."

"I feel I must apologize for our press." The serious tones of the First Lady made us all straighten. "They can be something of a trial." She was followed by a comet-like tail of White House secretaries and flunkies, and she wore a practical navy blue dinner dress. *I am a working woman,* that dress said, *not a clotheshorse.* Which was starkly at odds to the summation I'd heard in my Moscow briefing: *an aristocrat, a millionairess, a member of the exploiting class.*

Was she? This was our second meeting, and the first had not exactly ended well . . . but her smile was just as welcoming as it had been on our introduction this morning. If she was angry with me, she wasn't showing it.

"You are all invited to supper at the home of Mrs. Haabe, daughter of the former U.S. ambassador to the USSR," the First Lady continued, encompassing us all in her smile. "I thought perhaps you would like to proceed straight there."

A bustle of bilingual chatter erupted as details were discussed, and eventually I ducked out onto the nearest balcony for a cigarette, dying for a moment alone as much as the nicotine. Another party full of curious strangers, when the morning had begun with that awkward breakfast and then proceeded through an afternoon blur of meetings, photographs, speeches . . . I fumbled for matches and saw a silhouette of someone else on the balcony, already smoking—not holding a cigarette loosely between fingertips, but cupped in a reversed hand the way snipers smoked, to keep the spark from giving away your position. I lit up, took my first drag, and went to stand with my partner. Kostia was as still as a pillar, eyes going over the city. So many electric lights! Washington looked like a scatter of jewels in the dark. It should have been beautiful, but all I could think was that it ruined my night vision.

"Three," Kostia said at last.

"I make four," I answered. "Where are yours?"

He pointed to a rooftop across the way; to an upper window at a diagonal; to a street-corner phone box—all the best vantage points with direct lines of fire to where we stood. "Your fourth?"

I pointed almost directly up, at a sixth-floor window above us. "A good shot could make that, straight down between the window ledges."

"Crosswinds would make that tricky."

"I could make that shot. So could you."

There was so much I wanted to say. There should have been ample chance for us to talk—the hours of preparation in Moscow, the endless plane flights, those few days in Cairo where we'd all been trotted out for the British and American ambassadors and had our first whirlwind introduction to cocktail parties and cameras. But there had been no chance at all for Kostia and me to exchange more than a few hurried words. The first time I saw him, a mere two days after I'd proposed his name as delegation interpreter, the moment had taken me completely by surprise—he'd appeared at the secretariat's office, sun-darkened and gaunt, an Order of the Red Banner glinting on his chest. If we'd had a chance to fall on each other with a comradely hug and a few quiet moments to reflect on that last day in Sevastopol, all would have been well.

But we'd stood staring at each other, awkwardly—he barely seemed to recognize me in my new medals and skirted uniform; my eye was glued to the cane in his hand, the lines of pain whitening around his mouth—and the moment had passed. And ever since, there always seemed to be someone in the room, keeping us from talking: Krasavchenko rabbiting on about a Party memorandum, the British ambassador in Cairo wondering audibly if Pchelintsev and I were *actually* soldiers, Alexei glued to my side . . .

And now we finally had a moment alone, and we were pointing

out lines of fire to each other for imaginary duels. *Snipers,* I imagined Lyonya hooting, *you're all just a bucket of laughs!* A bolt of agonized longing went through me like a bullet. Without Lyonya, how would I ever remember how to laugh?

"You still have Vartanov's pipe?" Kostia asked unexpectedly, looking at the cigarette in my hand.

I drew the pipe out of my pocket; a good-luck talisman I still carried everywhere. "I never learned to smoke it properly, no matter how often he tried to show me." I stroked the amber mouthpiece, feeling my chest tighten. "You didn't say what happened to him."

"Shot in the thigh, the day before I was hit and evacuated. Femoral artery. He bled out before we could get an orderly."

I bowed my head for the old ranger, the way he could move through trees like a ghost. "The others? Burov, Volkonsky—" I listened as Kostia went down the list. I'd hoped maybe some would have been evacuated with him, but my heart sank as Kostia listed name after name. "Of the whole platoon, you're saying the only ones who lived . . ."

"Us." Just as he'd said when I rejoined him in Sevastopol after being evacuated from Odessa. "Just us."

How I wished for a bottle of vodka and a little privacy. We could have got utterly smashed as we did when Lyonya died, cried it out on each other's shoulders, grieved and raged and come out the other side. That was what you did when you lost your friends in war. But here we were on a Washington balcony, about to be called away any minute now for some blasted official function, and I didn't know how to fight through the grief that thickened the air between us like amber.

"Kostia," I began, not even sure what I was going to ask him. *I still have your copy of* War and Peace *if you want it? Do you forgive me for yanking you along on this trip, when you'd probably rather be at the front avenging our friends? Do you think I want to be here, either, with all the lights and the idiotic questions?*

"There you are." Krasavchenko's loud voice made us both jump.

"We're leaving for Mrs. Haabe's house, only the Cadillac won't hold the three of us delegates and the interpreters."

"I thought perhaps Mrs. Pavlichenko might travel with me," the First Lady was suggesting as I stubbed out my cigarette and came back inside, the frustration hastily wiped off my face. "I drove myself over, and my car has room for a passenger."

"Me?" I hadn't forgotten her words that morning: *It will be hard for American women to approve of you.* I'd taken that to mean that *she* didn't approve of me. So why was she inviting me to ride in her private car?

I looked at her now, really looked: such a tall woman, neat rather than fashionable, an air of energy around her like the crackle of a coming storm. Her teeth prominent, her eyes kind, her smile as she looked down at me unmistakably friendly. "I would welcome the chance to know you better, Lyudmila dear."

IT WOULD BE fair to say that I do not frighten easily. I'd lived through the siege of Odessa, I'd survived the fall of Sevastopol. I'd earned the nickname Lady Death.

Well, Lady Death had never been so certain she was about to die.

"Harry Hopkins will be present at dinner; he has been a great advocate of rapprochement between our countries." The First Lady rocketed her little two-seat convertible down the broad Washington avenues like she was piloting a tornado. We'd left the embassy Cadillac and both the Soviet and American security patrols behind at the first stoplight; it was all I could do to hang on and try to follow her English. Were presidents' wives allowed to do this? I tried to imagine Comrade Stalin's wife (should he have one) zooming around Moscow like an unescorted missile, and my imagination failed utterly. "Harry is keen to speak with you about the fighting at Leningrad, Odessa, and Sevastopol."

"I did not fight at Leningrad, Mrs. Roosevelt." I squeezed myself back into the seat as we approached a turn. For the love of Lenin, she had to slow down to turn, right?

"Wherever you've fought, he'll be glad to hear details." She threw the convertible around the curve very nearly on two wheels. I gripped the door handle. "He's long been advising the President that though you Russians may have withstood a blow of unprecedented German force, the time has come to offer help."

"Past time," I couldn't help saying, trying not to scowl.

"We do understand your country's dire need of a second front, Lyudmila dear." Mrs. Roosevelt's voice was mild but very firm, even as she flung the car down another long avenue. "Perhaps you are not aware of the difficulties we face in taking such a measure. We have our hands full in the Pacific—the fall of Singapore, the retreat from the Philippines. There are those who argue we must concentrate upon Japan, not split ourselves between the Pacific and Europe, and such concerns must be addressed."

I blinked. It was not something I had really considered—that the Americans too might be struggling to allot their resources in this war. They had so *many* resources that sending us aid had seemed a simple matter to me, something to be accomplished with the wave of a presidential hand. Of course it was not. In the dark, I felt myself reddening—maybe I'd knocked the First Lady off-balance at breakfast, but she'd done it to me now with a few deft words.

"A second front—it is an obsession with Red Army soldiers," I offered, struggling to find the right words in English. The words that would offer an olive branch for the narrowness of my focus, without apologizing for asking for what we *did*, after all, so desperately need from her country. "We are too close to the violence of the fight for objectivity. And of course I think like a sniper, focusing only on what is right in my sights—" I broke off again as a light turned red unexpectedly, and I braced myself before her stamp on the brakes sent me through the windshield.

"Naturally, your chief concern is for the men and women in the trenches at your side. And I would assure you that we have not forgotten them, either. At tonight's dinner, you'll find supporters of your cause, but you will also find detractors . . ." The First Lady took her hands off the wheel as she chattered, prominent teeth flashing, the very picture of a gossipy fifty-eight-year-old woman chattering about her grandchildren. Only she was breaking down anti-Soviet factions and which members I might expect to see at the dinner party, not stopping for breath when the light changed and she sent us bulleting off into the night again, at speeds I wasn't sure trains should be achieving much less automobiles. *The President's wife is a lunatic,* I thought, clutching the door for dear life. She threw me an amused glance as if she could tell what I was thinking, but I'd be damned if I asked her to slow down. And she didn't offer.

"Is your sniper's tally truly at 309?"

Yes. No. Maybe? I knew my official tally was over three hundred, but in the final chaotic days of Sevastopol's fall, I'd stopped taking note of official hits. Who had time for that with the German advance grinding forward? "But the Americans will want a specific number," the secretariat had insisted back in Moscow, so the number 309 was settled on. I didn't care enough to argue. My real count was probably over four hundred, but no one seemed interested in the complex answer over the simple one. "Three hundred and nine, *da,*" I told the First Lady now.

"You know, your English will put you at an advantage at events like tonight's," she said, hurtling us through a yellow light without slowing. "It's really quite good. Where did you learn?"

"My first lessons came from my mother, when I was a child."

"Is she a teacher?"

"*Da—*" I caught my lip in my teeth as we scraped past a dark green Packard. "Is this interesting to you, Mrs. Roosevelt?"

"Americans want to like people," she said unexpectedly. "We want to like everybody. It's one of our better traits. But we need a reason, Lyudmila. You Russians with your statements and talking points— that's all well and good for policy meetings, but the American people want to know *you*. The young woman behind the official statements. Who your family is, what food you like—"

"What underwear I wear?" I couldn't help saying, and imagined Lena chuckling: *She might be the First Lady, but she's still a cheeky Yank! And you can't let cheeky Yanks have it all their own way.* "That is the kind of thing Americans want to know about me—my underwear?"

"They would appreciate a glimpse at the underpinnings of your character," Mrs. Roosevelt said tactfully. "Questions about the underpinnings of your clothing may of course be ignored."

"But things about my character, my family—these things are not relevant. Not to the public." I tried to find the words as the convertible pulled up with a screech of tires outside a stately Washington home, all redbrick and vast expanse of lawn. The windows blazed with light; I could see women in satin gowns moving on the other side of the glass; waiters with trays of hors d'oeuvres. "What is important is the reason I am here. You say your presidential adviser Mr. Hopkins wants the details of our fight—why does no one else?" My voice rose despite myself. "Why does your press not care? Why don't their readers?"

"Let them get to know you," Eleanor replied. "Make them care."

"And do not fail?"

"I hate to put it that way, Lyudmila dear, but you are not here long. It's a short window you have, to win over the American people."

"Don't worry, Mrs. Roosevelt." I looked at the cocktail party inside, drawing a steadying breath. "When I take aim at something, I do not miss."

Notes by the First Lady

She did well. No easy thing to walk into a Washington dinner party (oh, how those elegant cocktail-sipping matrons used to make my knees knock, as the young Mrs. Roosevelt!) and hold one's own under all those idle, curious eyes. In a foreign language, no less—her English is painstakingly grammatical, if accented.

It's near midnight by the time I bring our Soviet guests back to the White House. They trail into their bedrooms looking utterly exhausted, but I still have hours of work ahead tonight—a draft of the speech I'm to give at the Brooklyn Navy Yard, the text for the "My Day" column still to be finished. Franklin will already be asleep, or at least I hope so, because it will not do to have him brooding about cabals of enemies in the shadows and what they may or may not be planning. The best way to stop him brooding is to intrigue him, and I know just how to do it. Pausing in the darkened hall outside his bedroom, I nod to the Secret Service officer patrolling the corridor and scribble a note for the Eleanor basket, pushing it under the door for tomorrow morning's perusal. My feet ache as I head off to my own study, already flipping the pages of my Navy Yard speech, and I can't wait to take off my shoes.

You'll like Lyudmila Pavlichenko, *my note to Franklin reads.* And she has given me one of my ideas.

CHAPTER 25

The headline: SNIPER LYUDMILA PAVLICHENKO ENJOYED HER FIRST NIGHT IN WASHINGTON UNDER THE PRESIDENTIAL ROOF.

The truth: Sniper Lyudmila Pavlichenko learned that even under the presidential roof, she was not safe from people wanting her dead.

FOR A MOMENT I just stared at it: the folded sheet of plain paper that had been tucked into an unmarked envelope and slid under my bedroom door while I slept. No salutation, no signature, just blocky Cyrillic lettering blaring into my sleep-fuddled eyes.

GO HOME YOU COMMUNIST WHORE
OR YOU'LL DIE HERE

I realized, remotely, that my hand holding the paper was shaking. Not at the words—I'd been called a whore before; I'd certainly been threatened with death before. It was that someone had reached me *here,* in the White House. Had approached my bedroom at some point after I retired from last night's press conference and pushed their hate under my door for me to find as soon as I woke.

Whoever they were, they wanted me to know they could get to me. Even here.

I looked around the palatial bedroom where Mrs. Roosevelt had ushered me just yesterday morning. "Mr. Churchill stays here when visiting, and so does Princess Märtha of Norway." I wasn't impressed by royals, but I was certainly impressed to rest my head where Britain's prime minister had. A big bed with a rosy canopy; striped couches and lace-draped occasional tables; a vanity and a dressing room. A private bathroom all for me, which didn't have to be shared with eight Muscovite neighbors across the hall . . . I'd done some unabashed reveling last night in the big bathtub and then the bed's unbelievably soft pillows, reflecting how different it was from the muddy dugouts of the front line. In a bed like this, even someone like me could drift off to sleep feeling safe.

I looked back at the scrawled threats in my hand. *Not anymore.*

"You look rather grim," the First Lady greeted me when I came down to breakfast. Krasavchenko and Pchelintsev were already digging into their eggs and bacon. "Did you not sleep well, my dear?"

"Your friend Mr. Hopkins poured me many whiskeys last night as he asked about the Sevastopol front." I put on a bright smile, unfolding the newspaper.

"The reports of yesterday's press conference are really quite favorable," said the First Lady, pouring hot tea into a delicate china cup. "Elsa Maxwell gave you a lovely write-up in the *New York Post*. Listen: 'What Lieutenant Pavlichenko possesses is something more than just beauty. Her imperturbable calm and confidence come from what she has had to endure and experience. She has the face of a Madonna from a Correggio painting and the hands of a child, and her olive-colored tunic with its red markings has been scorched by the fire of fierce combat—' "

The florid words made me flush, and the next article—the one that described me as having *the icy eyes of a cold-blooded killer*—made me burn. One day in Washington, and I already had people who disliked me. No, worse than that—I pushed the newspaper away, feeling the crackle of paper in my pocket: *Go home you Communist whore or you'll die here.*

One day in Washington, and I was already watching my back.

"YOU WILL RETURN to the White House for the student conference in a few days," the Soviet ambassador told us all when we gathered in his office after another press conference at noon. "But from tonight on you will be housed near the embassy—a hotel a few blocks from here. You may have the afternoon today for sightseeing on your own, but this evening there is a performance at the national theater which the entire delegation will attend." Checking notes. "The opera is *Madama Butterfly.*"

I hadn't attended the opera since *La Traviata* in Odessa on the day war broke out. I'd left at intermission then, not even staying to see Vika dance in the opera ballet. I wondered if Vika was still driving tanks or if she'd returned to her toe shoes and raked stages.

Or if she was dead. So many of the people I knew were now dead. And here I was going to the opera . . .

I felt a sudden violent need for fresh air and decided (once we were dismissed) on a walk through the city. High time I saw some part of America that wasn't glimpsed through a train window or over a bank of microphones—I couldn't get over how glossy and prosperous this city was. You'd never know there was a war on, looking at the men in gleaming shoes that had never been patched, the women in smart hats and ready-made frocks, the children with their plump well-fed cheeks. The shining automobiles, the buildings unmarked by bomb craters, the shops with no queues stretching out the doors . . . And I blended in here, passersby moving around me without a glance for my canvas shoes and lace-collared dress. I was just another window shopper, not the icy-eyed cold-blooded killer these people had read about with their morning coffee. Not a *Communist whore.*

I shook that thought away before it could darken the day. "Are you looking forward to the opera tonight?" I asked my minder gamely as he tramped along at my shoulder. "Do you like Puccini?"

"No, Comrade Pavlichenko. It is Western and therefore decadent."

I sighed. The delegation members had all been assigned minders, discreet Party men in heavy suits whose job it was to shadow us whenever we left the embassy. I'd made a token protest yesterday—what did they think I was going to do, defect? with my son still back home?—but the minder was mandatory, and mine was named Yuri Yuripov, who looked like a cement block in his gray wool coat, and had all the personality of a cement block, too. Having him trudge along behind me while I wandered a line of shops was like wearing a concrete bangle to the swimming pool. "What about some shopping, Comrade Yuripov? A few little luxuries for your wife in Moscow?"

He just stared at me stolidly. You didn't really expect a rollicking sense of humor from anyone who'd made a career in the NKVD, but the occasional smile would have been nice. *I bet he's a real thigh-slapper at parties,* I imagined Lena saying with a chuckle. I wished desperately that she was here instead. If she had been, she would have had her nose pressed up against the glass of the nearest boutique, ogling the dresses on the mannequins. *Look at this beauty,* she'd be crowing. *I'd look like Hedy Lamarr in that!*

"Yes, you would," I said aloud, lingering to look at the dress in the window: a yellow evening gown, heavy satin the color of buttery sunshine, scooped low at the front, skirt slinking toward the floor from a tight-molded waist. I couldn't take my eyes off that color—something a sniper would never wear; a color that painted you like a target. I'd spent an entire year trying to camouflage myself, blend in, and now suddenly I was yearning for color.

Well, why not? I had money in my pocket, all my army pay I'd never had the chance to spend, and Lady Death wanted some life for a change. Lady Midnight wanted to put on a little sunshine.

"Would you mind waiting out here?" I asked Yuri. "Or are you going to follow me into the dressing room?"

"No, Comrade Pavlichenko. That is not part of my directive."

"Small favors," I muttered, and went in. Coming out half an hour later with a shopping bag in hand, I saw an unpleasant sight: Alexei leaning up against the lamppost, smoking a cigarette with Yuri.

"Is the pretty lady out buying herself pretties?" my husband asked.

"What, you're going to report me for succumbing to Western decadence?" I retorted. "When half the men in this delegation raced out to buy lipsticks and nylons by the sack for both their wives in Moscow *and* their Bolshoi Ballet mistresses?"

"Everyone knows the perks of trips like these. Nylons and lipsticks are only the beginning." Alexei fell into step beside me. He'd already kitted himself out in a Western-style suit, a fine supple tweed that draped his long lean body with casual elegance. "There's one of those Hot Shoppes around the corner—a big improvement on the cheburek cafés in Odessa. Let me buy you a root beer." He glanced back as my minder fell into step a dozen feet behind us. "Yuri too."

"Root beer is not part of my directive," Yuri said stolidly.

"Mine either." I'd been told there was a park not far from here, so I reversed down Decatur Street instead. A sniper could look at only so many shop windows before yearning for trees and brush.

Or maybe it was cover I was looking for. The spot between my shoulder blades had been feeling itchy since I read that scrawled threat this morning, and now here was Alexei pressing me, too.

"Wait up, *kroshka*." My husband tagged along behind me, Yuri behind him. Thank goodness Alexei hadn't been deemed important enough to also have a minder (and oh, but that must be annoying him) or else it would have looked like I was leading a parade. "Have that root beer with me. You'll like it."

"What I *don't* like is taking anything from you, Alexei."

"You used to call me Alyosha. Not in public, but when it was just the two of us, and you weren't talking so much as moaning."

I stopped on the corner of Decatur and Blagden, nearly bumping into a woman with a patent leather pocketbook. "Alexei, what do you *want*? Why are you being like this?"

His eyes danced. "Being like what?"

I nearly shrieked. It wasn't fair that he could still get under my skin this way. It wasn't *fair*. "Forget it. I'm going for a walk in the park."

"Then I'll walk with you. Would you mind falling back out of earshot, Comrade Yuripov?" Alexei asked. "A man wants a private discussion with his wife, eh?"

Yuri fell back another twenty feet without consulting me. It wasn't broadly known in the delegation that Alexei was my husband, but clearly it was no surprise to the NKVD. I sighed, tempted to tell Alexei I'd rather walk out into a live fire zone than walk with him, but if my husband and I were going to have it out, better to do that away from the embassy. So I shrugged, taking a fast clip in the direction the hotel clerk had told me Rock Creek Park lay. I was expecting some tame stretch of city-bound grass, but it turned out to be a proper stretch of woods in the heart of the capital. What looked like miles of brush and boulders and trees, some clinging to their green needles, some weathering to red and gold autumn glory. Even trailing my irritating entourage, I couldn't help but be enchanted.

"Are you sure you wouldn't like a hamburger instead?" Alexei said, still ambling along at my side as I threaded in among the beeches and oaks. "I tried something called a Mighty Mo—charred meat and flavorless white bread, strangely addictive. I wouldn't mind trying more American food. Seeing more of this country . . ."

I ducked under a branch dipping over the path that barely deserved the name. "We're only in town another week or so."

"But this is just beginning for you, surely. You were approved by the Boss himself. That means there could be more trips overseas, more travel, more privileges . . . the wages of fame showering down on our family."

"Fame's fleeting." I ignored the *our*, still swinging my shopping bag at my side. "I intend to go back to the front. What are the odds I'll survive another year? My family will be the only ones to remember my name when I'm gone, and that's enough for me."

"The Party might have bigger plans for you." Alexei didn't seem fazed by the overhanging trees, he scrambled surefooted as a mountain goat up a slope toward a jutting rock. "Now that's a view!"

I scrambled up, ignoring his outstretched hand, and stood for a moment looking out over a steeper ridge below, all tangles of mountain laurel and the fluttering wing beats of thrushes. *What a perfect place for a stakeout,* I couldn't help thinking. You could lie flat up here with a rifle and pick anyone off on the slope below.

"How is Slavka?" Alexei asked, turning back his pristine cuffs.

"You have never once asked me how your son is doing." I turned to scramble back down from the rock, feeling all my senses tense at Slavka's name.

"I still have a right to know."

"Debatable." I resumed my brisk pace along the bending path. "He's healthy, if you must know. Excelling in his studies."

"It's been so long since I've seen him, but I'm sure he's growing up handsome. I always thought he had my eyes."

"I remember a time you said he looked nothing like you, and you asked me whether he was your son at all."

"I was an ass back then." Alexei gave a rueful grin, but I could hear the edge creeping into his voice. "Can you entirely blame me? Your father strong-armed me into a wedding I wasn't ready for; it was a choice between marrying you or worrying he'd send someone to cut my thumbs off. You wonder why I was just a little resentful about that? Having my hand forced?"

"No one *forced* you to seduce a girl barely fifteen years old." I heard my own voice scaling up.

"I'm saying I'm sorry, Mila." He made one of those little *calm down* gestures that made me want to hit him with the nearest blunt cement object. Right now, that would be Comrade Yuri Yuripov, trudging along behind doing his NKVD best to ensure that we didn't start divulging state secrets to the nearest elm. "I'm not here to quarrel with you," Alexei continued. "I'm here to make amends. I want to see our son when we return home."

I resumed my brisk pace. "No."

"Mila, a man can admit he's made mistakes. I wasn't a good husband and father then; let me make it up to you now. When all's said and done, Slavka's still my son."

Suddenly I was regretting this walk among the trees. There weren't the kind of crowds I'd envisioned, children playing, women with baby carriages, students with picnic lunches. Just a few hikers in the distance, spots of color in bright jackets, and a gangly bird-watcher with binoculars . . . but otherwise, not a soul among these sound-swallowing woods except Yuri. And I didn't think he'd interfere if Alexei tried to put hands on me. His directive was to stop me misbehaving, not get in between a husband and wife. I heard the babble of a creek somewhere close and pressed toward it. Running water meant open banks, and suddenly I wanted room to maneuver.

"Even you have to admit every boy needs a father," Alexei coaxed, seemingly unaware of my unease. "Someone to teach him how to play hockey, help him with his lessons—"

Lyonya would have shown Slavka how to do all that. It was so easy to see the future we'd never have, the three of us ice-skating on the pond at Gorky Park in winter . . . I gave a hard blink, willing the tears out of my eyes as I came out onto the creek bed. Not a deep current, more a winding stream littered with rocks, but there was a bridge spanning it to my left, ancient-looking arches slabbed together out of massive chunks of stone, and I made for it.

"You know Slavka needs a father. Why else did you take up with that lieutenant?" Alexei asked, reading my mind even if he couldn't see my face ahead of him. "But he's gone now, and that made me realize I let a good thing slip away."

I came to the middle of the bridge, looking out. A beautiful spot: huge trees spreading across either bank, the creek with its happy babble and scatter of stones, red-gold arches of autumn leaves fluttering overhead. Part of me marveled to see something so beautiful in the middle of a city, wilderness left pristine and perfect to restore a soul tired of stone buildings and pavement. And part of me was as wary as I had ever been, conscious of my husband beside me, his every move and glance.

"What do you want?" I asked at last, levelly. I knew perfectly well what he wanted, but I refused to make this easy for him.

"I want you back, Mila." Alexei laid his hand on the bridge parapet, palm up in invitation. "You, me, Slavka. A proper family again. And what better time for you and me to make a new beginning than on this tour?"

"No," I stated. "No a thousand times. No."

His smile didn't budge. "I know I'll have to win you back, *kroshka*. Court you properly, the way I should have done the first time."

"Aren't I a little old for you by now?" I'd seen the way his eyes followed the barely curved hips of the teenage girls we passed on Decatur Street.

"You were a girl then. Now you're a woman. A man gets to a stage in his life when he appreciates a woman—"

"When he appreciates a war heroine, you mean. A woman in line for privileges from the Party." If Alexei was already thinking about the overseas trips I'd earn if I survived the war, I was certain he was also thinking about a big apartment in Moscow; Party functions where caviar and champagne flowed; gifts and bribes and seats at the high table with glittering officials. Fame, comfort, wealth—maybe he'd rather have earned those things in his own right, but if it took hitching his troika behind a star rather than becoming one himself, he'd get out the harness and start buckling straps.

All he needed was for the mare to walk into the horse collar he was holding out.

"Imagine the life we'd have," he was saying softly, persuasively. "The gowns and jewels I'll give you, the privileges for Slavka—"

"I'm not as famous as you seem to think. This luxurious life you think is mine for the taking—"

"Ours for the taking."

"Even if it were possible"—I didn't believe my notoriety had any more staying power than the strike of a match—"why would I need you? Anything you promise for our son, I can already give him myself." I ignored Alexei's outstretched hand. "These privileges you're talking of, they all flow from *me*."

"Except the name." Something in his smile flickered. "The name under which you got famous, Mila. That's still mine."

"The world knows me as Lady Death, and I earned that myself. I don't owe you for your name."

"You owe me for something. Didn't I let you have your lieutenant in Sevastopol?"

Rage choked me momentarily. "*Let* me—"

"Anyone could see it wasn't going to last, so I let you have it. He was going to get the chop sooner or later, or you would, so I didn't make a fuss . . . and really most husbands wouldn't have been so understanding. But things are different now—"

A thrush exploded out from the nearby bushes as the birdwatcher with the binoculars came tromping along the bank, lenses flashing. I nearly jumped out of my skin at the sudden noise, and Alexei's smile widened just a little. "I'm going to divorce you the moment I get back to Moscow," I told him, wishing I hadn't shown any weakness, and reversed course back toward stolid Yuri on the bank. I wanted out of these woods. I wanted my private Washington hotel room. Somewhere both my husband *and* any anonymous hate-scrawling enemies could be safely locked on the other side of a stout door.

"You don't want that, Mila." I didn't turn, but I could hear the smile in Alexei's voice. The man it was impossible to anger, because he always knew best and was always in control. Always. "You don't know what you want."

That made me turn, even though I knew I shouldn't. His eyes sparkled. *Enjoy your little tantrum?* they asked.

"I want you to leave me alone," I snarled. "Because I will never, ever, *ever* take you back."

"I'm going to change your mind," he said softly. "And, *kroshka*, you're going to like it."

"I AM REQUESTING Dr. Pavlichenko be removed from the list of those attending the opera tonight," I told Krasavchenko in the embassy study he'd made his own. "I was instructed not to mention him publicly on this tour because the American press would disapprove of a woman who was separated from her husband. Very well, I want more distance between him and me on *all* forthcoming events."

Krasavchenko looked confused. "He made it clear to me that the two of you were considering reconciliation."

"*I* am not considering anything. *He* is pressing me when I am trying to focus on my duties, and *you* are to see that this stops."

I could see the look in Krasavchenko's gaze: *Look at her, overreacting just like a woman.* "If you would perhaps be calmer about this—"

"I am very calm, I assure you. Unless provoked, I am an exceptionally reasonable, calm, and quiet person. Dr. Pavlichenko, however, is beginning to provoke me. I guarantee that if he and I are in the same place, there will be a scene."

A sigh. "He will not attend the opera tonight."

"Thank you."

Just get through the conference, I told myself as I went back to my hotel room. Once I returned home and then to the front, Alexei would know my chances of surviving were too minimal to get much out of my fame before I was killed . . .

I paused, yanking a comb through my short hair, realizing it had been a while since I felt death's quiet shadow at my shoulder reminding me how little time I had left. I had this short space before battle consumed my life again; maybe it was all right to enjoy it for what it was: the long final breath before the last plunge down.

So enjoy the opera, I thought with a surge of tentative pleasure, and unwrapped the yellow satin dress I'd purchased from the boutique. The first pretty thing I'd bought myself in so long—I hung it up so the creases would fall out, then shimmied into my slip and spent some time powdering my face, applying lipstick. My hair was still cut short to the nape of my neck, but it had curl and shine in it again, and you could hardly see where it had once been shaved away from a splinter wound. I clipped it back on one side and let it fall on the other, over the ear that had nearly been ripped off by mortar fire and still showed stitch marks. Scars safely hidden, I pulled the dress over my head and reached behind me to do up the dozen little satin-covered buttons.

A knock sounded. Strange how you can know a man from his knock—Krasavchenko's knock was as self-important as he was; Alexei's knock insinuated, nearly curling itself under the door. Kostia's was almost inaudible, hardly more than a brush of knuckles. He didn't need to call out for me to know it was my partner.

"I'll be down soon." The room had only one small mirror; I stood twisting in front of it, trying to see my back. "Tell Krasavchenko I have to change."

Kostia's voice floated. "Why?"

I couldn't see my back. I blew out a frustrated breath. "Would you mind coming in?"

My partner came into the room, and the sight of him made my brows fly up: severe black-and-white evening clothes setting off his sun-swarthy face, the dark cane like a knight's sword rather than an aid to lean on. "I've never seen a wolf in black tie before," I joked.

He said nothing, just looked me over. I folded my arms over my yellow satin bodice, suddenly self-conscious. Strange to feel all this naked skin: bare arms; hair curling against bare neck; satin clinging

to stockinged legs—my partner hadn't ever really seen me in anything but uniforms. I'd had an evening dress for the formal events in
Cairo, but Moscow's idea of an evening dress and America's were very
different. Kostia's face was carefully blank.

"I bought this without trying it on," I burst out, filling the silence.
"The salesgirl assured me it would fit . . . I didn't think about the
back."

I turned around. The back of the yellow satin dress plunged in a
deep V, and as much as I twisted, I couldn't see how much of my back
it revealed. "Does it show?"

The splinter wound that landed me in a hospital cot in Sevastopol
had healed into a long, reddish, forked scar that snaked from my right
shoulder blade to my spine. Lena had angled a pair of mirrors so I
could see it. "Looks like a firebird clawed you," she'd said cheerfully.
I'd never had cause before to feel self-conscious about it. Why would
I? The only one to see it besides Lena had been Lyonya; he used to
trace it when I fell asleep at night with my naked spine curled against
his chest. Otherwise, my uniform covered the scar. All my clothes
covered it—except this foolish dress I'd bought on impulse, because
Lady Death wanted to look *pretty*.

No one would think *pretty*, looking at my scars framed between
the panels of yellow satin. I could cover the scars in my hair, the scars
on my ear, but not this. "Let them get to know you," the First Lady
had counseled me in dealing with Americans—but they wouldn't
want to get to know me if my battle wounds made them recoil.

"It shows, doesn't it?" I asked as the silence stretched.

My partner's voice came quietly, right behind me, close enough to
prickle my skin. "Yes."

"I'll change. Tell Krasavchenko—"

Kostia's hands came down on either side of my waist. He bent his
head, setting his mouth against the puckered skin of the scar, and
stood there for a long year of a moment. "Wear it," he murmured into

my skin. The kiss started at the blade of my shoulder and finished over my spine at the scar's tailing end. "Wear it with pride."

I stood utterly still, pinned in place, until I heard the quiet click of the door signaling he was gone.

THE MARKSMAN SLID onto the stool beside the tall fair-haired Russian silently nursing a vodka alone at the hotel bar. "Mind if I join you?" he asked in his bad Russian, flashing his falsified press ID. "You're Dr. Pavlichenko, right? The delegation physician." He'd plucked the name off the list Pocket Square had provided of the delegation's little people.

"The same," said Alexei Pavlichenko, clearly pleased to be recognized. "Sit, sit. It's always a pleasure to converse in my native language."

"Even as badly as I speak it, eh? I had the beat covering the American Communist Party a few years . . ." The marksman trotted out some pleasantries, letting the conversation eddy around the drinks. He didn't normally make contact with target-adjacent people like this—usually he operated by the rule that the fewer points of contact there were, the better—but he'd done enough research to talk like a newsman all night if necessary, and some careful changes in outward presentation (wig, shoe lifts, voice) meant Alexei Pavlichenko was very unlikely to recognize the marksman again once he'd reverted to his own accent and hair color.

"So, doc," he said after calling for another round of drinks, "I hear you're something of a war hero yourself. So why aren't you at the National Theatre with the others?"

The doctor's smile wavered. "One gets tired of these public events. All the press, the attention . . ."

You weren't invited. The marksman had already sat through the first act of *Madama Butterfly* tonight, keeping an eye on the Soviet delegation, which attracted more attention than the singers. At intermission they were urged onstage by the audience to take a bow. Lyudmila Pavlichenko, looking visibly nervous in yellow satin, had given a pretty speech through the interpreters about how pleased they all were to be in Washington, how dire the Russian need was for American aid . . . when the theater audience began passing the hat for donations to the Red Army, the marksman had risen in his seat and ambled back to the hotel where the delegation had been put up. Not just the delegation but their flunkies and minders.

"Say, about your name," the marksman exclaimed as if just struck. "It's the same as the lady sniper's. What are you, her brother, cousin—"

"Her husband." The doctor drank his vodka off in a quick motion.

"I thought she was a widow." Pretending bewilderment.

"It's complicated." A conspiratorial smile. "Aren't all things, with women?"

The marksman buried his own smile in his glass. He heard jealousy in the other man's voice, envy, spite, longing . . . that confrontation at Boulder Bridge *had* been a marital quarrel, then. He hadn't been entirely sure—bumbling around the banks of Rock Creek as a local birdwatcher hadn't gotten him near enough to eavesdrop, and he hadn't wanted to get close enough for anyone to see his face under the brim of his baseball cap—but the body language between the girl and the doctor had told its own intriguing story. Their meetup had surprised him. The marksman had been tailing the doctor that afternoon, not the girl—narrowing down his choice for who to approach on the delegation staff, what person could be used to fix the frame around Lyudmila Pavlichenko. And then to discover his top pick was her disgruntled, shunted-aside husband?

Sometimes fate dropped a gift in your lap.

Another round of drinks, and the marksman waited for them to hit before he leaned closer across the bar. "So, this student assembly . . ."

CHAPTER 26

The headline: THE INTERNATIONAL STUDENT ASSEMBLY OPENED TODAY WITH NEARLY FOUR HUNDRED STUDENTS FROM FIFTY-THREE COUNTRIES. LATIN AMERICANS, AFRICANS, ASIANS, AND EUROPEANS MINGLED IN HARMONY AND ENTHUSIASM.

The truth: The students from Bombay University nearly came to blows with the British Oxford contingent over the so-called Indian Question, and the only reason I didn't start swinging alongside the young man in the turban shouting, "We'll win independence eventually, you colonial curs!" was because Krasavchenko threatened to have me exiled to the Arctic Circle.

"MAY I STEAL you away, my dears?"

I blinked up at the First Lady, exchanging glances with Krasavchenko and Pchelintsev. The opening-day reception was far from over; the three of us stood with untouched plates of canapés and glasses of ubiquitous warm white wine like perfumed goat pee, besieged by questions from journalists, honorary guests from U.S. civic organizations, and fellow students. Krasavchenko was boring the ears off a White House aide; Pchelintsev was re-fighting all his Leningrad duels for an American general laden with medals; and I was fending off an avid society columnist who wanted to know what kind of makeup routine I followed at the front. "I bathe in the blood of my enemies," I wanted to tell her. "It's simply *wonderful* for the complexion!" But she would probably think I was being serious, because Americans seemed to assume all Soviets were as humorless as my minder, Yuri.

In other words, all was going much as expected, the first day of the conference. But now the First Lady was drawing the three of us aside. "Supper at the White House," she made our excuses for us, collecting Kostia along the way. I expected to be ushered into the familiar White House dining room and resolved that this time I wouldn't gape at the chandeliers and portraits and china—but we were led into a private oval-shaped study instead, and my jaw dropped for an entirely different reason.

In the center of the room, a man sat alone in a wooden chair with a high back, long-fingered hands resting on its wide arms, a tartan rug across his legs. "I'd like you to meet the President," the First Lady said simply.

I was already standing at attention, bracing without making the decision to do so. So were the others, all of us responding to the authority radiating out of that chair. The President's keen gaze passed over us as Kostia made introductions, and I knew he'd be able to produce our names and details a decade from now if he were asked. "Krasavchenko, Pchelintsev, Pavlichenko—how wonderful." He smiled, and I couldn't help smiling back as I stepped forward in turn to press that long, sinewy palm.

"I would hear the lady's experiences first." A courtly half bow from the chair. *You're a sniper with 309 kills,* I scolded myself. *Don't blush just because the American president is a charmer!* But for the love of Lenin, it was a close thing: I'd been told to expect a sharp mind and a strong will when it came to Franklin Delano Roosevelt, but I hadn't expected the warmth, the force, the unblinking attention as he aimed questions at me through Kostia. What fighting had I done; what actions lay behind my military decorations; how had my regiment fought? The press corps here found it hard to believe I did anything at the front but curl my hair for propaganda pictures; their president didn't bat an eyelash when I described how to dig a trench and wait six, seven, eight hours for the perfect shot. How our shortage of fire-arms was so dire that my first rifle came to me with the blood of its previous owner still wet on the barrel.

"Years of war," President Roosevelt said finally after grilling my fellow delegates in turn, "and our side hasn't succeeded anywhere in resisting their enemies as long as you Russians have done. Is it your military spirit, your training? The skill of your officers and generals? The unity between army and populace?" He tilted his head, looking at each of us in turn. "What would you say?"

"It's *will*," I answered when I saw Krasavchenko hesitate. "Because we hold and fight or we die. But no amount of willpower in the world matters if we have no bullets to shoot or rifles to fire."

"Tell me more," the President said quietly.

He'd won us all over in a matter of minutes. The First Lady's authoritative voice sounded in the background and chairs were pulled up; drinks poured; rough maps sketched with napkins and cocktail shakers as we talked and the President listened. "And how do you feel in our country?" he finished, looking from face to face again. "Are the Americans cordial toward you all?"

For an instant, I thought of the second hand-scrawled threat I'd received just yesterday morning: YOU'LL DIE SCREAMING YOU RED BITCH. Same scrawled Cyrillic, same handwriting as far as I could see, and they could apparently get to me just as easily in my Washington hotel as they could in the White House. I couldn't stop glancing over my shoulder now whenever I ventured outside, even if the Soviet ambassador shrugged and said it was likely nothing . . .

"We're greeted everywhere as welcome guests," Krasavchenko was assuring the President through Kostia. "You Americans are a very hospitable people!"

I wasn't going to bring up my death threats, but I couldn't resist saying in English, "Sometimes we are subjected to sudden attacks."

The President frowned. "Attacks?"

"From your reporters." I kept my face serious but let my eyes dance. "They are very persistent. They want us to bare everything."

President Roosevelt grinned. What a grin that man had. He liked women, we had been told in our reports in Moscow, and I could tell he liked me. He didn't think the cut of my uniform was unflattering at all. So I took a breath and said, "May I ask—"

"More active assistance for the Soviet Union?" he said, reading me without effort. "The opening of a second front in Western Europe to draw German divisions away from the banks of the Volga?"

I nodded. I knew that second front wasn't such an easy matter for him to put into motion as I'd first assumed when I arrived in this country, but neither would I pretend our need for it wasn't dire.

He looked pensive. "Mr. Stalin is already aware that it is difficult at present for us to render more active assistance to your country. We Americans are not yet ready for decisive action—"

"You acted decisively after Pearl Harbor," I couldn't help saying.

Another of those rueful grins. "Yet when it comes to expanding into a European front, we're held back by our need to aid our British allies. But in heart and soul"—another of those courtly bows from the chair—"we stand with our Russian friends."

"Well," Krasavchenko muttered later as we went down to our actual dinner and the President excused himself to another function, "that was useless."

"Did you think he'd put his hand on his heart and promise an army on the spot? If he had, I wouldn't have trusted him a centimeter." I smiled. "We're just students, not negotiators. All we can do is advocate. At least he listened, unlike his journalists."

Unexpectedly Kostia spoke up, his voice quiet over the muffled tread of our shoes on expensive carpet. "That's a man to follow into shellfire."

"He makes me think . . ." I paused, trying to find the words. "I might only be a student here, but I don't have to be useless. If one man like him can tow his nation single-handedly through a worldwide economic depression and then a worldwide war, I can learn to give speeches without feeling like a deer caught in klieg lights, can't I?"

Kostia didn't answer, but his eyes caught mine for the first time since the opera. There was something in his gaze now that scorched, and I couldn't stop my stomach from clenching in confused, chaotic response, even as we were ushered toward another long dining room table of White House officials and guests. The final day of this conference here would also mark six months since the day Lyonya had died . . .

I was relieved to turn away from my partner and take a seat beside the presidential adviser Harry Hopkins, who pulled out my chair with something of a twinkle in his eye. From our very first meeting he'd taken a liking to me, and despite my instinct to stay reticent with Americans, I'd taken a liking to him. He was another one, like his boss, who asked questions and actually listened to the answers. I'd been dropping as many facts as I could into that receptive ear. "What did you think of the President?"

"I am honored to call him an ally," I managed in my most gracious diplomatic tones, murmuring a *spasibo* to the server who filled my glass.

"Mrs. Pavlichenko, I've heard the tobacco company Philip Morris is offering you a contract," a woman called across the table. "They want to put your portrait on cigarette packets! What have you to say to that?"

"They can go to the devil," I said in English, abandoning the gracious diplomatic tone, and the table burst out laughing.

"Cigarette packets may only be the start of it," the First Lady murmured, and I cocked my head.

"What do you mean, Mrs. Roosevelt?"

"Oh, nothing." Her eyes positively danced. "I merely have an idea . . . and I believe the President, having met you all, is ready to agree to it."

THE SECOND AND third day of the conference. Long droning addresses, usually followed by heated debates. Answering questions about my uniform; trading university lecture stories with a bucktoothed girl from York and a smooth-cheeked boy from Beijing who barely looked old enough to shave. Applauding as the delegates adopted a Slavic Memorandum condemning German fascism. "So kind of them to conclude that fascism is bad," I whispered to Yuri. "I can't wait to inform Comrade Stalin of their decision. He'll be so relieved!" Even that didn't get a facial expression out of my minder, who continued to watch beady-eyed from the back of the room as flashbulbs went off.

The First Lady insisted on posing for photographs between Pchelintsev and me, taking our hands very firmly in her large, capable ones. Maybe her husband couldn't promise aid as quickly as we wanted, but she made sure no photographer left without that photograph of us all holding hands, a visible symbol of the Soviet-American military alliance.

"You're getting comfortable in the limelight at last," Alexei murmured on the conference's last day. The closing reception was being held on the green beside the White House; the warm, sunny evening threw my shadow ahead of me long and slanting. "Well done, *kroshka*."

"*Ta mère suce des ours*," I told him. A phrase I'd been taught by a French Canadian student on a cigarette break, when we'd been discussing how to get rid of handsy lecturers—a topic female university students could discuss across all global divides and language barriers. I'd taught her how to say *Put your pig paws back in your pockets* in Russian; she'd taught me *Ta mère suce des ours,* which apparently meant *Your mother sucks bears.* "It's even more insulting than it sounds in translation," she advised, and I grinned at Alexei's perplexed face now as I strolled off to join the group of students from Montreal. I was determined to enjoy this last reception. In Moscow it would have been an elaborate affair, white-draped tables and dark suits and long speeches, but the First Lady had made it all into a backyard party: students wandering the gardens with paper plates full of sandwiches and glass bottles of Coca-Cola, the sound of decadent, delicious ragtime drifting from an unseen radio. President Roosevelt had yet to join us, and I could sense a thrum in the crowd as the guests looked for him, but until he arrived, things could remain decidedly informal. I ended up telling a White House aide about my walk to Boulder Bridge in Rock Creek Park, blinking as the aide told me how President Roosevelt had once lost a signet ring there on a hike. "President Roosevelt was hiking?"

"This was his cousin President Teddy Roosevelt, forty years ago," the aide explained. "He lost a favorite ring there, so he put an ad in the paper: *Golden ring lost near Boulder Bridge in Rock Creek. If found, return to 1600 Pennsylvania Avenue. Ask for Teddy.*" He guffawed, and so did the students from Montreal. "The ring never turned up . . ."

I smiled, taking a deep breath to smell the fresh-cut grass, letting the aide press a sandwich into my hand—a sausage roll the Americans called a *hot dog*. American food looked Technicolor-bright to me, like it had been molded in plastic rather than cooked. "Not bad," I said, swallowing my first bite. "Actual dog?"

"Mrs. Pavlichenko, you're a card!"

"What? They eat worse than dog in Leningrad by now." As party chitchat went, that observation went over like a lead balloon, as the Americans liked to say, but Mrs. Roosevelt rescued me, smoothing the moment over.

"You know," she said, drawing me to one side, "I've been planning this conference a long while now. The idea was to promote American values in the context of international youth . . . but you Russians have changed that plan."

I took a sip of my Coca-Cola through a straw. Too sweet and too cold, like sucking on sugared razor blades. "How, ma'am?"

"All you delegates are eloquent"—ha, that was a lie; she was as bored by Krasavchenko's droning as I was—"but you Russians have a particular passion when you speak about the war, Lyudmila dear. It nearly hurts to listen to you."

"I am sorry if it *hurts* to hear truth," I began stiffly, but she put a pacifying hand on my arm.

"No, it's good if it hurts us. We Americans are used to viewing war from a distance—the privilege of living, as Chancellor Otto von Bismarck once said, with less powerful neighbors to the north and south, and nothing to the east and west but fish. Even the terrible attack on our own Pearl Harbor came thousands of miles away. You have helped put a visible face on the price of war viewed inside one's homeland. The bleeding and suffering of neighbors and loved ones in their own cities . . . You make it real and impossible to ignore. Thank you for that."

She paused, but I said nothing. I still wasn't entirely sure how to treat her, this observant lady who was so evidently bent on charming us all. President Roosevelt might have been a man of privilege, but his crippled legs had clearly left him with a keen understanding of suffering. I wasn't so sure about the First Lady. She was very friendly, very clever, very complimentary when she spoke of *putting a visible face* on war—but what did she know of it, really?

And I still hadn't forgotten her statement to me that first day over the breakfast table. Whether I could see the faces of my enemies through my sights, and whether that would make it difficult for Americans to like me.

She smiled, not offended by my silence. "It's my hope that our whole country will hear what you have to say."

"But we return to Moscow in a few days." I couldn't wait. This celebration on the White House green would be the end, and I was glad. The Washington journey might have had its pleasant moments, but I wanted home soil under my feet again. I wanted to know I was at least on the same continent as my Slavka.

"Your ambassador has yet to brief you officially, but other plans have been—" The First Lady broke off as Alexei bowed his way into our conversation.

"Do pardon me to the First Lady," he whispered in Russian with a bow over her hand. "I need to steal you away for a moment, *kroshka*. I've been asked to show you the Rose Garden before President Roosevelt arrives and the evening goes to chaos."

I was about to tell him that I had no intention of strolling any roses with him *ever*, but the First Lady broke in. She didn't speak any Russian beyond *da, nyet,* and *spasibo*, but she'd heard her husband's name. "Is he asking when the President is coming down?" she asked, looking at me. "He won't be able to drop by tonight as he planned, unfortunately. Some other business intruded—but never fear, you'll all have other chances to meet with him." She broke into a wide smile. "At my urging, the President has invited the entire Soviet delegation to extend their stay. You will tour more of our cities to give greater publicity to your fight against Hitler. Your ambassador tells me approval has just been granted from Moscow!"

In the face of her delight, I worked to keep the disappointment off my face. "How long is this visit extending, ma'am?"

"That will be decided later. The immediate plan is to send you all to New York City tomorrow morning, on the Washington–New York express." She lowered her voice. "I've requested that you especially, Lyudmila, get the chance to do more speaking. I think the American people will respond to a woman—and not merely to any woman, to *you*."

"I thought you were worried they would not approve of me," I couldn't help saying.

She smiled. "I think you have the power to change their minds."

"What's she saying?" Alexei asked in Russian. I ignored him, trying to match Mrs. Roosevelt's evident pleasure as my heart sank into my knees. I wasn't going home yet, after all.

POCKET SQUARE'S POCKET-SQUARE handkerchief was red today instead of blue, and his face was even redder. "Explain yourself," he hissed at the marksman without so much as a greeting. They'd met overlooking the Washington Monument today, clouds racing past the tip of the great stone spire, standing well out of earshot of the crowding tourists. "The conference done and not a shot fired! Did you lose your nerve or—"

"The President didn't attend," the marksman said calmly, tipping his hat to a pretty young mother steering her baby carriage toward the monument. "A last-minute schedule change." A great pity, because everything had been going like clockwork: the marksman poised to drift away from the cadre of photographers, disappear into the gardens, and begin setting up his long shot that would take Roosevelt between the eyes the moment the man appeared on the portico. That booby of a Russian doctor had been primed to lead his wife off to the Rose Garden so she would be suspiciously absent from the festivities once the shot was fired. "I'll lurk along behind, get some real good photographs of you two there for tomorrow's write-up," the marksman had promised him at the hotel bar; the doctor, full of vodka by that point, was so keen to see his own face in the paper alongside his wife's, he hadn't even needed the incentive of a folded bill or two. No notion he was being set up: the husbandly accomplice helping his assassin wife murder the president. Theirs would have made a pretty pair of mug shots in the papers, the marksman thought wistfully.

Ah, well.

"I warned you that even the best plans can go awry," he told Pocket Square, who was still apoplectic. "Fortunately the Soviet tour in the

United States has been extended, so we'll have plenty more chances while Pavlichenko's still here to take the fall. She's gone to New York; I'll need a copy of the new itinerary."

The marksman paused, frowning. The cover identity of a journalist had been a good one so far, but the First Lady seemed to have taken a liking to Lyudmila Pavlichenko, and if they appeared at events together on the road, then Eleanor Roosevelt would insist on *women* journalists. Another of the horsey bitch's peccadilloes, something about getting more females onto newspaper staffs. Like the world needed more yattering cows. "I may need a new cover," the marksman said, more to himself than to Pocket Square, and walked away from the stone needle of the Washington Monument without a goodbye. Lady Death was in New York City; there was plenty of time to plan.

"I WISH WE were in Stalingrad."

I spoke into the silence of the car, but even so, I wasn't sure Kostia could hear me over the wail of sirens, the rumble of motorbike engines from the motorcade that enclosed the Cadillac. Two vehicles had greeted our delegation at the train station in New York; Krasavchenko, Pchelintsev, and their minders had been shuttled through a tunnel of flashing cameras and shouting journalists to the first car, and I'd dived into the second with my partner as Yuri rode with the driver on the other side of the partition.

"I hear the Germans are storming for the Volga," I continued. "Pushing into the outskirts of Stalingrad." The Red Army soldiers would be falling back from street to street, skirmishing from rooftops and bombed-out buildings—perfect conditions for snipers. I could so clearly envision Kostia and me there, camouflaged against the rubble of shattered pipes and demolished walls, chewing dry tea and sugar, our rifle barrels twin eyes narrowed on the enemy.

Yet here I was in a Cadillac instead, moving at a crawl through the brightest, busiest city I'd ever seen. The closer we got to Central Park, the deeper the roar of the crowd became all around us. My heart was trying to climb up my throat. I'd thought Washington was overwhelming, but the noise in New York City had me wanting to dive into a foxhole.

And maybe my rising nerves had a little something to do with the *third* threatening note I'd found . . . this one waiting in my coat pocket as I boarded the train for New York City. Whoever it was had followed me from Washington—had been close enough to touch me—could have sunk a knife between my ribs rather than slipping a note into my pocket that read I'M GOING TO CORE YOUR SKULL WITH YOUR OWN RIFLE BARREL YOU MURDER-ING RED SLUT.

I didn't care that the embassy wasn't worried; that they'd wave it off as *another American crackpot.* I was being hunted, and I was weapon-less on unfamiliar territory, and for a sniper that was terrifying.

And on top of all of that, I had to give a speech in this huge, ca-cophonous park crammed with people who would probably agree that I *was* a murdering Red slut.

"Lyonya told me you gave your first speech in Sevastopol." Kostia looked straight ahead, voice low and calm, but his shoulder was pressed into mine as though we were lying on our elbows in a trench, waiting for our shot. He knew about the threats, but I'd made light of them—I didn't want him seeing I was afraid. "How did you prepare then?"

"I asked Lyonya—" My voice caught on his name; I swallowed hard. "I asked how someone like me who shoots people from a dis-tance, trying never to be seen, is somehow stuck under bright lights in front of a packed crowd, giving a speech."

"And he said?"

" 'Shut up, Mila, you'll be brilliant.' "

"He was right." Kostia looked at me squarely. "You'll always be brilliant."

"But—"

My partner raised his hand, holding it flat at eye level. I stopped speaking and raised mine. My pulse might be racing, but my hand was granite steady. Threats or no, crowd or no. Kostia smiled. Not with his mouth, but folded into the corners of his eyes, where only I could see it.

I couldn't resist a smile back, the strange chaos of conflicting emotions warring in my stomach again. Ease and awkwardness, tenderness and confusion, wariness and—

The Cadillac swung through the main entrance of Central Park, and the roar redoubled. Crowds were pressing all around, barely held back by the motorcade. I spared one look at them, then back to Kostia. Breathe in, breathe out. "You'll have my back?"

"From here to Stalingrad."

The car halted. "I wish I was armed," I groaned as the doors opened, and then I swung myself out, hoisting a smile into place. My ears roared at the noise; hands were pulling me forward and men in burly jackets lifted Kostia and me up onto their shoulders. They bore us along through the crowd up to the stage, where the mayor of New York was saying something through a microphone about the gargantuan struggle of the Russian people against the German fascists.

And then it was time for me to speak.

I looked out at a sea of faces, an ocean of cameras. *Don't fail,* I thought. *Don't miss.*

"Dear friends." I heard my voice soaring, as though it might carry all the way up to the spires of these vast skyscrapers. Kostia repeated my words into his own microphone, fierce and sonorous. "Hitler is making a desperate attempt to cripple our united nations before we

Allies do it to him. It is a matter of life and death for the freedom-loving people of every country to join forces and render assistance to the front. More tanks, more planes, more ordinance."

I spread my boots, clasped my hands at my back. I found the rage in me that a year at the front hadn't killed, and let it roar flame-red into my voice. I spoke in Russian, but even if these New Yorkers couldn't understand my words, they could understand my fire. My anger. My *will*.

You will aid us, I thought. *You will aid us in this fight, or I will die trying.*

I still stumbled in places. I still faltered. But it was better than the speech I'd given in Sevastopol, better than the statements I'd given for the Washington press conferences, and the scream of the crowd when I finished nearly blew my shell-damaged ears in.

Maybe they didn't think I was a murdering Red slut after all . . .

I stood on the stage with applause raining down on me like mortars, hearing thousands of Americans call my name, and I wondered for the first time if Alexei had been right. If this flash of fame I'd somehow accrued was something more than a matchstick's brief transitory flare.

CHAPTER 27

The headline: MAYOR FIORELLO LA GUARDIA OF NEW YORK CITY PRESENTED THE SOVIET DELEGATION WITH A MEDALLION STRUCK IN HONOR OF ALL WHO STRUGGLE AGAINST FASCISM, AND "BROAD IS MY NATIVE LAND" WAS SUNG BY PAUL ROBESON, WHOSE BASS IS AS DARK AND SHINING AS HIS VISAGE. BOTH TRIBUTES WERE ACCEPTED BY CHARMING GIRL SNIPER LYUDMILA PAVLICHENKO, WHOSE SPEECH WAS RECEIVED WITH ENTHUSIASM BY THE PEOPLE OF NEW YORK CITY. MRS. PAVLICHENKO PROCEEDS ON TO BALTIMORE . . .

The truth: When women become famous, it brings strange men out of the woodwork.

"YOUR ADDRESS WAS brilliant, Mrs. Pavlichenko, utterly brilliant!"

"Thank you, Mr. Jonson." I tried to remove my fingers from the man in front of me, but he seemed determined to wring them off my hand, eyes glowing with fervor over his starched collar and pinstriped suit.

"Quite as brilliant as the speech you gave in New York."

"Mr. Jonson, it was the same speech—"

"I first heard you in New York, and I followed to Baltimore just to hear you speak again!"

"How . . . dedicated!" My welcoming smile was slipping; I hitched it back in place as Kostia translated. Usually I tried to speak English when conversing at these receptions and parties, disliking the embassy's instructions about using the interpreter for all questions, but Mr. William Patrick Jonson—American millionaire, dedicated eccentric, owner of a metallurgical company, and apparently smitten with *the girl sniper*—had me diving to take refuge behind the dual shields of my native language and Kostia. Not that Kostia was much help; he was so entertained by my new suitor he was actually almost smiling. "I will hand you your molars on a wreath if you keep smirking," I warned him in Russian, still beaming at Mr. Jonson.

"Mr. Jonson wishes to know if you will visit his home on the outskirts of New York," Kostia said, straight-faced. "He has a fine collection of artwork by Russian avant-garde artists from the beginning of the twentieth century."

"Tell him he can jump into Baltimore Harbor."

"Mrs. Pavlichenko prefers the work of the Peredvizhniki artists," Kostia translated, "particularly Vasily Vereshchagin."

"I will *acquire* some Vereshchagin, Miss Pavlichenko, if only you will agree to visit." The American millionaire was still chafing my hand as though trying to warm it back to life from frostbite. "And then you can meet my mother—"

For the love of Lenin. "Mr. Jonson, I'm afraid I am leaving very soon. The Soviet delegation has been invited to spend a week at the President's family estate."

"She would love to meet your mother when she returns," Kostia translated. He was quivering with laughter by the time I managed to scrape free.

"Number 310 on my tally is going to be you," I promised Kostia in a whisper as we moved off through the thronged Baltimore reception room. "Because I'm going to *shoot you in the back* as soon as we are sent to Stalingrad after coming home from this circus."

"Lady Midnight, I'm always the one at *your* back."

We traded quick smiles. We weren't uncomfortable with each other, but we were *aware*; we were making conversation rather than slipping in and out of comfortable silence, and I heard myself saying brightly, "Are you coming to Hyde Park? If Alexei inveigled his way along, surely you can."

"Alexei's coming?" Hyde Park was where the Roosevelt country estate was located on the Hudson River; the First Lady had invited the Soviet delegation, the students from Britain, several from Holland and China . . . "I thought Krasavchenko agreed to leave him behind."

"He claims he needs to tend Pchelintsev's recent illness."

"Pchelintsev has hay fever."

"That's what I said, but did anyone listen to me?"

Alexei was right there with the rest of the delegation, squeezing himself up between Kostia and me when we all arrived at Hyde Park. I saw his eyes go narrow and acquisitive at the sight of the gracious colonial house with its pillars and porticoes, its surrounding acres of green lawn and waving trees. "Never mind having a dacha someday," he breathed, putting a caressing hand at the small of my back as the party crowded toward the entrance hall. "We'll have something like *this*. Spacious, well-appointed, near the woods for a little hunting . . . what do you think, *kroshka*?"

I moved away from his hand without saying anything, because words did no good. Clearly his plan was to wear me down with sheer persistence until I got so tired of refusing that I gave in. Insults didn't put him off; silence didn't put him off—and maybe he'd gotten a warning from the delegation not to make any embarrassing public fuss around me, but that left plenty of time away from cameras and American eyes to continue his campaign. *That's my wife,* he was always saying casually to the other delegation members. *We've been separated, but she was very young . . . you know how fickle young girls can be, eh? We get on so well now . . .*

Avoid him, I thought, looking around the vast green spread of the Roosevelt estate, the guest quarters where Yuri and the other minders were already tramping with the luggage. *At least there's plenty of room here to do it.*

The fresh country air should have been a restorative after the choking noise and smoke of New York and Baltimore, but somehow my dreams that first night were full of cobwebs and nightmares. Lyonya died in my arms, over and over, and when I twisted out of that dream, I fell into another where a shadowy figure stalked me through Washington's empty streets, snarling *Commie slut . . . Red bitch . . .* I woke up gasping, on the whisper of *You'll die here.*

"I am not going to die here," I said aloud into my shadowed bedroom. No crackpot could get his scribbled notes or his murderous intentions anywhere near this remote presidential hideaway surrounded by Secret Service and forest. But I knew I wouldn't sleep another wink, so as soon as the dawn broke, I tugged a flowered day dress over my head and slipped out of the house for a walk—only to run right into the cement pillar of Yuri.

"Really?" I exploded. "We're on the presidential retreat. Everything is entirely locked down—there is no way I could meet any undesirables on these grounds, even if I wanted to, *which I don't.* Can't you just sleep in for once and let me go on a walk alone?"

"That would countermand my directive, Comrade Pavlichenko."

Well, it had been worth a try. "Would you mind staying a bit back, then?" I sighed, and headed toward the gardens, away from the bustle of breakfast preparation I could already see at the main house as servants streamed in and out.

The surrounding park was laced with paths, beds of autumn flowers, gazebos for dallying, all standing sunlit and peaceful in the morning light against the surrounding darkness of the woods. I took a deep lungful of air, not realizing until now how badly I'd missed quiet—silence—space to breathe. Snipers are loners, after all, and between Yuri, the ever-present journalists, and my speaking schedule, I hadn't had much time to myself. My night terrors were melting away fast as I wandered toward the water; one bank was choked with reeds, while the other sported a bathing shed, a row of small boats, a small dock. At the end of the dock, looking out at the water—

"I should have known I'd find you out here away from everyone," I said to Kostia's back, wandering out to join him as I motioned Yuri to stay on the bank. My partner was smoking a Lucky Strike; we'd both taken to American cigarettes, so he lit another off his own and passed it to me. We stood looking over the water for a quarter hour's companionable silence, smoke drifting up from our cupped hands.

"Three," he said at last.

"Three," I agreed. "Bathing shed—"

"Back behind the tree line—"

"And among the reeds on the far bank." I narrowed my eyes at the spot, mentally planning a foxhole. "Hard to keep your weapon dry there."

"Good thing we don't have to shoot anyone this morning."

I finished the cigarette, grinding the butt under my heel as I looked at the row of small boats. "When I was a child in Belaya Tserkov, my sister and I took a flat-bottomed rowboat out on the river sometimes. We called it the *Cossack Oak*, pretended we were rowing to the North Pole to find Morozko." I remembered telling Kostia in Odessa how he reminded me of the winter god from old times, snow-silent and dangerous. I cleared my throat, nudging the nearest craft—a narrow leather-covered thing with two short paddles that I was fairly certain Americans called a canoe. "Shall we try it? The First Lady did say to make ourselves at home."

Kostia jumped down into the canoe before I was done speaking.

I took the seat behind him as he gave us a push off the dock. "Only room for two!" I shouted toward Yuri just in case he had any thought of joining us, and we got our paddles in a rhythm, aiming for deeper water. I enjoyed the burning in my shoulders even if I did favor the unscarred side, savoring the glassy expanse of water and the rustle of reeds. "Lyonya would have liked this," I found myself saying. I could almost see him here in the canoe with us, fair hair ruffling in the wind.

"He didn't like water," Kostia said over his shoulder. "I used to tease him about that."

"Oh." Something I hadn't known about the man I thought of as my second husband. In my mind's eye he reached out and tucked a lock of hair behind my ear. *There are a lot of things you didn't get a chance to know about me,* milaya.

And now I never would. I'd missed my chance—my second chance at love, the world giving me Lyonya after I'd made such a monumental mistake in my first attempt at marriage. You hardly ever got a second shot after missing your first; life as a sniper had taught me that, but the world had been kind enough to give me one and I'd missed that, too . . .

"Mrs. Roosevelt says there's a very fine library at the house," I said just to be saying something. "I could use some new books to read, to practice my English. Maybe we can find you something other than *War and Peace*."

Kostia's shoulders continued to flex and relax, flex and relax as he swept his paddle through the water. "I'm going back to Washington tomorrow."

I blinked. "You're leaving the delegation?"

"Only for a few days. I'll make a private fuss to Krasavchenko that it doesn't sit well with me, staying in a presidential palace built on the backs of the masses, and ask to go back to the embassy for the rest of the week." A brief thread of amusement laced his voice. "The real reason . . . I mean to take a day in New York City, on my way to catch the New York–Washington express."

"New York City?"

He stopped paddling, and the canoe drifted to a halt in the middle of the glassy mirror of water. "My grandmother. Remember the one I told you about?"

The American girl who had come to Russia before the revolution with a missionary group, full of romantic ideas about Siberian snows and white nights, marrying a revolutionary and staying behind. I nodded, remembering the night he'd trusted me with that story—a forest camp outside Sevastopol, celebrating with Vartanov and the rest of our platoon when they'd all still been alive and laughing. Strange to think I'd nearly forgotten Kostia was part American, though he'd spent the last few weeks among Americans, deploying his fluent English instead of his rifle.

"I have family in New York," Kostia went on, still sitting with his back to me. "Cousins I've never met. They probably don't know I exist. I've done some digging, very quietly. I know at least where my grandmother's sister lives. She's still alive, living in Ridgewood."

"Kostia, the risk . . ." He'd managed to conceal his American ties for so long, lost or destroyed all the relevant documention—clearly he'd passed all the background checks, to be allowed to join this delegation at all. If, after all that, it were found out he had undisclosed American relations . . . I didn't even want to imagine the consequences. They would assuredly be hideous.

"I won't have trouble getting permission to return to Washington alone—they don't assign minders for little fish like me. And I'll concoct a story about missing the last train, having to stay the night in New York City. They won't suspect."

"And—what? You'll just walk up to your great-aunt's house and knock on the door?"

"Maybe I'll knock. Or maybe I'll just walk the streets where my grandmother grew up." He hesitated. "I don't know."

I tried to imagine an Irish family in New York finding this sinewy Siberian wolf on their doorstep, a cousin from halfway around the world. *They'd better not slam the door on you,* I thought. "If you need a story I'll cover for you," I began, digging my paddle into the water again to turn us back toward shore.

"Careful," Kostia began, "it's got a very shallow draft—"

Too late. The canoe slewed sideways from my paddle, and before I knew it, I was in the drink.

The famous Lady Death and her sniper partner, Lyonya hooted fondly as Kostia and I floundered and splashed. *May I present the deadliest shots in Sevastopol!*

The water was barely up to chest height, so there wasn't much hurt but my pride as I surfaced spitting water. Yuri, on the bank, didn't move; his orders were to stop me from defecting, not drowning. Kostia righted the canoe, pushing back his soaked sleeves and tossing the paddles in before they could float away. "We'll tip that over again if we try to climb back in," I said, grabbing for my felt hat before it could sink. "Good thing the Hitlerites can't see us like this. They'd be dead of laughter, not lead shot."

Kostia tossed my soaked hat into the canoe too, angling the boat so it blocked out Yuri on the bank. My partner reached for my hand under the water and pulled it against his chest, then he bent his head and kissed me. He tasted like iron and rain, his other hand tangling briefly in my hair, and I felt the sniper-calluses of his trigger hand against my scarred neck before he pulled away.

"You already know," he said. "What I feel for you."

I did know. I'd known a long time.

"No reason to say it in Sevastopol." He untangled his hand from my hair, reaching for the canoe before it could drift away from us. "You were my sergeant. You were my partner. And you loved my friend." A pause. "It feels too soon, saying this to you now. Lyonya has only been dead six months."

Lyonya. I realized my hand had bunched into Kostia's wet shirt, and I pulled it away.

"I wish I could wait a year, wait until the grief is less. But we don't have a year. We barely have tomorrow." Kostia hesitated. The fire in him had always been leashed, banked; now it was blazing high in his gaze, almost too bright to look at. "I'm out of time, Mila. When we return to Moscow—in a week, two weeks, whenever it is—you'll be headed back to the front, and I won't. We'll be pulled our separate ways. So I have to say this now."

"But you're coming back to the front, too." I don't know how I fastened on that first when everything he said had cracked me and tumbled me like an earthquake, but the thought of rejoining the fight without him sent a pang of utter terror through me, pushing past everything else. "You're my *partner.* I'll ask to get you in my platoon, they'll transfer you—"

"Not with this knee. I couldn't make a two-kilometer march, much less an all-day advance. I'm done as a soldier. It'll be sniper instructor duty for me, and you'll be heading back to the fight." He pushed a strand of wet hair off my forehead. "It's too soon. I know that. But this is what we have. Before there's danger and bullets flying again, and we run out of life."

Lyonya, I thought. Kostia was thinking it, too.

"You still love him. You still miss him. So do I. Six months or six years or six decades, we'll still miss him." Kostia's eyes were black and still. "I wasn't even jealous, him winning you. You picked the best man I knew. I wasn't going to break with my friend over that, or my partner."

There was pain there in his voice, but well-buried. He'd paved it over at the time, matter-of-factly, because in his eyes it didn't matter that he'd lost. I remembered Alexei's narrow-eyed glance assessing every man who visited me in the hospital battalion: a dog keeping an eye on a discarded bone, not wanting anyone else to have it . . . while Kostia had just quietly gone on being my other half, being Lyonya's friend, keeping it complete: the three of us.

And now it was just the two of us, the ones who'd loved Lyonya best.

"That's all." Kostia blew out a long breath. "I'm just—I'm not waving you off to war without telling you I love you. "

I was shivering with cold and something else. My mouth burned. I reached out, tangling my hand in his shirt again, but unable—for the first time in our partnership—to look my shadow in the eye. "I feel it, too," I heard myself say, so quietly. "Maybe I've felt it for a long time. But I'm still . . . mourning my dead."

All my dead, not just Lyonya. Still fighting my way free.

Kostia's fingers folded over mine. "So am I."

He released my hand, took the canoe by its prow, and began towing it back toward shore.

"LYUDMILA!" MRS. ROOSEVELT'S voice suddenly sounded. I looked up as I crossed the lawn toward the big house and realized she was leaning out of a first-floor window. "What on earth happened?"

"Swimming," I said through chattering teeth, arms crossed across my soaked dress. "Without a bathing costume." Yuri, tramping along behind, hadn't offered me his coat. Wasn't part of his directive.

"It's far too cold for bathing," the First Lady scolded, sounding like my mother. "Come here at once. "

I was too numb to resist. I followed the wave of Mrs. Roosevelt's hand toward the vestibule on the side, where she met me and began clucking. "You may stay outside," she told Yuri politely but unmistakably, and even he didn't say a word about his directive to the First Lady as she wafted me into her private quarters. I gave a disjointed explanation about the canoe, hesitating to walk on her exquisite carpets in my soaked shoes, but she shooed me into the attached bathroom and put a big soft towel into my arms. (American towels! I never ceased to marvel at their fluffiness. I was still undecided about hot dogs, but American towels, now . . .) "Undress here, I'll be right back."

"*Izvinite*, I can go to my room," I began, but there was no stopping her. By the time I came out of the bathroom, wrapped up in towels, leaving a pile of wet clothes on the edge of the First Lady's bathtub, she was back with a pair of pajamas and a sewing box. She smiled at my scarlet face, called a maid for my wet clothes, then turned with a matter-of-fact expression as if she was entirely accustomed to have half-naked Soviet snipers dripping on her Persian rugs. "Change into my pajamas, dear."

"W-we are not the same height," I said, teeth still chattering.

"No matter, I'll take a hem in the sleeves and legs."

"B-by y-yourself?"

"*Da,* my Russian friend. Or do you imagine that Roosevelt women are ladies of leisure who never lift a finger?" That was exactly what I'd thought, and she smiled again at my expression. "I assure you, American women know how to work! Now, into the bottoms first . . ."

I was still too bemused to argue as she tactfully turned her back to rummage through her sewing box, and I swam into the pajama bottoms. Heavy rose-pink satin, clearly never worn, with violets embroidered down the seams—I'd never seen anything so lovely in my life, just for *sleeping* in. Normally I slept in one of Lyonya's old shirts, or if it was cold, my winter uniform's woolen under-layers. I left the towel around my torso as the First Lady whipped out a tape measure and took the length of my arms. "You do not need to do this, ma'am," I assayed feebly, but she paid no attention at all, so I submitted to the measuring.

"Goodness," she said behind me, and I knew she was looking at the scar on my back. "What's that, Lyudmila?"

I felt Kostia murmuring against my spine, *Wear it with pride*—felt it so keenly, a shiver went over the entire surface of my skin. "The result of a scrap of metal," I said finally, unable to find the English words for *scar* or *splinter*. "Last December, Sevastopol."

"A mechanical accident?" Mrs. Roosevelt came back around to the front, folding her measuring tape. "Or did it come from fighting the Germans?"

"From battle."

"My poor girl," she said simply. "What dreadful things you've had to endure."

She hugged me. *Hugged* me—I hadn't been hugged since my mother embraced me on the train platform in Moscow. And it shattered me. I felt my shoulders shake, felt the First Lady's arms tighten around my back as I buried my face in her bony shoulder. I had so many broken pieces stabbing me inside, I didn't know what to do but dissolve into that hug and try not to weep. "I lost—so many," I managed to say around deep gulping breaths. Lyonya, Vartanov, Lena, my platoon . . . and now, when I went back to the front, I was going to lose Kostia. Not tomorrow, not the next day, but soon. We'd never fight together again.

The First Lady said nothing. She just held me until I stopped shaking, and then she passed me a handkerchief, just like Mama would have done. I laughed shakily. "You and my mother—you would like each other."

"I'm sure I would. She raised a fine daughter, after all." Mrs. Roosevelt stepped back, going to her sewing box to give me time to scrub at my eyes. "Is your mother pleased at your war record, Lyudmila?"

"She is proud," I said, perching on the edge of the bed as the First Lady seated herself on the other side and threaded a needle. "But she grieves for the history student she waved off to university." I hesitated, wondering if it was defeatist counterpropaganda to say what I wanted to say. "I grieve, too," I admitted finally.

"Do you?" Mrs. Roosevelt took up her scissors, measuring where to cut the too-long sleeves.

"People think I hate the Hitlerites," I said tiredly. "I do hate them. I have to. But I didn't ask to hate them. I grew up dreaming to be a historian, not of killing 309 fascists."

"I know it hurts you when you read articles that call you a killer. Don't look surprised; I saw your face when you read the accounts of your first press conference." *Snip* went her scissors; the ends of the cuffs fell away. "I advise you not to go into politics, where one has to get used to reading such things about oneself."

"You are used to it?" I couldn't help asking.

"If I worried about mudslinging, I would have been dead long ago." The First Lady folded the cut edges of satin over for a new hem. "But I was a shy girl, Lyudmila, and the sight of my name in newspapers once made me cringe. Eventually I grew into my role, but in those early days as a politician's wife . . . well, public criticism had a way of stinging. It takes time to grow a thick skin for insults."

"But your poll numbers are higher than the President's." I remembered hearing that in a Moscow briefing. She was rated "good" by 67 percent of Americans polled, as opposed to her husband's 58 percent.

"I've still been called impudent, presumptuous, meddling. A traitor to my class, a bucktoothed horror, a Negro lover, a Jew lover." She shrugged. "I have heard it all."

"Have they called you *a cold-blooded killer*?" I couldn't repeat the worse ones to her: *Red bitch, communist slut . . .*

" 'A cold-blooded killer with no mercy for the poor enemy soldiers who are merely following the orders of their senior command'?" Eleanor quoted. "I thought that one bothered you the most."

"What do these journalists think I should do, nicely ask all those enemy soldiers to leave? Do they think that would *work*?"

"I believe they didn't know what to think, meeting you. But they're beginning to change their tune, thanks to all your recent public appearances."

"What, because they are starting to get to know me? To like me?" My words came out mocking, but she nodded.

"Is that so impossible? I wasn't at all sure I would like you when I first met you, but I have gotten to know you . . . and now I do like you. The American people are beginning to do the same. Which is why, if you wish to help sway public opinion about sending American soldiers to Europe to aid the USSR, you should consider extending your speaking tour even further."

"I do as my delegation and the Party dictate," I said, heart sinking. Yuri wasn't the only one who had to follow a directive.

"I know you don't want to. I know you dislike the spotlight." The First Lady bit off a thread. "I disliked it, too. I remember my knees shaking the first time I gave a speech."

I could not imagine it, not at all. "How did you do it? Become good at it?"

"I reminded myself that you must do the thing you think you cannot do," she said simply. "Always. And generally you find out you can do it, after all."

"But what if you can't?" I burst out. "What if you fail?"

"You try again—"

"No." I shook my head, reflexive. "It does not work that way. You cannot count on the world giving you second chances when you fail."

She looked thoughtful. "Is that a rule you've made for yourself?"

"The most important rule there is." I quoted the words that breathed in my bones. "*Don't miss.*"

"Oh, my dear. That is no rule to live by."

"It is for a sniper!"

"You think such a rule is exclusive to snipers? *Most* women are haunted by the fear of missing. Of failing."

I blinked, taken aback. "It kept me alive."

"And clearly made you into a brave soldier, but a frightened woman." The First Lady laid down her needle, looking at me with those piercing eyes. "Everyone fails, Lyudmila. I've failed. My husband has failed—you think all his New Deal proposals were dazzling successes? He has proposed initiatives that have fallen flat; he has espoused positions for which he has rightly been condemned; he has hosts of enemies who would happily see him dead." A shadow crossed her face at that. "He has failed at more than most men ever try . . . but better that than not to try at all."

"He is a man," I said harshly, "and an American. He makes mistakes, and the world makes him the only three-term president in your history. The world is not so kind to a woman's mistakes."

"Agreed," she said, surprising me again. "Which is why we women are especially prone to believe we must never stumble. But constant perfection is something at which we will *always* fail, all of us. And despite what you may think, the world won't smite you for the occasional misfire. I daresay you didn't down every enemy you ever had in your sights on the front—yet you're still here, alive, wearing my pajamas. You lost the man you loved—yet I daresay you don't regret loving him, and you may very well have another chance for love someday, because you are very lovable." She picked up her needle and began stitching again. "If at first one doesn't succeed . . . well, I'll spare you the somewhat obnoxious little rhyme I learned in childhood, but *trying again* is something we Yanks believe in very strongly."

"In Russia we believe that if we fail, we die," I stated. "And I have seen nothing in this war to make me disbelieve that."

"But life isn't always going to be war, Lyudmila," she said gently. "And you'll do yourself a grave disservice if you live your every moment—not just your wartime moments, but your gentler ones— by a standard as harsh as *never miss*."

I stared at her, clutching the towel around me, shaken to my core.

"Now let's get these cuffs done." Clearly seeing my distress, the First Lady adopted a brisker tone, holding the pajama top up to my face. "This pink is a lovely color for you . . ."

An hour, a pot of tea, and a plate of biscuits later, there came a knock at the door. But we didn't hear it, because we were talking up a storm. "But to my understanding, women do not regularly serve in the Soviet military," Eleanor was saying. "Even in your own country, it is not entirely common. So how is it that you were able to make the choice to enlist so easily?"

"Because in my home, women are respected not just as females but as individuals." To my relief, the First Lady and I had moved into less

sensitive topics of discussion: first color palettes and fashion dispari-
ties, then the differences between American and Soviet cinema, and
now the complexities of serving in the military as a female. "We do
not feel limitations because of our sex. That is why women like me
took their places beside men so naturally in the army."

"You need to work this into your next speech. I would emphasize
that word *individual*—we Americans are enamored with the idea of
the individual, and assume you Soviets are all about the collective—"

The door opened, and I looked up at the creak of hinges. "What's
this?" said President Roosevelt, looking amused.

I jumped to my feet, shedding biscuit crumbs. I was now wearing the towel around my lower half, upper body draped in the friv-
olous pink flower-embroidered top as Eleanor set the final stitches
on the bottoms. I watched the American president look around his
wife's room—pink satin scraps scattered over the bed, reels of thread
everywhere, teacups drained to the dregs, a half-dressed Soviet sniper.
"Hello, dear," Eleanor said tranquilly, as if she hemmed pajamas for
foreign-born killers every day before dinner.

"This is one of those scenes," the President mused, rubbing his jaw
with that sinewy hand, "that just defies description."

I began to apologize, side-slipping into Russian, but he burst out
laughing. So did Eleanor. And then so did I.

When I went back to my own quarters in my pink satin splendor,
I found my felt cap, which Kostia had scooped from the water into
the canoe, carefully dried now and sitting on a chair beside the door.
I folded it tight in my hands, heart thumping—but I could feel the
First Lady's arms around me in a surprisingly strong hug, and my
battered heart was cautiously exploring the words that still echoed
through my bones in her forthright voice: *The world won't smite you
for the occasional misfire.*

Notes by the First Lady

Something dear Lyudmila said today bothered me deeply. It was when she was departing for her own room, looking no more than sixteen in her pink pajamas and damp hair, and Franklin asked how she was liking Hyde Park. "I sleep well," she replied, straightforward as one of her bullets. "No one can harm me here."

She doesn't know Franklin, so she didn't see the shadow on his face as he answered jovially, "Or me."

When she is gone, I look at my husband and ask, "Who do you think would try to harm you?"

He shrugs the question aside with a tilted grin. "We'll be late for lunch."

"Another Zangara?" I make myself ask. "Another MacGuire?"

Zangara was the assassin who fired five shots at Franklin in Miami in 1933, seventeen days before his inauguration. MacGuire was the American Legion official at the head of a plot to depose my husband in 1934 and install a military dictator. Zangara killed the mayor of Chicago instead of my husband; MacGuire's coup folded and was disappeared into a flurry of House committee hearings. Those men failed.

But there have always been rumors that bigger names—industry names, Wall Street names, names any American would know—were behind both.

"Franklin—" I begin, pulse beginning to pound, but he is already silently taking himself away.

CHAPTER 28

The headline: THE SOVIET DELEGATION RESUMES THEIR GOODWILL TOUR THROUGHOUT THE CITIES OF AMERICA. MR. KRASAVCHENKO AND LIEUTENANT PCHELINTSEV WILL CONTAIN THEIR TRAVELS TO THE EAST COAST, BUT FAMED GIRL SNIPER LYUDMILA PAVLICHENKO HEADS TO DETROIT, CHICAGO, MINNEAPOLIS, SAN FRANCISCO, FRESNO, AND LOS ANGELES. SHE WILL BE ACCOMPANIED ON THE FIRST LEG OF HER JOURNEY BY NONE OTHER THAN THE FIRST LADY . . .

The truth: Thank goodness the presidential limousine had a driver, because if Eleanor Roosevelt proposed to get behind the wheel herself, I'd *walk* to the Midwest.

"I DO NOT understand," I complained as the limousine eased down the highway. "Why have me visit the headquarters of the Ford Motor Company if the workers would not even talk to me?"

"Of course they wouldn't talk to you." The First Lady chuckled. "Ford pays well, and they have a great deal to lose. They worry it will seem suspect if they show too much interest in a visitor from communist Russia, much less her notions about workers' rights!" Mrs. Roosevelt was already taking rapid notes from our tour through the aircraft works and our meeting with Mr. Ford. I came to America assuming the President's wife would be an idle society millionairess, but from what I could see the woman never stopped working. "Your speech went over well, I thought."

I was less certain, but I was already starting off this tour on a sour note: another of those ominous threats had found its way under my hotel-room door this morning. IT'S NOT ENOUGH TO LEAVE WASHINGTON, YOU MURDERING CUNT. GO HOME NOW OR YOU'LL GO HOME IN A BOX.

Was my enemy stalking me across the country now? Or was it someone inside the delegation? Darkly, I thought of Alexei. I wouldn't put it past him to try to terrify his own wife, just so she'd feel like fleeing into sheltering arms. If he thought *that* would work—!

"Five hours to Chicago," Eleanor said, interrupting my brooding, and I looked through the bulletproof glass at the flaming autumn trees by the roadside. Five hours . . . I wished I'd brought a book, like Kostia. He had a leather-bound copy of some poems by a Mr. Walt Whitman, on loan from the First Lady's library. "How is it?" I asked, slipping back into Russian.

"Perplexing." He had my English dictionary on his other knee and kept flipping back and forth between the two. The watery autumn sun slanted through the bulletproof window over his black hair. "What's *pokeweed*?"

"I don't know. I feel like I should get a sample of it for Slavka." I took a deep breath—no one in the car would understand us; neither the First Lady nor her secretary spoke enough Russian; the driver and guard were separated by a partition; the ever-present Yuri was riding in the security car behind us with Alexei (who had somehow talked himself onto my half of the tour)—but I was still shy to voice the question. "How was your visit to New York?" My partner had been at the Soviet embassy in Washington when we returned from the Roosevelt estate, but I hadn't dared ask a thing about his family within embassy walls. "Did you . . ."

His smile stayed invisible as he turned a page. "Yes."

"Lyudmila, do look out the window," the First Lady called. "This flat land in Michigan, does it remind you of your native steppes?" Kilometer after kilometer, the limousine rolled along as Eleanor pointed out the cities she knew from her coast-to-coast traveling.

She was proud of her country, I could hear it in her voice—certainly she thought it superior to anything found in Russia, which made me grin privately. The towns and cities ticked by, *Ann Arbor, Albion, Kalamazoo* . . . then the vast shores of Lake Michigan like a sea, and my eyes blurred as I remembered the Black Sea bordering Odessa.

"You're homesick," Mrs. Roosevelt said, reading my face with a glance. "You'll be home soon enough, my dear—and if we're lucky enough to see this war end soon, you'll be able to return to your studies rather than your platoon."

"I would be able to finish my dissertation." I sighed. "Would you like to see? A study of Bogdan Khmelnitsky, the Ukraine's accession to Russia in 1654—"

I could have sworn Kostia gave a cough of warning on my other side, but the First Lady listened with every appearance of fascination, only interrupting me to point out the high sand dunes that had begun to appear on the landscape the farther south we drove.

"It is a beautiful country," I admitted, leaning past her to look out. "You people here live in such peaceful conditions. I keep looking around and wondering where the bomb damage is . . . such a land of luxury."

"But?" she said, hearing the note in my voice.

"A land of destitution, too." I looked her in the eye. "I see enough of the poorer parts of your cities to know that American Negroes live very badly."

"It's true we have a long way to go," she acknowledged calmly. "America fights prejudice abroad but tolerates it at home. Segregation warps and twists the lives of our Negro population; that is beyond doubt. Things must change."

"How?"

"Work," she said, flourishing her pen. "It isn't enough to believe in equality and peace and human rights—one must work at it."

I grinned. "For an American millionairess you have a work ethic a Russian would approve of."

"And you have an ability to laugh that any American would approve of," the First Lady replied. "*Punch* cartoons and Hollywood would have us all believing that Soviets have no sense of humor."

"Life can be hard for us. We have to laugh at it." I remembered a joke my darling Lena had told me. "What did one German soldier say to the other when they reached the Russian front?"

"What?"

" 'Look at that cute Russian girl eyeing me over there.' His friend says, 'Why not go say hello?' His friend replies, 'Because she's eyeing me with her scope.' "

Eleanor laughed. More kilometers slipped by; conversation giving way to silence and then to drowsiness. At some point I dozed off, giving a great start when the limousine stopped. My eyelids were gummy, and I felt a weight against my shoulder—Kostia's dark head.

"You dropped off at the same time," Mrs. Roosevelt said, eyes crinkling down at me, and I realized I had fallen asleep with my head on *her* shoulder. "Wake up now, my darling," she continued as I sat upright, pink with embarrassment, thinking *Please let me not have drooled on the First Lady!* "We are in Chicago. A famous American poet once called it 'the city of the big shoulders,' you know."

"We have bad poetry in the Soviet Union, too," I consoled, and she burst out laughing.

DON'T THEY LOOK *fresh and rested,* the marksman thought sourly, watching Lyudmila Pavlichenko and the First Lady take the bunting-draped stage, waving to the cheering crowds below. He'd spent five hours following the presidential entourage in a shoebox-sized Packard, cramped and irritable—*he* hadn't arrived in Chicago bright-eyed and rested like the girl sniper.

A dazzle of flashbulbs went off, and the marksman noticed she no longer flinched as though grenades were exploding in her face. He'd thought she'd be more nervous, especially after he'd bribed a hotel maid to get another of his anonymous threats shoved under her door. In Washington, it had seemed to be working. She'd been visibly nervous at the opera, and at the conference reception she glanced repeatedly over her shoulder as though looking for her stalker. She'd looked off-balance, which was precisely his aim. But now she appeared poised and professional as she gave a short speech through her interpreter—and people were responding, damn it. The marksman had been convinced she'd never be the success the Soviets hoped for on this goodwill tour—asking an American audience to warm to a woman who had supposedly killed 309 men was absurd. But the audience here in Chicago was ecstatic.

"All right," he mused aloud under the hubbub of the crowd, jingling the little rocks of uncut diamonds in his pocket. "So she's a success." That just proved she was a seasoned propagandist, not a sniper. Only a professional could have pulled this off . . . and she'd charmed the First Lady, to boot. They kept putting their heads together in conversational lulls onstage, sharing some private joke. *Let's see how you're smiling by the time we hit Los Angeles,* thought the marksman. It was the new plan: slip into the cortege of hangers-on shadowing the presidential entourage as it snaked west and insert himself so that he became part of the scenery, unremarkable and unremarked upon. He'd already contacted Pocket Square, made sure his name passed the First Lady's security without a hiccup. No one would give him a second glance, and he'd have all the time in the world to stay in the background until they came to the City of Angels . . . where President Roosevelt, who had been making a private tour of the nation's defense plants, was scheduled to arrive for a joint appearance with his wife and Lyudmila Pavlichenko.

That was when the shot would now be fired.

And wouldn't the First Lady be surprised to see her new friend plummet from the heights, no longer a national heroine but a Soviet John Wilkes Booth. MRS. ROOSEVELT BEFRIENDS HER HUSBAND'S KILLER—that would be a headline worth reading.

The marksman realized, watching the two women leave the stage, that he was looking forward to that with a visceral, spiteful satisfaction. He hadn't felt much of anything about Lyudmila Pavlichenko when he first watched her disembark at the doors of the White House a few weeks ago, only a mild curiosity as he set about framing her for the assassination of the century.

Now, having been dragged all over the country tailing the Red bitch and already planning his next set of anonymously scrawled Cyrillic threats, he wanted to see her fall.

"MRS. PAVLICHENKO, SO delightful to gaze on your face again!"

At first I didn't recognize the man—linen suit, slightly pop eyes—but then I felt the damp, fervent fingers wringing mine, and remembered the millionaire I'd met in Baltimore. "Mr. Jonson, here you are . . . all the way from Maryland."

"I would have greeted you in Detroit," he said, starry-eyed. "But Mr. Ford's headquarters have very strict security."

"Don't they here?" I couldn't help asking. The First Lady and I had been invited to visit the Chicago Sharpshooters' Association; you'd think a firearms club would have more armed guards at the door. "How did you—"

"Oh, I bought a ticket. And I would buy a dozen for a chance to meet with you again. Would you like a handkerchief, it's very hot—"

"*Nyet*. Mr. Jonson—"

"William!"

"William, I have been asked to visit with the association chairman." I extricated my hands from his clammy ones and made my way toward the weapon racks, shaking off journalists piping *Mrs. Pavlichenko . . . Mrs. Pavlichenko . . .* like a chorus of baby birds. So many of them! I kept trying to put faces to names, but they were simply too numerous to keep straight.

"Smile for the camera, *kroshka,*" Alexei murmured, managing to get his arm around my shoulder and turn me neatly toward the nearest flashbulb, thumb caressing the back of my neck. I shrugged him away with a warning glance and finally managed to find the head of the Sharpshooters' Association, waiting not too patiently to have his picture taken with me.

"What do you think of our American weapons, Miz Pavlichenko?" he harrumphed, and I wasn't surprised to see skeptical glances between the clubmen. Did they think I couldn't hear the whispers? *That girl they're calling a sniper doesn't know one end of a rifle from another . . .*

"Is this a M1 Garand?" I asked the chairman through Kostia, strolling along the club's gun racks. "Very similar to the Sveta we use on the eastern front—the diverting propellant gas through the port in the bore to unlock the breech." I took the self-loading rifle off the rack, gave it a quick inspection, lifted it to my shoulder to sight along its length. "Weaver sights, very nice."

Surprised looks, which I pretended not to see. "What do you think of this one, Miz Pavlichenko? Our M1903 Springfield."

"Yes, much more like the Three Line I used. I prefer a sliding bolt in field conditions. The nonautomatic safety catch here is very similar to the German army Mauser Zf. Kar. 98k, as well—"

I chatted about Soviet rifles and how they compared to various Allied models, urging the chairman to break the 1903 down with me so I could examine the trigger mechanisms and exclaim over the pull weight, the crispness, the feel of the hammerfall. The older men were grinning by the end. Even the watching corps of journalists looked grudgingly impressed, and William Jonson was starry-eyed. "Oh,

Mrs. Pavlichenko, how I wish you would favor us with a demonstration."

I hesitated. I'd always refused such invitations before today. I wasn't
a trick pony performing on command; I was a soldier. A journalist in
Detroit had compared me to some American circus shooter he called
Annie Oakley, asking if I could shoot over my shoulder while looking
at a mirror, and I told him that skills like mine weren't meant for
big-top tents or party games. But these shooting club fellows looked
so keen—the older men had the look of veterans, men who remembered what blood smelled like when mixed into mud, and the younger
ones were so cherry-cheeked and innocent . . . yet they were the ones
who'd go off to fight, if the First Lady's plan to sell the idea of a second front through me succeeded. Mrs. Roosevelt was speaking with
an Army colonel on the other side of the room, but I could have sworn
she gave me a tiny nod from the corner of her eye.

"*Nu ladno*," I said with a grin, and the men cheered.

My hands were trembling just a little by the time we'd hashed out
the demonstration's details: 100 meters distance, prone unsupported,
ten shots, ten minutes to shoot, iron sights. *You haven't fired a rifle for
a month and a half,* the voice inside my head scolded. *A professional
needs to shoot at least twice a week to keep in practice!* Was I supposed to
defend my own reputation and the honor of the Red Army with rusty
skills and an unfamiliar weapon?

"She'll need someone to shoot against," Kostia volunteered in En-
glish as we came to the range, unexpectedly. I blinked as a clamor of
Americans jostled forward. "No, someone she'll have trouble beating.
Another Russian." He grinned, provoking just the right chorus of
laughs and catcalls. "If you'll lend me a 1903, I'll join Lieutenant
Pavlichenko. Comrade Yuripov, would you care to join us?"

"That is not part of my directive," said Yuri against the wall.

"Our delegation doctor, then." Kostia gave a bland smile. "He fan-
cies himself a keen shot."

My head jerked up as Alexei sauntered forward in his western pin-stripes from the cluster of delegation hangers-on, taking a rifle from the nearest hand. "Delighted," he said in the English he was clearly making an effort to pick up on this tour.

"And I'll join you," William Jonson said eagerly, coming forward so fast he nearly tripped over his own shoelaces. "I fancy I can match any embassy doctor, ha-ha! Done a little pigeon-shooting in my boy-hood, 'deed I did . . ."

"What are you doing?" I hissed to Kostia in Russian, but he just carried on loading his own rifle with a quick flash of his hands. We all took position, settling ourselves on the ground belly-down, and took five or six calibration shots to familiarize ourselves with our weapons, then waited for new paper targets: me lying between my husband and my partner; Mr. Jonson, who kept shifting his rifle's barrel with a carelessness that made me twitch; and a handful of the older Americans who proclaimed they had fought in the Great War. The call to begin went out, Lady Midnight began the countdown, and the world fell away.

Ten shots. My first went a few centimeters wide of the bull's-eye; from how the round landed, I could tell I'd jerked the trigger rather than squeezing it. I steadied myself, not letting the miss sting me. This wasn't the battlefield; death wouldn't claim me because I was a few centimers short of perfect. By the second shot, the unfamiliar rifle whispered, *There.* When I saw the bullet hit that time, I was grinning. Kostia was already sighting his third shot alongside me, an American with gray brush-cut hair just behind us. Kostia's 1903 and mine thundered in unison, and I knew that was a pair of bull's-eyes. Our hands flew in tandem, our rifles barked in tandem, and it was just like old times. No, better—cleaner, the smell of gunpowder unmarred by the smell of blood.

I didn't need ten minutes to make my ten shots. I didn't even need five.

Everyone rose as the last shots from the stragglers tailed in and crowded around the paper targets. Whoops went up as the hits were tallied. "Lady Death takes it!" I grinned, dusting off the front of my dress and wondering what my scarred firearms instructor would say if he could see his pupil now. Wondering if he was still training snipers in Kiev, if he still lived . . .

"Goddamn, I ain't lost a contest that bad since aught nine." The American with the gray brush-cut hair hair offered me a hand like oak. He'd come third, right after Kostia, and I could hardly understand his odd drawl. "I reckon your Siberian boy here could shoot the eye out of a muskrat at three miles if the wind was right, Miz Pavlichenko—and you could probably do it at five. I'd ask you to marry me, if I didn't have a missus at home already who wouldn't care for no Russki sniper gal bunking in her spare room. Care to raise a glass with me instead?"

"And me," gushed William Jonson, who hadn't even managed to hit the target most of the time. He lit up a Lucky Strike, waving it enthusiastically. "A wonderful demonstration, Mrs. Pavlichenko!"

Bottles of brandy and whiskey began appearing; up in the gallery with Colonel Douglas, the First Lady looked faintly disapproving. I waved up to her, unrepentant. This was a soldiers' gathering, a shooters' gathering, and for the first time since coming to America I felt honestly at home. One of the delegation flunkies bleated a reminder at me to let Kostia interpret rather than use my English, but I ignored him. I didn't want a filter between me and these men; I was done with filters. Out of the corner of my eye, I saw Alexei toss his 1903 aside with a curt gesture, and grinned. He'd come in fifth out of ten.

"Good try," I called to him in Russian. He glared and I fluttered my fingers, murmuring to Kostia, "Why *did* you invite him to join?"

"Because you were nervous," my partner returned. "But once he stepped to the line there was no way this side of the Arctic Circle you'd let him win."

I laughed, tossing down a shot of American whiskey that tasted like a wood fire. "I gutted him, didn't I?"

"Like a fish."

"Will you be able to give your usual speech tonight?" the First Lady asked as we settled back into the limousine, giving a disapproving shake of her head.

"It was not very much whiskey. Americans, they don't know how to drink. Forty milliliters is not enough for a proper toast." Just enough to warm my cheeks, which were still smiling from a half hour with the American shooters. The chatter over the glasses had all been war stories—they asked for mine from this year; I asked for theirs from the Great War—and then they had presented me with the mahogany box now sitting in my lap. "Have you ever seen anything so pretty?" I burst out, lifting the lid on my gift again: a pair of Colt M1911A1 pistols, brand new and gleaming, and two magazines with cartridges.

"In New York you were given a full-length lynx coat." The First Lady looked amused as I gleefully took one of the Colts out and began examining it right there in the passenger seat. "In Detroit, you were given six dozen roses. Yet you turn starry-eyed over a pair of pistols?"

"This is much better than the last time I got a pistol." That had been in Sevastopol, when General Petrov told me to keep the last bullet for myself rather than be taken alive and suffer what the Germans did to women snipers. I blinked that memory away, examining the various mechanism parts of my new Colt. "Ah, .45 caliber! Made by Browning, you know that? Adopted by your army in 1911, then by ours in the last war . . ."

Mrs. Roosevelt laughed. "Play with your new toy later, my dear. We're almost at Grant Park."

Maybe it was the whiskey, maybe it was having the reassuring song of a rifle back in my ears, or maybe it was the fact I'd finally, *finally* managed to wipe the serene look off Alexei's face—but something went through me when I found myself in the park on yet another flag-draped stage, looking out at yet another crowd of middle-aged men.

"The floor is yours, Mrs. Pavlichenko—"

"Lieutenant Pavlichenko, *spasibo*." I stepped forward and began my speech, painting the war raging in my far-off home as Kostia translated. One of the men in the front row stood jingling his hands in his pockets, watching me with a cold gaze; a journalist stood fiddling with his camera and looking bored; a cluster of city officials were eyeing my uniform as though it were a costume. *None of you believe I've really fought in a war,* I thought. The men I'd met at the range today, they believed me. Many of them had been veterans; they knew a real soldier when they saw one pull a trigger. But these audiences I faced in city after city, these people I faced armed with nothing but my voice—what did they know?

Let them know now, I thought, and the thought for once was not bitter or angry. It filled me with a fierce pride.

"Gentlemen," I called sharp and loud, abandoning my planned speech. I waited until I had all the eyes that might have wandered, and then I planted my boots wide on the platform with a sound like a coffin knock, clasping my hands behind me in parade rest. "Gentlemen, I am twenty-six years old. At the front, I have already eliminated 309 fascist soldiers and officers. Don't you think, gentlemen, that you have been hiding for too long behind my back?"

I let the challenge hang in the air.

For an instant, the crowd was silent. Then a roar of applause drifted out across Grant Park, men surging to their feet, ladies waving their hats, journalists raising their cameras. I looked at Kostia, and meeting his eyes through the flashbulbs, I could have sworn I saw Lyonya at his shoulder.

He was smiling.

THE BITCH CAN *shoot.*

The marksman hadn't been able to think anything else since watching Lyudmila Pavlichenko sink ten superb shots at 100 meters with an unfamiliar weapon in three minutes. He'd gone through the motions of admiration with the rest of the crowd at the range, but the words had pounded through him over and over: *The bitch can shoot.*

He couldn't even tell himself he was watching a target shooter, a gun-club competitor. There was range expertise and there was *real* expertise, the cold kind practiced until it was part of the blood. He'd seen a flash of it when she first handled her rifle—and then she'd taken position on the firing line, and he'd seen Lady Death unhood her eyes. The sparkling brunette with her warm gaze had disappeared; the sniper with 309 enemies on her tally flared to life. By the time she sank that last bull's-eye, he believed she'd bagged every one of those kills on the eastern front.

God damn, the marksman thought numbly, watching her stand on this Grant Park stage as half of Chicago howled her name, *she's the real deal.* A hundred small impressions were slotting into place now: the way she held her cigarettes in a reversed, cupped hand, to keep the ember from showing; the way her eyes flicked as she entered new rooms, establishing exits and movement lines. Why hadn't he realized?

You didn't want to, the answer came. *You didn't think it was possible.*

Well, it was. Lady Death, here in the flesh. A pint-sized Russian woman who had just thrown back her head on an American stage and told every red-blooded man in that audience to stop hiding behind her back.

I would happily shoot you face-to-face, the marksman thought, watching her fierce eyes prowl over the wildly applauding crowd like those of a predatory lynx. *But tomorrow I have a president to kill in Los Angeles, and a slip of a Soviet girl to pin it on.*

CHAPTER 29

The headline: IN THE WAKE OF HER NOW-FAMOUS CHALLENGE TO THE CITIZENS OF AMERICA, LYUDMILA PAVLICHENKO TRAVELS TO THE CITY OF ANGELS. HOLLYWOOD ROYALTY THE LIKES OF DOUGLAS FAIRBANKS JR., MARY PICKFORD, AND CHARLIE CHAPLIN ARE LINING UP TO HOST THE GIRL SNIPER . . .

The truth: "You were wonderful in *The Mark of Zorro,* Mr. Fairbanks" was not my best conversational opening, considering the actor's drunken response was "That wash my father Douglash Fairbanksh Shenior."

"BRILLIANT AS ALWAYS, Mrs. Pavlichenko! Champagne?"

"*Nu ladno,* Mr. Jonson," I sighed. In a dinner jacket, no less, but he just looked even more pop-eyed and irritating. I hastily took the flute of champagne before he could seize my hand. "I did not think you would come to Los Angeles."

"I submitted a request to the First Lady herself! I had something very particular to ask you, and her people put me on the list today . . ."

I blinked, coming down from the now-familiar sensation of having shaken two hundred hands, posed for two hundred photographs, and answered two hundred inane questions. "Ask me what, Mr. Jonson?"

"Lyudmila, I've invited you to call me William," he chided.

"William, are you intending to hear every speech I give from Washington to Fresno? How much free time do you have?"

Too much, clearly. I bolted half my champagne, hoping it would kill the headache I'd been nursing since Chicago. I hadn't slept well after the Grant Park event—the First Lady assured me it had been a resounding success ("I wouldn't be surprised if Reuters reported that speech worldwide, my dear"), but ever since, I'd felt like I had spiders running down my spine. It wasn't even due to the appearance of yet another ugly note in my hotel room (I'M GOING TO RIP YOUR SPINE OUT AND CHOKE YOU WITH IT, YOU STALIN-LOVING BITCH)—I realized I was becoming almost inured to the hateful things. Given that whoever sent them was following me on the road, it seemed fairly obvious it was someone in the delegation, and even more obvious that that person was Alexei, and though I'd registered this suspicion with delegation security in no uncertain terms, I refused to be frightened by the notes anymore, *or* give my husband the satisfaction of confronting him. No, it wasn't the anonymous notes. Something else was bothering me, at a level so low I could hardly register it.

Something I'd seen, something I'd heard? On the front line I could keep watch so closely that not a single leaf's fall in the nightscape before me would pass unnoticed, but this tour had been such an avalanche of sights and sounds, something easily could have got lost in the hubbub. And I felt like something had, but couldn't put my finger on what.

"You know I am a widower, of course," Mr. Jonson was still yattering.

"I do? That is, yes, *da*—"

"And I read in the newspaper that you too were married. You lost your husband at Sevastopol—"

My second, unfortunately. Not my first. "Yes," I said, thinking how Lyonya would have roared with laughter at this entire exchange.

"Then, my darling Lyudmila, why should we not salve our mutual loneliness? If you would but make me the happiest of—"

"*Chto?*" My attention snapped back to the man who was now gripping my hand regardless of the empty champagne flute in it. "Mr. Jonson—"

"William!"

"Mr. Jonson, you are out of your mind."

"From the moment I saw you speaking in New York, my heart told me you were the only possible wife for me. Will you marry me?"

"YOU COULD ACCEPT his offer, you know."

I paused, buttered roll halfway to my lips. "Are you serious, Eleanor?" The First Lady had invited me to use her first name, but this was the first time I'd done so.

"Why not?" Across the small table from me, Eleanor unfolded her napkin. The delegation had taken to having meals privately after these receptions, since whenever the First Lady and I turned up to dine at a restaurant, the entire meal turned into hours of autograph signing. Kostia, Yuri, and the rest were already tucking in at the table across the private dining room. "Mr. Jonson is perhaps a trifle eccentric, but pleasant and well-bred," Eleanor went on. "He has not deceived you as to his background and prospects: he is a widower, he does in fact own a metallurgical company, his finances and reputation are sterling. Such men are investigated," she answered in response to my puzzled look, "when they begin following my entourage from state to state. Mr. Jonson's proposal of marriage may be sudden, but it seems sincere."

I snorted. "I have only met him a few times!"

"But to marry a gentleman of means who is madly in love with you—it's as much a guarantee of security and safety as the whims of fate give a woman." She smiled, reaching for her salad fork. "You would remain here in our country, and I would welcome the chance to continue our friendship."

"So would I, but—" I dropped my roll, rising to pick up a copy of the *Chicago Tribune* I had carried off the plane. "Look at this: *Mrs. Pavlichenko is in raptures over American food, eating five helpings at breakfast every morning.* Blatant lies. Where do they even get such things, and why are they obsessed with such nonsense?" I laid the paper down again, cheeks heating, fighting for the right words in English. "In your country I am the object of idle curiosity. A circus act, like a bearded woman. At home I am an officer of the Red Army. I have *fought*, and I am not a freak because I have fought. There are other women like me." I thought of what I'd told her about how Soviet women had full independence as human beings, not just as women. "This tour—this is my fight now. But soon I will go home, and I will go on fighting for the freedom and independence of *my* country. Not join yours, as much as I have grown to appreciate it."

I realized the other table had heard my outburst. Kostia's face was still, watching me. I flushed and sat back down, tearing my discarded roll into scraps. When I looked up at Mrs. Roosevelt, I saw a strange wistful smile on her face. I'd said there were no women like me in America—well, there were no women here like her, either. Was that why she had befriended me, why she had so liked the idea that I might stay in this country? Because she too felt like a circus act at times?

"We will forget Mr. Jonson," she said simply, pushing the bread-basket across the table. "I'll have his name struck off the list of any future events here, before I return to Washington."

"Thank you," I said, feeling rather embarrassed now for my impassioned words. "You aren't staying through the President's arrival?"

"Yes, about that . . ."

GOD DAMN THAT *Soviet bitch to hell and back,* thought the marksman. He'd just received word: President Roosevelt had quietly canceled his Southern California appearances. His tour of the nation's defense plants had been under a press blackout, but alert Washington operators already knew the President's special train had headed back toward the capital, and Pocket Square had duly telephoned with the update. Maybe it wasn't Lyudmila Pavlichenko's fault that the presidential cripple hadn't felt up to a press leg at the end of his private tour, but the marksman decided he'd blame her anyway. Lady Death was murdering his usually excellent luck on the job.

Idling through the hotel lobby, avoiding the NKVD minders and their stony eyes, he flipped through the remainder of the itinerary. Some Hollywood party; more speeches; then the trip to Fresno . . . *Fresno*, for Christ's sake. The marksman remembered a two-for-one job there a few years back, knocking off a couple of executives who'd been dipping in the company funds. Lousy town full of lousy farm hicks, and now he had to go *back*, after already trailing that woman from Detroit to Chicago to Los Angeles? That was a hell of a lot of travel considering how little he had to show for it: a lot of nights in anonymous hotels, a backache from so many hours behind the wheel of that tin-can Packard, and no damned shot at Roosevelt. He might as well have cooled his heels in Washington and waited for her to return, not run all over the country trying to manufacture a chance at a target that never showed up. And now fucking *Fresno*.

It's your own fault, he told himself, still fuming. Normally he *would* have stayed in Washington rather than follow the tour: kept well back, gathered any information he needed from third parties. Less contact, less trouble, less danger. But no, he'd decided on a more personal approach with this job. Had he really let *curiosity* get the better of him, after so many years of distant professionalism?

The Soviet delegation came rolling through the doors, back from the evening's reception. The marksman eyed Lyudmila Pavlichenko over the edge of his newspaper as she paused at the front desk. The night clerk passed over a sealed envelope; the girl sniper raised her eyebrows as she reached for a paper knife. The marksman sat forward a little, knowing exactly what words greeted her: WATCH YOUR BACK, SOVIET WHORE. He'd never seen her open one of his missives before. He hoped she'd blanch, tremble, look over her shoulder . . .

She rolled her eyes. It was unmistakable—she *rolled her eyes.* "An-other one," she said in Russian to the blocky minder at her shoulder, balling up the letter and tossing it at him, and then she was sweep-ing off toward the hotel elevator. Heading upstairs to her luxurious whore's bed and a good night's sleep, no doubt. Having herself a good *chuckle.*

The marksman came to a sudden decision as she disappeared from sight. Tossing down his newspaper, he made for the hotel doors and the warm night outside. "Taxi," he told the bellboy curtly. No more orange groves, no more Beverly Hills chatter, and no goddamn Fresno: he was abandoning the Packard and his current cover identity and getting a flight back to Washington. Lady Death had to return to the capital at some point—he'd get her (and the President) then.

It occurred to him, settling into the taxi, that getting Lyudmila Pavlichenko now seemed just as important as getting FDR. Before, he'd left his plans open: frame her or kill her, whichever proved sim-pler.

He reckoned he'd just decided.

"ARE YOU TIRED of signing autographs yet?" Laurence Olivier gave me his trademark burning glance: every bit as handsome in person as he was on the screen. Lena would have had him up against the wall and his trousers down by now. His hand drifted to my lower back as he remarked, "I always thought autograph hunting was the most unat-tractive manifestation of sex-starved curiosity."

Slide your hand any lower, and you'll be drawing back a stump, I thought. A popping sound made me start, but it was only a cham-pagne cork. Beside the wide French doors thrown open to the balmy California night, I could see the actress Mary Pickford throw her head back in laughter at something the silver-sequined Myrna Loy was whispering in her ear: this graceful Italianate house was packed to the rafters with film stars. Not that I knew who half of them were; I hadn't seen many Western films. My poor friend Sofya from Odessa, she'd have known every face after all her covert poring over Western film magazines—she'd have been thrilled to her toes for a chance to meet Mary Pickford at a Hollywood party. I'd just been bemused. And missing Sofya . . .

"Charlie Chaplin is throwing a bash for the delegation at Breakaway House—that's his home in Beverly Hills," the staff of the Soviet consulate had told me giddily that afternoon after a luncheon event, an embassy meeting, and a speech at a hotel overlooking the long blue rollers of the Pacific. "Now that the First Lady is away"—Eleanor had had to depart for Washington that morning, leaving me with a fond hug—"we'll have a chance for a little fun!" So far I'd had my hand kissed by Charlie Chaplin, my champagne poured by Tyrone Power, and my backside appreciated by Laurence Olivier.

I smacked his hand off as it drifted downward, but the Englishman didn't appear offended. He just laughed, tucking a strand of my hair behind my ear. "No need to be so tense and watchful, darling. You might get stabbed in the back at a Hollywood party, but no one's going to shoot you."

"Very clever, Mr. Olivier."

"Do call me Larry."

"*Nyet,*" I stated. The film star reminded me far too much of Alexei: the same glitter, the same charm, the same complete inability to hear the word *no.*

"Charlie's got a swimming pool at the bottom of the slope," Call Me Larry was purring, oblivious. "Why don't we slip away for a little private party while your friends are enjoying themselves?"

The Soviet consulate people certainly *were* enjoying themselves, taking over this sumptuous space with its French doors, its ink-black grand piano, its silver platters of hors d'oeuvres and ice buckets of champagne on every surface. Even Yuri was positively giggling as he watched Charlie Chaplin grip a bottle of champagne between his teeth and walk on his hands across the marble floors.

Hollywood people, I mused. If Americans sometimes seemed strange to me, these film stars seemed even stranger. Breezy, informal, not nearly as inclined to bristle at socialist ideas as guests at a Washington party . . . but they seemed to perform more than exist, and I wasn't sure they saw my uniform as anything more than one of the outlandish costumes they were all wearing.

Suddenly I wanted some fresh air. "Excuse me, Mr. Olivier"— peeling his hand off my hip again—"I need more champagne."

"Drink *me,* you darling little killer. I'm like a vintage wine—you have to swill me down before I turn sour!"

I managed to fight my way free, through the crowd on the terrace outside and toward the long, sloped lawn leading away from Breakaway House. "I see we're both looking for some quiet," Kostia said, melting out of the shadows in his silent way.

"At least Yuri's not breathing down my neck for once." My partner and I wandered down the long stretch of grass, which did indeed lead to a swimming pool far below. "Who'd have guessed he was so starstruck?"

"Apparently he used to shadow a Moscow bigwig with a liking for private showings of forbidden Western films," Kostia said.

We'd had our own private cinema showing tonight: *The Great Dictator,* Charlie Chaplin's most famous film, showed in his small personal theater. I'd seen some strange things in my life, but not much was stranger than watching a man strut and posture across a flickering screen, then turning and seeing the same man sitting on my right, all friendly smiles, watching for my reaction. I'd never seen a Chaplin film before; he seemed like an odd pop-eyed little man, not how I envisioned a film star.

"What did you think of *The Great Dictator?*" Kostia asked, reading my thoughts.

"I don't know if I can laugh at Hitler." I shortened my stride to match Kostia's slight limp, since he'd come outside without his cane. "Maybe we should—laughter makes men small. But I've seen too many Hitlerites coming at me with rifles and tanks to find them funny."

"You're philosophical," my partner observed.

"Only at noisy parties." I didn't feel alone in a sniper's nest at midnight, but I frequently felt alone in crowds—which was why I was here outside, and Kostia, too. That's where you find two snipers at a party: away from the crowd, in the dark, alone. And happy to be there.

"I hate almost all parties," Kostia confessed. I was still in uniform, but he was in black tie again. He'd left the jacket somewhere inside and his sleeves were pushed up, hands stuffed in his pockets.

"You didn't seem to hate this one so much when you had two film stars draped over you earlier," I couldn't help saying. Myrna Loy and Mary Pickford, learning that my interpreter was a sniper himself, had asked to see the hands of an expert marksman, had gushed over his calluses, had cooed like doves when he cracked walnuts effortlessly between his cast-iron fingers. "Myrna Loy was nearly sitting on your lap."

"Charlie Chaplin kissed your hand," Kostia pointed out. "And went down on one knee."

"That was embarrassing." The actor had proclaimed he was ready to kiss every finger on my hand for those 309 Fritzes I had put into the ground—and then he did it, lingeringly, damply, as cameras flashed and I resisted the urge to wipe my fingers on my uniform.

Another champagne cork popped in the distance. It made my partner and me tense briefly; we traded smiles and Kostia handed me down the half wall above the swimming pool at the bottom of the long lawn. The house at the top of the slope was barely visible from here; I saw bouncing shadows of half-drunk actors—I could have sworn I saw Yuri's square silhouette dancing on top of the piano—and heard the distant strains of "Song of the Volga Boatmen," undoubtedly being played in Soviet honor. The night was warm; autumn had already come to the Midwest, but it had yet to touch down in the City of Angels. The swimming pool shimmered only faintly in the dark; it was a new moon, almost no light at all. That didn't matter. Kostia and I, we could see in the dark like it was noon.

We sat down at the edge. I kicked off my heels so I could lower my feet into the cool water, and Kostia rolled up his trousers to do the same. "Your visit in New York," I began, thinking maybe he could tell me about his family now—no one in earshot here, much less anyone who could speak Russian—but he shook his head.

"Later."

I nodded, looking down at the water, dark blue and shimmering. I'd never seen a private swimming pool before, marble-tiled and sumptuous, all for one person to enjoy alone—or *not* alone. My heart ratcheted up into my throat, and I swallowed. "Let's swim."

I peeled out of my uniform, down to my new silky American underthings, and entered the water with a neat dive. Kostia shed his black-tie finery like a fish leaving its scales behind in a scatter of silver, slipping into the water seemingly without disturbing the surface. A second later I felt steel-strong hands link around my wrist and yank me into the deep end; I pivoted underwater and got my heels into his ribs, yanking free as an underwater laugh surprised me in a stream of bubbles. We thrashed and fought and finally fetched up gasping for breath on the far edge of the deep end, arms folded side by side on the lip of the pool, bodies hanging light in the water. My heart was still cannoning inside my chest.

"Your leg," I managed to say, nodding down through the ripples toward the livid scar I'd seen on his leg when he dived in. The gash gouged from the knee almost to the ankle. "From the end of Sevastopol . . . I know all your other scars but that one."

A drop of water slid down his sharp jaw. I resisted the urge to smooth it away. "Do you?"

"Of course I do. I was never more than a few meters away from you whenever you were wounded." I wasn't sure exactly what I was saying, just that I had to keep putting words into this dark, bottomless silence. "You didn't usually get hit badly enough to land in the hospital battalion; you were always luckier than me. But you got the bad cut on your trigger hand at the beginning of the Sevastopol siege—" I was talking too fast. Forcing myself to slow down, I nodded at the ridged line running along his thumb where it rested on the pool's tiled edge. "The slash from a German combat knife, clearing out that nest of snipers on No-Name Height." I reached up to touch the puckered seam running along the crown of his head under the razored-short hair. "And the splinter wound on the back of your neck, the one I stitched up for you in Sevastopol." Sliding my fingers across the jagged mark on his neck. I let my hand stay there, resting against his pulse. "Four near misses," I said quietly.

He didn't name my scars, but his hand found them under the water—sliding over the hip I'd wrenched outside Gildendorf; running up my spine along the forked shrapnel scar, up through my wet hair to find the splinter wound from Odessa, coming to rest on the side of my face, fingers brushing the ear that had had to be stitched back to my head. "Those are just the scars we can see."

Lyonya, I knew we were both thinking.

And then Kostia was looking at me through the dark, thinking *I love you.* He didn't need to say it for me to hear it. I took a deep, unsteady breath, looking down at the tiled ledge where my hand had found his and linked finger to finger.

"You're my partner," I said unsteadily. "You're my shadow. My other half. I trust you like no one else in this world. No one can do what we've done and not be closer than two humans can ever be, in this world or the next." My parents, my child, my friends, either of the men I'd called husband—none of them knew me like Kostia. No one would ever know Kostia like me.

His trigger-calloused forefinger caressed my knuckles. "You could have just said *I love you,* Lyudmila Mikhailovna."

"I do," I whispered. I loved Lyonya, too. Maybe I'd loved them both all along, my husband *and* my partner. Maybe it wasn't moving too soon; maybe it was *this has always been.*

The second kiss, slower and fiercer than the one by the canoe. "Why are we always in water when we do this?" I murmured as he pulled me against him through the silky ripples of the pool. He still tasted of iron and rain. We clung, coiled together, mouths locked, silent as a countdown. With Lyonya, things had been all jokes and laughter, even curled in bed; falling into Kostia felt like falling into a well down to the middle of the world. My fingers skated over his skin, satin over granite. He'd looked deceptively slight next to Lyonya's golden height and breadth, but naked in my arms, Kostia looked like he'd been forged rather than born, bolted together out of piano wire and iron rivets rather than tendon and muscle. My head fell back against the lip of the pool as his mouth found my breast, and that was when we heard tipsy shouts from the house above. Yuri's voice, calling my name—the delegation, tipsy and happy, was returning to the hotel.

Kostia gave a soundless wolf's snarl into my throat, and then we were breaking apart, splashing out of the pool as quietly as possible, wrestling back into our dry clothes. I gave him one last dark, drowning kiss, murmuring "Room 114" into his mouth even as I wrestled my damp limbs back into my uniform—thank goodness for sturdy gabardine that could withstand a Russian winter, much less a little Beverly Hills chlorine. A fast scoop of his own clothes and Kostia was limping back toward the house the long way, while I shoved my wet hair out of my face and shouted "I felt like a swim!" to the cross-looking Yuri as he tramped out of the shadows.

"It is not part of your directive to swim."

A drunken, weaving drive out of Beverly Hills, every centimeter of my skin singing like I was crawling on my elbows through no-man's-land again, feeling my partner in the seat in front of me like he was a missing limb, everyone around us drunk and oblivious in the crammed car . . . then I was in my hotel room in the dark, waiting, *alive*. I knew when he was there; he didn't have to knock. He was moving into the room like an arrow before I even had the door fully open, tumbling me to the floor in a midnight blackness that felt as bright as day. Grappling and pulling at each other, sniper eyes flaring, rifle-roughened fingers teasing out cries of response the way we'd once teased out ballistic arcs through icy winds. Folding our bodies together into a nest, a foxhole, like we'd done so many times—only this was a foxhole of crisp sheets and fierce warm arms and a silence so complex it wiped away the world.

No one spoke until nearly dawn, and then it was me, arm curled around Kostia's waist, his lips in my hair. "When I said I was still mourning my dead, I was really thinking, *What would Lyonya say if he saw us?*"

My partner's voice in the darkness was quiet. "I've been thinking that, too."

I knew he had. Our thoughts, in the few private moments to be found around the edges of this noisy, exhausting, exceedingly public goodwill tour, had probably been much the same. Thinking in somber reflection, in bitter grief, in tensile silence, imagining Lyonya's smiling face, holding entire unspoken conversations with the man we'd both loved.

"I think," Kostia said slowly, "he would be glad for us. He'd say no one should waste time if there's a chance to be happy."

"I was thinking the same thing," I whispered as Kostia's lips touched my temple, my scarred ear. "I can hear him saying it."

CHAPTER 30

The headline: WHO WOULD HAVE THOUGHT THAT AMERICA'S NEXT SWEETHEART COULD BE A SOVIET GIRL SNIPER WHOSE HAND (NOW KISSED BY HALF THE COUNTRY!) HAS ENDED THE LIVES OF 309 NAZIS? LYUDMILA PAVLICHENKO RETURNS TO WASHINGTON AFTER CONCLUDING HER TOUR OF THE WEST WITH CROWDED STOPS IN SAN FRANCISCO AND FRESNO . . .

The truth: I think San Francisco had a bridge. Fresno I don't remember at all, but even the people who *live* in Fresno probably don't care to remember it. The only thing that rose above my daze of quiet happiness at being with Kostia was the question the entire delegation asked the moment we returned to Washington: When can we go home?

"THE TOUR HAS been extended." The Soviet ambassador beamed, looking at the three student delegates who had been reunited. We had traded stories of our respective tours, and the stories had been largely the same . . . except that my leg of it had gotten considerably more newspaper coverage. Krasavchenko was the only one who looked pleased to be continuing in the public eye; Pchelintsev scowled openly, and I couldn't keep my face from falling. "My friends, this is good news," the ambassador protested. "You have accomplished the near impossible: shifted public opinion in the USA in favor of the USSR. Opposition to a second front is subsiding. We would be foolish not to capitalize on—"

"Send Lyudmila on the tour," Pchelintsev interrupted. "She's the one they want to see. Have her trot round the spotlights and send me to Stalingrad."

I looked at him. "If anyone's going to Stalingrad, it should be the better sniper, and that would be me."

The ambassador waved our objections aside. "No one is going to Stalingrad yet. Our directive comes from the Kremlin; we will continue on to Canada and then Great Britain . . ."

I wilted, hearing the details: we were to fly to Montreal, then Halifax, then Glasgow, then London . . . I saw a long line of receptions, dinners, and speeches stretching out in front of me. Would Slavka think I didn't want to come home to him? At this rate he'd be a man grown by the time I returned. "I serve the Soviet Union," I replied, sighing, when the ambassador paused for a response.

"Did you manage to say that without cursing?" Kostia asked later. He'd come to my room as discreetly as ever, knocking only after Yuri had trundled off duty. (What *did* Soviet concrete blocks do, off duty? Perhaps a little light reading: *Winning the War Against Capitalism*, I. K. Volkov, 9th edition.)

"Barely." I curled into Kostia's shoulder. We were lying in a mess of sheets, cold Washington sunlight slanting through the blinds, still damp with sweat from recent exertions. "Then I got a scolding because the ambassador somehow got wind of the marriage proposal I got from that ass Jonson, and feared I meant to accept it and defect!" I pleated the sheet between my fingers, shaking my head. "Imagine thinking I'd jump at the chance to stay in the United States."

"It's not so bad here."

I smiled. "If I have to eat another hot dog, I'll run shrieking around the Washington Monument. I want white nights, Kostia. I want ponchiki in a paper cone, all dusted with sugar. I want people who know about Bogdan Khmelnitsky and the Pereyaslav Council—"

"Mila, even in Russia no one knows about the Pereyaslav Council."

"They will once I finish my dissertation. If you can even read my dissertation anymore through the bloodstains and the gunpowder burns." I shook my head. "All my schooling would mean nothing if I stayed here—I could never be a historian, and that's all I've ever wanted to be. Yet even people like Mrs. Roosevelt seemed to think I'd be grateful to stay."

"Some people would." Kostia's voice sounded odd.

"Not people like us." I tugged my partner's head down for a kiss, but he'd gone utterly still. "Kostia . . ."

He reached over suddenly and turned on the radio. The sound of Kay Kyser warbling "Jingle, Jangle, Jingle" filled the hotel room as Kostia cranked up the volume, then rolled over in bed and pulled me beneath him. Laying his cheek against mine and his lips to my ear, he spoke in a voice that was barely more than a thread. "I want to tell you about New York."

I didn't know if my room was being listened to by our minders, but Kostia was taking no chances. He told me in the vaguest terms possible, in a nearly soundless whisper right into my eardrum so not even the most sensitive microphone could pick up his words . . . but the picture was clear enough.

He'd summoned up the nerve to knock on the door of his grandmother's sister in Ridgewood. He'd shown her photographs: his grandmother; his mother. He'd been welcomed, embraced, introduced to others.

It hadn't been explicitly said . . . but they would welcome him if he stayed.

He fell silent then, his face taut and stony, and I had no idea what I could say. There were too many things to say, all of them impossible. *How can you think of walking away from your country?*—but I could see why he was tempted. The motherland could be great, I believed that with all my soul, but I wasn't going to pretend in a moment like this that it wasn't a hard, unforgiving place to make a life. *You're in danger*—but Kostia knew that; he knew he risked a bullet even for revealing he had family here, much less for visiting them. And my final desperate question: *How can you be with me and then threaten to leave me?*—but that wasn't important. This was a life to consider, his life—I had flesh and blood in Russia pulling me back there by an invisible steel thread, but he didn't. His only blood family was here. His tie to Russia was . . . me.

He must have read the shock in my face. I couldn't voice anything, not here in this room where there might be wires and listening ears, so I only shook my head mutely. He switched off the radio, then leaned back to cup my face in his hands. I don't know what we might have said, but there was a key rattling in the lock, and suddenly the door swung wide.

Alexei Pavlichenko stood there with an armload of pink roses.

He could have been an illustration in a romantic novel. The suitor in a sharp suit, flowers in his arm, a charming half-smile on his handsome features. But the smile disappeared like a doused light, and a wave of dead anger swept over his face.

I was already near tears, brimming with various churning emotions. I did not, *not*, need Alexei added to the mix. "No," I snarled before he could say a word. "Not now. Not today. Not *ever*. I don't care what you want, just get out."

He stood looking at Kostia as if he were vermin. "How long have you been fucking your pet wolf behind my back, Mila?"

Kostia sat up slowly, the sheet sliding to his waist as he rested his elbows on his raised knees, and maybe my husband missed how that movement put my partner closer to his Finnish combat knife lying on the nightstand, but I didn't.

I threw the sheet back and got out of bed. My naked skin was crawling, but I refused to cower in the bed like a guilty wife caught in an illicit romp. "How did you get in here?" I knew I'd locked the door.

"I charmed the housekeeper into giving me a passkey. So I could leave these as a surprise." He tossed his armload of roses to the floor, a careless scatter of thorns and petals over the carpet. "I wonder how many other men you've paraded naked for in this room."

Kostia tensed behind me, silently asking me what I wanted. My fingers tapped against my leg twice, as if we were back in a sniper trench communicating in silence: *wait*. I stalked across the room naked, head held high, and pulled my robe off the wall hook. "Don't pretend you're jealous, Alexei. This grown woman's body of mine is ten or twelve years too old to arouse you." I knotted the sash about my waist with a snap. "Now get out."

"No." He took a step closer, turning away from Kostia now. Kostia hadn't moved from the bed, stone still and watching everything . . . but his combat knife had disappeared off the nightstand.

"I am the one saying no, Alexei." The storm of roiling emotions in me was tipping rapidly in favor of rage. From the damp-handed Mr. Jonson's blind insistence to Alexei's smug persistence to Laurence Olivier's hand returning over and over to my hip—why could I not seem to make anyone hear the word *no*?

"You're still my wife."

I made myself laugh in his face. "Who do you think you are? I'm the famous sniper; the war heroine; *America's sweetheart*. I'm the one being feted all over the *world*, helping Comrade Stalin get his second front. You're the delegation pill pusher. A dog being towed behind on a leash."

"Shut your mouth. You sound like a spoiled little girl having a tantrum."

"Spoiled little girl, is that all you can call me? What about all those lovely things you wrote in your unsigned notes? *Red bitch, murdering slut*—"

"Act like a slut, don't be shocked when you're called one." His eyes tightened. "But I didn't write those damn things. I answered enough questions about them from delegation security; I won't stand here and listen to you—"

"You had better listen to me, Alexei." Now I was the one to overrun him. He'd once loomed in my life like a mountain, the biggest obstacle I faced in making a new life. Now, after everything else I had confronted this last year and a half, he was a pebble. Yet that pebble was still lodged in my shoe, doing its best to prevent me from moving forward. I was done with it. "You're not my husband anymore, and as soon as we get back to Moscow, we *will* make it official. Because I'm the one with friends in high places now, and I will make you stop stalling."

He took one long stride toward me—and stopped, because Kostia was behind him. My partner, who had silently slid out of bed as I was speaking, angled himself to one side and moved the moment Alexei came at me. My husband froze. Kostia had never looked more like the old myth of Morozko, ice-silent winter standing frost-cold and naked, knife growing from his fist like an icicle, its razor tip resting gently over Alexei's jugular.

My husband started forward. Kostia pressed the knife a millimeter deeper, and a trickle of blood slid down Alexei's throat toward his snowy shirt collar. Alexei stopped, eyes moving from me to Kostia. "You know what?" he said. "Take her. Take her and choke on her."

Maybe now he'd finally leave me alone. Now that *he'd* decided he was done with me. Whatever I'd decided up till this moment didn't count, of course. Over the roaring in my ears I stretched out a foot toward the nearest discarded flower on the rug and kicked it toward him. "Get out, and take your cheap lousy bribe with you."

But the door slammed behind him and left Kostia and me staring at each other, and the rage drained away to leave me cold and shaking. I wanted Alexei to leave, and he finally had. I wanted Kostia to stay . . . and I had no idea, looking at his closed face, if he would or not.

THE MARKSMAN FELT his luck returning when he saw Alexei Pavlichenko bang into the hotel bar and call for a double vodka in a tone barely above a snarl before he even sank down on the barstool. The

marksman ambled over, sifting his fingers through the uncut diamonds rattling in his pockets. "Bad day?" he asked in his execrable
Russian.

Alexei glanced over. "The journalist," he said, visibly recalling their
last conversation here. Nearly two months ago now, before the international student conference that had started all this off. "What's your
name?"

The marksman showed his falsified press credentials. He was back
to the journalist identity again, the one he'd backed with extensive
research and cover from above. "I never did get those pictures in the
White House Rose Garden of you and your wife," he said, just to
be saying something. "You want to try again? The delegation's getting one last dinner at the White House before leaving, right? A nice
photograph of you and the wife for the Sunday edition . . ."

"If you think that bitch needs more flattering press—" the doctor
paused, eyes suddenly sharpening. "I've seen you before."

"Sure," said the marksman amiably. "Right here, couple of months
ago."

"No. After that. Chicago, the sharpshooters' club. You're the one
who was trailing after Mila like an idiot." A long moment. "You're
Jonson." Alexei Pavlichenko blinked.

"No, I'm not," the marksman said, genuinely startled. The changes
in his clothes, posture, hair, voice . . . he'd been so careful. He was
good at disguises, damn it. He sank into each new cover like a be-
spoke suit. "Who's Jonson?" he asked, swirling the ice in his lowball
glass.

"You are." The Russian doctor's eyes were flicking rapidly over the
marksman's face. "Surgeons see bone and muscle, not hair color and
posture. You're him."

And you're good, thought the marksman in some dismay. Lady
Death certainly hadn't seen past William Jonson's dark wig with its
receding hairline, the honking upper-crust voice, the eager-to-please

scurry that put her would-be suitor two inches in height under the tall, ginger-haired, mustachioed newsman who had tailed behind her at so many public functions. Then again, he'd taken care that Lyudmila Pavlichenko never saw the newsman except as one more form hunched behind a camera across the room.

But the doctor had put two and two together. The marksman rattled the ice in his glass again. Kill him, bribe him, or find a way to use him?

"So which one are you?" Alexei Pavlichenko demanded. "William Jonson or—"

"There is a William Jonson," the marksman decided to acknowledge. A metallurgical businessman living as a near-total recluse in New York State. The man never went anywhere, he never met anyone, so his identity was useful whenever the marksman needed one that would come out both genuine and whistle-clean when investigated. A wig, a clean shave, and some expensive suits were all it took to match the out-of-date photograph.

"There's a rumor going around here that you proposed marriage to her. To my *wife*." Alexei was still looking at him as if waiting for the final punch line of a prank. "Was that a joke or—"

"I needed an excuse to follow the tour. Journalists don't typically follow even a presidential entourage all the way across the country, and ordinary citizens are liable to get asked some hard questions if they keep turning up." Even with all the backroom handwaving from Pocket Square's employers, making sure the First Lady's security passed the marksman without question onto any necessary lists, he'd wanted additional cover . . . and nobody looked as harmless as a lovestruck idiot who picked up more than his share of restaurant bills. Especially a lovestruck idiot who popped the question. "Besides," the marksman said with complete honesty, "I wanted a closer look at Lady Death." Squeezing that small hand with its trigger calluses, seeing the annoyance masked in those big brown eyes. Thinking how

those eyes would flare in fear if they realized what was going on behind William Jonson's earnest pop-eyed stare. Thinking: *You have no
idea, you Red bitch.*

Yes, the marksman thought—he had definitely let curiosity get the
better of strict professionalism on this job. A bad thing, considering
it was the biggest target of his career . . . Yet somehow he wasn't dis-
mayed. This turn of events was going somewhere, he could feel it.
Weeks of dead ends and failed plans were all leading here.

Alexei Pavlichenko sat back on his stool now, tilting the vodka in
his glass. Sudden calculations going through that handsome head,
without a doubt. "And why did you need to follow my whore wife?"

"Just looking to make a little trouble for America's Soviet sweetheart." The marksman leaned closer, still speaking in his bad Russian,
feeling the pulse quicken. "Not everyone here wants her to go home
a heroine, you know."

The doctor's gaze sharpened. "Really."

There it is, thought the marksman. And leaned closer.

CHAPTER 31

The headline: THE GIRL SNIPER AND HER COMPATRIOTS RETURN TO THE WHITE HOUSE FOR A FAREWELL DINNER AND PRESS APPEARANCE WITH PRESIDENT ROOSEVELT BEFORE DEPARTING OUR FAIR SHORES TOMORROW MORNING . . .

The truth: My last trip to the White House was not quite that uneventful.

THE WIND WAS blustering outside as the delegation gathered in the hotel court in black tie and evening finery: our final night in America. "Pretty fitting weather for Halloween, eh?" the concierge said.

"What's Halloween?" I asked, distracted by the delegation baggage piling up behind the front desk. Most of our things were already packed, ready for our flight to Halifax tomorrow morning. There was nothing left to do in this country but say our goodbyes to the President and the First Lady at tonight's White House dinner. Krasavchenko and the other men were already joking about getting a bottle or two of vodka here at the hotel afterward, since we'd have a long flight to Canada to sleep off any hangovers. I searched among them—Yuri, Pchelintsev, a glowering Alexei—but I didn't see Kostia.

"Mila."

I turned. My partner looked rumpled, his sleeves pushed up to his elbows, a dark shadow of stubble on his jaw. "You're not dressed for dinner," I said inadequately.

"I begged off," he said. "They have plenty of interpreters . . . I'm going for a walk."

Are you coming back? I thought, stepping closer. I couldn't read his face. I knew him so well and I couldn't read his face. "Take a coat," I said instead. "It's cold."

"Not to a Siberian." His eyes went over me like a kiss. I was back in my yellow satin dress, and I hadn't flinched when the elevator operator gasped at my scars.

"Will I see you later?" I meant my room—I wondered if he'd come to me after I was back from the White House dinner. Maybe if we were pressed skin to skin I could say all the things through our blood-bonded silence that I couldn't voice aloud . . . But as soon as the words were out, I realized it sounded like, *Will I see you tomorrow morning?* Would he be here, waiting for the embassy car to take us to the airfield, or would he be . . . gone? Here we were the night before departure, and I still didn't know. I knew he was avoiding me. I knew I couldn't beg. Beyond that—

"I don't know," he said. I stepped forward and kissed him in the middle of the crowded hotel court, long and desperately, and his hand came around my waist and touched the scar over my spine.

Then I broke away, ignoring the glances all around us, and joined the delegation for my last visit to the White House.

PRESIDENT ROOSEVELT RAISED his glass. "To new friends."

The delegation murmured in response, toasting. We sat in the same small dining room where we'd been welcomed to our first American breakfast. Had that really been only two months ago? When I first sat at this table, I'd been grieving, angry, resentful, convinced I'd hate America and all Americans. Well, I'd given speeches in more cities than I could count, in front of more journalists than there were stars in the sky, and I'd seen the beauty in rolling American hills, towering American skyscrapers, and friendly American faces. I no longer flinched to see my name in print, or a microphone standing in the circle of a spotlight awaiting my voice, or a crowd of eager faces turned up toward mine to listen. How very far Mila Pavlichenko had come.

Although I was still grieving and still angry, even if for different reasons.

"Are you quite all right, Lyudmila?" the First Lady asked in a low tone. She'd placed me on her right, the seat of honor. "You look strained."

"Quite all right, Eleanor." I saw Alexei looking at me from his place at the far end of the table, his gaze speculative rather than sullen—I hadn't spoken to him since he scooped his rejected roses off my rug and stormed out of my room. He'd probably decided he'd come out on top of it all . . . no one could beat Alexei when it came to twisting an argument around so *he'd* won it.

Three courses, more toasts, and then the President excused himself to the oval reception room, where the press would take some final photographs. I knew by now—though Eleanor certainly never said any such thing—that her husband would situate himself in an arm-chair in advance of the photographers, so they would find him at ease with his trademark cigarette holder clamped between his teeth, not struggling with his braces and cane. A respectful wait, then the Soviet delegation followed into the big oval room with its vaulted ceilings and graceful fireplace, beside which the President gave his famous fireside chats. One last bank of photographers and journalists flooded in, snapping pictures—not just of us but of the gifts we'd accrued during the goodwill tour. A long table had been piled with plaques, city seals, mayoral keys, commemorative albums of all the cities we'd visited. I smiled to see the mahogany box of the twin Colt M1911A1 pistols that had been given to me by the Sharpshooters' Association in Chicago, and the soft silver pile of the lynx coat I'd been awarded in New York.

"Two more gifts for you, Lyudmila." The First Lady drew me

aside, lowering her voice as Krasavchenko approached President Roosevelt for his farewell handshake. "I have many photographs of you by now, but I thought you might like one of me, to remember our friendship."

I blinked down at the framed picture she placed in my hand: an image of Eleanor in the black dress she wore tonight, seated at her desk like the hard-working woman she was, inscribed in her own hand. *To Senior Lieutenant Lyudmila Pavlichenko, with warm good wishes from Eleanor Roosevelt.*

My eyes prickled as I looked up from the picture to its smiling subject, and for a moment my own troubles faded away. "I will miss you," I said simply. "I will not miss hot dogs, or your press—" Casting a glance at the hubbub of journalists and flashbulbs all around. "But I will miss you, Eleanor. You have taught me so much."

"And you me," she said with a smile. "I'll miss all of you, even Mr. Krasavchenko and his rather endless anecdotes of his Komsomol days . . . but of everyone, dear Lyudmila, you're the one I wish I could keep."

You might be keeping my partner, I wish I could have said. *If he stays, look after him.* But I couldn't say that. If Kostia asked for asylum here, our delegation would be in utter uproar; it would have to look like he'd told no one of his plans. Besides, I knew I didn't have to ask the First Lady to extend a helping hand if he needed it. If there was one thing Eleanor Roosevelt knew how to do, with grace and tact and unending sympathy, it was how to *help.*

"One more gift arrived for you," she said with a mischievous smile, lightening the moment of farewell and passing me a flat silk box. Pchelintsev was now having his photograph taken with Roosevelt; I'd be next. "From a certain brokenhearted American suitor, once it was made clear to him that you would never accept his proposal!"

I eyed the case like it was a snake. What surprises had the damp-handed Mr. Jonson left for me now? When I lifted the lid, my gasp made the Soviet ambassador drift closer.

A collar necklace of tiny diamonds. Twin bracelets like bands of diamond lace. A brooch with hanging diamond tremblers to catch the light. A diamond ring like a drop of cold fire.

To Lyudmila with great love from W. P. Jonson, my businessman suitor had written on the accompanying card. *We will meet again.*

"I cannot take this," I began to say, but Eleanor shook her head.

"The man's covering note stated that he refused to take anything back."

"A fitting tribute to a heroine of the USSR," the Soviet ambassador said, looking envious. I made a mental note to offer the brooch to him for his wife or his mistress. That was the way things were done in the Soviet Union, and I was fairly sure it was the way things were done in Washington as well.

Alexei's voice sounded, sharp-edged and mocking on the ambassador's other side. "Try them on, Mila."

"Yes, do," Eleanor enthused. "For your final photograph." She looked innocently pleased, and for her I clasped the necklace around my neck, fastened a bracelet around each wrist, pinned the brooch to my yellow satin bodice, and tried on the ring. It ended up fitting my trigger finger, perfectly.

I looked at the handwritten card. *We will meet again . . .*

"Your American suitor picked well, Mila," Alexei said, still mocking. "Diamonds for a girl with a heart like a diamond."

"I would disagree," Eleanor said when I translated for her. "I think I have come to know something about snipers by now. An eye like a diamond, yes. But a heart"—she led me toward her husband for my final photograph—"for friendship."

"Agreed," President Roosevelt boomed, grinning around his cigarette holder, and for the last time I felt the clasp of that strong, sinewy hand. We turned toward the bank of journalists, smiling as flashbulbs went off, and before he released my hand, he gave it a final squeeze along with a low-voiced promise: "Go home, keep fighting, and tell your friends that America is coming."

THE MARKSMAN, METHODICALLY setting up behind a thicket of shrubs on the edge of the South Lawn, wondered why he'd given her the diamonds.

He'd get them back, of course, but why do it in the first place? He was finished with the William Jonson persona, at least as far as this job was concerned; there wasn't any need to extend the facade of the mooncalf suitor. Yet when he made his preparations for this evening, packing up his disassembled rifle into the case specially modified to look like a carrier for camera equipment, he'd gone on a whim to his private safe, pushed aside the uncut gems into which he routinely converted most of his cash payments, and reached for a jewelry case at the very back. Payment for a job back in 1927; some stockbroker's inconvenient wife. The marksman had made it look like an interrupted robbery; the grateful husband had paid him with the now-dead wife's diamonds, then gone on to collect the insurance and a dewy-fresh fiancée; everyone had gone home happy. Well, except the wife. The marksman remembered how her eyes had widened, the moment she realized he was going to kill her . . . Would Lady Death's eyes widen in the same way, when she faced his gun muzzle? On impulse, he took out the jewelry case, scribbled out an accompanying card, and sent it all off in the name of that booby William Jonson. A whim.

Maybe he hadn't been able to resist telling her *We will meet again.*

Or maybe he was old-fashioned. You gave a woman a present, after all, when you took her on a date. And wasn't this a date, in a way?

His hands had never stopped moving, assembling the rifle from its pieces. He'd separated from the other journalists as soon as they were admitted onto White House grounds; it shouldn't have been so easy, but it was. The Secret Service weren't on high alert for small functions like this, and his path had been smoothed for him by his shadow-suited employers, who made sure his name made the night's list and gave him the routes in advance where he would need to avoid security points as he melted into the gardens.

He checked his watch, timed down to the second. The Soviet delegation would be finishing up their last photographs in the oval reception room just inside the South Portico. After that they'd spill out onto the lawn, a last informal mingle with Halloween punch before everyone departed . . . and the President and his wife would wave farewell from just above the portico stairs.

The shot across the south lawn would be long, but he'd made longer. He just needed Mila Pavlichenko out of the way first . . . and if her husband did his part, that should be in about ten minutes.

I HAD THE feeling, once again, as if I had spiders crawling down my spine. We were all mingling on the South Lawn now, sipping cups of highly spiked Halloween punch for a final informal aperitif as the delegation's mountain of gifts was packed into the embassy cars pulled around front. Eleanor was spinning one of her amusing, informative anecdotes about the celebration of October 31 in America: costumes, harvest parades, candles placed in hollowed-out turnips or pumpkins . . . but I couldn't focus. That unsettled feeling was back, stronger than ever, and I couldn't shake it. I lit a cigarette and looked up at the moon rising over the tipsy, triumphant crowd of celebrating Soviets and eager journalists. The moon was waning gibbous—it had been months since the moon's phase was a matter of my nightly survival, but I still couldn't help tracking her wax and wane. The wind had died down; it wasn't cold by Russian standards, but the yellow satin dress was flimsy enough that I'd shrugged into my lynx coat before coming down to the White House lawn. I took another deep inhale of a Lucky Strike, watching the sparkle of Mr. Jonson's diamonds on my wrist in the moonlight.

We will meet again . . .

Where exactly did he think we were going to meet again, when tonight was my last in his country? I shook my head at my pop-eyed suitor, who had probably thought he was being very romantic. Anyone could have told him that the line between *very romantic* and *vaguely creepy* is not one you want to land on the wrong side of when you are courting a sniper. Kostia would split himself laughing.

Kostia. Surely he was the reason I felt so unsettled. I side-slipped a journalist cajoling *One more smile for the camera, Lady Death?* and turned back toward the columned portico of the White House's southern side. President Roosevelt had not, of course, followed us down the stairs to the lawn; he sat under the awning between the portico columns, chatting with someone or other. I could see the confident line of his profile all the way from here. If Kostia were with me, we'd be automatically assessing potential angles of fire.

"There," I said aloud, nodding at a series of hedges to the east of the lawn. "Better yet, there." A thicket of trees and shrubs on the other side, near the West Wing. I lifted my cigarette for another drag and stopped. Even here, even now, I turned my lit cigarette inside the curl of my palm, hiding the ember . . .

And it slid into my memory with a click: William Jonson in the sharpshooters' club in Chicago, laughing at himself for shooting so badly during the demonstration, lighting a Lucky Strike—which he held in a cupped, reversed hand, like a sniper.

It's not just snipers who smoke that way, I thought. Any battle veteran who had stood a night watch did. Had Mr. Jonson been a soldier? He was too young to have fought in the Great War. And he'd shot so badly in the demonstration, half his shots missing the target altogether . . .

Which is exactly what a trained sniper would do if he wanted to look like something else.

We will meet again.

"Mila!" Alexei was trying to get my attention from across the crowd, but Krasavchenko had waylaid him about something. My husband beckoned me, but I turned the other way, stubbing out my cigarette in the grass underfoot, looking up at President Roosevelt on the portico. I didn't know what I was doing, just that the sense of wrongness was stronger than ever, and my eyes were flicking back and forth between the potential lines of fire so automatically parsed by my sniper's eye (*an eye like a diamond*, Eleanor's voice whispered).

The hedges to the east; the trees and shrubs to the west. I hesitated.

"Lyudmila!" Eleanor sailed up to me, cheeks flushed with the night's chill. "Would you like more punch, or—"

I cut her off, something I'd never done before. "Get him inside," I said, pointing to the seated figure of her husband on the portico. "Inside, *now*—" and without waiting for a reply, I arrowed off toward the western side of the White House lawn. A white-aproned server stood at the edge of the grass with a tray, and among the glasses I saw a small paring knife for peeling lemon twists or taking the foil off wine bottles. I plucked the little blade off the tray and kept going, past the startled server and straight into the thicket of trees. I wasn't thinking, not in words. I was following something so deep I couldn't name it, or maybe I could. Maybe I already had, to Captain Sergienko when he asked if skills like mine were instinctive and I'd scoffed that it was simply training.

Well. Dozens of months of practice, hundreds of hours of training, thousands of shots fired under a blood moon on the other side of the world had all joined voices, singing a song down deep inside my veins.

And my feet followed it.

Notes by the First Lady

She gave an order. I find myself obeying it. Is it because the tone of absolute authority issuing commands will get feet moving whether they intend to or not?

Perhaps it is simply that when a woman with the name Lady Death looks suddenly and fearsomely alert, mortals formed of mere flesh and blood know it is time to run.

I hurry up the steps toward the South Portico, heart hammering, and I cannot help but think of that crisp night in Miami when a shot was fired at my husband's heart as he stood making a speech from his open car. That night. This one. Franklin's unspoken fears over the last few months—yes, he has been afraid. Of what? Of this?

I reach the top of the steps, and my husband looks toward me. His careworn face, etched with pain and humor, so alive. I call out quietly but urgently: "My dear, you are needed inside—" and then I turn to the nearest Secret Service officer.

I don't know what your diamond eye saw, Lyudmila, but do not miss.

CHAPTER 32

His luck was back; the marksman could feel it. His Packard was waiting for a quick, discreet getaway; it had already been vetted on the way in, and he thought he could manage to exit in the chaos after the shot. If not, people inside were already prepared with cover stories to smooth his way. He could hear the tick of the clock inside him, counting down toward the squeeze of the trigger.

Perhaps ten more minutes. The girl sniper would arrive, puzzled, directed by her husband: *I'll tell her that her precious partner is here to speak with her; she runs like a bitch in heat when he calls.* A fast, silent arm-bar from behind to choke her out without overt bruising, then the long-range shot toward the South Portico, where the President and the First Lady were both standing, heads bent close in some discussion. The marksman had already prepared his weapon: a Mosin-Nagant with PE sights, the same type Lady Death would have used on the front. He'd put in thousands of practice rounds on it—a good weapon, workmanlike, unfussy. The moment the President fell, the marksman would fire another shot, this one through Lyudmila Pavlichenko's unconscious mouth, and leave the rifle behind in her hand: an assassination-suicide. The newspapers would eat it up. Reaching for the rifle with gloved hands, he smiled as he loaded five rounds. He should only need two.

He didn't know why he looked up. It was too soon for her to be here yet, and not so much as a rustle of leaves or whisper of twigs had sounded against his ears. But some unknown trip wire twanged in his silent depths, far below the level of clocks or plans or even thought, and his head whipped around.

There she was: Lady Death gliding across the shadowed grass in rippling lynx fur, the glitter of his diamonds at her throat like star-dust. Bleached silver in the faint moonlight, but her eyes pitch-black. They didn't widen in shock or take in his face in stunned disbelief. She knew. She already knew.

How did she—

His hand on the rifle twitched—he couldn't shoot her; the report would ruin everything—and in that instant's hesitation she moved shadow-fast. Not away, running for safety. *Toward* him. He lunged to meet her, and the two snipers collided under the gibbous moon.

IN THAT SPLIT instant I saw the skull under the face: William Jonson without the darkened hair, the eager gaze, the supplicant stoop in his shoulders. A coat hanger of a man considerably taller than Jonson, bony-shouldered, scoop-faced, with eyes like mud. And at his side, the long, glinting, unmistakable shape of a rifle's barrel and telescopic sights, aimed through the bushes toward the White House like a half-hidden snake poised to strike. A Mosin-Nagant.

One glance, and then we were grappling.

I got out a piercing, wordless shout before his fingers clamped over my mouth. I bit as hard as I could and heard his strangled curse. I nearly lost my grip on the paring knife in my hand; before I could bring it up in a fast stab between his ribs or into his throat, he flung himself sideways to shake me off. He didn't wrench free, but I lost my footing and went to my knees in the grass. He kicked once, twice, and I felt something in my side go white-hot. I gasped for breath, and then the inside of my head filled with sparks as he clubbed me across my bad ear.

Dimly, I felt him hauling me up by one arm. I fumbled inside my coat, feeling instinctively for the eight-shot Tula-Tokarev that hung at my belt in case I ever fell into enemy hands, the weapon I'd jam to my own temple before I ever let myself be taken alive. But I wasn't wearing the TT; I was in cocktail-party satin and diamonds halfway around the world from my battleground, and I wasn't supposed to be among enemies—yet I was. Here in the velvet heart of America's capital, Lady Death had finally fallen into enemy hands.

And President Roosevelt was sitting just a bullet shot away. Eleanor's husband, who had gripped my hand and said, *Keep fighting, and tell your friends that America is coming.*

Get him off the balcony, Eleanor. Get him off the balcony—

I felt the man lock his arm around my throat from behind, grip tightening like a steel band. My sight darkened. My lips parted but I didn't have enough air to scream.

I fumbled the paring knife in my numbing hand, and stabbed down hard and straight into the meat of his calf.

He shouted, arm loosening around my throat, and his shout disappeared into a chorus of whoops: Krasavchenko and Pchelintsev and the rest of the delegation, kicking off the round of heartily bawled patriotic songs without which no evening with Russians present can conclude. I managed to tear myself out of the slackening choke hold, gagging for breath, ripping the knife out of his leg with another savage twist. My enemy scrambled backward with a hiss of agony, head jerking toward the sound of Russian voices—they were loud, close, coming closer—and then he wavered another split second, eyes whipping back toward me as I struggled up to my knees with the little bloody knife still gripped in my hand.

My gaze flickered toward the White House portico. So did the marksman's. In the same split second we saw it was empty. Or rather, it was rustling with swiftly moving dark suits, but no seated figure with a cigarette holder. *Thank you, Eleanor,* I thought disjointedly, gripping the knife even as another verse from the half-drunk delegation roared skyward.

"Mila?" Even closer than Krasavchenko and the others, I heard Alexei's irritated voice. The bushes rustled, and I saw the decision pass through my enemy's mud-colored eyes. He scooped up his rifle and its case in one swift movement and half a heartbeat later was running jerk-legged and stumbling in the opposite direction.

I tried to stand and nearly collapsed. My side was on fire from where he'd kicked me—*cracked rib,* I could hear Lena diagnosing, *maybe two*—and my throat was ablaze with pain from his half-throttling. Worse was the dizziness from his blow across my head; the world wouldn't stop spinning. But I lurched to my feet and went reeling after the man who'd attacked me: my suitor William Jonson, who had given me diamonds; the man who had aimed a rifle exactly like mine at the American president on the grounds of the White House. Nothing made sense.

Except his note tonight—written, I realized hazily, in the same writing that had scrawled so many epithets in Cyrillic. His latest note, saying: *We will meet again.*

"Mila, I've been looking for you—" Alexei caught me by the arm as I came staggering out of the bushes onto one of the gravel paths. "I was going to tell you, Kostia is . . ." But my husband stopped, staring at the marks on my throat, the knife in my hand.

"The man we called William Jonson tried to kill President Roosevelt," I managed to say, and saw the look of utter horror on Alexei's face as I began half running and half stumbling after the man with the mud-colored eyes.

I SHOULDN'T HAVE done it that way. I should have stopped in my tracks and started screaming until White House personnel came running. But I'd already warned Eleanor; it was up to her and the Secret Service to shield the president now. The man who'd tried to kill him was getting away, fast, and I didn't want to waste even the precious moments it would take me to explain what had happened to White House security. And it wasn't in me to *stop and scream* when death reared its head around me and bullets threatened to sing—everything I'd learned in a year at the front told me not to stop and scream, but to run in silence.

So I went after him.

Alexei hurried along beside me as I arrowed through the dark gardens toward the front of the White House. My husband was pouring out words in a disjointed torrent—"He said he'd knock you out, get some embarrassing pictures of you like you were drunk. I just wanted to see you taken down a peg. I didn't know, Mila, I didn't know he was—" and even with my attention fractured into slivers, I took it in for what it was. If an assassin were looking for someone to take the blame for a presidential hit, a girl sniper from the Soviet Union fit the bill. And if you needed a way to get to that girl sniper, her disgruntled husband fit the bill, too.

"Mila, you have to believe me, I'd never be part of something like this, I don't have a damned *death wish*, I wouldn't piss about with American assassination plots—"

I kept thinking we'd run into presidential bodyguards, White House staff, whoever was responsible for protecting these grounds. NKVD would have had any assassin up against a wall and half his fingernails yanked out by now. But there was no knot of guards with a handcuffed figure, no matter how my eyes hunted, and I wondered if someone had taken care of that. A change of roster to clear his path . . .

Even so, he couldn't go far. These grounds were fenced.

And then I realized someone had taken care of that for him too, as I came out through the dark gardens to the front of the White House where the Soviet embassy cars were pulled up for our departure . . . and saw, beyond them, a blue Packard driving fast but not suspiciously fast for the entry gates.

Stop and scream—that's what I could have done, even then. But the car would be through the gates and gone before anyone could hear me out, and I was still in the grip of that raging imperative to *fight*, not stop. This man had been under my nose for weeks, and I'd missed him. Missed a threat to Eleanor's husband, to the whole fragile alliance that was the only thing that would save my homeland, and now I had him on the run. I couldn't have stopped myself going after him if he'd leaned out the driver's side window and shot me in the head; I'd still have crawled blood-blind and dying after that Packard.

So I whirled and grabbed Alexei by the lapels, feeling an instant's twisted howl of frustration that Kostia wasn't here at my side tonight of all nights. "Alexei," I panted, dragging him toward the nearest embassy car, where the White House stewards were loading up the last of the delegation gifts. "That man nearly made you into an assassination's patsy. Help me now and you become the hero instead."

I swear I saw calculation go through his eyes. Even now he was looking for the angle that benefited him most. "What—"

In the open trunk of the embassy car, I saw a familiar mahogany box: the twin pistols from Chicago, complete with two magazines of .45-caliber ammunition. I yanked the box out, slung it under my arm, banged the trunk, and stumbled around toward the passenger side. I'd never in my life had cause to regret not learning to drive, but I regretted it now. Too late. "Get the president into a bunker if he isn't already, and tell your people to ask who drove a blue Packard onto the grounds," I said to the nearest astonished White House steward, then collapsed into the seat. "Alexei," I roared, slamming the door, "get in and *drive*."

CHAPTER 33

The marksman swore when he realized the embassy car had caught up with him as he turned onto 16th Street. "What the hell do you think you're doing?" he asked her. She should have stayed on White House grounds; raised the alarm. She didn't have a weapon beyond a *paring knife*, yet she'd come after him anyway?

Well, he'd made a study of her over the last few months—that very first morning he'd seen how she lost her temper and her script when surprised.

The fingers on his shooting hand were bleeding from the marks of her teeth, and his leg was a roar of pain. He'd strapped it tight with his tie, stanching the blood for now, but she'd stabbed him deep: if he hadn't been limping too badly to run, he'd have easily beat her to his Packard and been gone into the night before she could follow. Rage was beating through him in unsteady pulses as he blew through a stoplight past Dupont Circle and saw the embassy car blow through the light, too.

You cocked it up, he told himself brutally. He'd ignored his own rules about keeping his distance; he'd underestimated her from the start and let it make him careless. And now the chance at Roosevelt was gone, and he *hated* to miss a mark. He caught himself wondering if she was the same way. He didn't think they had much else in common—he shot people for hire; she shot people because they'd invaded her home, and he was well aware of the difference there—but he would have bet every diamond in his pocket and around her throat that she hated to fail as much as he did.

He was the one who'd failed tonight. He'd never be the man who killed a president. Instead, he was the man running away from a woman armed with a paring knife.

He almost wished she had a gun. He'd never gone up against some-one with skills like his own before.

"Not rolling your eyes at me now, are you?" he said aloud.

The car behind ghosted along in silence. No horn-blaring, no try-ing to force him off the road. Just following as the marksman blasted down 16th Street. This late at night, the Washington streets were clear enough to drive fast and smooth. The marksman looked at his fuel gauge. A full tank; he could make for the city limits and lose her on the highways.

But what was the fun in that?

He made a sudden, vengeful turn onto Decatur Street, knowing exactly where he was going.

"STOP HERE," I told Alexei, gripping one of the now-loaded Colt pis-tols in my lap. I was still loading the other, but it slithered off my lap and under the seat in a cascade of loose bullets as Alexei stamped too hard on the brakes. He'd seen what I'd seen: the Packard ahead, aban-doned at the side of Colorado Avenue, driver's door open.

"Where did he go?" Alexei gripped the wheel, white-faced. He was still imagining his future, if it got out that he'd aided a would-be presidential assassin, however unwittingly. I didn't know if he was en-visioning an American electric chair or a Soviet bullet, but I doubted he liked either prospect. "Why would—"

"He wants to lose me in the woods." Rock Creek Park loomed on the other side of the street, a dark wall of trees. I'd walked here before, with Alexei—the day I'd bought the yellow satin dress I was wearing now. I wondered if the man we were tailing had been tailing *us*, back then. If he'd picked this place for a reason: because he and I both knew it. I cursed, fumbling under the seat for the fallen pistol.

"Maybe he just ditched the car and doubled back into the city be-tween buildings," Alexei was muttering, staring at the Packard.

"He's in the woods." Because it was what I would have done. And he hoped I'd follow. *We will meet again.*

I abandoned scrambling for the second pistol, swept up as many of the loose bullets as I could, and got out of the car.

"Mila—" Alexei began.

"Go back to the White House and tell the ambassador everything," I said. "Raise the alarm. If I come out of these trees, that man is dead. If I don't, *I'm* dead and they can pick up his trail from my body. Either way, the President is safe and you get to be the hero who carried the warning." And I slammed the door and began walking toward the trees.

For the love of Lenin, I asked myself, *what are you doing?* I could focus my eyes again, but my head still pulsed. My ribs throbbed with every step. I was in my stocking feet since I'd kicked off my flimsy heels; I was decked out in yellow as bright as a traffic light rather than my sniper's camouflage, and I had a weapon I'd never fired before . . . but I didn't stop walking toward the trees, not hurrying, watching every shadow, because if this man were smart he'd wait for me just inside the tree line in case I came crashing down the street and into the wall of woods without looking around me. But I wasn't going to do that. Even caught at a disadvantage like this, I still knew my trade, and I knew something now about my enemy. He'd been hunting me since I came to this city, and he'd been hunting Franklin Roosevelt, who wasn't my president but was still—as long as I'd pledged friendship to his wife, and as long as he'd pledged friendship to my country—under my protection. And this man who'd thrown a challenge down to me with his diamonds and his hate-filled notes wasn't a sniper like me. He wasn't even an assassin, because he hadn't killed anyone—not tonight, anyway. He was just another marksman, and I was Lyudmila Pavlichenko.

And with every step toward the trees, I felt my sniper self filling me back up. Maybe I wasn't at my best with my injured ribs and ringing head, and maybe I looked like just another Washington elite hurrying home from a dinner party—some politician's pampered wife swathed in dappled furs, diamonds glittering at her throat under the streetlights. But it was All Hallows Eve, when dangerous things supposedly walked the night . . . and the most dangerous of them here was me. A woman who wore a lynx pelt like the predator she was, who strode under the waning moon not with a socialite's bustle or a housewife's scurry, but with a gunslinger's glide, shoulders swaying easy, hips loose and rolling below, pistol swinging ready at her side. I pulled the diamonds from around my neck and wrists and stuffed them into my coat pocket so their sparkle wouldn't give me away, and as I slid from the paved surface of Colorado Avenue into the dark choir of trees, the glossy propaganda poster-woman so at ease in the national spotlight disappeared. Breathing through her skin was Lady Midnight, Lady Death, the woman who had terrified Nazi invaders from Odessa to Sevastopol.

Even if I'd been living soft on tour for two months, the muscles of my legs remembered what it was to clamber Kamyshly gully and No-Name Height under fifteen kilos of snipers' gear. My feet were being sliced and bruised beneath me, but I put the pain away along with the pain of my cracked ribs, finding the nearly invisible trail and noiselessly following its bend. I went slow, keeping low to the ground and taking cover behind every tree trunk and boulder, listening for the faintest rustle or creak that was out of place.

Where are you?

I remembered the way to Boulder Bridge perfectly, even in the blackness of night. I was edging past the jutting rock where I'd lingered the last time to gaze over the ridge, pressing through tangles of mountain laurel toward the bend that would lead to the creek and the stone bridge, when instinct raked the back of my neck with dark claws. The barest rustle of leaves, a faint slide of pebbles, the tiniest click of metal where no metal belonged in the tapestry of night noises—I threw myself flat on the earth without a second's hesitation.

An instant later the crack of a gunshot echoed through the dark, and I heard a bullet bury itself in a tree trunk just beyond me.

I rolled hard to my left and didn't stop. Another shot whined as I went into a tangle of mountain laurel, scrambled through it with twigs raking my face, and finally wedged myself in a ball behind a boulder of rough granite.

He's up on that rocky outcrop, I thought, mentally tracing the shot's angle. *The one where I stopped to take in the view. The one that made me think,* "What a perfect place for a stakeout."

IT WAS A perfect place for a stakeout. The marksman lay flat, the Mosin-Nagant's barrel braced, the ground spread below in a perfect arc. If she moved from behind that boulder in any direction, he'd split her through the eyes—at this distance he couldn't miss, even in the dark.

Now it was a waiting game. He almost called down to her, in sheer curiosity. But what was there to say? The question had been asked silently: *Which of us is better?* The answer would come at the tip of a bullet.

Again, he wished she had a gun. It would have made things more interesting.

HE HAD A Russian rifle; I had an American pistol. The irony was not lost on me. My Colt wouldn't be effective past fifty meters, but it was better than no firearm at all. I lay behind the boulder, going through the pockets of my lynx coat to verify what else I had: the paring knife, a handful of loose bullets, the discarded jewelry I'd pulled off at the tree line . . . and among the rattle of diamonds, a matchbox.

I heard a rustle of leaves as he moved in his nest and thought about trying for a shot—but in the dark, aiming uphill with an unfamiliar weapon, I'd have to expose myself to get clear aim, and that meant the marksman's shot was far more likely to hit than mine. He had picked this ground, not me; it favored him, not me, and I didn't want to tip my hand until the ground was mine. Right now he thought I was cowering here unarmed, the quivering fool who'd rushed blindly, rashly into the night after her enemy.

The air between us shivered with unsaid words. I almost called out to him—*Who are you? Why did you do this? Are you a fanatic or just a hired gunman?*—but there was no point. It didn't matter who he was or why he did this dark work. I'd been driven by war to find the midnight side of my moon; he'd followed his willingly. That was all I needed to know.

But I could still feel the pulsing beat of his curiosity all but touching me through the dark. He was watching, he was eager . . . and the time was now.

I squeezed my eyes shut and struck the entire bundle of matches to life by touch. Feeling the flare in my fist, I thrust my hand up above the rock and flung the burning handful out like a scatter of fireflies. The minute the marksman's night vision was wrecked by the flashes of light I was moving, eyes still shut, bursting out from behind the boulder and flinging myself down the slope toward the creek in the direction I'd already mapped out for my feet. His shot went off somewhere behind, nowhere near me; I heard him grunt, heard the uneven thump of his boots crashing off into the trees at the wrong angle. Heard what I thought was a gasp of pain and smiled at the thought of the knife wound through his calf. I opened my eyes then and went still against the nearest tree, listening with all my senses to the living dark. Distant crunching of leaves; the marksman was still pressing the wrong way, but he'd soon get his bearings.

The forest is like a temple, I remembered Vartanov saying. *Be respectful, and the woods will reward you.* I used every trick the old ranger had ever taught me about how to move through trees, making my silent way down to the creek and then stealing along its pebbled bank. I knew exactly where I needed to be.

The frozen moon slid out from behind a cloud, and I saw the dark arch of the bridge. I scrambled through the boulders and rocks of the bank, freezing water numbing my bruised feet in their shredded stockings, dead leaves clinging to the sodden hem of my furs, and then I was onto the bridge and moving across it at a flat sprint. If the marksman was already behind me, this was his chance to drill me between the shoulder blades—but there was only the burbling rush of the creek below as I melted off the bridge and down onto the far-side bank beside the stone arch.

It was near midnight and icy cold, the ground beside the water hard-frozen and glittering with frost, but I stripped off my lynx furs, dropping the loose bullets into the bodice of my dress. I gathered an armload of wet leaves and driftwood, casting it all on top of a rock beside the bridge and just above the water. I worked frantically fast, going still every time I heard a new sound. Once or twice a distant drunken shout came to my ears; once I thought I saw the outline of some passerby in the distant trees—this park wasn't completely deserted, even late at night—but it was too dark and cold for anyone but the odd tramp or troublemaker. However this duel finished between the marksman and me, there were no innocents here to get between us. I was almost grateful to him, for moving the game to an arena where we could fight things out alone.

I finished up my heap of leaves and driftwood under the bridge and tucked my coat around it to look like a woman huddling under the stone arch. I took the diamond brooch with its flashing tremblers (had I really put it on only a few hours ago at the White House, as Eleanor beamed over the table of gifts?) and pinned it to the fur collar, where it would catch the moonlight. I added the necklace and bracelets too, tucking them around the coat's sleeves, and stood back to examine the effect. *You're no Ivan,* I thought, remembering the dummy soldier Kostia and I had built together for the duel with the German sniper overlooking a very different bridge outside Sevastopol. *But you'll have to do.* From a distance, to my enemy's eyes, it would with luck look like I'd crossed the bridge, slid exhausted to hide underneath on the far side, and waited there trembling and praying for him to cross . . . unaware, of course, that my diamonds were catching the moonlight and giving away my position, stupid commie bitch that I was.

He was the stupid bitch, to come at me like this. To assume a real sniper would ever, ever enter a duel unarmed.

I found a big lightning-forked beech tree on the bank—plenty of foliage, perfect vantage point. I'd never mounted a stakeout in a satin evening dress before, but at least the bright yellow turned to gray in these deep shadows. I wriggled up into the tree, feet wedging painfully against the bark, and then I nested into a fork in the branches and turned myself to stone.

CURSING, LIMPING, AND increasingly cold, the marksman reminded himself that all she could do was hide. It was a smart trick with the matches—he'd gotten turned around in the dark, losing his night vision and arrowing off a good quarter mile in the wrong direction before getting his bearings—but he was back on her trail now, heading toward Boulder Bridge. Two months ago he'd stood on the bank of Rock Creek covertly watching the Russian woman argue with her husband on that bridge . . . Following her at the time, he'd noted how she wore no perfume that would linger in the air and make her trail easier to follow. She still wasn't wearing any, and he cursed, wishing she were.

He'd ceased enjoying himself. He wanted a beer and a painkiller for this leg; he wanted to telephone Pocket Square and tell him the job was off. He just wanted this duel done.

I WATCHED THE moon slide behind a cloud, plunging the world into midnight. The bridge was a dusky arch against the black silk rush of the water, and the cold sang a high freezing note, moving into my body like ice fronds creeping across the surface of a lake. An October night in Washington wasn't cold the way a Crimean January was cold, but without the lynx coat my bare flesh was marbling. I had to keep shaking out my hands, rubbing them together to keep them from trembling. My side burned. My throat ached. My legs cramped. My skin froze. I wished I had my Three Line rifle, not this unfamiliar pistol braced rock-steady in the crook of a tree branch. The last time I'd fought a duel I'd been padded in camouflage and wool with Kostia at my back, idly talking in the lulls about whether a face-off between two snipers constituted a fair fight. I yearned for a pinch of dry tea and a lump of sugar to chew; for a heel of black bread with strips of fatback and salt. I yearned for Kostia.

I held my position. I'd hold it all night if I had to.

A rumble of thunder sounded overhead in the rushing black clouds. Even as I prayed for rain not to fall, I adjusted my Colt against the branch and took aim at the central bridge stone. I got three shots off in the masking roll of the next crack of thunder—three shots weren't going to teach me enough about this weapon, her unique variations to the song they all sang in my hands, but it would have to be sufficient. My shots landed high; I was bracing my wrist up. I could compensate for that, but how much? A pistol was so unforgiving compared to a rifle; the tiniest movement could throw my shot off. For a sure hit, I would have to let him get close. Very close. Calculations split and slid through my mind as I shivered under the rising snap of the wind and thunder continued to peal.

And then I saw a limping shadow moving down the far side of the bank, and I went utterly still as the countdown began. Lady Midnight's countdown, the one I'd sung softly to myself from the days I'd been shooting at wooden targets to the day I killed my first enemies outside Odessa, all the way through 309 officially tallied kills and who knew how many unofficial ones, to *here*, to *now*, to this black, ghost-filled night on the far side of the world.

One . . . the first cool, measuring glance at the target, the moment the soul falls silent and the eye takes over.

Two . . . measuring the horizontal sight line; I didn't have telescopic sights tonight, but I could imagine the lines framing the marksman's shoulders as he stepped out of the trees.

Three . . . using that benchmark to calculate distance. Hardly any distance at all here, but still not close enough. My heavy .45-caliber bullet would drop fast as soon as it left the barrel, but I hadn't put in thousands of rounds of practice with this weapon to learn how fast.

Four . . . checking the bullet in the chamber.

Five . . . nestling the barrel forward a hair through the foliage as he stepped onto the bridge with his rifle leveled.

Six . . . watch him stop, watch him catch the flash of the diamonds just barely visible beneath the far arch of the bridge.

Seven . . . become stone, become ice, become so still frost could gather on me—all as I watched the President's would-be killer raise his weapon, satisfaction in every line of his body because he thought he had me dead in his sights.

Eight . . . final adjustment for wind, normally. No need here.

Nine . . . take aim.

Ten . . . breathe in.

Eleven . . . breathe out.

THE MARKSMAN WAS smiling as he fired, straight into the huddled heart of the lynx-fur mass. The girl sniper toppled on one side in the sluggishly moving stream, and he felt the slow, ecstatic beat of his heart as her arm flopped out. *Got you, you Red bitch.*

Then he saw the diamond bracelet slide off the fur sleeve without catching on a limp hand. Saw the fur collar gaping around a mass of pine needles. Saw the necklace he'd given her, wound around a sodden bundle of pine branches and sparkling up at him with a cold, merry light.

He looked wildly up from the dummy and saw the glitter. Not of diamonds, but of moonlight off a gun muzzle. *Oh, fu—*

TWELVE.

My shot took him clean through the right eye.

CHAPTER 34

want to go home.

All my light-footedness was gone as I began making my way out of Rock Creek Park. Every ache and pain had flooded back into me the moment I slid half frozen and shaking with aftermath out of that lightning-forked beech tree. I'd still made myself wade down into the creek where the dead man had toppled, heave him onto his back, and go through all his pockets. No identification, no keys, not so much as a handkerchief or a book of matches to tell me who he was or where he'd come from—only his rifle, and a scatter of bullets and odd little rough rocks in one pocket, which I transferred to mine so I'd have something to show the Soviet ambassador. Shrugging my cold-marbled arms gratefully back into the sodden lynx sleeves, I stood for a moment looking down at the man I'd killed. Number 310, looking up at the sky with his blank, unremarkable face, the moon reflecting glossy and empty from his open eye. He looked surprised. They so often did. Even when you were the one used to dealing death, you were still surprised when it came for you.

What's your name? I wondered, looking down at him. And then in a sudden surge of exhaustion and distaste, I didn't care. I didn't care who he was or who he'd been working for. I didn't care about anything but going home and holding my son in my arms, cradling his beautiful head between my hands as I promised him on my life that I would never leave him again.

So I left the marksman behind, jamming the pistol that had killed him into my coat pocket and limping on my torn soles back toward the city street and the abandoned Packard. Once I got there, it was some six or seven kilometers back to the hotel on foot . . . I'd walked it before, swinging my yellow satin dress in its shop bag, but that had been on a warm day in comfortable canvas lace-ups, not in utterly shredded American stockings on a blustery midnight. But I'd have to walk it now; I couldn't drive and I didn't have a single coin for a taxi. Would the delegation have returned to the hotel by now, or were they embroiled in uproar at the White House? Had the White House even realized they'd had an assassin on their grounds, or—

"Mila!" Alexei's voice, sharp with alarm through the trees. "Is that you?"

"Alexei?" I pulled up, swaying with exhaustion—he stood just inside the tree line at the edge of the park, a silhouette against the shadowed saplings, streetlights not far behind. "Why didn't you go raise the alarm?" Even as anger went through me in a spasm, relief did, too. Now I could collapse into the embassy car and he could drive us wherever we needed to go to make our report. I'd make him a hero in the telling, just for that—give him all the credit he liked, as long as I could sit down.

"Is he dead?" Alexei asked, coming a step closer.

"Dead under Boulder Bridge," I said wearily, and that was when my husband shot me.

The bullet whisked through my hair. It should have sunk through my left eye socket but I'd seen his arm rise, seen the glint of metal where there shouldn't have been metal, and that dark claw-rake of instinct sent me lurching sideways before I'd registered what was happening, so the bullet grooved the tip of my ear instead of burying itself in my brain. There was nothing controlled this time about my flight; I went half scrambling and half galloping into the thicket of brush on all fours, crashing like a panicked deer.

"You're wondering how I got a weapon." Alexei's voice was shockingly conversational. "The Colt that fell under the seat . . . along with a few rounds of ammunition."

I fetched up behind a big half-rotted tree stump, both hands clamped over my mouth to stop my ragged gasps from escaping. The tip of my earlobe dripped hot blood down onto my shoulder. My husband had shot me. Alexei had *shot* me. And I wasn't even surprised. He knew he'd never win me back, and even if he had, he'd never have been satisfied living the rest of his life hanging on the arm of a more famous wife. Maybe he wouldn't have thought to kill me on his own, but the marksman had handed him a chance on a silver platter: either I'd have died in the duel with the President's would-be assassin and Alexei would get to raise the alarm alone, the grieving widower and heroic messenger—or I killed the marksman, Alexei killed me when I was exhausted and off guard, and the rest went according to script. Either way, he didn't have to share the glory with me, and he was free of his bitch wife.

Or maybe he hadn't even thought it through that much. Maybe he just wanted me dead and thought he could get away with it.

"Don't run, Mila." I heard Alexei reloading his Colt, and I scrabbled for my own in my sodden pocket. "I saw how wet that coat was. You'll freeze to death out here if you run, and it won't be pretty. I'll make it quick."

I got my pistol into my cold-numbed hand, frantically reloading, still fighting for breath. I risked a glance over the stump, and he was nowhere in sight. He wasn't stupid; he knew not to give me a silhouette. I'd be foolish to underestimate him simply because he wasn't the marksman I'd just left dead. My husband was no sniper, but he'd already winged me in near-total darkness, from thirty paces, with an unfamiliar weapon. And he was warm, rested, alert, committed; a man with dry clothes, sturdy shoes, and the prize of a lifetime—freedom, fame—within his grasp. Not an exhausted, half-frozen woman with two broken ribs and pulverized feet, who'd left a blood trail clear from Rock Creek while driving herself to the breaking point dispatching *another* man bent on killing her tonight.

For an instant, I felt my whole shivering body contract in on itself, and I understood why animals sometimes froze in a predator's path and waited with dulled eyes for death to claim them. I was so tired. I'd shot so many enemies in Odessa, in Sevastopol—now I'd crossed half the globe and I was still shooting enemies. When did they stop coming? When would I look around and see no one advancing to kill me? Could I just close my eyes and let it all stop?

But Alexei wasn't any enemy; he was the first enemy. The one I'd outgrown, the one I'd stopped being afraid of a long time ago when larger monsters entered my sights . . . but still the first. The one whose gaze had prickled me as I pulled a five-year-old Slavka away from him at the shooting range, the one who made me think perhaps it would be just as well if I learned to shoot. Not only so I had a father's skills to teach my son someday, but if the moment came to defend us.

Well. Here it was. Die here, and Alexei would try his best to swan home a hero and claim my son.

"Mila?" His voice sounded again, impatient, taut. "Don't play dead. I know I didn't hit you. If I had, you'd be screaming."

I drew a deep, slow breath. "You have no idea what makes me scream. In battlefield or in bed, you pathetic sad sack of a man."

I *felt* his surprise through the shadows. Him behind a rocky slope somewhere to the southwest of me; me behind my tree stump: this was another waiting game, like the one I'd played not even an hour ago with the marksman in his nest and me pinned behind a boulder. Only the marksman could have waited forever. I hadn't known his name, but I'd known he'd had a sniper's patience. I'd had to play my trick with the matches to change the game, change the ground, change the beat.

I no longer had any tricks up my sleeve, just a pistol and a few remaining shots. But this was an enemy I knew, right down to his bones.

"You'll never get away with killing me," I called into the dark. "Everyone in the delegation knows how I despise you. They'll never believe you had nothing to do with my death."

"I'm going to be the hero of the night," he called back. "Once I tell them where to find the man who tried to kill the president—"

"You're still just the messenger. They'll know I'm the one who took care of him. They'll fete me in Red Square with a citywide parade and make me posthumous Hero of the Soviet Union. You'll be playing second best even at my funeral."

"You're my wife." His voice rose, despite himself. I was getting to him. "That famous name you're boasting of, that's *my* name."

"Not anymore." I flexed my right hand, shaking out the tremors. "You dreamed of making your name famous, Alexei? You dreamed it would be known from Moscow to Vladivostok? You dreamed of Lieutenant Pavlichenko, Hero of the Soviet Union? Well, it's all coming true. But for me, not you." I hissed the words through the dark between us like a viper, sinking each one deep. He'd never listened when I said no, never heard when I begged *please*, but he'd hear this. Maybe it was the only thing he was capable of hearing: that his grand dreams had blossomed for someone else. "I didn't even want fame. All I wanted was to defend my home. I didn't want fame, but I still got it—not you. You're still just what you've always been: a dog eating scraps from someone else's table. You don't have a drop of real heroism in you. All you've ever been is a collection of pieces scavenged from someone else—mostly me."

I heard him breathing faster, felt the pulse of his anger rising. *If you were clever, Alexei, you'd abandon this madness and go back to the hotel,* I thought. *Leave me out here waiting; concoct a story to tell the delegation and get in front of whatever I might say.* But he wasn't going to do that. Whatever had pitched him over that final edge and made him want me dead—the sight of me in Kostia's arms, maybe, or the sight of my name in one too many newspaper headlines—he wasn't going to let me leave Washington alive. He'd made his choice, and he was in it till the end.

"How does it feel?" I taunted, voice rising. "Knowing that the Pavlichenko recorded in the history books won't be you? It'll be your child bride instead. It'll be *me*."

The marksman wouldn't have broken at a schoolyard taunt. My husband did. I heard Alexei come out from behind the rocky slope to close the distance, saw his arm level, his teeth bared in a snarl of utter hatred—and I was erupting to my feet, bracing every exhausted muscle in my body behind the pistol as I fired once, twice, three times.

It happened in the space of a heartbeat, in the blink of a sniper's eye, in the flash of light off a diamond. He swayed—my husband, my first fear, my last shard of an outgrown life—and then he fell.

Alexei was dead.

I SUMMONED THE invisible steel, force, and spirit of Eleanor Roosevelt as I came into the hotel court at nearly two in the morning: my feet bloody, my face bruised and filthy, my sodden lynx furs wrapped over a destroyed satin gown. As my furious minder and half the delegation staff flooded toward me in a storm of Moscow suits and questions, I drew myself up as if I were six feet tall, pulled my coat collar around me like I'd seen Eleanor settle her famous fox stole, and put my hand out with all the absolute authority of the First Lady of the United States.

"Bit of a to-do with my husband," I said breezily, cutting off Yuri's *Where were you?* and Krasavchenko's *How dare you?* and Pchelintsev's *The First Lady said.* "I started feeling unwell at the White House, he offered as delegation doctor to drive me back early, and he ended up picking a quarrel and shoving me out somewhere near Rock Creek Park. The car's still there on Colorado and Blagden; it's full of delegation gifts, so I suggest you send someone to retrieve it. We will all assemble in Comrade Krasavchenko's room in forty-five minutes for a fuller report, but right now I intend to clean up."

The men parted for me as I made for the elevator, still spilling questions which I ignored. No one was saying anything about President Roosevelt or a hullabaloo at the White House, and that told me he was safe. Eleanor's husband was sleeping between crisp sheets right now, safe and sound . . . or perhaps he was hard at work at his desk despite the hour, and Eleanor was right there beside him. Making plans, perhaps, for when they could broach the matter of a second front to lend aid to my countrymen.

My glowering minder made to get into the elevator with me, and I put out my hand again. "Yuri," I said mildly, "*no*." And he stepped back and let the doors shut between us.

Tonight I'd survived two duels, countless minor injuries, and a seven-kilometer midnight walk on my shredded feet—yet the thing that nearly felled me was arriving at my hotel room two floors up and realizing I had no idea where the key was. I sagged against the door, shaking with exhaustion, wondering if I could curl up and go to sleep right here on the threshold—and then I nearly collapsed in a heap as the door opened inward and I fell right into Kostia's arms.

"Mila—" He gripped me, pulled me into the room and against his chest. My teeth were chattering too much to say anything, so I just clutched him. He was warm against me, granite-solid and night-silent in his dark shirt with the sleeves rolled up. He'd clearly let himself in with the key I'd given him days ago; waited for me in the chair by the desk where his borrowed copy of Walt Whitman lay facedown.

"You're h-here," I said, still shaking with cold, and the import of that struck me like a blow. He was *here*, not on his way to New York or to his family. He was here. With me, his face turned toward mine, not turned away to find a new future far from our homeland.

"I'm here," he said quietly, and that was all.

When I'd returned from my duel with the German sniper in Sevastopol, it had been Lyonya who peeled me out of my ice-stiffened clothes, wrapped me in a blanket, and began rubbing the life back into my cold feet and cramped shoulders. Now it was Kostia who stripped the creek-soaked lynx fur off my back, peeled away the destroyed yellow dress beneath it, and without comment laid aside my pistol and the little pile of diamonds all tangled up with loose .45 slugs and Alexei's wallet and ID. He didn't burst out with questions like the men downstairs; he just stripped me down and tucked me under the blankets, then crawled in and pulled me against him to warm me. "They said you hadn't come back from the White House, Mila. The First Lady told the ambassador you'd taken off running." His voice was normal, unconcerned, but I felt the tension humming through him like steel hawsers. Because unlike the men downstairs, he could recognize the aftermath of a sniper duel when he saw one.

I told him what happened. I'd go through it again in half an hour, for the benefit of the whole delegation, but this was a chance to get my facts in a row . . . figure out what I'd say, and what I'd leave out. Kostia pulled back when I finished, looked at me. I looked back, my teeth still chattering, reactions finally setting in now that I'd stopped long enough to let my guard down. "I killed Alexei," I repeated, stark and plain, not having to care if there were ears listening in this room. I couldn't stop shaking; I couldn't stop seeing his face. But I felt not one straw's worth of guilt. *He's gone. He's finally gone.* He wanted me, and if he couldn't have me, he wanted me dead, and now he was the one dead.

"You left them?" Kostia asked.

"Where they fell." I'd tell Krasavchenko and the Soviet ambassador where, and they could do what they liked about retrieving the bodies or leaving them to rot unidentified; involving the White House or not. Whichever way they decided to handle it, I knew it would be done with maximum discretion. This was one escapade by the Soviet girl sniper that would *not* be written up in any American newspapers.

The only thing I'd insist on, when I gave my briefing, was a full and comprehensive warning to Eleanor: *your husband has enemies who want him dead.* I'd taken care of one, but I was leaving American shores. She'd have to take over the watch.

But I trusted she could do it.

It occurred to me that when I pulled the trigger tonight—first on the marksman, then on Alexei—I had not once intoned my desperate prayer of *Don't miss.* Perhaps Eleanor's lesson had finally sunk home: the knowledge that even if I'd missed, I'd have gotten up, fired again, kept going until I succeeded. Until I saved the American president; until I saved myself.

Kostia was still looking at me, gaze urgent enough to burn. *What do you need?* he was telling me. *How can I help?* I just nestled into his chest, floating somewhere between warmth and cold, between the dregs of old fury and the restlessness of a finished hunt, burrowing into this oasis of warmth and safety before I'd have to rise and make my report. I saw the marksman lying in the creek, an enigma to the end. I saw Alexei's eyes staring up at the gibbous moon, empty as glass. I wondered what the official excuse would be when he failed to return to the Soviet Union. Would they say he'd defected or—

My eyes snapped suddenly wide at the word *defected,* half stupefied though I was by the warmth creeping through my limbs and the leak of adrenaline seeping out of them. "Kostia, where have *you* been tonight?" He'd skipped the farewell dinner and he'd clearly come to some decision during that time, but how?

"The Soviet embassy," he said into my shoulder blade. "I've been heading back there every week, whenever I had a few hours free. I needed a Cyrillic typewriter."

I blinked. "A Cyrillic typewriter?"

"I can't give you diamonds." Kostia nodded at the glittering heap on my desk, raising himself on one elbow to reach a pile of paper sitting on the nightstand. "All I could think of was this. I finished it tonight."

I snaked an arm out from under the coverlet to take the pages, reading the title at the top in neatly typed Cyrillic letters. " 'Bogdan Khmelnitsky, the Ukraine's accession to Russia in 1654, and the activities of the Pereyaslav Council: a student dissertation by Lyudmila Mikhailovna Pavlichenko,' " I read in astonishment. "You . . . you retyped my dissertation?"

"Pecked it out with two fingers." Kostia kissed the back of my neck. "You had blood all over the last one."

I wondered if this had been intended as a goodbye gift. Maybe, as he typed through my final footnotes tonight, he'd changed his mind about leaving. Or maybe finishing it had been a way to keep himself from turning toward the life that beckoned here.

Time enough to talk about that later, once we had real privacy.

"Thank you," I whispered, smoothing my hand over the pages. The marksman had given me diamonds. My husband had utterly ignored anything I told him I wanted, because he always knew better.

My sniper partner had retyped my dissertation with two fingers on a borrowed machine.

Kostia was sliding toward sleep in the way that snipers did, still full of questions, and full of tension too, but the body taking any opportunity for rest that it could. Careful not to wake him, I slid out of bed and into some fresh clothes, wondering if we'd all still be departing for Canada tomorrow or not.

As I stood sorting the bullets from the diamond jewelry and those odd little rough rocks I'd taken from the marksman's pocket, I found an unfamiliar lump. In Rock Creek Park, I'd automatically collected the shells from my shots that killed Alexei and the marksman—my hand had evidently swept up another lump of metal from the dead leaves. I blinked in bemusement at the modest gold signet ring with tiny dirtied chips of diamond, sized for a man's finger, metal dulled as though it had been buried from sunlight for decades. Inside the band were worn English letters—I couldn't make out the first, but the second was definitely an R.

I held it to the light, a memory nagging for a moment before it slipped into place: a White House aide on the mansion's lawn, telling me the story of President Teddy Roosevelt on a hike, losing a ring near Boulder Bridge forty years ago. Could this be it? I turned it over in my hand. It was a lovely thing, this marker from my final dueling ground. A sign, perhaps. I'd had two husbands, one in law and one in my heart; one who had fallen in Washington's woods where I'd never walk again, one who had fallen in Sevastopol where I might never walk again either unless it could be wrested out of Nazi hands. I should never have married the first husband, and time had stolen my chance of legally marrying the second.

I wouldn't make a mistake like either of those again. I wouldn't miss this third precious chance.

I leaned over Kostia, dozing so lightly, and folded the signet ring into his loose-curled hand. "When we get back to Moscow," I whispered softly, preparing to go meet with the rest of the delegation and pass on my full account, "marry me."

Notes by the First Lady

I watch my husband's chest rise and fall in sleep. He'll get far less rest than usual tonight—the hullabaloo behind closed doors, after Lyudmila's exit, was considerable, and there have been confused telephone calls winging back and forth from the Soviet embassy and Franklin's private line. The picture is far from complete, but one thing is clear: the immediate danger has been taken care of, thanks to the young woman who leaves our shores tomorrow.

Welcoming her to my home, I had no idea the service she would render me and this country. I only thought she might be of interest, another useful female of the type Franklin likes to collect and hone and use—use up, sometimes—in this great work of his.

Franklin's women. I am sure many books will be written about him someday, but I hope there will also be books about us. The woman who was his wife, his eyes and ears . . . the women who served on his cabinet and at his side in the White House . . . and the woman from a nation halfway around the world, a nation entirely foreign to us and sometimes frightening, who held no oath to him but nevertheless threw down her life in his defense.

I watch his chest rise and fall in the dark for another long moment, smiling. Then I close the door.

There is still much work to be done tonight before I find my bed . . . but a Russian bullet has given me peace and safety to do it.

CHAPTER 35

I t was a long two months more before I found myself back on Soviet soil, disembarking from a four-engine B-24 Liberator bomber
after an endless night flight from Glasgow to Vnukovo airfield.
Twelve hours in the bomber's belly, the inside sparkling with frost
like the Snow Queen's bedroom, the entire delegation wrapped in
furs to the whites of our eyes and talking of the tour we'd finally, *finally* completed. But I wasn't thinking now of the glittering functions
we'd attended in Montreal and London, Cambridge and Birming-
ham, Newcastle and Liverpool—not as we touched down at last in
an enormous frosty field ringed by a blue belt of snowy woods. *Home*,
I thought. I was supposed to be gone only one month—it had been
four.

A lifetime.

Disembarking, gloved hand linked with Kostia's—I could feel the
hard circle of the gold signet ring on his finger. My heart pounded as
I saw shadowy figures breaking away from the waiting crowd, running toward the bomber. Pchelintsev was already embracing his wife,
Krasavchenko kissing his father on both cheeks, but I had no thought
for them. I could see my mother with her long plait, bundled like a
round little owl . . . and breaking away from her, sprinting toward
me, a smaller figure.

My hand tore from Kostia's as I broke into a run. I shed Lady
Death behind me, I shed the famous sniper of a thousand photographs, I shed my proud hopes of seeing Allied soldiers in Europe
soon to buoy our eastern front—I shed everything but the sight of the

child running toward me, ten years old, lanky with growth, his face alight. I flung my arms around him and then my legs buckled underneath me and I crashed to my knees in the snow, holding my son in a hug like steel, weeping unashamedly into his hair.

Mila Pavlichenko was finally home.

EPILOGUE

Eleanor Roosevelt Arrives in Moscow

October 10, 1957

Mrs. Roosevelt, may I present Lyudmila Pavlichenko, Hero of the Soviet Union."

We looked at each other for a long moment—long enough for whispers to ripple through the Committee of Soviet Women clustered around us in the airless public hall. Fifteen years since the former First Lady and I had set eyes on each other. I took in the plain suit and black hat, the lines of grief that the loss of her extraordinary husband had carved on her face, and knew she was absorbing the changes time had wrought in me. I was forty-one now, no longer the angry young lieutenant who had eyed her so warily over the White House breakfast of eggs and bacon. My dark hair showed wings of gray at the temples, and my medals were pinned to a businesslike suit instead of an olive-drab uniform.

But I could feel my face cracking in a huge smile, a smile that mirrored in her face under the white hair. "Darling Lyudmila," she said, coming forward.

"Eleanor," I breathed, leaning into the embrace, and there was a ripple of applause as the two of us beamed at each other. Perhaps fifteen years was not so very long, after all. We had met once more during my English tour when Eleanor came to visit the Churchills, and we had corresponded when I returned to the Soviet Union. I'd sent a letter of condolence on the death of President Roosevelt ("Eleanor, I remember

the press of his hand as though it were yesterday"); she'd congratulated me after the war on the news that as a fifth-year student of the
Kiev State University history faculty, I'd finished my dissertation with
a grade of Excellent ("Lyudmila, I confess I do not remember who Bogdan Khmelnitsky is, and I pray you will not tell me!")

And here she was in Moscow, a First Lady no longer but still a
diplomatic force to be reckoned with, our positions reversed: now she
was the one on a goodwill tour of my country.

There were speeches to sit through (there are always speeches);
there were hands to be shaken (there are always handshakes); there
were commemorative plaques to be presented (for the love of Lenin,
no more plaques—where is a Hero of the Soviet Union to put them
all?). But at long last the former First Lady and I were permitted to
retire to my Moscow apartment, sitting with our feet up, drinking tea
from the samovar in the corner, security details and NKVD minders
alike waiting outside.

"You have a beautiful home, Lyudmila." Her eyes took in the apartment I'd been awarded: four whole rooms near the center of Moscow,
not far from the Soviet Navy department where I'd worked, an entire
wall filled with nothing but my books. "Does your son live with you?"

"He has a place of his own now. Graduated with distinction from
Moscow University's law faculty." My Slavka, a young man now,
so steady and kind, his dark hair and stocky build marking him a
younger version of my father. Nothing, fortunately, like his own.

"He must make you proud." Eleanor studied me, stirring her tea.
"You look happy, Lyudmila. I confess I worried that it might make
you bitter—the fact that you never returned to the front, after your
goodwill tour."

"It was determined that I would be of more use as a sniper instructor." Yes, I'd been bitterly disappointed at the time . . . but as Kostia
pointed out, if I'd returned to sniping, I would probably have died in
Stalingrad with so many other sharpshooters, and that would have

been a great propaganda victory for the Germans. Instead I was assigned to train new snipers—and not just boys. Girls passed through
my hands, cherry-cheeked girls like I'd once been, so fierce and burning bright. I'd poured my skills into them, told them how to manage
the shakes in their hands when they made their first kills, and that
shaking hands didn't mean they lacked courage. I taught them how
to camouflage themselves and care for their weapons; how to scavenge
battlefields for spare cloth, because the Red Army would never give
them enough for their monthlies; how to avoid amorous officers and
how to cross no-man's-land on lynx feet so silent that the long-dead
Vartanov would have blinked tears of pride.

I taught them to try again without shame when they missed a shot.
That failure was not always a death sentence.

I taught them everything I knew and I saluted them when they left
me and I grieved them when they died . . . and the ones who lived, I
hosted here in Moscow to drink vodka and trade stories of old nightmares and comrades in arms long gone, and we'd part with tears on
our cheeks and smiles on our lips: the girl snipers who lived.

Maybe I could have added more Nazis to my tally, but more than
two thousand women fought for their homeland as sharpshooters by
the end of the war, and a good portion of them were trained by me.
The tally of every woman I trained stands alongside mine, and as a
woman of forty-one I cannot look back and see my switch from sniper
to sniper instructor as a waste.

"Besides," I said now to Eleanor, smiling, "I wanted to be a historian, not a sniper. And I became one."

"Certainly you did—Lyudmila, are you putting *jam* in your tea?"

"It's the Russian way." I added a heaping spoonful of cherry jam
to her cup. "I hope you'll have time on your visit to meet with the
Committee of War Veterans?"

"Of course. You work with them now that you're retired from—
what was your position again?"

"Research assistant in the Soviet Navy fleet history section." I'd retired a few years ago, my old war wounds acting up. All those concussions, all that shell shock, all that scar tissue . . . it sank deeper as I got older, rather than fading away. "But retirement is no reason to sit around doing nothing."

"I could not agree more," said the former First Lady.

Kostia slipped in then, still lean as a wire, his hair now iron gray, our dog bounding in front of him. He'd finished his war at my side, my shadow to the end, helping me train young snipers . . . and then he found himself at the Red Star Kennel helping train military dogs, who he said were much smarter than most military recruits. We had a big black Russian terrier puppy of our own now; Kostia romped with her all over Gorky Park every day, ignoring his old limp. "My husband," I introduced him as he came to drop a kiss on my hair and shake Eleanor's hand, but no more than that. For many reasons, Kostia kept a low profile.

"He looks familiar," Eleanor said thoughtfully as Kostia nodded farewell and took the dog into the next room for a brushing. "Was he on the Washington delegation?"

"Mmm," I murmured.

"Perhaps I'm thinking of your first husband . . . I didn't realize until later that *he* had accompanied the tour to Washington."

"Mmm." I smiled.

"You didn't paint a very flattering portrait of him, little as you told me." Eleanor's eyes regarded me calmly over the rim of her glass. "Perhaps it's no great tragedy that he didn't end up leaving with the rest of you."

"Mmm." Alexei Pavlichenko had officially died on tour of a burst appendix—all part of the frantic behind-the-scenes scurrying to make sure nothing from Rock Creek Park surfaced to embarrass either the Soviet delegation or the White House. Nothing at all, of course, was said of the marksman.

I still woke at night sometimes thinking of his mud-colored eyes, wondering what his name had been. Who had hired him. Eleanor and I had never had the opportunity to speak of such things, even when we met afterward in England.

Now . . .

"Remember that eccentric American businessman who proposed marriage to me?" I mused, stirring my tea. "I always wondered what became of him. Who his friends were, the people he worked with."

(It would be foolish to assume there were no listening ears tuned to hear this conversation. Eleanor and I might be friends, but our nations no longer were, much as that grieved me.)

"My husband had a good idea who your suitor's friends were," Eleanor said. "He spoke with a few of them, after your departure. There was a certain settling of accounts . . . I don't believe anyone gave much trouble after that."

Clearly not. If there were any further attempts on his life, they had evidently failed: he had sailed unharmed into a fourth term, after all. "I wish President Roosevelt could have lived to see the end of the war." I'd saved him from death on Halloween night of 1942, and he'd lived long enough to fulfill his promise that American soldiers would come to aid my countrymen . . . but he'd died before Hitler's fall.

"He might not have lived to see victory, but he lived long enough to ensure it." And Eleanor raised her cup to me, in silent thanks.

I raised mine in return. We held each other's eyes a long moment, and then we both began clattering our saucers like the middle-aged ladies we were. "Such good weather for your visit, Eleanor—"

"Yes, and I do hope I can see more of this country in your company while I am here, Lyudmila!"

"This time I will be *your* tour guide. There's so much I want to show you. Leningrad, Tsarskoye Selo, the Hermitage, and the Russian Museum . . . But for tonight," I said, "the opera. I have tickets for *Eugene Onegin,* since my friend Vika is dancing a variation in the ballroom scene. She was a tank driver in the war, you know—decorated three times for bravery, and now she's a Bolshoi ballerina."

"What extraordinary women your country produces," Eleanor observed.

"I'll introduce you to more of them." I knew so many now through my work with female war veterans: Vika, prickly and incorrigibly elegant despite the fact that she'd lost an eye during the final drive toward Berlin; a dark-haired Hero of the Soviet Union named Yelena Vetsina who had flown nine hundred bombing runs with the Night Witches . . . and best of all, my darling friend Lena Paliy. She hadn't died in the fall of Sevastopol after all. She'd turned up emaciated but alive after retreating into the hills from the German invasion, and now we went walking every month in Gorky Park to talk about old times. I was usually late, and she'd pound on my apartment door with a shouted, *Wake up, sleepyhead!*

"Vodka during the day?" Eleanor shook her head disapprovingly when I proposed a toast before we headed out. "Very bad habit, Lyudmila dear."

"You can't call yourself a veteran until you have at least one bad habit you can't kick." I grinned.

In truth, I have more than one. I drink too much, this I know. I wake at night gasping from the old memories of battle, or dreams where I am frozen in that lightning-split beech tree beside Rock Creek until the marksman comes to put a bullet through *my* eye instead of the other way round. On those nights Kostia has to hold me until the shudders subside, and on other nights I do the same when his own demons of war come snarling and red-clawed through the land of sleep to hunt for him. I still tense up whenever I hear anything that sounds like a shot, and I can't enter a room, a building, or an open space without parsing the movement lines and the potential threats. But that is the cost, as much as the old physical wounds that still sometimes cause me pain. The invisible wounds can hurt just as much—if not more.

The Party is encouraging me to write my memoirs. *A straightforward account of your heroics on the front line, Comrade Pavlichenko, with suitably stoic reflections on courage, duty, and the bright future of the motherland.* But, as I have frequently reflected in the years since my war concluded, there will be a great difference between any official account of my time in the Red Army and the version that lives in my memory. I can write honestly about the friends I lost, about my work as a sniper and the demands it places upon the soul. I can write about the extraordinary people I met on my goodwill tour from America to Canada to Britain, from Charlie Chaplin to Franklin Roosevelt, from Paul Robeson to Winston Churchill. I will not lie in my memoir . . . but there is much I will leave out.

Alexei Pavlichenko will not appear in those pages, except in a line or two as the infatuation of a foolish girl hardly out of childhood and the father of my son. Let him disappear from memory, from the pages of history, into the leaf mold of a Washington park.

Kostia will not appear in those pages, either, for very different reasons. Not long after we returned from our overseas tour, he had quiet word that his unofficial father, that Baikal fur trapper who had passed his diamond eye and savage skill to the son he'd fathered in Irkutsk, had been denounced for speaking against Comrade Stalin. It took half my diamonds—the uncut ones I'd scavenged from the marksman's pockets, and the bracelets from the jewelry set he'd given me in a duelist's challenge—to keep Kostia's name off the warrants that swept up the rest of his father's family, the sons and daughters who bore the name *Markov* and not *Shevelyov*. I keep the rest of my jewels in reserve, and Kostia lives quietly, not drawing on the fame that could be his as a decorated sniper and the husband of Lady Death. I sometimes look at him and wonder if he has regrets: the children we weren't able to have, the family he left behind in America . . . but if so, he never voices them. I hope I have been enough for him, and since he made the choice to yoke his life to mine, I have sworn to keep him safe. Red Army records may say I was intimate with my sniper partner, but the partner in my memoir won't be named as Konstantin Shevelyov. I'll give that title to one of my other platoon members instead—one of the men too long dead to gainsay my word—and I'll keep my husband anonymous.

And finally, there will be no word in my memoir of the muddy-eyed man who courted me, stalked me, and fought me in Rock Creek Park.

Because people love war heroes . . . but even in my own beloved homeland, war heroes are supposed to be clean and uncomplicated. Those urging me to write my memoir will want a patriotic young woman who fought to defend her country, a heroine to root for with a story clean and simple as a full moon—and I was that young woman, but I was more. My moon had a midnight side.

To the world, Lyudmila Pavlichenko's tally officially stands at 309, a list achieved without bloodthirstiness, every shot fired in simple defense of hearth and home. Only a few know that there was another duel fought under a waning moon on the other side of the world, a duel fought in rage and desperation and savage self-preservation against two very different men . . . and that my true tally stands at 311.

But that is my secret, a sniper's secret, and it dies with me. Eleanor knows, but I saved her husband's life, and perhaps our nations along with it, so she will take my secrets to her grave. So I put down my tea and head to my wardrobe with a smile. "I don't have that old yellow satin dress anymore, but let's see what I can rustle up to wear to the opera tonight . . ."

"I'm here to tack up a hem or let down a sleeve if you require it," said the First Lady.

AUTHOR'S NOTE

Odds are, you've never heard of Lyudmila Pavlichenko. A few years ago, I hadn't, either—it wasn't until my research into *The Huntress*'s Night Witch pilots that I ran smack into the astounding story of another Soviet war heroine: this celebrated library-researcher-turned-sniper who was responsible for 309 kills during World War II, took America by storm during a publicity tour in 1942, hobnobbed with Hollywood stars, and became White House besties with Eleanor Roosevelt. I knew at once that I had to write her incredible story.

The Soviet Union's record before, during, and after the war isn't pretty, so it's easy to forget that in the early days of World War II, they were the underdog. The Third Reich regarded Russians as racial undesirables fit only to be exterminated; Soviet soldiers were routinely slaughtered or starved if they were taken prisoner, unlike the more by-the-book treatment of French and English POWs. The Russians responded with equal savagery once the tide turned in their favor, but at the beginning of Germany's terrifying and overwhelming invasion, all the under-equipped Red Army could do was mount a fighting retreat, letting the harsh terrain and Russian winter do to Hitler what it had done to Napoleon. That strategy came at a horrifying cost: millions of Soviets died wearing down the German advance.

And many of those front-line lives at stake were women.

The USSR was the only Allied nation to employ women on the front line in their actively fighting military branches. Approximately 800,000 women served in the Soviet Armed Forces during the war, or about 5 percent of the total military personnel. They were more likely to be shunted into communications and medical personnel, but many managed to play a more active part: bomber pilots, like the Night Witches; tank drivers, like Mila's friend Vika—and snipers.

Hollywood has colored our view of sharpshooters. We imagine them as militarized serial killers; at best they're the odd man out on a squad of regular guys, the one described as having ice water in his veins—see Barry Pepper's Scripture-quoting sniper in Steven Spielberg's *Saving Private Ryan*. And the idea persists that killing from a distance, from hidden nests, is somehow dishonorable or unfair . . . but skilled marksmen have been used by every army since the invention of firearms (and before that the bow and arrow: think of the English archers bringing down French knights at Agincourt, or Robin Hood's Merry Men downing royal soldiers from hidden forest hideouts!). The use of snipers isn't a violation of the Geneva Convention, but the stereotype persists: snipers are cold-blooded, remote, pitiless. As Eleanor Roosevelt said when meeting Lyudmila Pavlichenko: If you have a good view of the faces of your enemies through your sights and still fire to kill, how can ordinary people approve of you?

But the woman known as Lady Death defies such stereotypes. She comes across in her memoirs and the anecdotes of her peers as warm, funny, charming, a bookworm, a loving mother, an introvert who savored her alone time but could nevertheless be the life of the party. She did not even have the requisite ice-blue or cold gray eyes most snipers are described as having!

She was no naïf who learned to shoot at the front; she arrived in uniform already an accomplished markswoman. Neither did she come from the kind of rural family where a daughter might be expected to wield a rifle right out of the cradle. She was Ukrainian (though she described herself firmly as Russian when asked), a city girl and a booklover whose ambition was to be a historian, but she enjoyed the occasional outing at the gun range with her friends—enjoyed it enough that she decided to apply for an advanced marksmanship course. Though she acquired her skills as a hobby, she lost no time volunteering them in her country's defense: a young woman went to the beach with her friends in the morning, heard the declaration of war at noon over lunch at a nearby café, and by nightfall was leaving *La Traviata* early to go enlist. It didn't take long for the girl from Odessa—the graduate student who had been finishing the world's nerdiest dissertation on Bogdan Khmelnitsky, the Ukraine's accession to Russia in 1654, and the activities of the Pereyaslav Council—to begin racking up a serous tally.

A sniper's official tally consisted only of confirmed kills, so Lyudmila's true list of enemy dead probably did not stand at the official 309: fighting in two desperate sieges, she would not have had time or opportunity to verify all of her kills, and the enemies she downed fighting as a soldier rather than a sniper wouldn't have been counted at all. Her true tally might have been less than the 309 eventually finalized for official purposes; it could also easily have been much more. What seems certain is that in less than eighteen months of fighting, Lyudmila Pavlichenko buried hundreds of enemies, was wounded at least four times, and earned the nickname Lady Death. Many of the feats described in this novel—her training of a platoon, the assaults on Gildendorf and No-Name Height, her recruitment of the ranger Vartanov whose family had been murdered, the Kabachenko homestead and the bond she formed with a young girl who had been raped by German soldiers ("Kill them all")—are drawn directly from the memoir Lyudmila wrote later in life.

Soviet memoirs are long on fact and short on emotion; it isn't the Soviet way to gush about feelings. Yet Lyudmila's response to becoming such an efficient taker of lives come through as far from ghoulish. Making her first two kills under the eye of Captain Sergienko, she didn't hesitate to down the two officers, yet admitted that firing on a target and firing on a human being were very different things. She disliked her own growing fame, viewing herself simply as a soldier with a job to do: the enemy were invaders who had been ordered to attack; she was a defender who had been ordered to push them back, and that was that. Her anger at the Germans flowered into hatred as she saw the damage Hitler's forces inflicted on her homeland, but Lyudmila still prided herself on clean kills and utter professionalism. The only time she gave the order to shoot to wound rather than to kill was in the final defense of Sevastopol, where it was the only way to slow down an overwhelming enemy.

The Russian front was pure hell: the casualty rates were appalling, the weather brutal, the troops ill trained and under-equipped, almost as likely to be shot by their own officers (if they showed a single sign of faltering) as by the Germans. Women soldiers had an especially tough time of it. Red Air Force women like the Night Witches served together in all-female regiments or were at least grouped with their sister pilots in mixed regiments, but Red Army women were vastly outnumbered by male soldiers and commonly regarded as sexual perks for the officers. Turning down a superior's advances could result in anything from physical assault to being left off lists for commendations and promotions. Lyudmila was intensely admired by the men in her company, whom she apparently handled with friendly but steely authority, but at least one source states that she incurred resentment for turning down men who outranked her. This could explain her lack of military decorations early in her fight . . . until a three-day duel with a German sniper catapulted her to fame.

Detractors disputed both that fame and her achievements. Even now, some insist that Lyudmila Pavlichenko was a fake, a pretty propaganda-department brunette with a memorized story designed to inspire the masses. Such claims nitpick at the inaccuracies in her memoir's timeline, insist that the kind of platoon she described leading wasn't yet formed, and cite her refusal to demonstrate her sharpshooting skills in America as proof she didn't actually have any.

To me, Lyudmila Pavlichenko comes across as the real deal. Her memoir bears the stamp of Soviet propaganda, but her technical recall of a sniper's skills, weapons, and routine is exactly where her voice is the most precise and vividly individual. There are inaccuracies in her timeline, but a woman piecing her memories together through the fog of war and the PTSD of multiple battlefield concussions is bound to get a few details wrong. The kind of sniper platoon she described leading didn't exist yet in the Red Army, but Lyudmila was fighting in the early days of the war when everything was slapdash, and she was probably making up procedure as she went along. As for her on-tour *nyet* whenever she was asked to shoot on command (except for one gun-club demonstration in Chicago), her reasons come through loud and clear in her memoir: Lady Death scorned the idea of being trotted out like some show-pony circus shooter, and she absolutely refused to reduce her deadly skills to a parlor trick.

Her war wasn't all mud, blood, and pain. Lyudmila had a sense of humor, which shines through when she recounts butting heads with oblivious superior officers or relaxing with her platoon in an evening of song, vodka, and scavenged treats after a successful raid. And despite her mandate of no fraternizing with male colleagues, she broke her own rules for a spectacularly romantic front-line love affair.

At twenty-four, Lyudmila had already endured a minefield of a love life. She says extremely little (and nothing good) of her first husband Alexei Pavlichenko, the older man who seduced and impregnated her after a dance when she was barely fifteen. Lyudmila's only comment about Alexei, after he abandoned her and their son Rostislav, is: "Fortunately, my son is nothing like his father." As a single mother she remained focused on her work, her education, and her son—so romance hit like a thunderbolt when she met a tall, funny, good-looking Red Army lieutenant in Sevastopol. Enter Lyonya Kitsenko, the man who wooed and won the most dangerous woman on the Russian front.

Kitsenko is frequently described as her junior sergeant and fellow sniper, her partner with whom she hunted night after night as part of a lethal, inseparable team—but Lyudmila described him as the lieutenant who commanded her company. My conjecture is that two men may have been confused, and that Lyudmila was romantically involved with both her company commander and her sniper partner at different points. Thus I separated the two and described Kitsenko as Lyudmila did: Lieutenant Alexei Arkadyevich Kitsenko, nicknamed Lyonya, her superior officer and eventually second husband. Whether they were legally married or not (he is not listed on her grave as her spouse), Lyudmila regarded Lyonya as her husband in every way that counted: they had a whirlwind courtship culminating in the attack where Lyonya carried the wounded Lyudmila off the front line, gave blood for her surgery, visited throughout her recovery, and invited her to dinner in his dugout (complete with flowers in a shell-casing vase!) the day she was released. He proposed that night; he and Lady Death were inseparable from then on.

It was the best time of Lyudmila's war. She wrote that love was good for her shooting; while she was coming home to Lyonya she seemed to hit every target she aimed at, including the tense three-day duel where she and her sniper partner (to whom I gave the name of Konstantin Shevelyov, a name later crucial in her life) outwitted a German sharpshooter. But after barely three months together, Lyonya was hit by mortar fire right before Lyudmila's eyes. He died in her arms hours later, and she nearly went mad from grief. She wasn't able to return to shooting until she and her sniper partner grieved together at Lyonya's grave. Then she returned to the front lines with a new fury: as she later told Eleanor Roosevelt, every German in her sights after that might as well have been the man who killed Lyonya.

Sevastopol fell months later, and Lyudmila likely would have been killed there (women snipers in the Red Army had about a 75 percent chance of dying in combat) had she not been wounded and evacuated a few weeks before. Despite her wish to return to the front, the propaganda department had other ideas. A missive had recently landed on Stalin's desk from Washington, D.C., inviting a deputation of Soviet students to join Eleanor Roosevelt's international student conference, and the Boss saw an opportunity: Lady Death was headed to America.

She certainly felt like a fish out of water, and the White House welcome breakfast did not go well: Lyudmila's terse response to the First Lady's comment about how a woman sniper could be relatable to Americans is drawn directly from her memoir, as are her responses to the astonishingly asinine questions she was asked at her first press conference. But one woman turned things around for Lyudmila: the First Lady, who offered her Soviet guest a ride in her convertible to that evening's dinner party. Though her driving apparently alarmed Lady Death more than an entire panzer division, it signaled the beginning of an unlikely friendship.

It was Eleanor who introduced Lyudmila and her fellow delegates to FDR for a private meeting where they could discuss the hoped-for second front in Europe, and who escorted her on part of her subsequent goodwill tour around America. The idea of a First Lady and a Russian sniper becoming friends may seem wildly improbable, but many of their scenes in *The Diamond Eye* are taken directly from Lyudmila's memoir: their discussions on American segregation (which appalled Lyudmila, as did British colonialism in India); Lyudmila falling asleep in the presidential limousine with her head on Eleanor's shoulder; Lyudmila tumbling out of a canoe at the Hudson estate and ending up in the First Lady's bedroom as Eleanor hemmed a pair of pink pajamas for her and they chatted for so long that FDR had to retrieve the unlikely BFFs for dinner!

Under Eleanor's wing, Lyudmila found her feet in the spotlight. She met everyone from Charlie Chaplin to Woody Guthrie (who wrote a song for her, "Miss Pavlichenko"—find it on YouTube!) and became a passionate public speaker, never forgetting her mission of asking for American aid on behalf of her fellow soldiers. In Chicago she brought an audience roaring to their feet with the speech that cemented her fame: "Gentlemen, I have killed 309 fascist invaders by now. Don't you think, gentlemen, that you have been hiding behind my back for too long?"

Eleanor and Lyudmila bid goodbye at a farewell dinner at the White House in October 1942. They continued to correspond for the next fifteen years, as FDR carried through on his promise to send American soldiers to Europe and Mila finished her war as a sniper instructor. In 1957, the widowed Eleanor came to the USSR on a goodwill tour of her own, and the former First Lady and the former sniper embraced with cries of welcome.

My author notes usually take time to explain where my fictional characters weave in with the historical ones. *The Diamond Eye* is different, because nearly every person named comes straight from the historical record. Lyudmila's fellow delegates Pchelintsev and Krasavchenko; her officers General Petrov, Lieutenant Dromin, and Captain Sergienko; her platoon mates Fyodor Sedykh and old Vartanov; her Odessa friend Sofya and medical orderly friend Lena Paliy . . . all real. My only substantial fictional additions to the record are Vika, the ballerina turned tank driver (a heroine I have in mind for a future novel!), and Kostia Shevelyov, who is a fictionalized composite of two real men.

I have taken some liberties with the historical record to serve the novel. A few of Lyudmila's front-line adventures were condensed and reordered: the Romanian attack with priests was slightly moved up, and her subsequent recovery moved to the hospital battalion rather than back in Odessa. The first sortie she fights with Kostia was fought with another recruit, and Lyonya is introduced earlier in *The Diamond Eye* than he appeared in real life—his time with Lyudmila was so limited, I couldn't resist bringing him onstage sooner! Some events on the goodwill tour are also reordered: Lyudmila's meeting with Laurence Olivier likely didn't happen until she went to England, and FDR's private tour of U.S. defense plants ended somewhat earlier and wasn't intended to coincide with any of Lyudmila's California press engagements.

Wherever I have conflicting information, such as the exact name of Lyudmila's regiment or the precise evening of the Soviet delegation's White House farewell, I have used Lyudmila's version—likewise, I generally use her spellings of location names and Russian names, which may appear differently in modern maps and transliterations. Some of the facts and figures she quotes may not be accurate, but they are the facts and figures she would have believed were accurate at the time, so I have used them. There are also incidents in Lyudmila's memoir which I have chosen to leave out, like a meeting with Stalin that probably didn't happen. It has been something of a delicate dance to treat Lyudmila Pavlichenko's memoir as the concrete original source of its heroine's memories, yet also a document with which the propaganda office took some liberties.

Her memoir contains tantalizing gaps and silences which I've filled in with artistic license. Lyudmila states that she last saw her husband Alexei Pavlichenko three years before war broke out, and she makes no further mention of him. Likely he was one of the millions of Russian men who disappeared into the Red Army and died on the front—there is some evidence suggesting he was a doctor, so I brought him into the novel as a combat surgeon. His ultimate fate was unknown, so I crafted what I felt was a suitably satisfying end for the man who seduced a fifteen-year-old and abandoned her and their child.

The other place I filled in a historical gap is around Lyudmila's sniper partner, and around her final husband Kostia Shevelyov. Lyudmila's partner is named in her memoir as Fyodor Sedykh: such a relationship would have been as intimate as a working relationship could possibly be, yet she makes no mention of him after Sevastopol. Likewise, the man who became her husband after the war is a complete blank: we know nothing about Kostantin Shevelyov except his birth and death dates. Why does her memoir contain so little about two men who would have been so important to her?

I gave her a reason: Konstantin Shevelyov had good cause to fly under the radar, and his famous wife was doing her level best to keep him out of her own limelight. In the carnivorous Stalinist regime, there could be any number of reasons a man might want to lie low. Thus I turned Kostia into Lyudmila's sniper partner so I could introduce Lady Death's final husband into the story and pay homage to the records that indicate a romantic link between her and her partner, but also gave him a background that explains why she might list another name as her partner.

Lastly, the marksman: there was no known plot against President Roosevelt in 1942, though he narrowly escaped assassination in 1933 when Giuseppe Zangara fired on him from a crowd in Miami, and he also managed to escape being deposed the following year by a shadowy cabal (allegedly including some of America's most prominent heads of industry) who hoped to replace him with a military dictator. By 1942, Roosevelt still had plenty of enemies who would have celebrated his death: isolationists, American fascists, political rivals who believed him a traitor to his race and class, and anti-communists who saw even a wartime alliance with the USSR as treason. Creating the marksman also allowed me to make sense of one of the most bizarre episodes of Lyudmila's goodwill tour: the American millionaire William Jonson who fell in love with her on her tour, followed her from city to city, proposed marriage, and sent her a spectacular set of diamond jewelry with a note stating: "We will meet again." According to Lyudmila's memoir, they did not. But this was too good a story to ignore, so in my version they do meet again: first at the White House (which had *much* less stringent security in the forties than it does today) and then in Rock Creek Park, a stretch of wilderness slicing through the nation's capital that has swallowed its share of bodies over the years. Murdered Washington intern Chandra Levy disappeared there for a year, despite modern search capabilities. Another park mystery is the lost ring of Teddy Roosevelt, which fell off during a presidential hike in 1902. It remains missing to this day, and I enjoyed crafting a possible fate for it, too!

I owe heartfelt thanks to many people who helped in the writing, researching, and production of this novel. My mother and husband, this book's first cheerleaders. My wonderful critique partners Stephanie Dray and Stephanie Thornton. My beta readers and marvelously knowledgeable subject matter experts: Erin Davies and Outlaw, Charles F. A. Dvorak, Annalori Ferrell, Elena Gorokhova, and Shelby Miksch. My agent Kevan Lyon and editor Tessa Woodward, and the marvelous team at William Morrow. I would be lost without you all!

I would also have been lost without Lyudmila herself. I recommend her engrossing autobiography *Lady Death: The Memoirs of Stalin's Sniper* for those wishing to know more about this fascinating woman. The English translation by David Foreman (Greenhill Books) proved invaluable in the research and writing of this novel. Lyudmila Pavlichenko was far more than a killer of men, and she paid a price for her tremendous courage. Although she survived her war, finished her dissertation, and achieved her dream of becoming a historian, she saw many of her friends die, she struggled with PTSD, and she outlived Kostia . . . but she devoted her later years to war veterans, recorded her story for posterity, and died in the arms of her beloved son, surrounded by family and swearing at death until the very end.

It's sometimes said that World War II was won with British intelligence, American steel, and Soviet blood. This sweeping generalization bears a kernel of truth. Since the USSR became America's enemy in the Cold War so soon after WWII's end, it's easy to forget that without them, the war against the Axis powers might have been lost. Of all Hitler's mistakes, his colossal Napoleonic error in taking on the USSR was perhaps the most pivotal: without the eastern front soaking up so much of Germany's manpower, the Allies might never have prevailed. The cost of that victory was millions of Red Army dead as Soviet blood gave American steel and British intelligence time to turn the tide. In *The Rose Code* I wrote about the war through the lens of British intelligence. *The Diamond Eye* is seen through the lens of Soviet blood—one woman's fight to stanch its flow, first with her rifle and then with her voice as she crossed an ocean to bring American steel home to help her countrymen.

HISTORIC PHOTOGRAPHS

Lyudmila Mikhailovna Pavlichenko
(© Shim Harno [Mr Robert Kemp] / Alamy)

Lyudmila Pavlichenko, propaganda photograph, Sevastopol, early 1942

Sniper platoon commander Lyudmila Pavlichenko with her troops
(32nd Guards Parachute Division), Moscow military district,
August 1942 (Courtesy of Greenhill Books)

Lyudmila Pavlichenko and Eleanor Roosevelt, USA tour,
1942 (© ITAR-TASS News Agency / Alamy)

Lyonya Kitsenko and Lyudmila Pavlichenko,
Sevastopol, January 1942

FURTHER READING AND ENTERTAINMENT

Nonfiction

Alexeivich, Svetlana. *The Unwomanly Face of War,* trans. Richard Pevear and Larissa Volkhonsky. Random House, 2017.

Cook, Blanche Wiesen. *Eleanor Roosevelt, Volume 3: The War Years and After, 1939–1962.* Viking, 2016.

Fitzpatrick, Sheila. *Everyday Stalinism: Ordinary Life in Extraordinary Times: Soviet Russia in the 1930s.* Oxford University Press, 2000.

Fitzpatrick, Sheila, and Yuri Slezhine, eds. *In the Shadow of Revolution: Life Stories of Russian Women from 1917 to the Second World War.* Princeton University Press, 2000.

Glantz, David, and Jonathan M. House. *When Titans Clashed: How the Red Army Stopped Hitler,* revised and expanded ed. University Press of Kansas, 2015.

Goodwin, Doris Kearns. *No Ordinary Time: Franklin and Eleanor Roosevelt—The Home Front in World War II.* Simon & Schuster, 1995.

Markwick, Roger D., and Euridice Charon Cardona. *Soviet Women on the Frontline in the Second World War.* Palgrave Macmillan, 2012.

Nikolaev, Yevgeni. *Red Army Sniper: A Memoir on the Eastern Front in World War II.* Greenhill Books, 2017.

Obratztsov, Youri, and Maud Anders. *Soviet Women Snipers of the Second World War.* Histoire and Collections, 2014.

Pavlichenko, Lyudmila. *Lady Death: The Memoirs of Stalin's Sniper,* trans. David Foreman. Greenhill Books, 2018.

Vinogradova, Lyuba. *Avenging Angels: Soviet Women Snipers on the Eastern Front (1941–45).* Quercus, 2017.

Wacker, Albrecht. *Sniper on the Eastern Front: The Memoirs of Sepp Allerberger, Knight's Cross,* reprint ed. Pen and Sword Military, 2016.

YouTube

"Lyudmila Pavlichenko—The Extraordinary Sniper." Dubistic, September 23, 2016. https://www.youtube.com/watch?v=rYnn BpxsI7s&ab_channel=dubistic.

"Lyudmila Pavlichenko Speech in New York City." Pietrossino, YouTube, February 12, 2010. https://www.youtube.com/watch ?v=jDO6n7GuslA&ab_channel=pietrossino.

Film

Battle for Sevastopol, 2015 biographical war film.

Enemy at the Gates, 2001 war film.

**If you loved *The Diamond Eye*, why not try
Kate Quinn's other books . . .**

The Rose Code

1940, Bletchley Park, Buckinghamshire.

Three very different women are recruited to the mysterious
Bletchley Park, where the best minds in Britain train to break
German military codes.

Vivacious debutante Osla has the dashing Prince Philip
of Greece sending her roses – but she burns to prove herself
as more than a society girl, working to translate decoded
enemy secrets. Self-made Mab masters the legendary
codebreaking machines as she conceals old wounds and
the poverty of her East-End London upbringing. And shy
local girl Beth is the outsider who trains as one of the
Park's few female cryptanalysts.

1947, London.

Seven years after they first meet, on the eve of the royal
wedding between Princess Elizabeth and Prince Philip, disaster
threatens. Osla, Mab and Beth are estranged, their friendship
torn apart by secrets and betrayal. Yet now they must race
against the clock to crack one final code together, before it's
too late, for them and for their country.

The Huntress

On the icy edge of Soviet Russia, bold and reckless Nina Markova joins the infamous Night Witches – an all-female bomber regiment. But when she is downed behind enemy lines, Nina must use all her wits to survive her encounter with a lethal Nazi murderess known as the Huntress.

British war correspondent Ian Graham abandons journalism to become a Nazi hunter, yet one target eludes him: the Huntress. And Nina Markova is the only witness to escape her alive.

In post-war Boston, seventeen-year-old Jordan McBride is increasingly disquieted by the soft-spoken German widow who becomes her new stepmother. Delving into her past, Jordan slowly realizes that a Nazi killer may be hiding in plain sight.

The Alice Network

1947. In the chaotic aftermath of World War II, American college girl Charlie St. Clair is pregnant, unmarried, and on the verge of being thrown out of her very proper family. She's also nursing a desperate hope that her beloved cousin Rose, who disappeared in Nazi-occupied France during the war, might still be alive. So when Charlie's parents banish her to Europe to have her "little problem" taken care of, Charlie breaks free and heads to London, determined to find out what happened to the cousin she loves like a sister.

1915. A year into the Great War, Eve Gardiner burns to join the fight against the Germans and unexpectedly gets her chance when she's recruited to work as a spy. Sent into enemy-occupied France, she's trained by the mesmerizing Lili, the "Queen of Spies", who manages a vast network of secret agents right under the enemy's nose.

Thirty years later, haunted by the betrayal that ultimately tore apart the Alice Network, Eve spends her days drunk and secluded in her crumbling London house. Until a young American barges in uttering a name Eve hasn't heard in decades, and launches them both on a mission to find the truth . . . no matter where it leads.